Milk
in My
Coffee

Also by Eric Jerome Dickey

Sister, Sister
Friends and Lovers

Milk in My Coffee

Eric Jerome Dickey

Tonya,
09/01/98
Hey, o ye talented one. I
wanna learn to write hot & steamy...
Stay Blessed
Keep on sharing that gift
Eric Jerome D

A DUTTON BOOK

DUTTON
Published by the Penguin Group
Penguin Putnam Inc., 375 Hudson Street, New York, New York 10014, U.S.A.
Penguin Books Ltd, 27 Wrights Lane, London W8 5TZ, England
Penguin Books Australia Ltd, Ringwood, Victoria, Australia
Penguin Books Canada Ltd, 10 Alcorn Avenue, Toronto, Ontario, Canada M4V 3B2
Penguin Books (N.Z.) Ltd, 182–190 Wairau Road, Auckland 10, New Zealand

Penguin Books Ltd, Registered Offices:
Harmondsworth, Middlesex, England

First published by Dutton, an imprint of Dutton NAL, a member of Penguin Putnam Inc.

First Printing, September, 1998
10 9 8 7 6 5 4 3 2 1

REGISTERED TRADEMARK—MARCA REGISTRADA

LIBRARY OF CONGRESS CATALOGING-IN-PUBLICATION DATA:

Dickey, Eric Jerome.
    Milk in my coffee / Eric Jerome Dickey.
        p.   cm.
    ISBN 0-525-94385-4 (alk. paper)
    I. Title.
PS3554.I319M55 1998
813'.54—dc21   98-5258
                                                                    CIP

Printed in the United States of America
Set in Sabon
Designed by Leonard Telesca

PUBLISHER'S NOTE
This is a work of fiction. Names, characters, places, and incidents either are the products of the author's imagination or are used fictitiously, and any resemblance to actual persons, living or dead, events, or locales is entirely coincidental.

This book is printed on acid-free paper. ∞

For Vardaman and Lila Gause
Miss y'all
Always

Acknowledgments

Once again, Virginia Jerry's grandchild wants to thank everybody. So grab a Snapple, eat some fat-free chips, and be patient.

Thanks to the Creator for allowing this dream to come true. From a humble boy who grew up on Kansas Street.

Always, I want to thank my editor, Audrey LaFehr, for doing such a fantabulous job. Peace and light to you eternally.

To my agent, Sara Camilli, thanks for all the hard work and reminding me to take my vitamins. (Smile) And my car is finally out of the shop. Eternal blessings to you and all you touch.

Tracey Guest, thanks for working hard at pubbing me from coast to coast. ((((((((((((((((Tracey))))))))))))))))))))

Shout outs the LA running crew—My Inglewood Ten Friends: Richard "Stomach Man" Scott, Dwayne "Poppa" and Evelyn "Lady" Orange, Raymond "Coach" Bell, Karla "with a K" Greene, Glenda "Trainer Girl" Greene, Vince Owens, John "The King of Diamonds" Marshall, Jodie "Alright, Alright" Little-Williams, Karl "Mr. Alright, Alright" Williams, Juanda Honere, Victor "Shortcut" Miller, Stella, "Running" Ron Streeter, Mellie Mel Melanie, Stephanie (the attorney that will not be outrun) Myers, Stephanie (Rob's wife, AKA the Marathon Queen), Malaika (Where R U?) Brown, Samuel Jones, Lawrence and Brenda Doss, Rafael Morales, David (DEA) Brown, Tracy, Neiko, and Stephanie "Miss Thang."

Thanks Licia "Triple Threat" Shearer for kick starting this idea. You probably don't even remember when you said, "Write a story about a brotha going out with a white girl. . . ." Hope I didn't go too far. But you know me. . . .

Thanks for the years of support and chicken soup—Brenda Denise Stinson (She reads with me in Los Angeles, and is the BOMB!), April (Down in Miss'sippi) Wiggins, Tiffany and Danielle (Out in Vegas) Royster. Hey Danielle! And my LA "daughters," Chiquita Martin, Gina.

The Fances (Tyrone, Taylor, Delia, Devin).

At my home away from home, 24 Hour Fitness; Maria and Tanya—thanks for keeping these buns tight!

Special SPECIAL thanks to Yvette Hayward in NYC—thanks for the east coast hook up and taking me all over the joint.

And Lolita Files, author of *Scenes from a Sistuh,* you know you be my twin! ^5 a 1000 times, thanks for the support and conversations. U B a genius. And you got me ROFLMBAO 24-7-365.

To my fellow writers and friends—E. Lynn Harris, Shonda Cheekes, Suzette Webb, Victoria Christopher Murray, Lolita Files, Yvette Hayward, Kimberla Lawson-Roby, LaJoyce Brookshire, Sharon Mitchell, Franklin White, Omar Tyree, Sabrina Lamb, Jacqueline Powell, Van Whitfield, Jerry Craft, Malaika Browne—and many others I've met in one way or another on this journey down the Yellow Brick Road of publishing, thanks for the friendship and advice. Let's keep the ball rolling!

TNT Driving Service in Dallas (Theresa, Dianna, Tina)—Y'All SISTAS ARE THE BOMB DIGGITY! Why can't y'all go on tour with me?

To my Grandmother, Virginia "MaDear" Jerry, LOVE YOU!

Audrey Cooper, my friend, my brother, thanks for everything.

Emil "Jake" Johnson. ^5 and ( ) Thanks, bro.

Bobby Laird. Okay Music Man thanks for—hey, you know what you've done over the years to make this happen.

Shirley "Poetry Lady" Harris—thanks for reading this in its roughest form, then still talking to me. :-) Keep writing from your heart and moving onward and upward toward the light.

Hugs to some more of my southern fried family—Verna Pigues, Keith and Monica Pigues, Kevin Pigues, Darrell V. Jerry, Regina Quinones.

Tywla, Pat, and Taylor. Love y'all.

AOL buddies—you know who U R here's a hug (((4you)))

I wish I could thank all of the book clubs (Sister, Sister—nice name by the way—in Texas was the hook up!) but that would be another book in itself. Thanks to all of you.

And just in case I forgot you, grab a pen. Special, special thanks to _____ for whatever you did to make this happen. (For real, s/he helped. Couldn't have done it without him/her.)

If you're online, feel free to hit me at EDickey142@AOL.COM. Give me your comments. Go into amazon.com and do the same for myself and other writers. We need to know what you think/feel, and we want the people who are watching us (Big Brother, is that your breath on my neck? Take a Tic Tac and chill out) to know that this New Renaissance is more than a trend. At least I do. :-) Send money if you got it. Small bills. Unmarked. Not in consecutive serial numbers. To my POB in Switzerland. Just jokin'. Send large bills. LOL.

Thanks for the love and support.

Peace and blessings to you and all you touch.

Now, good people, go out and buy some books.

part one

Preconceived Notions

1 Jordan Greene

Before I could make it to the 42nd Street station in Times Square, my damn fingertips were aching. Every one of them had turned more purple than Barney, that stupid dinosaur that everybody over three loved to hate. And I'm not lying. I'm serious. About hoofing it up to Broadway and 44th and being cold. The wool lining in my trench coat was doing the right thing and keeping my five-foot-nine inches of middle-ground-brown body warm, but I was carrying a couple of packages, things I'd bought from R.A.G. and the Official All Star Cafe. Presents for my best friend. My friggin' hands were bare; my fingers were swollen and ready to burst like microwave popcorn. I should go by Fino's, right up the way between Fifth and Sixth Avenues, and buy some more gloves made of that soft Italian leather, but I hate to buy what I already own and left at home. It's amazing how pain in one part of your body can make you miserable all over. To make it worse, I could see my brown Italian boots stepping on the gray asphalt, could hear the crunch when I slipped and slid in some leftover filth and slush on the edge of the pavement, but I couldn't feel my toes.

It was the first Friday of December, and a bone-chillin' twenty-four degrees. This was the warmest it'd been all week.

If I wasn't so miserable I would've stopped moving across the grating on the sidewalk long enough to glance up at the mountains of larger-than-large billboards polluting Manhattan's skyline. Man, when I first came here from the South, I swear to God, I'd never seen this many billboards in my life. And they were stacked stories high, taller than most buildings, one on top of another. Outside of the big-ass advertisements for the Broadway shows and the huge neon Coke bottles that faced the red and white TKTS booth, there was a big-ass ITT video screen stacked on top of a colossal Cup O' Noodles, stacked on a gigantic bottle of Budweiser, stacked on a colossal Panasonic TV screen that was showing whatever was on NBC, stacked on an immense movie billboard, and all of it hovering over the itty-bitty NYPD substation.

A bad-tempered breeze from the direction of the East River kicked in, making everybody in Times Square bend, walk like hunchbacks, curse, and shudder, but nobody slowed down. Since I've been in New York, I've never seen anybody slow down. Even the dead keep moving. And no matter when, no matter where, there are so many damn people.

When I gripped my bags and rolled my hand into a fist, pain shot up my arm to my neck. Head to toe, a shiver quaked through me and I thought I was about to have a freaking stroke. The hawk was kicking my butt like I owed it some serious money. My stiff-shouldered hustle toward the subway station across from the Disney Store wasn't working. Another minute of this shit and I'd be a nut-brown Frosty the Snowman. I had a packet of subway tokens in my jacket pocket, but even if I made it from here to Queens's Roosevelt Avenue station, I'd still have to wrestle with my gifts, scramble up from that musty tunnel into the streets at Roosevelt and Broadway, wait in the freezing air for the Q33 bus, ride another fifteen minutes, then get back into the cold and slip and slide by all the corner stores to make it to my apartment on White Oaks Court. Shit. I was about to lose my mind. To get home from here a cab would cost a grip, at least thirty bucks, but enough was enough. It was time to break out the wallet.

I hopped off the curb, dodged a brother in army fatigues who was trying to sell me a Rolex watch for two hundred dollars, ignored another blue-haired white guy trying to hustle gold chains, and tried to flag down a cab. I didn't have time to haggle. If they weren't selling gloves, there wasn't a damn thing they could do for me. A swarm of yellow taxis and Lincoln Town Cars—those were taxis too—were going by, moving like a sirocco. There were always more cabs than regular cars on the city streets, so the avenue looked like a sea of yellow. I stepped off the curb, lurched deeper into the street, and made sure one saw me. The driver slowed, made eye contact, slightly shook his head, sped up, stopped, and picked up a white man about thirty yards down. Bastard. Paranoid punks never stop for a black man because they're afraid we might make them do something unreasonable, like drop us off in a black neighborhood. This is bull. I'm twenty-nine, work a nine-to-five, and have a wallet full of legitimate cash, and I still can't get a damn cab.

I was ready to kick butt and take names later, whatever I had to do to get home and find some fire. I let the packages rest in the web of my arm and jammed my right hand back inside my pocket, stuck it right next to the Rachelle Ferrell CD I'd just bought at the Virgin Megastore, dodged people and strutted by the Merry-fucking-Christmas decorations hanging from storefronts, stomped by a crew of Salvation Army Santas.

Finally, a yellow taxi swerved and stopped a few feet from me. I didn't miss a beat. I maneuvered through the sidewalk traffic and broke into a numb-toed jog. A heavyset sista leaned forward to pay the driver and wiggled out into the breeze. The wind tossed her Mary J. Blige–looking blonde weave, blew her ankle-length wool overcoat open, whipped her orange dress, and let me catch a view of her dark nylons and thunder-thighs. She fought to adjust her clothes and I struggled to catch the door before it shut me out. The door bent my fingers; I dropped my packages, grunted to keep from howling with the pain. Felt like three fingers cracked down to the bone. I smiled at the sista. She didn't smile. Bitch must be from New York.

She'd left somebody inside the taxi. A white woman. I sighed. Damn. When my head shot inside the cab, her earmuffs leaped off her neck and she shrieked, cringed, and dropped her magazine. Her wavy red hair slipped free, dropped around her shoulders and covered most of her round face. Then she sucked in her pouty lips and trembled back into the corner.

She frowned and snapped, *"The air is cold. Get in."*

"What?"

"Get your stuff off the ground and get in. Get in or close the damn door."

She adjusted her green coat and scooted over closer to her door. Inside reeked with the fragrance of Passion. J'nette used to wear the same brand, so I knew it very well. I'd been dating J'nette for the last few months, but our relationship wasn't exactly on the rise. Sugar had changed to shit. Anyway, the softness of the red-head's perfume stood out from the cab's rank—a wet-sock and athletic-foot—stench. And I felt something else I'd kill for. Warmth.

"Already got a fare!" That was the driver. I didn't know what nationality he was, but the I.D. over his visor was thirty letters long and needed Vanna White to sell him a few vowels.

She leaned toward me and said, "For the last time, where?"

I started to say I was going to the black boroughs, either Jamaica, Queens, or Strivers' Row in Harlem, but it wasn't the right kinda weather for games.

"Jackson Heights." My teeth clattered with my moan as I grabbed my bags. A teaspoon of moisture ran from my nose down my face. But I was too cold to be embarrassed. "Seventy-fifth Street and Twenty-third Avenue."

She rattled off, "Near La Guardia."

I nodded, sniffled, said, "Near the Brooklyn-Queens Expressway."

She made an impatient motion, her fingers quivered with the cold, told me to hurry up and close the door. "That's a couple of miles from where I'm headed. We can split the fare."

On the other side of the clear bulletproof barrier, the driver gripped the wheel and growled. His scarred, bearded face tensed up while he shook his head and yacked in his own language. My wool scarf loosened around my neck when I relaxed into the back-seat. My bags fell at my feet. The driver let out a few American curses, which was just a typical East Coast hello.

"What was that?" she said, then jerked her hand up to her ear like she was trying to improve her hearing. That made me nervous. The driver didn't say another word. She sat back on the cracked seat, re-opened her magazine, and said a sharp, "And *don't* take any so-called shortcuts. I'm watching you and I know my way."

The driver glared into his rearview mirror. Snow crunched under the tires as he pulled away from the curb. I moaned. She cut her eyes at my suffering, then went back to trying to find her place in her magazine. It was a *New Yorker*. I rubbed my hands together, but it felt like I was massaging a block of ice with a block of ice.

She peeped at me, sighed, reached into her purse, grabbed a pink tissue, handed it to me. "I feel the cold coming off you."

"Thanks." I wiped my nose. "I've been out there begging cabs to stop for at least thirty minutes."

"Why?"

"Because." I glanced at the driver. "Because."

She nodded. "For all they know, I could be a serial killer."

"Are you?"

She gave me a stone-faced "What do you think?"

"I'll take my chances." I bent my fingers. "Hurts."

"Where're your gloves?"

"Lost 'em."

She shook her head. "New York. Winter. Naked fingers. Not a sane combination. You might be the serial killer."

"If I'm not wearing gloves, then I'm trying to kill *myself*."

With full lips and a round face, she reminded me of that actress Kim Basinger, but her voice was perky and quick, like the actress Geena Davis's. She sported rainbow-hued mittens that let her fingers wiggle around in harmony and share the same space. I was a glove man. A segregated compartment for each finger. That was how my momma raised her three boys up. Wearing either black or brown gloves.

She said, "Let me help."

Before I could figure out what she meant, she pulled off her mitts, reached over, and took my right hand. At the moment of first contact, I wanted to snatch it away, but her hands were warm. Damn warm. I tried to make myself relax. For now.

I chilled and let her become my furnace. Her hands were soft. Thick fingers, short nails, manicured, clear polish. Her ankles were thick too.

When the warmth she was giving up faded, she rubbed her hands some more, made them super-duper warm again. She was running her mouth, but the throbbing inside my body had made me deaf.

I said, "What?"

"I said"—she grinned—"my name is Kimberly Chavers."

I looked at her hazel eyes and repeated. "Kim?"

"No." She held one finger up to correct me. "Kimberly."

I didn't smile. I was still checking out her eyes. Hazel. From a certain angle they looked silvery, from another emerald.

I blinked away my amazement and said, "Jordan Greene."

"Nice to meet you, Jordan."

"Likewise."

My forehead was dank. The sweat came from the pain of my fingers aching, coming back to life. Fingertips stung like they were being jabbed with hot needles. It had been so long since I'd been this cold, not since me and Solomon went skiing in Vale, that I'd forgotten that the torture increased with the thawing. It would get worse before it got better. I bent my fingers, tried to get some circulation going, set free a few orgasmic-sounding "oooohs" and "ahhs." She smirked, picked up her *New Yorker*, flipped through the pages.

I leaned away from her. "Thanks."

She nodded and said a definite, "You're not East Coast."

"Accent?"

"A little. Mannerisms. You're too nice to the cabbie."

"I was cold as hell."

"Don't matter. Keep that 'tude with them or they'll walk over you. Where are you from?"

"Brownsville."

"Is that in Texas?"

"Small town right outside of Memphis."

"Tennessee, huh? Ever see Elvis?"

"Yeah. Want to see the pink Cadillac he bought me?"

We shared paper-thin laughs. I could feel my toes again. Piece by piece, my body was coming back to life.

I said, "You're pretty nice yourself. Where you from?"

"Seattle. Oakland. San Antonio. Few other places."

"Military brat?"

"Yep." She smiled. "What brought you up to New York?"

"Came up here seven years ago to work for CompSci Enterprises. Software. Been here ever since."

"Sounds like a bomb job. I need to get my own computer to do some graphics. I've had classes in QuarkXpress. I was thinking about taking a few more at La Guardia Community College."

I nodded. Then I smelled another kind of funk, a leftover Marlboro stink. I didn't have to lean forward and see the driver's overflowing ashtray to know he was a chain-smoker, just like my older brother Darrell. I tried smoking back in high school, but asthma put an end to that idiocy. Thank God for that. Anyway, the cancer smell was bad, but not strong enough to dilute Kimberly's sweet aroma.

She continued chattering. "I want to learn some of the latest computer software, and to get online, maybe eventually do my own Web page and get my work out there." She went back to reading. "It sounds so exciting. Being on the 'Leading edge of technology.' "

"Leading edge of technology?"

She held up her magazine. It was open to a full-page CompSci advertisement.

She raised a brow. "Don't you know your own motto?"

"Well," I said and shrugged, "I didn't make it up."

"I hope not." She laughed, folded the magazine, and stuck it in her coat pocket. "It's so damn corny."

"What do you do?"

"I'm an artist. Visual."

"No shit?"

"Yep, shit."

"What style?"

"Stuff like Norman Rockwell."

All I knew about art was Ernie Barnes, Varnette Honeywood, and Salvador Dali. I owned two Barnes prints. Both were in my dining area. I had the one with the young girls playing Ring Around the Rosie and the party scene that was used as a cover on one of Marvin Gaye's albums.

She raised a brow. "You've heard of Norman Rockwell?"

"Name's familiar. Is he from New York?"

"Actually, he's dead."

"Oh, sorry."

"Don't be. Anyway, in layman's terminology, I do what you call real-life stuff," she said matter of factly, then touched a reddish freckle on her right cheek. "Depends on my mood. I haven't done anything lately. Artist's block. My mind's cluttered and it's hard for me to get a good groove going."

I had wanted to draw comic books when I was a kid. I had a T-square and a drafting board set-up next to about a thousand comics. Hadn't thought about that in years. After I went off on a mental tangent, I was brought back to the present by her giggles.

I flexed my fingers and said, "Whu'sup?"

"Your eyes lit up."

For a minute or two, while we headed down three lanes of madness crowding Park Avenue, then on East 57th Street toward the Queensboro Bridge, I yacked, told her that when I was a kid I wanted to draw comics, make up a million black superheroes, and work for either D.C. or Marvel. While we laughed those subtle, polite, distant laughs, the driver gazed at us through the rearview mirror, shook his head like we were crazy.

I said, "It would be nice to see some of your work."

"Hold on for a sec." She reached inside her purse, pulled out a bulky leather wallet, handed it to me. "Here."

When she stuck her wallet in my face, I thought she was setting me up for a downfall. "What's up with this?"

"I keep snapshots of my work with me."

They looked like real people. The colors, the details. A lady in a swing nursing her baby. A woman crying as her lover walked away, suitcases in both hands. The sun rising as a couple sat on a hill. Silhouette of two lovers in a shower, getting it on at the break of dawn. There were about twenty 35mm pictures. None of them had any real facial features. I guess that was to make her work more salable. Their skin tones were varied. No doubt another business move.

I mumbled, "Wow. You did these?"

"Typical male response." She smiled, then rattled off a very feministic, "Don't think women can do much, huh? If I was, what do you call those things, a *man*, you would have—"

I raised a hand. "I didn't mean it like—"

She laughed. "I was joking."

"Good."

"And yes." She smirked and replied, "I did them by myself."

"These are smooVe."

"Smooth?"

"No, not smooth. *SmooVe*. With a capital V."

"SmooVe?" she mimicked me. "Well, thanks. SmooVe. I'll have to use that. SmooVe. With a capital V."

When she said she was going to use *my* expression, that made me wish I didn't say smooVe. I glanced forward, glared at the two lanes of traffic trudging over the Queensboro Bridge, put my eyes on the East River for a moment, toward Silvercup Studios, then back toward the IDCNY building so I wouldn't have to make eye contact with her. *SmooVe. I'll have to use that.* My momma used to say white people would steal everything down to your last breath.

A moment later, I kept my attitude from showing by placing a log on the conversation's fire. I cleared my throat, flexed my fingers, and asked, "Is your work out on exhibit?"

"Not yet. I've been lucky and sold quite a few lately on consignment through a few places in the Village."

"So you do this full-time?"

"I've had a few part-time jobs off and on, but I'm freelancing for magazines and corporate layouts. Individuals aren't buying art because of the economy, but businesses are always in the market; it's in their budget. They overpay and write it off. Have to pay the rent until I get that career-making *Life* cover."

"I wish I could see these. I just might buy one, if I can afford it. What medium do you work in?"

She sounded distracted when she muttered, "Oil and canvas."

"Nice," I said. Her hazel eyes lit up. When she grinned, I asked, "All right, whu'sup?"

"Wanna see the rest?"

I nodded. "Let me know when they go on display."

"I can do one better. I was just thinking, we don't live far from each other. You could stop by my place for a couple of minutes, then catch another cab the rest of the way."

Underneath my smile, I felt a chill of discomfort. I tried to think of a lie, come up with a quick line and fake that I had something to do, but the lie wouldn't come. Especially since we were eye to eye, no room for an alibi.

She continued, "I don't know if you have any plans, or a date, or have to get home to your wife or something."

I thought about how J'nette hadn't returned any of my calls, remembered the nothing I had to do from sunset to sunrise on a Friday night, then I laughed, low and easy.

She tilted her head, "What?"

"No, I'm not in a hurry to get home. No, I don't have any plans." I held up my empty ring finger. "No, I'm not married."

Her eyes widened; her hand went up over her face. "I didn't mean for it to sound like that. I didn't know where you were going. Not that it matters. Business is business, right?"

I nodded. "Business is business."

A hard breeze swooped down the moment we stopped in front of her three-story, red-brick building. She lived right by a European-American deli. Not too far from Bulova Corporate Center on Astoria Boulevard. A row of necessity shops—things like a fish market, nail shop, a Chinese wash and dry, and a florist—were less than a block away. We lived about three miles apart, were both equidistant from the Waldbaum's where I did my food shopping, the Bank of New York where I did my money transactions, and the Boston Market where I bought my ready-made food when I wasn't in the mood to cook. From what I could tell, her middle-class side of the borough had the same demographics as mine—Italian and Puerto Rican, with a side of Negro tossed in to add flavor. I noticed that because it seemed like every other mile, the nationalities changed. If you go left it's Italian, go right it's East Indian.

But no matter where, wall-to-wall rectangular houses with itty-bitty rooms and two feet of front yard were sandwiched together on every block. Air-conditioners jutted out the front windows. Like most of the area, Kimberly's building was surrounded by winter-brown grass. Under a family of naked trees, two rows of six-foot bushes were on either side of the chipped, red-brick walkway, all topped with slush and patches of dirty snow.

"Be careful." Kimberly pointed at the ground. "There might be ice patches in the shade."

There wasn't an elevator. My toes weren't ready to work so I moved like an old man while we hiked up to the third floor. When she opened the three locks on her door, good-feeling heat welcomed us. This was worth the delay, because I'd turned my heat down and I lived in the basement of my building, so my cave would feel like a freezer. My fingers and toes wiggled. The scent of old coffee seasoned the room. And its odor was strong enough for me to know her brand of hazelnut was full of caffeine.

Voices were coming from the bedroom. At first I thought she had a couple of people waiting for her to get home, but the noise came from talk radio. Her walls were painted with the standard off-white color. The wall facing the streets had a mural of New York. Statue of Liberty. The Apollo Theatre. Other places were outlined, but I couldn't figure out what they were. Kimberly saw me eyeing it and walked over next to me.

"I mess around on that wall when I'm bored."

I pointed. "What's that?"

"The one on the right is a real bad version of the Roman Colosseum. The one on the left is a Mexican pyramid."

The dining room was small, typical for New York, and didn't have a table. Her apartment had some size, which meant she could be paying a grip, and I wondered how much rent-control had controlled her rent. A beige cotton drop cloth that had been splattered with all the primary colors and their cousins covered part of the hardwood floor. Canvased paintings leaned against the wall at an angle. One was on an easel.

My shoes echoed while I strolled her dull floors.

She told me to get comfortable. I thought about it, hemmed and hawed, put down my packages, flexed my hands again, then slid off my trench and suit coats, dropped both across the pastel futon in the living area. Saw a stack of aerobics tapes—"Booty of Steel," "Stomach of Steel," "Arms of Steel." Books were on the floor—*Gauguin Masterworks*, *The Far Side*, *Works of Norman Rockwell*. I squatted, heard my knees pop like baby firecrackers, and picked up the book on Rockwell. I knew who he was, but didn't know his work. It took a second, then I remembered his down-home and true-to-life style, because he'd drawn a picture of the little black girl being led to a newly integrated school; being safeguarded at the school's front doors by the National Guard, back in the civil rights era. I remember that it was on the cover of *Life*. Yep. We had to be escorted during integration. Another one of my people's liberties that had been taken for granted.

I had hoped she had a roommate, but she lived by herself. That made me nervous. I stepped over a few CDs that were scattered at the base of her stereo—Harry Connick, Jr. En Vogue. Diane Schuur. The Fugees. Bonnie Raitt. Alanis Morrisette.

They reminded me that my new Rachelle Ferrell CD was in my pocket. That was part of the reason I'd been out in Times Square freezing to death. Rachelle Ferrell was a sista who had it going on. All that and a fat can of turtle-wax; she could shine me anytime. I loved her strong, black-woman look, her got-quite-a-few-octaves voice, her full lips, the arousing way her mouth moved when she hit all those sexy notes as she crooned. Part of the reason I was attracted to J'nette was because she had that same look. Ain't nothing like a strong black woman. Nothing.

Kimberly had taken her coat off and strolled into the bedroom. She called out, "You can put some music on if you want."

"Can, uh," I corrected myself. "May I put my CD on?"

She called back, "Sure. You know how to work it?"

"Yeah. I can work it."

Since she wasn't in the room to watch me, I checked her place out. From the red oriental rug to the fuchsia curtains on her windows, all of her decorations generated warmth, life. No pale grays, dark blues, or nasty browns. She stepped back in long enough to adjust the blinds to let in what was left of the natural light; then she went back into the bedroom.

The music started. I flexed my fingers, made sure they were still okay. They ached a little, but not enough to worry about. The tips were still somewhere between dark red and light purple. I stood up and caught Kimberly's reflection in a rectangular wall mirror. She moved her scarlet hair from her eyes and sat on her white lacquer bed, a bed that was unmade on one side.

I heard some clicks followed by a beep. A digital voice said she had five messages, then started to play. A couple of the messages sounded like business, galleries calling. Another was from a scratchy-voiced woman named Sharon: "Sweetheart, I told my husband I was coming out to visit you for the night. I wanted you to know just in case he calls over there looking for me, but I doubt that he will. Call me and we'll do lunch. Ta-ta."

That voice sounded as white as Wonder bread.

The next message was from a woman named Kinikki. She sounded like a sista with a strong Caribbean accent and left a chatty girl-to-girl message. Nothing personal, nothing scandalous, just enough to let me know they were as tight as me and Solomon. So I guess Kimberly had friends on both sides of the color bar.

Then the last one sounded like a white man who was on his last leg: "Kim, why won't you return my calls or let me see you? Baby, it's almost Christmas and I'd love to meet you down at Ricky's Cafe so we could at least talk—"

Kimberly cursed, then either she cut the begging message short or turned down the volume. I didn't see her, but I heard her harsh breaths. By the time she came back and crossed into the kitchen, I had made myself comfortable on the floor, was humming along with the sounds of Rachelle Ferrell, thumbing through the first stack of Kimberly's art.

I said, "I see you like Rachelle's music."

"Love her to death." She perked up a notch. "She's awesome. Saw her in concert with George Duke and Jonathan Butler. That's her first CD. Don't tell me that you're just now buying it?"

"Just getting around to it."

I was about to be impressed because she liked jazz, but most of the jazz concerts I'd gone to were packed with white folks who knew more about jazz than all the hip-hop and gangster-rap'n brothers I knew combined. Made me wonder that if it weren't for Europeans, some classic black music would be extinct.

There were several stacks of work, each at least twenty paintings deep. All on canvas, all unframed. I was straight up amazed. It was sort of like reading a good book, then meeting the person who'd written it. I guess I was starstruck, in awe.

"Take your time, Jordan." Kimberly yawned, did a slow, lazy walk by. Now she had on pink house shoes with bunny ears. "But don't force yourself to look at all of 'em."

"Well, I don't know if you have something to do, or if you're expecting company. Maybe your husband is on the way home."

"Ha-ha." She shook her empty ring finger. "I travel light."

We smiled at each other.

"Jordan, are you hungry?"

"A little."

"Have some spaghetti here. It's meatless, in case you don't eat meat, but I have sauce with turkey meat if you do."

"Sure. Turkey meat's fine."

Kimberly turned her back, bent over. That made her butt apple up big time. I stole a peek, made sure it wasn't my imagination running away with me. Or the angle. Or the jeans. With her defined waistline and tight butt, I knew brotha after brotha had been trying to get her phone number, beeper number, cellular number, Social Security number, any number she had, wherever she went. Damn nice. Right about now, there was a sista in Harlem with an ironing-board butt, crying every hour on the hour, trying to figure out who stole her portion of the ancestry.

Kimberly took a cast iron pot out, then closed the cabinet by bumping it with the side of her foot. Rachelle was crooning a song about her father. Kimberly was humming, hitting the idiosyncracies of the melody like she'd written the tune herself. Every now and then she shook her head along with the groove. Her rhythm matched the beat. Surprise, surprise.

I pulled out a couple of pictures I might be interested in, then slid over to the second stack. After I got about three deep into the stack, I froze. Most were oil paintings of Africans. Black people in villages. In cities with fast-food stores and American banks. Ceremonies and rituals. Families. Adults. Children. Babies.

Each one was labeled with a few lines of descriptions and dates. Ghana. Accra. Cape Coast. Takoradi.

"I did those back when I visited Africa."

Kimberly's soft voice scared the hell out of me, but I don't think I jumped too much. Either she floated across the room, or I was busy with the voices inside my head. The smell of spaghetti and turkey meatballs had filled the place. My stomach growled. Folding trays were in the living area, in front of the futon. For a few minutes, I'd been lost in time. Lost in Africa.

"Okay, SmooVe, would you like soda or wine or water?"

I blinked out of my stupor. "What are you having?"

"Wine."

"That's cool." I almost corrected myself and said "That's fine" because I thought I was getting a tad bit too relaxed. Maybe I was. I straightened my down-home posture, made it echo my profession, then asked, "You said you visited Africa?"

"For almost three months. Ever been there?"

"I've been to Detroit."

She laughed. "Detroit?"

"Hey, it's got more black people than Africa."

We sat on her futon, me in my corporate America costume, and I wondered how she saw me. In this room with closed doors and walls, where, for the moment, this was the world, we were just two people kicking back and having fun, enjoying each other's company. Which I needed, especially since J'nette seemed to have a different agenda and I wasn't on her yuletide program. But still, Kimberly's being friendly for no reason made me feel awkward. If she was a sista I'd be asking for her phone number, offering a dinner date later in the week. If she looked like me.

I slipped into a liberal moment and wondered why that mattered so much. My boundaries. I didn't know. I was like that, and that was that. I guess a man gets so used to feeling one way, that whether it was right or wrong, politically correct or incorrect, it was the only way he knew how to feel. Sometimes things unwritten became your personal law. I'd grown up in a small town that separated *us* from *them*. They lived on one side of the railroad tracks, we on the other. Right now, I was lounging on the wrong side of the tracks.

In between heartbeats, I was ready to grab my coat and get the hell out of there. But I chilled. Kimberly had me irked all of a sudden. She hadn't done or said anything to piss me off. What bothered me? Could've been her openness. Might've been her relationship with Africa. Had to be Africa. I'd read about the motherland. The closest I'd been to it was the reruns of *Roots*. She'd eaten there, slept there, touched the people.

Something else that pissed me off was that part of my mind had defrosted, had started feeling, and I admitted what I'd been denying since she'd touched me inside the cab—I was aware of her. She was a fine woman. I couldn't make her invisible, not the way I did a lot of the people I worked with, or like I did the strangers I passed on the streets.

After a strong helping of spaghetti and meatballs, garlic bread, salad, white wine, and store-bought apple pie, she kicked back and led me through each picture, explained what she saw, what inspired her to create each piece.

The next thing I knew, we had gotten comfortable. I'd slid my shoes off, and we were yakking about our families. She was an only child, had an older brother who had leukemia, but he died three years before she was born. Her father was in the Air Force. Her mother gave up her real estate career to make a family. Kimberly had lived on damn near every base in the U.S., plus a couple in Europe.

Outside of New York, I'd lived in Brownsville and Memphis.

I told her I had two older brothers, Darrell and Reggie. Didn't break into a song and dance about any real issues, kept it shallow, but I did tell her that my momma had died right before I turned eighteen. Tuberculosis. She wasn't blessed with the chance to see me graduate. Anyway, I told Kimberly that I was the first in my family to finish high school. Both of my brothers had dropped out to work. Darrell had to. Reggie wanted to.

She asked, "What about your pops?"

"Never knew him. He died in a car accident right after Momma found out she was pregnant with me. We all have different dads."

As soon as I said the different dads thing, I wished I hadn't. The wine I'd sipped was doing some of the talking.

She spoke before the moment turned awkward. "You've done a lot by yourself. I mean, I never would have guessed."

"You've done more."

"Not. I was born middle-class."

"Silver spoon in your mouth, huh?"

"I wouldn't say that. My family has had a few ghosts hanging from its trees."

White people always had it made, then complained about it. I yawned at what she was taking for granted, then glanced at my watch. I said, "It's after three."

She yawned. "Well, this has been fun. I rarely do much other than work and hang out with boring people."

"Boring?"

"Yeah. My girlfriend Sharon always talks about charities and my girlfriend Kinikki always talks about work. Both of them are married, and I'm not, so you know how that goes."

"What about your man?"

She gave up a shamefaced expression, twisted her lips a touch, spoke a soft and flirty, "I don't have a man."

An awkward moment was born between us. I twitched. She did the same at the corners of her lips. She flipped her hair from her face, eased away from me, whispered, "Thanks for asking."

"Then maybe, if you want to, since we don't live but a hop, skip, and a jump from each other . . ." I started, stopped, cleared my throat, then found some nervousness creeping into my words, yanking on my tongue. "Maybe we can get together again. Maybe hook up, get something to eat or go into the city. We could catch a play or something. I think Whoopie Goldberg is still doing *A Funny Thing Happened on the Way to the Forum*."

Kimberly said, "Whoopie's not. David Alan Grier is."

I paused. "If you want to hook up, let me know."

She lost eye contact and didn't say anything else.

I was definitely walking on the wrong side of the tracks. I was stepping in soil that wasn't meant to be on the bottom of my shoes.

It felt like my words were bumbled when I said, "I mean, that's if you'd like to."

Then she looked at me. Her voice was still satiny. "That would be cool."

A little more silence stood between us.

"Let me help you with the dishes," I insisted.

"No, I can handle them."

"I don't mind. Actually, I insist."

"I'll wash; you dry," she rebounded and motioned for me to follow her. "Can you handle that?"

"Sounds like a plan." I rolled up my sleeves and asked, "What are you doing for the holidays?"

She hesitated for a moment. "Not much this year."

Kimberly turned off the water. Her shoulders slumped a little. So did her smile. Mouth twisted a bit.

"I'm sorry," I said, "I didn't mean to—"

"That's all right." She chuckled. "Holidays make me a little sentimental. Holidays and birthdays. Especially my birthday. And PMS. Especially PMS."

"Thanks for sharing that with me."

She elbowed me. "You're welcome."

I laughed. "When's your birthday?"

"New Year's Day. I'll be the big two-eight."

"Really?"

"Yep. When's yours?"

"March tenth," I said, and felt like we were playing the are-we-compatible-by-the-Zodiac-signs game. She's Capricorn; I'm Pisces. If we could be in astrological harmony, it would be a shame, but then again, it wouldn't matter. What made us incompatible went beyond astrology. Way beyond. I held my grin and asked, "So what're you doing for yours?"

"Both my girlfriends celebrate Christmas with their husbands' families, but we get together the day after. It's our tradition. But on Christmas, I guess I'll be by myself." She shrugged. "Maybe I'll hang out in the Village. Catch a bite of Thai food at Toons, if they're open. Might rent some movies. Sip some wine and work until sunrise. Don't know. Hadn't given it much thought."

She turned off the faucet and stuck her hand in to test the water. Kimberly rolled up the sleeves of her shirt, folding the right one above a bruise on her inner arm, above her elbow. It was plum-sized, the color of a ripe cherry.

"You hurt your arm?"

"Birthmark." She held it toward me.

"My brother Darrell has a similar mark on his neck."

When I reached over to touch her skin, just so I could show her the exact location, something happened. My hand grazed her flesh and I felt a chill pass through her. A mini-convulsion. I felt its ripples. Then the sensual glow that swept across her face made me shudder. Her eyes fluttered. A soft moan slipped through her pouty lips. Again, I noticed her in a different way. That made me quiver. That feeling more than anything else made me take a step away, shift my stance south of where she lived. South of where I lived.

She moved away too, fingered the spot I'd touched, stuttered, "I-I'm a little sensitive on my neck."

"I didn't mean to—"

"That's okay." She blew air again. "Guess I'm—"

I whispered, "Delicate?"

"Yeah." Her voice was a whisper too. "Delicate."

We shut up. I wished I'd left ten minutes ago. No, two hours ago. She washed the dishes. Slowly. Handed me a plate to dry. Touched me when she gave me the plate. I touched her hand when I took it. Our flesh grazed. She paused. Her breathing changed. Mine was almost asthmatic. She didn't say a word. Didn't move her hand. And I returned the favor.

She looked me in the eyes, moved closer, tilted her head. I kissed her. A nervous kiss. Her tongue crept into a slow groove, moved like it was a brush and she was creating art. She led, then switched gears and followed my savoring, put her arms around me, pulled me closer, tighter to her, a little at a time. I did the same and brought the curvature and firmness of her womanhood into focus. Felt her breasts squeeze against my chest. I know she felt my manhood coming to life. Her hips moved. She kissed my neck. Made me throb. She eased away. Went back to humming and washing dishes. No smiles or blushes.

After the dishes were washed, I wafted through my awkwardness and called a taxi. Since I'd touched her, after I'd tasted her, my thoughts had been everywhere, but had settled. Almost. I'd made myself stop looking at her, killed the eye contact. Kept my distance. It was best for me to not go for the obvious. Best for me to get the hell out of Dodge before the sheriff and his posse came with a rope. Yep. I yawned. It was late. Damn near the beginnings of early morning. The mystical sexual hours had arrived and I was in the company of an enticing creature I knew so much about, but in reality she was just a stranger. A different kind of stranger at that. If we were of the same tribe, I would've made my move before midnight, but we weren't from the same tribe. She wasn't any shade of black. And she wasn't J'nette. I didn't know if either of those were good, or bad. Didn't know if any of it should matter.

We held on to thin conversation and awkward smiles. Part of me couldn't wait to get back to my own cotton-picking reality. I said, "Hope I haven't kept you up too late."

"Not at all. Tomorrow's a nothing day. I paint late nights, early mornings. I'll be up for a while. What about you?"

"I'm off until Monday. I work another week, then I'm on vacation until after the New Year."

"Leaving town to visit your family in Tennessee?"

"Nope." Other feelings breezed through me. A weird longing. A missing of the family ties I had when my two brothers and I were growing up. We haven't been in the same space for a positive reason in years. My smile was getting harder to hang on to, so I turned it into a yawn and said, "I'll be in town. Might kick it with Solomon."

"Is he your brother?"

"A friend who's closer than a brother. He's from Arkansas."

"Call me. We'll do something if you're not busy."

"Sure."

A horn blew downstairs. My taxi. Kimberly walked me down. Outside, we stood between the six-foot bushes. She handed me her business card, wrapped her arms around me, gave me a kiss. I filled my hands with the packages I had brought upstairs with me, filled my hands to give myself a reason not to want to hold her again. But she put her head into my shoulder, held me while her fingers made circles on my back. I glanced left and right to see who saw us.

"Thanks for coming by. Remember, you owe me a play."

"And don't forget, you promised you'd hang out with me. Hold those two paintings I pulled out. How much are they?"

The taxi's horn blew again. I nodded toward the driver.

Kimberly chuckled. "We'll talk business later, and if you're as sweet as you are now, I might cut you a deal."

The cab's horn blew like somebody was losing their mind, kept honking in rapid succession. Again I looked around to see who could see us, then I put down my bags long enough to give her another kiss. Shorter than the first, but more intense. Deeper and more soul stirring. As in good-bye.

She caught her breath and smiled when I was done.

"Good night," she said in a wispy tone. "Talk to you soon."

"Good morning." I paused, then winked. "Sleep tight."

She let out a naughty giggle. "Stay smooVe."

After we broke our staring at each other, I rushed and met the chill of the hawk head on, sliced through the winds and made it to the cab. Kimberly was standing in the cold, one arm folded across her chest, bunny house shoes on, shivering, smiling, and waving. I waved. Felt like I had jogged to my freedom.

I tossed my packages to the far side of the car and spoke to the driver. "How's it going?"

The brotha tugged the gray part of his inch-long beard and glowered back at me. "Where to, my *brotha*?"

We exchanged glowers. In the middle of our tension, with stiff words, I told him my address, 23-57 White Oaks Court. Told him where to drop me off. He nodded once, like dropping me off would be his pleasure. Our eyes stayed on each other for a few seconds after that.

I asked, "Does there seem to be a problem, my *brotha*?"

He did a slight shake of the head, hard enough to make his dreadlocks sway, then put his eyes on the road.

My accent came alive. "And don't take no damn shortcuts."

He chuckled, like he gave a damn.

This was the first time I had been on this side of racism. It hurt for a brotha to look at me like that. Felt like my character had been assassinated without cause. No due process or question of intent or purpose. But I couldn't play off what he'd seen, me and a red-haired woman kissing like we'd been getting it on all night long.

I was wondering how the hell I'd ended up here, considering where I started out this morning. Soon the sun would come up on the morning and melt away the memory of what I'd done like yesterday's snow. I yawned, a real one this time, then felt Kimberly's business card in my naked hand. Smelled her perfume on the front of my coat from where we had hugged. Tasted traces of her lipstick on my lips. I wiped my mouth. Closed my eyes.

It was over and done with. My best bet was to wipe away the flavor, toss her business card to the winds, and move on.

The brotha in the front seat was sucking his damn teeth, cutting his eyes at me in the rearview.

2 Jordan Greene

All thoughts were on Kimberly when I thawed out and dozed off. I tried to think about something else, but couldn't help but fantasize about what would've happened if she'd ask me to stay, or if I'd asked her if I could stay and she had smiled.

Damn. That ignorant desire had made its way into my apartment. I'd hoped that hunger would've faded with distance, that the confusion would stay outside on the curb. With every spin of the cab's wheels, I'd thought about shredding her card and throwing it out the window. I didn't. I kept thinking about the way she kissed. How she tilted her head, eased her mouth open. The way she moved her tongue. Her voice. The way she moved. The kindness from the cab to her crib. How, when she told me about the motherland, her words were so intellectual, so invigorating. I wanted to put all those wishes under house arrest, but I let those thoughts of a stranger and feelings for somebody I didn't have the right to feel anything for take me into a dream.

I kept thinking about Kimberly. Wished I wasn't so guarded and knew how to be open and free like she was. Dreamed we were having an intellectual conversation. A meeting of the minds.

Then I was scared awake.

Something dropped, rattled, and rolled. Clatter came down the hallway. The apartment was dark, but a light was on behind the bathroom door. A light I hadn't left on. I tugged my blankets off me, jumped up and bumbled in the darkness, tried to find my bearings and grab the lamp on my nightstand for a weapon.

The toilet flushed.

J'nette stepped out of the bathroom, her jeans drooping off one of her arms. She clicked the bathroom light off, turned the hall light on. She didn't look surprised to see me standing bubble eyed, lamp raised up over my head, scowling.

I caught my breath and blinked.

"How'd you get in?"

"E train, then cabbed it up from Roosevelt Avenue station."

"I meant the front door."

"Extra key. I forgot to leave it."

We looked at each other. Neither of us spoke again. Nobody smiled. I got back into the bed. She pulled off her sweatshirt, dropped her pants where she stood, tugged off her pink flowered long johns. She kept her heavy socks on. I cleared my vision and regained more of my reality. The rest of her winter gear and trendy military boots were piled on the floor in front of the chestnut dresser, meaning she'd been here a few minutes.

I said, "Why didn't you put your stuff on the wingback or hang it up like I've asked you to do over and over again?"

She made an irritated sound, but didn't answer.

I said, "Turn the light off."

"Why don't you have the damn heat on?"

"It's on."

"On what?"

"Sixty. Sixty-five."

"It's cold."

I talked through my yawn, "The waterbed is warm."

"What's it on?"

"Eighty-something. Turn the light off."

"Okay, already. I heard you."

She was stripped down to her boxer shorts and bra when she clicked off the light, and continued bitching about the cold. J'nette jumped up and down, rocked from foot to foot while she took off her watch, golden bracelets, then her big hooped earrings. All her jewelry rattled and clanged when it dropped on the dresser. When she unsnapped the front of her bra, freedom made her scoop-sized breasts bounce to separate rhythms. She jerked back the covers, giving me an unwelcome blast of brisk air, and slid her small, four-foot-eleven, honey-brown frame under the comforter and dual blankets and snuggled up to me. A second later, she realized she'd missed getting under the top sheet. She bounced back out and got it right the second time. She kissed my shoulder, rubbed her cold nose against my back. When I turned toward her and ran my hand across her head, I realized her hair was different. Shallow. Missing.

"You cut your hair?"

She ran her hand over her mane. "Yeah."

"When?"

"Got it bobbed."

"When?"

"Don't remember," she slurred. "Three, four weeks ago."

I pushed her smoke-smelling hair out of my face. She scooted closer, tighter. Cold nipples poked deep into my chest. She ran her feet across my legs; her socks were moist, cold. Her words were blurry. We kissed and I tasted the same rum that had perfumed her skin. Smelled it coming out of her pores.

I asked, "Where've you been?"

"Out."

"With?"

"Elaine. Zoe. My sister Toni."

"Where?"

"The Shadow."

That club was on 28th, between Seventh and Eighth Avenues. Big-ass Elaine and cutie-pie Zoe work in Relations with her. Toni's her identical twin sister. Elaine lives down in SoHo, where all the wannabe artists have fled, and she doesn't hang out as much with the regular nine-to-five crew, but she's part of their sista-girlfriend team. Elaine's a wannabe actress, so she's always off somewhere trying to get famous on somebody's soap opera.

I asked, "What time is it?"

"Don't know." J'nette yawned. "Sun's coming up."

I blew air and asked, "Why haven't I heard from you?"

"Been busy thinking about shit."

"Why didn't you return my calls?"

"No reason."

"No reason? That's bull. You could've e-mailed me."

"You want me to go?"

"You're here now."

She positioned herself with her clitoris firm against my leg. Started a slow grind. Her body was cold all over, except down in the Y. The heat came through the boxers. My hand eased inside her underwear, rubbed her rotund butt; she eased me a mechanical tongue kiss. Pulled me on top of her.

We kissed and undressed. She yanked off my pajamas. I helped her wiggle out of her boxers. We held each other closer as she stole the rest of my body heat. I kissed her neck, nibbled her breast, licked across her chest. She put her hands on my shoulders, pushed me south. I didn't go. She pushed harder. I didn't go. When I came back up to give her a few more kisses, she turned her face and moaned, "No."

"No?"

"No."

I asked, "What's wrong?"

"Go downtown. Lick me."

"No. I told you, I have to be in the mood."

"Oh, so I can go down on you, but you can't go down on me."

"I never asked you to go down on me."

"You didn't *have* to ask."

"I told you, I don't do windows."

"*Why* are you trippin'?"

"Why are *you* trippin'?"

"Look, I've been up front and told you what I liked. Why can't you lick me a little bit to get me in the mood? You act like it's poison."

"Tastes funny."

"Get some honey or something. Hell, be creative."

"You know damn well brothas don't get into shit like that."

"No, *you* don't," she said, then pushed me off her and pulled her body from under mine at the same time. "Real brothas do. And jump to it without a sista having to beg. Damn. Real *brothas* are down with the program."

"What *program*?"

"Program six-to-the-nine. Check the menu and step into the nineties."

"Hey, look, I tried."

"Once. And you had to get drunk first."

"And you told me to stop."

"I told you to slow down. Hell, you were gnawing me raw."

"I wasn't. You just weren't responding."

"Look, I know the difference between *gnawing* and *licking*. One feels good, the other don't."

"So, you didn't like it?"

"You have to be gentle. Slow n' easy. And it would help me if you could at least pretend like you wanted to do it. You make it seem like a hassle, instead of a damn good thing."

"J'nette—"

"I know my shit is good."

"—you gonna bitch all night?"

"I'm not bitching. I'm telling you how to satisfy me. I'm asking you to, you know, listen to my body and listen to me. We'll let you know what we like and what ain't right."

"I thought I satisfied you."

"Well, yeah. You make me come. But you don't one-hundred-percent satisfy *all* my needs. I need to go to another level."

"Like?"

"*Like* I said, for starters, I love to give and receive oral sex. This is bullshit."

"What's bullshit?"

"*This.* Look. One of us is being selfish."

"Oh, okay. Now I'm selfish?"

"I didn't say you. I said *one of us*. As in, one of the occupants of this inconsiderate, cold-ass room. If you happen to feel guilty, then hey."

She moved to the far side of the bed, hugged the cushioned rail, turned her back, hiked the covers up above her tiny nose. I grabbed some of the covers she'd yanked off me, laid back on my side. It was a motionless waterbed, but I felt the vibrations from one of her feet bouncing up and down on top of the other.

"J'nette?"

She stopped bouncing her foot. "What?"

"Nothing."

"Nothing what?"

"Nothing nothing."

"It must've been nothing-something."

"Nothing nothing."

"You make me so—arrgh."

"So what?"

"Nothing."

She started back to bouncing her foot. Yeah, this was bullshit. I could and would cooperate. I'd love to please one hundred percent by tickling her fancy cravings, but I didn't appreciate her belligerent attitude. Her lack of consideration for this thin relationship. My special sexual treatments were for special people. Plus, when we're sexing, she always sounds egotistical, makes me feel like I'm making love to a commanding officer. I don't know if I should salute before or after I come. It's not what she said, it was how she said it that put me in a rebellious, defensive mood. I'm very giving, and would love to tongue-stir her black pudding, but she was too demanding.

Maybe I didn't want to do anything for her because I really didn't understand this new mood of hers. She'd become so drastic. Nobody knew why her personality had done a complete 180-degree turn, for no apparent reason. I'd even sat down at work with Solomon and talked it out, told him the 411 on me and J'nette's problems, and hoped he could drop some of his southern-fried wisdom on me and make me see the light. He thinks I get too wound up in the women I date, especially the Miss Wrongs, and always end up on a street called heartache. Might be some sprinkles of truth to that. I should adopt a more disposable attitude about relationships. But that nonchalance just wasn't in my blood. I guess if I didn't have that attitude after Sabrina—that's the sista I was seeing when I was at the University of Memphis—dogged me out, it probably wasn't in my blood. Sex has always bonded me to a woman. Probably always will until I turn to dust and get blown away by a summer breeze. Some nights I wish I had inherited gypsy carnality like my brother Darrell.

I twitched, moved around a touch. J'nette's leg touched mine. She was warm. I scooted a little closer toward her. She moved her skin from mine, inched away and balled up like a knot. Her attitude was colder than the city's streets. A moment passed, stillness filled the room, and I thought she was asleep, but her leg started bouncing again. J'nette did that over and over. She reminded me of a worn-out child that was fighting sleep. I pulled my pillow to my face. Tried to suffocate my irritation. A minute or two later, her rocking felt more soothing. Sleep was on top of me, and I felt like I was floating through a cloud. Reminiscing days gone by.

It's hard to believe, but J'nette used to be the sweetest woman I knew. Our southern-northern personalities have clashed, and we'd had some ten-minute arguments, but I'd assumed that those bits of fire were part of our thrill. Our opposites attracting. Now, she did have a hard East Coast way about her—a way that only seemed hard to me, I guess—and a time or two she'd said a few things that pissed me off to the extreme. I'd even canceled out on seeing her one evening when we were supposed to go to Solomon's for one of his house parties, but that was the nature of the beast. In relationships, people have little spats, don't want to see each other for a day or two, but I'd thought she'd get over it. Yep. Everything has gone down-fucking-hill. Back when we first hooked up, we held hands from Yankee Stadium to the Bronx Zoo; even went to Rockaway Beach and counted the syringes being washed ashore. Now I'd be lucky to get half a smile from her.

I dozed off. Rode that cloud of peace. Right when beautiful images were taking form, J'nette gently touched my shoulder, shook me a little, pulled me toward her.

"Jay, you sleep?"

"What you need?"

She pushed me over, crawled on top. No kisses. She rubbed between my legs, massaged it back to life. Again, I massaged her buttocks, put soft kisses on her breasts, did a slow and easy move with my tongue and licked her nipples back to attention. We were getting into something serious, but she cut short the foreplay, reached down and felt I had a pretty decent erection, then inserted me quick and dry. J'nette put her head into my chest, slid both hands around the small of my back, jerked me like she was trying to pull me through her. She grunted. Said something vulgar and religious. I groaned at the painful good feeling.

I knew what was up. The way she was built, the nature and orientation of her G-spot, she could only orgasm on top. She got pleasure and enjoyment from other positions, but this was the only way to make her come. And the way she went into the bump and grind, the way she dove into a frantic rhythm, she was trying to get right to the point. Before anybody broke a decent sweat, she winced, moaned, gasped, caught her breath, bit her lip, praised Jesus, cursed the good feeling, put her face deep into my chest, growled, held my hands tighter-than-tight, then sighed out the last of her wind as she let my hands go. Her body relaxed; her vaginal muscles slowed the violent twinging. She rolled away and lay next to me panting, one hand holding down her heart.

J'nette regained control of her breathing and stared straight up at the ceiling without a blink. She sat up and looked at me. At first I thought she wanted to switch positions, either ride doggie or go missionary, but when I put my hand on her to call her back to the loving, she snarled and yanked away.

"Wait, I'm not through."

"Too bad," she sneered. "Get some lotion and finish."

"What?"

"You heard me."

"What's wrong with you?"

"Think about it."

She snatched the covers back hard, off me and damn near off the bed, jumped up, wiped her face and stumbled over to her clothes, grabbed her long johns and jerked them on backward.

"Where you going?"

"None'ya."

She tugged her clothes off, put them back on, rumpled, crinkled, crooked, bunched-up and wrinkled. J'nette finger-combed her hair, slapped on her baseball cap, stormed down the hall. The front door opened.

She said a savage, "I just want you to know. I probably shouldn't even tell your selfish ass. I missed my damned period. Again. I didn't tell you last month, because. That's what my dumb ass gets for messing with you."

"You sure? I mean, have you taken a test?"

"Don't worry. I'll get it taken care of."

I called her name. The door slammed hard enough to rattle the oval mirror on my dresser. By the time I jumped into my pajama bottoms and bolted to the front room, she was long gone. My extra door key frowned up at me from the top of the dusty end table.

I got back into a funky bed that reeked of alcohol and perfume. I sifted through the four pillows, found one that didn't smell of her. The odor was strong, in my skin. My shaky hands and still-awake penis were overwhelmed by the spicy aroma of her angry vagina.

I ran my fingers through my hair, looked at the ticking wall clock. 7:45 A.M. I turned the heat up to eighty.

3   Jordan Greene

I called J'nette, left message after message. Begged her to call me back. I thought about apologizing, but I didn't know what the hell I'd be apologizing for. The only thing I had to be sorry about was meeting her in the elevator at CompSci six months ago, the day she started working there. Her arrogance at work turned me on. I just hated that she kept the attitude after five. She dressed striking and professional at work, and radical and hip-hop when she got off. That turned me on too. Instead of being a slave to the system, she'd mastered two worlds.

This feeling sorry wasn't anything new. Me and J'nette Barrett were on the downs. Way, way down. I'd been seeing her a little over four months—if you could call it dating—but the last two hadn't really been worth a subway token. We worked in the same building, her on the sixth floor in Employee Relations, me on the sixty-second. But before last night, we hadn't shared two decent words over the last two weeks. And those were over the phone. Which said much about the quality of our relationship, because the Christmas holidays were right around the corner. I hadn't looked for a Christmas present for her. Didn't matter. Wasn't her birthday anyway.

I was already in the begging zone. And a brother could only beg so long before he got all begged out.

Since I had been up most of the night, it wasn't too hard for me to fall back to sleep. Unfortunately, it was a restless sleep I wish I'd stayed awake to avoid. I dreamed about the night that we had sex and the condom broke. She hated using condoms, always complained about it feeling like an inanimate object being pushed inside her, so we only used extra-thin condoms during her ovulation. Anyway, I was dreaming that J'nette walked into a room, her flat stomach swelling like a balloon on helium. She growled, had a contraction, raised one leg, and plopped out a baby girl who looked exactly like her. Same size. Same attitude. Same clothes. Both attacked me.

I was getting my ass kicked when the phone rang. Now it was hella hot and stuffy, the air was thick, and my throat was dehydrated. I wiped the sweat from my face, cleared my throat, leaned over to pick up the cordless from the nightstand. It was somebody who didn't speak a speck of English. I hung up. Then I paged J'nette and waited. Watered all the house plants. Waited. Cleaned up the bathroom. Paged her again. Washed the dirty dishes. Thirty minutes later, I paged her again. Thirty more minutes. Nothing.

I wiped down the glass on the living room end table, then the frames on both my Barneses, had a bowl of Fruit Loops, sprinkled carpet deodorizer, ran the vacuum to pick up the dirt speckles J'nette had graced the beige carpet with. Her jewelry was scattered on my dresser. I dropped it all into a drawer.

Around one, I called J'nette again. Her twin sister Antoinette, better known as Toni, answered.

"J'nette left a message for you."

"What did she say?"

"*Go to hell.*" Toni laughed and slammed the phone down.

This shit had me rattled. I had to vent, so I called Solomon. He also worked with me, but downstairs in Systems Planning. I wanted to see if he felt like shooting into the City and catching a movie or something. He didn't. His woman—J'nette's best friend Zoe—was over snuggling, keeping his yuletide warm.

"How long has Zoe been over at your crib?"

"Came home with me Friday after work."

"Oh. What she do last night?"

He said a very proud, "Me. What you think?"

J'nette had lied about kicking it with Zoe last night. I kinda figured that, because most people party so much during the week that nobody hits the clubs on the weekend. Weekends are for recuperating. Her fake scenario didn't really matter. It did, but not that much. She needed to learn that when she was running a game, she had to contact all the players in advance, let them know they were on the weekend lineup of lies. Mistreatment and lies have no alibi. I'm through with her ass. Guess that's easy for me to say, especially since she was already through with me.

Solomon said, "I'm throwing a card party Sunday."

"It's cold as hell out. Ain't it supposed to snow again?"

"You better be here. We gonna have dinner and everythang."

"All right."

After I let Solomon get back to his woman, I couldn't think of any real reason not to, so I called Kimberly. Just to say hi. And to thank her for the northern hospitality.

I could hear the smile in her voice. "I was hoping I'd hear from you today."

"You sound wide awake and I'm dragging."

"I went running and I was just getting out of the shower when the phone rang. I'm drying off."

There was something about people telling you they had just gotten out of the shower that made you imagine them butt naked. I wondered if her hair was natural red, or Lucille Ball red.

"Oh, you run?"

"Three to six times a week. Depends on my schedule."

"How far?"

"At least thirty minutes. Just down to the subway and back."

"You can do that in thirty?"

"Maybe twenty-seven on a good day."

"Go on with your bad self! You tired?"

"Stir crazy. I'm going to meet a friend to talk some business. Chit-chat. Want to go hang out in the Village?"

My emotions crept back to that place, that zone where I felt uncomfortable. My brother's wife had been assaulted by a white man. Growing up, white people in Brownsville called us niggers and threw bottles out of their pickup trucks at us, just for fun. They hit us just to hear us holler. My mind was screaming it was a no-go, my finger was about to deliberately push down on the telephone's button and accidentally disconnect us, but my mouth had already answered a smooVe, "Yeah. That's cool."

She caught a cab over to my place. After she walked down the six chipped concrete stairs into my basement apartment, I gave her a friendly hug at the door. Nothing too tight, nothing like last night. She blushed. The chemistry was still brewing.

"Your place looks nice."

"Thank you."

Kimberly was staring at some books I had left on the sofa, manuals for finance and tax software. I wished I had swept them under a rug because now I felt like a nerd without a pocket protector. But my *GQ*, *Newsweek*, and *EM* magazines balanced me out.

She asked, "You use a Mac or an IBM?"

"IBM."

She chuckled.

I asked, "What's funny about that?"

"I use a Mac. Guess we're not compatible."

I laughed. "Guess not."

She hummed a Christmas tune as she wandered around, then picked up a gold-framed picture that was sitting on a shelf above the stereo inside my oak entertainment center. "Is this your mother?"

I was glad she said *is* instead of *was*. I liked to keep the memory alive. I nodded. "Yep."

"You have her complexion."

"Pretty much."

She smiled. "Pretty. Very beautiful woman."

She stared for a while. Moved and found better lighting.

I said, "What's wrong?"

"Nothing. Do you have American Indian in your ancestry?"

"I think my great-grandmother was Cherokee. Why?"

"Most of the African-American people I've met have said they have some Indian ancestry, that's all." She said that like it was no big deal, paused, nodded. "Your mother is really lovely."

I felt a little heated in my chest, felt a fire brewing when I started wondering how many brothas she'd hung out with, how many she'd kissed and held.

I said, "Thank you."

She winked. "Now I see where you get it from."

Her heavy jeans and turtleneck sweater were an even-toned, fresh black and seemed to blend in perfectly with her dark, chocolatey-colored lipstick. A beautiful, modelesque avant-garde flair was what she had. She was perky and peaceful and positive, reminding me of the way J'nette was at first, only with a Caucasian twist. J'nette was dynamite, and Kimberly probably wasn't even a firecracker. I was definitely attracted to Kimberly, but I didn't know why. Probably because I didn't know her. The mystery she radiated was definitely an aphrodisiac. If she was a black woman, I wouldn't question the sensuous feeling that was sneaking up on me. Wouldn't be wondering if going out in public with her was such a bright idea.

"Nice cords." She took her earmuffs from around her neck.

"Thanks." I pulled a loose string off my pants. "Does this shade of green look all right with the gold sweater?"

"Yep. And it goes with the hiking boots."

A beat later I had on my wool overcoat, scarf, and gloves. We talked and walked to the bus stop and caught the Q33, rode 82nd Street to Roosevelt Avenue with Italian and Puerto Rican kids and people who had too many bags and took up too much space. For the whole ride we stood side by side, held on to the rail for fifteen minutes, bumped shoulders, and bounced to and fro in a plethora of odors. Relative to yesterday, today was a very warm thirty degrees. No harsh wind; plenty of sunshine. Crisp air. While we passed by the shops, with each word, our breaths fogged from our mouths.

We went down to the subway platform, practiced being patient, waited so we could hop on the E train with a mass of aloof strangers and rattle our way into Greenwich Village. My soul's from Brownsville, that's the part of this earth that's my foundation. A small town. A simpler lifestyle. And no matter how far from home I roam, the spirit of Brownsville is in me like drawings etched into the walls of an Egyptian tomb. That's why I could live in New York a hundred years and still feel like a visitor. That's why it still amazed me how so many people could be in one spot and nobody would say a word to anybody else. If you smiled they'd think you were crazy. If you spoke you might as well be talking to yourself.

Kimberly playfully bumped me. "How're your hands?"

"Much, much better."

She raised a brow. "Thought you lost your gloves?"

I laughed. "Busted."

"Yep." She laughed. "Busted."

Kimberly kept hold of her petite purse in a strong New York style, with the strap over the opposing shoulder and the bag held tight into her front, making it a hard target for snatchers. Back home, down south, things like that were much more relaxed. Used to be anyway. I remembered seeing women walking with their handbags in one hand, dangling. Down south when people walked, it seemed like they moseyed along or meandered aimlessly, unlike the northern East Coast where everybody walked with the steady brisk pace of pedestrian expressway traffic. Get out the way or you would get run over and trampled. All New Yorkers walked like they had shit to do and were ten minutes late to do it. Even when they didn't have a damn thing to do. Here, subway shoving was mandatory, and stomping on toes required no apology. Took me a while to get used to that.

She said, "I should've worn shades. It's damn bright outside."

"Yeah." I nodded. "The sun reflects off the pavement."

"Worse in the snow. Right after the snow, it's blinding."

"Definitely need shades then."

It felt sorta odd standing out on the platform with her. We were both standing like we were together, but we really weren't together. Not too close, but not too far. A very, just-friends stance, and matching outer body language as we laughed and talked. But I still felt odd. Like everybody was watching me, judging. Like they knew I'd kissed her.

Kimberly was talking, but my mind was on J'nette. I'm not sure if it was J'nette, maybe it was me, but there'd been a serious lack of attention paid to what used to be a damn good relationship. Aside from us not talking as much, our off-and-on sex had become more of a physical activity than an emotional bonding. That disappointed me. I'd hoped for more than drive-through satisfaction.

Last night wasn't the first time she'd done a hit and run. Actually, I expected her to jet before the sweat dried. The last few times, she didn't even spend the night. She got up, smiled at me through the darkness, made an excuse to leave, cabbed it home. Or wherever. Everything had changed. We'd switched from psychedelic love-making to colorless fucking. Experimentation had tapered off. Now it was like jacking-off in somebody. Non-emotional, but still better than having sex with your hand.

Kimberly bumped me again. "Our train's coming."

I smiled to keep from frowning with my memories of J'nette. Then I coughed, moved a few inches away from Kimberly.

In the Village, we stopped off at a semi-crowded, trendy coffee shop near Washington Square Park, decorated with round, mauve tables, soft orange chairs, and green walls. The place looked like a well-drawn cartoon. The strong fragrance of exotic coffee and pastries lived throughout. Four girls, all in oversized NYU sweats, were at a corner table with their psychology books open, bopping their heads and sipping hot chocolate.

Original, abstract, and still-life pictures, with price tags hanging from the bottom right corners, were on each wall. A trio consisting of a pint-sized drummer, a heavyset saxophonist, and a too-tall bass player played instrumental, seasonal jazz. The kind that Coltrane would've thrown down.

I said, "Hey, I just thought about something."

"What's that?"

"Why didn't you have photos of your family up in your apartment?"

She paused, shrugged. Tilted her head like she hadn't ever thought about it. I was hoping her folks didn't throw barbecues at annual KKK rallies or something. Then I wondered why my mind went in that uncomfortable direction. The way I was raised, I was taught to believe the white man always had a secret agenda. Never knew who took the sheets off of their beds and put them over their heads at night.

She answered, "I've never been big on photos. I didn't even take pictures for my senior year in high school."

"Those snapshots capture moments that will never be again."

"True. Hadn't thought about it like that. Lately, well, I guess I've always used my wall space to put up my work."

"If I had your skills, I'd be self-serving too."

"Self-serving?"

"Proud?"

She laughed. "Much better description. And it's not like you have a lot of photos up yourself."

I nodded in agreement. Hadn't thought about that. But the kind of people in my family weren't the type I wanted to put on public display. She probably had the same thing; a family filled with problems that she didn't want to broadcast.

We sat around and talked over cappuccino and blueberry muffins as others played cards and dominoes. We used two of the chairs at our table to hold our coats and scarves, then scooted our chairs closer to each other so we wouldn't have to talk loud, maybe keep whatever secrets we revealed to ourselves. Sipped and eyed each other. Her warm flirting blanketed me. I didn't grin. But I didn't frown either. Kept it cool. Stayed real. Relaxed.

I said, "Penny for your thoughts."

"Eh, excuse me?"

"You look like you're thinking about something."

She smiled and blushed. "You kiss nice."

"You're pretty good yourself."

"Why didn't you kiss me when I came over?"

I paused. Felt a little awkward because she was so forward. But I liked it, because something about her stirred me from the inside out. So I set free my smile, then said, "Day's not done yet."

She patted my hand with hers, touched me and said, "That a promise?"

"Most definitely."

"Good." She grinned. "Day's not done."

While I eased up, relaxed, and rubbed my hand across hers, a couple of brothas walked in. Both had on bland-colored slacks and dull ties, and looked like they were in retail sales on the strip. Either that or Jehovah's Witnesses on break. I nodded my head and mouthed a cordial, "Whu'sup."

That speaking to strangers crap was a southern habit I had to get rid of. I kept forgetting I was in New York; being friendly to strangers wasn't en vogue. Frowns were the mood of the day. Smiles made you stand out like a tourist ready to get jacked. The brothas nodded. Hard-faced nods, no smiles. I stopped gazing that way, but felt all eyes on me.

When Kimberly rubbed my hand and excused herself to go to the bathroom, I watched her stroll. She had a tempting walk. Much more relaxed than the bumping-through-pedestrian-traffic strut. A more feminine sway. A lot of women had lost that artistic side of being a lady. Kimberly was definitely a lady. Her shoulders stayed firm. She brushed her hand through her frizzy red hair once or twice, led with her hips, and had a slight, easygoing sashay that sucked me into its rhythm. I was so busy watching her, so caught up in the rhythm, that I didn't notice that one of the brothas had come over and was standing over me. His eyes were filled with chastisement.

I said a tight-lipped, "Whu'sup?"

He winked. "Baby doll got it going on."

He grinned enough to let me see his crowded teeth.

I shifted, said a stiff, "Yeah. She's tight."

I was about to say that we were just friends, but alligator mouth winked again and walked away. I didn't get the message he'd delivered. If Kimberly was a sista, smile or no smile, I'd know what he meant. Maybe it was the same compliment and I was making a big deal out of it, making something out of nothing at all.

We walked around awhile, did some window-shopping in SoHo, passed by the buildings that have Ralph Lauren's six-story pictures of supermodel Naomi Campbell and the male model Tyson plastered on the fronts, both half-naked and advertising Polo Sport, then ended up stopping by a chic art store on Eighth Street. It was a rainbow-colored place that had practically no furniture. A huge, pastel-colored, oriental-style carpet covered the floor, and many matted paintings from local artists were hung on the walls. Kimberly had three of her works up front on display. I recognized the pictures. The woman and man in the shower. The lovers at sunset. The couple breaking up. Each going for over a grand apiece. On my budget, I wouldn't be able to afford the two I'd pulled out, not without a serious layaway plan. I might just have to settle for a fifty-dollar reprint and a Kmart frame.

Kimberly was talking with the owner, a middle-aged Italian woman named Clair, who looked as unique in dress and flair as Kimberly. Plus she had green hair. Looked like she'd been dipped in a bucket of lime Kool-Aid. Clair peeped over Kimberly's shoulder, smiled. Both of them giggled.

While Kimberly took care of her business, I tipped away to the pay phone, checked my messages to see if J'nette had returned my call. She hadn't. The hint was obvious. I think I'd better let it go. My eyes went to Kimberly and, despite the nippiness of the weather, I felt a warmth brewing head to toe. Felt that kind of feeling you get when you're sipping herbal tea and listening to a good instrumental sax song in the middle of the night.

I made myself comfortable in a worn brown loveseat by the front door, flipped through several of the artsy magazines on the golden coffee table. The sensor buzzed when the front door opened, bringing in a strong breeze of cold air. A very James Dean–ish looking guy in jeans and a military jacket took the final draw from a cigarette and flipped it back out onto the pavement before he primped inside, pulled off his gloves, went directly to the counter, eased behind Kimberly, snuck a kiss on the side of her head. That made me shift around. My blood warmed. First she smiled, but when she turned and saw him, she stopped laughing. Her body tightened. Fingers rolled into fists. She sidestepped.

"I thought that was you." He smiled and tried to hug her.

"And I thought you were somebody else," she snapped and stepped farther to the side. "Don't ever touch me again."

He took a breath, then nodded. "Clair."

After she cleared her throat, Clair moved her green hair from her face, destroyed her smile, and nodded back. "Hello, Eric."

Without another word, Kimberly glanced to see if I was paying attention, then breezed toward me.

I stood up, took a step her way.

"Kimberly," Eric called. "C'mon now. We need to settle this. Let's work it out."

"Keep away from me."

"Don't do this to us, Kimberly."

She flipped her hand in his direction and growled, "Away!"

He didn't move far from the counter. Clair said a few things to him, almost as if she was trying to calm the lion to keep the peace. Eric ignored Clair the same way Kimberly was ignoring him. I wasn't sure how I felt about this situation.

Kimberly walked to me, took my hand. Thick lines rose in Eric's face. Felt like he was frowning at me, maybe at my skin tone. I held on to my firmness in both stance and voice.

Eric dropped his head, nodded. He twisted his neck to flip his hair away from his face.

I asked Kimberly, "You okay?"

"Oh, I'm fine. Let's go."

I said an uncomfortable "Okay."

"Clair," she said without looking back. "I'll call you."

"You take care," Clair said without taking her eyes off Eric.

"Ah, Kimberly—" Eric grumbled and sprinted toward us, trying to beat us to the door. "Can I talk to you for a minute?"

"Keep the hell away from me."

She was shivering. I felt the tremors because I was holding her hand. Eric gazed at me, flipped his 90210-looking hair from his eyes before running his hand through it, made hostile eye contact with me, and said a cold-faced, "You mind if I talk to her for a minute?"

His voice sounded much more mature than he looked. I couldn't figure out how old he was, but I guessed he was a couple of years younger than me. He sounded and looked East Coast in accent and body language. Before I could answer one way or the other, Kimberly stepped around me.

"Eric, go to hell. Nobody controls my mouth. Nobody owns me. I talk to who I want to talk to. Now, I've told you for the last time, I don't want to talk to you. Ever."

"Kim, why—"

"*Kimberly*. My damn name is *Kimberly*, fuck you very much. Have a nice day. Now get the hell out of my face."

Eric moved side to side, glared like he was trying to feel me out. His eyes shifted back and forth. I matched his attitude. Nodded. He dropped more weight on one leg, fell into a trite Dean-ish pose. Half of his face smiled. "I'm her boyfriend."

Kimberly interjected, *"Ex-boyfriend."*

She pulled my arm and we exited the store into the crowd on Eighth Street. As we moved up Avenue of the Americas through pedestrians and walked by two blocks of homeless people, street musicians, and poets, bumping by Salvation Army–posted Santa Clauses, Eric followed, marched on her other side, kept away from me as he bumped around people and continued pestering a non-hearing Kimberly. He was yelling her name over and over. Sounded like a scratched record. He'd pissed me off, but I did the right thing and chilled out. Last thing I wanted to do was get into what might look like a race war.

Eric said, "Look, Kim, please—"

"Kimberly. My name is Kimberly."

"Please," his voice sputtered. "Kimberly, I want to get back together. I need you."

Eric faded into the cold when we did an abrupt turn and dashed into a cab that Kimberly had forced to stop by leaping off the curb with a wide-armed body-block. She didn't even glance back or respond to his cries or beats on the trunk for a second chance. Other than wanting to know where we were going, the thin, female, Russian-sounding driver didn't seem to care one way or the other. The frantic scene rated a yawn. She was used to madness.

Kimberly sat on her side of the cab, me on mine. Several minutes passed before she said a word.

"I'm sorry about that." Kimberly bit her lip. Bounced one leg on top of the other. Slapped a mitten across her knee.

I cleared my throat. "What was that all about?"

Kimberly loosened her scarf and leaned forward to the driver. "Could you please turn the heater down?"

The driver raised her hand. "Yes."

"Kimberly," I started, "what was—"

"He doesn't understand the meaning of good-bye. He's one of those men who doesn't want it to be over until *he* wants it to be over. Reason or no reason, it's over when *I* say it's over."

"That gooder?" the cabbie asked.

"Ah, I," Kimberly was flustered, struggling to unbutton her coat, "eh, yeah. Thank you. Much, eh, gooder."

"No problem. Let me know if it get cold for you."

We both said, "Okay."

I asked, "How long did you go out?"

"Almost six months. Too long."

"What happened?"

"Let's just say," she rattled in a dry, sarcastic tone, as she stared forward, "he wanted to be in my bed, but he didn't want to participate in my life."

"So, he's your boyfriend?"

"Hell, no."

I laughed.

She scowled at me, "What's so damn funny?"

I smiled. "You look so damn fine when you're mad."

She stopped her fidgeting. "What?"

"Your skin lights up. Eyes get tight. Voice gets deep, and you kick in a real professional tone. You rattle nonstop. I like the way your lips move when you talk fast. You get those hot, bedroom eyes."

She groaned. "Corny."

Seeing her fire had turned me on. Damn. I've always been attracted to that in a woman. "Why don't you come over here and make it fresh? Or don't you like the way I kiss anymore, huh?"

A smile rose in her face. She scooted over close to me and punched my shoulder.

"I'm sorry for the situation."

"It's okay."

A moment later, we stared at each other. She moved closer and tilted her head, just like she did the first time.

Kissing crosses a thick, personal line. As you sample the flavors, as you taste each other, it definitely gives a different, deeper level of familiarity. It lets you inside. Everybody can kiss, but not everybody understands the art of kissing. The listening. The talking. Knowing when to give, knowing when to take. And with all the passion involved, with all the desires and fantasies the tongue massage can create, kissing is an art form within itself that isn't necessarily the prelude to sex. Kissing is kissing. And sex is sex. One's not necessary for the other. But when mastered, they both work oh so well together. And depending on how skillful, how tasteful, or how sloppily the exchange is done, it could be the slow beginning of something magical. Or a very abrupt ending. A sweet turn-on, or a hard turnoff.

After many minutes of savoring each other, I looked up at the smiling cab driver. My face was smeared with chocolate lipstick. The cab driver turned her mirror away. Kimberly eased her hand on the side of my face and called me back to the kissing. Her round face looked so sensuous as she slowly parted her full lips. She sucked my ear, kissed my face, and made her way back to my mouth. Then my hand had grazed the top of her blouse, had stopped wandering long enough to squeeze her breast. She moved my hand, eased up a portion of her sweater, slid my fingers under and into her warmth.

It's hard to digress from intimacy without looking hypocritical. Especially when you didn't want to back off, and had no desire to deviate from what you felt. Right or wrong, it felt right. My mind and heart were both in agreement on that.

But I knew one thing for sure. With Kimberly, the curiosity was not the attraction. The attraction was the attraction.

4 Jordan Greene

From the front door, our clothes were scattered. We'd left a lusty trail across her living room, through her work area. Never turned a light on. I was going to kiss her good-bye, then head on home, but we never stopped kissing. I followed her toward the bedroom. Maybe she was following me. No music. The only sounds were the ones we made.

Kimberly had a peach body fragrance. I kissed the side of her face, inhaled the fresh smell of her hair when it tangled into my mouth. We'd been kissing so long and so strong that we were sweating like we'd been working out. Like mine, her breathing was erratic, choppy.

We slowed at the bedroom door, caught our breath. Her eyes had the same wanting as mine, but the closer we made it to the bedroom, the more her face had a what-the-hell-are-we-doing pout blossoming underneath the passion. I felt the same, but that male part of me didn't want to punk out and walk away from a woman. But I know I felt the same way she did, so each of us was waiting for the other to change their mind.

And I paused, let some fresh air come between us, waited for her to pull her scarlet mane from her face and put some soft and tender words with the we-can't-do-this-because-we-just-met expression swelling in her face. Hoped my expression told her that this didn't have to happen. Not today, anyway.

But she kicked out of her French-cut panties, underwear that made her long legs look longer, then used her foot to drag my boxers from around my ankles. Damn, she had a glow. Like she was on fire from inside. That made me want to know how my nakedness appealed to her; if the heat I felt in the pit of my stomach was radiating in my eyes. I tried to pretend that one more kiss wouldn't send me over the edge, acted like I wasn't aching to slide inside of her, but my erection was in her hand. Being caressed. She held on to me, pulled me toward the bed. I followed the feeling.

A car's horn was blowing outside. Another car was riding over broken snow, crushed ice.

When she broke free long enough to pull her sheets back, I stood behind her, kissed up and down her spine. Her back arched, she sucked air in short pants, released a long breath, dropped the covers, tilted her head forward for more kisses. I massaged her breast with one hand; she led the other between her legs, to begin a slow finger massage on her love. She was wet. Soft. Hot. I pushed her facedown on the bed, licked up and down her back, made a trail to her butt. Back down to her calves. Across her thick ankles. To her toes. She pulled her foot away.

I asked, "Ticklish?"

She nodded.

More licks, sucks, and nibbles on her butt. Kimberly squirmed, moaned, and tried to wriggle away. I chased. Kimberly turned over, put a hand under each of my armpits, and pulled me up to her, face to face. We kissed and she reached down to find me, but my rigidness had already self-guided itself to her opening. It touched, slipped across her wetness, moved inside. Her breathing sped up; her grip on me tightened, pulled me deeper into her soul. I stopped breathing. She had done the same. Had scraped the bottom of my soul. Neither of us was breathing or moving. Then at the same moment, we gasped back to life.

We'd connected, had become the same person. I was inside of her, but she was deeper inside of me. She bit her lip and let out a scream of wispy moans. The sounds of her loving matched mine, ran chills through me. With one hand on my butt and the other around to my back, she orchestrated the rise and fall of our loving, controlled the depth of the ins and outs.

The winds whistled against her window for a long while. Then calmed. Another car started tooting its horn. Somebody's heavy bass echoed gangsta rap from their car when they passed by.

My rhythm was still slow in, ease out. All my nerves had migrated, were working to drive satisfaction out of my body and into hers. I pulled out. Caught my breath. Wiped her face. She took my hand, nibbled my fingers. Her hips were anxious, rotating. She tried to bring me back toward her honey.

I told her, "I don't want to come yet."

She took a deep breath and smiled, then puffed out her breath and whispered, "I don't want you to."

Kimberly held the tip of my penis, pressed right under the hat. Did that until the sensation died and I had my control.

She whispered, "Better?"

"Yep. Better."

She turned me on my belly, then eased out of the bed.

"Where you going?"

"Keep your eyes closed. Be patient."

She opened the fridge and its light brightened the hallway. I closed my eyes. Heard the cabinet click open. Glasses clacked. Fluids poured. Then she came back. Giggled. She took several swallows and let out a satisfying, "Ahhhhh."

When she kissed up and down my back, I gripped the pillow hard and groaned, tensed my butt and stomach muscles. Her mouth was freezing. She had ice inside. She ran a cube up and down my backbone, held it so it barely glanced my skin. The room filled with her giggles and my moans. Damn. I was gone. Far gone.

She whispered, "You like?"

I wrestled her down to her back, slid my tongue down to her moist navel, stole her sweat, pulled her leg over my shoulder.

She sang along with her shudder, "Mmmmmhmm."

First, soft licks and kisses on her thighs. Then back and forth over her love. I became the artist. Pretended my tongue was a paintbrush and her womanhood was my canvas.

We placed both pillows under the small of her back. Stared into each other's eyes.

She blushed. "I don't believe we're doing this."

"That makes two of us." I kissed her neck. She jerked. I asked, "Want to stop?"

She held me tighter. "What do you think?"

"You don't scream, then I won't holler."

The naked trees outside her window looked like they were pointing at us while they stood motionless and watched.

With her hand around my neck, she pulled me close and kissed my face. Again my heartbeat moved south. We pulled each other into a frantic kiss. Her tongue chased mine, and when she caught it, she trapped it, sucked it deep into her mouth.

I put my hand on her waist, and pulled her hard to me. Her eyes bucked open and she grunted, jerked away, then relaxed.

"Do it again."

I did. Over and over. What started off slow had become wild and primitive. Short breaths. Vicious groans. Rough grunts. Uncivil squeals. Headboard banged the wall.

The creaks of her bed died. She collapsed on me, rested her sweat on my sweat. I felt her heart beating through her chest. It was running almost as fast as mine. We fanned each other. Wiped away sweat. Most of her sweat was on her lower back, draining around her sides.

Kimberly giggled and covered her face.

"What?"

"We were loud. *Real* loud, I think."

It's not until the quiet that you realize how much noise there was. We laughed, cuddled tighter. I felt like a high school kid who had just had his first orgasm. Wide-eyed and amazed at the feeling that another body could give to mine. Women are so damn extraordinary. In the afterglow, all of our after-touches and after-words were mellow. Soft spoken.

I asked her, "Did you?"

She elbowed me and said a sarcastic "You couldn't tell?"

"Had to be sure."

"Why do men always ask that?"

"Because we're creatures of detail."

"You're creatures of insecurity."

She leaned, clicked on the bedside lamp, then we pulled the covers back up on the bed. I didn't want the lights on, not that soon. I wasn't ready to shed light on what we'd done.

I was on my back, playing connect-the-dots with the dark freckles on her back and breasts. She was tracing her fingers across my arm, my chest, my legs.

She whispered, "Your skin has so many colors."

"What do you mean?"

"Your fingers have about three shades. See here? You're darker around your knuckles than on the other parts. Your back has at least three distinct colors. Your forearm is lighter on this side than on that side."

I guess I should've been offended, should've become defensive at the way she was mesmerized by me, but I wasn't. She was open; I was the one with the hang-ups, shut off from being real. And I was too busy staring at my hands. At my arms. Regarding my many shades of brown. I said, "I never really noticed."

"And your face is a little darker than your chest."

"My face is darker because of the sun. It's always exposed."

"Then why is your penis the darkest part of your body?"

We laughed.

She cackled, "It's the color of chocolate. Is it always exposed too?"

She flopped it to the side, compared it to the color of my thigh. We laughed while she played doctor and roamed my body.

She said, "Your butt doesn't get any sun, but it's the same color as your legs. How the hell does that happen?"

I shrugged.

She was still playing with me, touching me here, feeling me there, massaging me with her hands and words; I went back to touching her freckles. Most of them were on her neck and back. A few on her breasts. Some were as brown as me; a couple were milky; others varied from dark brown to the color of red clay. Her skin wasn't as doughy as I thought it might be. But next to mine, it needed some color, especially down in the areas a bikini would cover. Especially down in the Y. Whoever said that white meat was dry lied. The flesh around her eyes and cheeks was windburned. The rest a tad lighter. Lighter, but not close to being pale. Her breasts were firm; the nipples were light brown.

I said, "Where did you get your freckles from?"

"Daddy. My mother has a few, but Daddy has the most."

She cuddled next to me. The wind whistled a long, unmerciful song. I thought I heard a tree bend in agony. Her phone rang, we twitched, then her answering machine clicked on. It did that three times, back to back. That made me wonder what kind of life she led. Made me wonder what she'd be doing if I wasn't here. The volume was down, so all of her late-night messages went unheard. She ignored the machine, so I did the same.

I craned my neck to look at her digital clock. It was a few minutes before one A.M. We'd been teasing and touching and sharing whispers for almost two hours.

She yawned, then asked, "Are you staying?"

"Yeah. Is that okay?"

"Yep. I'd like that. I mean, you don't have to if you don't want to. I'll understand. This wasn't expected, so I'm not going to try to make you feel obligated."

I thought I'd want to break for the door, but I didn't. I couldn't remember the last time my life felt this agreeable. The feeling in my belly was like what I imagined parasailing over the ocean down in the Bahamas would be like. I touched her frizzy hair, traced my fingers over her dried sweat, and said, "I want to. Maybe we can get breakfast in the morning."

Her words sounded like a smile of relief. "Okay, SmooVe."

She leaned across me, kissed me, then clicked off the light. A few moments went by. Damn. I liked this woman. At least I did tonight. I was wondering what tomorrow's sunrise would look like in her eyes. Part of me wondered how I would see her in the morning; another part wondered how I would see myself.

"Jordan."

"What?"

"Nothing. I was just thinking your name; wanted to hear it out loud, that's all."

"Really?"

"Yep. Really."

A little while later I whispered, "Kimberly."

"Jordan." Her hand traced down my chest, touched my penis. Held my handle, moved it up and down, helped it grow in her hand. Made it tingle with heat, feel strong and powerful. She kissed me and said, "Let's make love again."

"Are we making love?"

She chuckled, kissed me, became real serious. With my eyes closed, I tried to taste the difference.

We jumped awake at about three A.M. That was when somebody lost their mind and rang her doorbell nonstop. When the ding-donging eased up, the banging began. It started soft, then grew into a demanding rhythm. Whoever it was wasn't going away. The drumming had a personalized pattern. And that made me shudder harder than the New York winds had ever done.

Kimberly jerked awake, jumped up, yanked her hair from her face and grumbled, "Shit."

Her voice, the shift in her body, told me it was trouble making a late-night run. My heart pounded in my throat. After we had gone another round, Kimberly had fallen asleep with her head in the small of my back, using me as her pillow. The room was cooler because the heat had kicked off, which made the snuggling much more appreciated. Minutes ago the room smelled of pleasure; now it reeked with terror.

The pounding was still going on. Harder. Stronger.

"What's wrong?" I asked.

She peeped out the window, then stared back toward the knocking. "Asshole."

"Who?"

"Eric."

In the scattered light, Kimberly stepped into her closet and pulled out a thick, red, hooded house coat.

She said, "I'll be right back."

She pulled the bedroom door to, but it didn't close. Kimberly's bare feet slapped hard and fast across the wooden floor. She stubbed her toe on something, yelped and cursed hard when it fell. I was about to call to see if she was okay, but I didn't want my voice to carry. Sounded like she moved something, maybe kicked it out of the way. Her smooth walk changed into an irritated, one-foot-limping-while-the-other-led stride.

I was about to move my clothes closer to me, when I remembered they were scattered in the front room. Dropped everywhere. I was a brotha trapped in a white woman's bed, butt-naked and defenseless. I wondered how this shit would read on the front page of the *New York Times*. I probably wouldn't get any sympathy from the NAACP or the UNCF, no matter how many donations I made.

"*What?*" I heard her snap. She hadn't opened the front door. Then I heard mumbles from the other side. First it sounded like cursing, then it changed to begging. Kimberly's voice came through loud and clear; it dropped back into her business tone. More vicious mumbles sprinkled in.

A couple of minutes later, she stormed back in and opened her closet. I was on my stomach, arms folded around her pillow.

"Jordan?"

"Yeah?" I raised my head when she whispered my name. "Whu'sup?"

"I have to step outside for a minute."

"Want me to leave?"

She wrenched a sweater over her head and said a soft "No."

She yanked sweats over her naked bottom, tightened the drawstring. I sat up and asked, "What's going on?"

"He knows I have company. That's why he's tripping out and won't leave. I don't want my neighbors in my business, so I'll, I don't know. I'll talk him out of the building."

"Want me to stick my head out of the door and—"

"No. Thanks, but no. I can handle this."

The doorbell rang several times, followed by the knocking. With each beat, the slamming was louder. I shifted, tugged the sperm-stiffened sheets back, and sat up, putting my feet on the cool floor. The way the winds were singing, it had to be damn cold, with a serious windchill outside. Too cold to be anywhere this time of morning starting some shit. But a fool was a fool, no matter what the time or temperature.

I asked, "Want me to leave?"

"I wouldn't give him the satisfaction."

"We could talk later."

"Everything's okay." Her words were faster than speed-dial.

I turned on the small light on her nightstand. It was a three-way and I clicked it to the softest setting. Waited for my pupils to adjust to the brightness. We both looked over at her digital clock at the same moment. She shook her head, tsked.

I asked, "He always drop in this time of the morning?"

"No. Well, when we went out, he did a couple of times, because he knew I'd stay up and work late."

"Oh."

"I haven't seen him in months," she interrupted. "The only reason he's here now is because he saw me with you today."

Kimberly hurried back to the doorbell. When the door opened, it sounded like he tried to push his way inside, but she made him go out. Their voices faded. They must've gone down the stairs.

The bedroom light killed enough of the shadows so I could hunt for my clothes. I brought them all in from the living room and piled them at my feet. Waited. It was late. Cold as fuck. I was tired as hell. Common sense was common sense. I dressed, waited a couple more minutes, then crept through the living room. Stood by the front door. Listened to their voices.

I opened the door and the breakneck-paced, overlapping argument that was echoing up from the bottom floor shut off. I glared over the rail. They stared up. Kimberly moved her hair from her face, turned, and jogged up the stairs, left Eric talking to himself. Eric held on to his glower, grimaced at me.

I was a quarter of the way down and Kimberly was in front of me. Face redder than her hair. Her breath steamed. "Don't go."

I shook my head. "I think I better."

We stood and stared, shared deep looks of shame and uncertainty. The poetic bonding ran deep. Almost as wide as the boundaries I had slipped and crossed. She came up a step and kissed my lips. "Okay."

Eric grunted. His pang and pisstivity rose from the bottom. Sounded like an echo from the pits of hell. I didn't move. Kimberly didn't flinch. I was about to head back up and give her a few minutes to work things out, when Eric's heavy shoes thudded up the stairs. He stopped near us, shook his head, and snapped out a bitter "I thought you were by yourself?"

Kimberly glanced at me, then sulked back to him. "No."

"Kim, why—"

"Fuck, my name is Kimberly."

He stomped up to the landing, *"All right, Kimberly—"*

Kimberly said a firm "Eric. Go. I'll call the police if you don't—"

Eric sprang past her, thrust both his gloved hands at my throat. Kimberly shrieked, slipped down to one knee, tried to grip the wall to pull herself back up. I had twisted and slapped down both of his arms, shoved his ass backward and downward, made him lose his balance. He fell to his knees and bounced down a couple of steps. I threw a right hook, kicked at his face, but I missed both times and slipped. I caught the railing and regained my balance. Long johns, pants, and coats didn't make for good fighting. With him lower than me, if nothing else, gravity was in my favor and I could drop-kick his ass.

We went after each other. Before I got to him, before he got to me, Kimberly jumped in between. My chest was about to explode. I focused on the fool, glowered at the woman who was keeping me from dropping my foot smack dab in the middle of his face. Thought about who I was and where I came from.

Them. Us.

It was on.

"You don't know who you fucking with," I machine-gunned and headed down toward him. "I'll ram my foot so far up your ass you'll be coughing up shit."

Eric cringed, scooted backward, bumped off the walls like a pinball, bumbled, tried to gain a better position for fighting. I'd forced him from offense to defense. I'd been forced from defensive to being offended. Kimberly hopped in front, indignant, blocking me and the ignorant asshole from each other.

Kimberly yelled, "Don't! Jordan, please, I'll—"

"Kimberly," Eric backed away and said, "I'm sorry. It's just that I don't want to live without you—"

"Eric, get your immature ass the hell out of my building. It's over between us and I don't want—"

I jerked from her, shuffled past him, hurried down the stairs and out the front of her building. Stormed along the fence lining the Bulova plant. Didn't look back.

Three miles later I was home. My fingers were beyond numb.

5 Jordan Greene

By the time I'd cabbed it back from the laundromat, rolled my laundry cart down to my apartment, and put up three loads of Downy-fresh clothes, I had two messages.

One was from my older brother, Darrell. The time tag said he called at one P.M., almost ten minutes ago. That was his second time calling all year. We hadn't actually talked in about fifteen months. No hostility. It was just that since Momma died, we all strayed our separate ways. A lot of families do that when the glue that held them together passes on to a better place. And Darrell had been difficult to talk to after the incident that happened to his wife. Or I should say ex-wife. Another page of tragedy in our family. If not calling to complain, he might be phoning to tell me our middle brother, Reggie, had overdosed again. Last time I saw Reggie, he'd blown up and looked like a chocolate Pillsbury Doughboy, and his arms had more tracks than a Hot Wheels set. No one ever knew where Reggie was. He popped up, stole what he could, disappeared. He stole the TV out of my dorm room when I was in college. That was my freshman year. And it was my roommate's TV. I slaved too many less than minimum-wage-paying hours at the Student Union's game room to pay Jefferson back. Maybe Reggie was why I never called. Sometimes I just wasn't in the mood for bad news.

Still, my brothers were my brothers. Blood was blood. So I gritted my teeth and called Darrell back. He was gone. I left a message saying I got his message. Tag, you're it. Guilt removed.

The other call was from Solomon. His country ass was definitely throwing another impromptu gathering at his apartment. And the weekend crew was definitely coming out to hang out.

Two hours later, I was huddled in my black wool coat, hopping off the 2 train at 110th and Lenox, passing by Central Park North and heading into the Collard Green Projects—that's what my people called Harlem. A beat later I was hoofing it on the east side of the city that had a low life expectancy for black men, outside Solomon's crib, a bottle of Spumante in my hand, buzzing his apartment. On the twentieth floor, I stepped off the elevator and was met by the sound of laughter seeping from inside his place. The smells of fried chicken and broccoli mixed with cabbage filled the air, crept out into the hallway. Solomon's antique three-speed phonograph was playing his collection of albums. Special Delivery's song "I Destroyed Your Love" was loud and clear. He had a CD player, but the brother was nostalgic at times. His Temprees collection was out next to a dusty Isaac Hayes album.

Other than the music, everything was newer than new. Furniture was leather, money green. His color. Solomon had huge pictures of Billie Holiday, Sarah Vaughn, Dinah Washington, and Nina Simone on the off-white walls. His women. A bootleg copy of an action movie that hadn't made it to the movie theaters yet was playing on his television, but there was too much talking to hear the sound. Plus the picture's quality was so bad that it made me think I had cataracts and glaucoma.

Everybody was wearing either jeans or designers sweats, and shoes were lined up at the front door. That was one of Solomon's pet peeves, people who wore shoes in the house. The first two people I saw were J'nette and Toni. They were a few feet away in the tiny dining room, by the four-foot-high Christmas tree, playing dominoes with a couple of guys I didn't know. Toni accidentally spoke. Accidentally because she'd opened her mouth and said something nice before she raised her eyes to see who she was talking to. She cringed like she wished she could take the words back. The brothas nodded, no attitude. J'nette wrinkled her mouth, dropped her head. Zoe peeped out of the kitchen, chuckled her svelte, bowlegged self over and kissed my face. I'd never seen a woman look so happy.

I hugged her. "Where's Sol?"

"My man's in the kitchen." She tiptoed and pulled at my coat sleeve. "Hand me your coat."

Solomon walked in and took it from Zoe, but she took it back from her man and said, "I got it, Sol. Baby, kick it with your homey. Take the wine in the kitchen and finish your plate."

He joked, "See, that's what's wrong with the black woman. Won't let a brother treat her like a queen. Won't let a brother shower her with affection."

"Don't start with that nonsense."

"All right." Solomon winked at her as he stroked his thick moustache. "It's your world. I'm just a squirrel."

She came back, "Trying to get a nut."

I said, "Sounds too freaky for my virgin ears."

They looked cute standing side by side. Like little African-American dolls. She was all of five feet on a good day. She used to look like Salt N' Pepa. Both of them, plus Spinderella. Together. Side by side. She was that big. But she hit the gym six days a week, hired a personal trainer, went on an Oprah-diet mission and lost fifty-some pounds. Solomon's five-two, but the way he talks, the thickness of his voice, you'd think he was at least six-three. Because of its shine, I could tell Solomon had slapped another coat of Dark N' Lovely in his hair. He'd been fighting a battle with premature gray.

Zoe paraded off with my coat and brown leather gloves. For a moment, I thought about Kimberly's mittens. Saw all the colors. Remembered her compassion, how warm her hands felt on mine. Thought about her kisses more than anything else.

I made my way around the room and spoke to damn near everybody, especially the people I didn't know. Yasmean was the mulatto in the green sweats and golden pageboy cut. She had three moles on her freckled face and a relaxed posture. Solomon had wanted to introduce me to her a few months ago, but I had already hooked up with J'nette. Yasmean smiled and shook my hand, held it too long.

J'nette and Toni looked up from the butcher block table. Their scowls matched, every line engraved in their foreheads was in duplicate, only Toni's expression looked like it came from the heart. J'nette needed to find the Wizard to get a heart.

"Whu'sup, J'nette?" I said as politely as I could. "Toni?"

"Not a damn thing," Toni said, then slapped down a bone hard enough to shake their wine glasses. She pulled a few strands of her shoulder-length hair out of her face and boasted an arrogant, "Twenty-five points."

"I didn't know you were coming," J'nette said without looking up. There was a frown in her voice. I smelled her attitude. It reeked. Made Nurse Ratchid look like Snow White.

I returned a dry "That makes two of us."

She asked a sarcastic "Anyone have any lotion?"

Toni snickered, slid J'nette an easy high five. Solomon followed me into the kitchen. Dominoes slammed hard on the table.

Solomon asked, "What's that all about?"

"Food smells good," I redirected the conversation.

"Knock yourself out."

I grabbed a paper plate, went to the gas stove and took the lids off several pots. From his windows that faced Fifth Avenue, I could see the bare trees in Central Park, Mt. Sinai Hospital, and parts of the East River. Some days I could see clear to 40th and parts of Trump Plaza. The brother had the view of all views. That was why he didn't have any curtains up, to let whatever the weather was shine in.

I said, "You cooked?"

"Hell, naw. I don't cook on Sundays."

"But ten minutes after you run out of Second Baptist, you walk across the street, throw a party, and listen to the blues."

"Damn skippy."

"Hypocrite."

"Zoe did the chicken. Yasmean brought the cabbage. Sweet potato pie is in the fridge."

"J'nette and Toni cook anything?"

"Those leeches don't never bring nothing; you know that."

"Then it's safe. No cyanide."

"Yeah." Solomon picked up his plate. We stood and ate. The record changed. The Temprees crooned "Thousand Miles Away."

"So, whu'sup with you and Zoe?"

"Right now," he said with a grin, "everythang and a bucket o' wangs."

"I see."

Solomon said, "She's melting like ice on a hot griddle."

"What's next?"

"I'm gonna meet her daughter, Sierra, one day this week."

"How old?"

"Four."

I asked, "DaReus is four, right?"

"Little man's three. He'll be back up for the summer."

"Sounds serious."

"I looked at some rings. Saw one I liked."

"You ready to get married again?"

"Like I done told you, Zoe is gonna be my future."

Solomon had been chasing and trying to romance Zoe for the last six months. Hard chasing. Big-buck romancing. While she had two consecutive boyfriends, he went after her. Said she was what he wanted and that he would chase her to the ends of the Earth. Looks like it paid off, both ways. They had serious, life-changing glows. Personally, I think she was playing harder-than-hard-to-get because she knew she could do no wrong when it came to him.

Solomon switched subjects. "What's up with you and J'nette?"

"Ain't shit up with us."

"She ain't you. You can do better."

"Tell me about it."

"I didn't think she would come over. You know I didn't invite her. She walked in with a big-ass 'tude on. She got a bigger 'tude when I told Zoe you were on the way out. I was kinda hoping she'd leave before you got here."

"I'd like to catch her waiting on the subway and accidentally drop-kick her wicked ass to the third rail."

Solomon laughed, pulled me deeper into the kitchen. J'nette cut her eyes at me, then back toward her identical stern-faced sister. They looked like evil bookends.

I asked, "Who's the guy with J'nette?"

"The one facing the wall is Carlton. The other one is Rodney. They were arm-in-arm with them when they walked in. I started to call to let you know the four-one-one, but the way you sounded on the phone, I didn't think you'd bundle up and bring your thin-blooded butt out in this weather."

"It's cool." I took a swallow of soda. "Don't matter."

"Sho 'nuff?"

"Yeah. J'nette's off the menu. History. I'm switching channels. She was cool at first, then all of a sudden changed up and started playing hard to get. Now she won't get got."

Solomon frowned, "Want me to kick her out? I'll do it."

"They'd call big-ass Elaine, she'd be here from SoHo in a poof, and they'd be all over your ass like you done stole something."

I told him about Kimberly, leaving out the race part. I told him about the cab ride, about her job, about us running into her ex, about the sex, about her ex showing up in the middle of the night, about him jumping at me, about me walking home before I started a riot.

Solomon beamed. "Call the sista up. She sounds like a damn good thing. Bird in the hand."

"Think I should?"

"See, see. That's what wrong with the black man. Always have to wait for the sista to chase him. Pursue and flatter, that's what the black man is supposed to do."

"She's not a sista."

His voice dropped and a brow rose. "Puerto Rican?"

I shook my head.

He dipped his voice another octave. "Italian?"

I thought about it, and shook my head.

"Jewish?"

I shook my head and let out a trite chuckle.

He dropped his voice a lot more. "Plain old white?"

I cringed, nodded.

A stupid grin came over his face. "You're lying harder than a three-day-old dead man. You ain't got with no Betsy Ross. You just trying to gas me up."

"Serious as a heart attack."

"You putting me on."

"Do I look like I'm joking?"

"You ain't into white women. Not the man with the Malcolm X picture on his office wall. As much as you dog out all the white people we work with. You shitting me, right?"

His tone changed from brotherly to a fatherly concerned. The bottom line was that we were from the South. Bad feelings about cultural mixing ran deep in our veins: was injected into our system nine months before we were born. Solomon let out a moan, then dropped his voice to a serious whisper. Like the way Grandmomma and Granddaddy and all the other old blacks down South would do whenever they got together and talked trash about white folks, even if the closest white person was two counties away.

He said, "Look, your business is your business is your business, but you know what sistas always saying about educated brothas getting successful and as soon we get paid, we hanging out in Bensonhurst trying to cross over to the pop chart."

"It's not even about that."

"You going public?"

"You make it sound like I'm undercover."

"Got jungle fever?"

"If I did, I'd take an aspirin and call a sista."

"Remember. If you go white, stay outta sight. 'Cause once you've dissed black, ain't no coming back."

Solomon didn't sound like a revolutionary, just concerned.

I said, "Just because I might be attracted to another race or color doesn't mean I don't like my strong black sistas."

"Wait, ain't that on a record?"

"En Vogue. Maxine, Cindy, Dawn, and—"

"Terry Ellis." He rubbed his crotch. "Lawd knows I'd love to dip that southern girl in some gravy and sop up her loving."

"I just switched the words around a little."

"Thought so." He gave a broad smile. "Is she fine?"

I imitated him, "Finer than a broke dick dog."

"Good. Don't need no more brothas dragging no tired-ass

mud-ducks over to the dark side. We don't need no ugly babies with funny shapes. She got back?"

"Is J'nette a bitch?"

We laughed and joked it up. I told him about how smooVe Kimberly was. Then we started funning about how much brothas loved the butt. It's a black thang. Loved the booty so much we always wrote songs of lust and celebration about it. "Baby Got Back." "Doing Da Butt." "Rump Shaker." "Bertha Butt Boogie."

While we were high-fiving, J'nette stepped in with a rude mood and stood by us. She cleared her throat several times, each time a little louder. I didn't look at her. Solomon did, then shifted away. She rolled her eyes at him, released a glower that made him squirm. She stepped to me with even less respect.

"Jordan." Her tone was scathing. "We need to talk."

"Y'all get your chit-chat on," Solomon said as he was leaving. "I need to check on a few thangs."

He eased by J'nette without touching. She shifted away from him like she couldn't stand anybody who associated with me, then stared at my essence like she wished me harm, sucked her teeth.

I said, "Whu'sup?"

"What you think?"

"You tell me."

"Well, I'm short and I've got to take care of this. I need to get three hundred dollars from you."

"For?"

"What do you mean, *for?*"

"I mean why do you need three hundred dollars, and why do you think I should be the one to loan it to you?"

"Loan?"

"You understand the concept, right? If I don't owe you, and I give you, then I loan you."

"No, no." For a split second she looked brittle, then she went back to her no-nonsense expression. "You need to *give* me the money so I can take care of this in the next couple of days."

"Take care of what?"

"Don't play stupid, Jay."

"So, did you take a test?"

"Why do you think I need the money?"

"Why should I give it to you?"

"You're the man, so be a man and act like one."

"Who're the guys you're with?"

"Friends who came out with us from Jersey."

"Friends?"

"So we wouldn't have to ride the subway by ourselves."

"So, are you pregnant?"

"I told you I missed my period, plus I'm gaining weight."

"But you haven't taken an EPT?"

"No."

"I don't have three hundred, anyway."

"Why not?"

"Spent it all on lotion."

She stormed away, headed into the living room, went right back to laughing and talking with a few more people who had just come in. Like nothing had happened.

We didn't speak a word to each other the rest of the evening, but I caught her stabbing her eyes at me, sending me a sneer that was colder than January in Alaska.

I had a bad feeling about her. One that rose up from the pit of my stomach and told me I never should've gotten involved with her. We were physically attracted to each other, but didn't like each other. At least not out of bed. Never have, never will. One-dimensional compatibility was a definite incompatibility.

A few minutes later, I'd had enough of my loud and raunchy friends and was saying good-bye to everybody. I loved to party, but I can only take loud noises in measured doses, and this prescription had been filled. Most of them will party until two A.M, then drag in to work by nine; I *needs* my seven-to-eight hours of sleep every night.

At the door, again, Yasmean gave me a long hug and a wanting look. I gave her a one-armed hug and ignored the way she kissed the side of my face.

Just as the elevator opened, J'nette appeared out of nowhere and jumped on with me. She wasn't wearing a coat or shoes. Lines were in her forehead.

J'nette said, "Jay, can I please have a minute?"

Her face was harsh, but fear was dancing in her eyes.

Before I could answer, she'd pushed the button for the top floor, the twenty-fourth.

"Jay, I'm sorry for being difficult, but I need your help."

"J'nette—"

"Hear me out, okay?"

The elevator stopped two floors up. J'nette took my hand and pulled me off when the building superintendent and a couple of rough-looking brothas got on. In the hallway, she stood on the beige tile, fell silent. Searched for words while she leaned against the concrete wall.

"All right," I said. "Go. I've got to go."

"I know we don't have a relationship. I'm not trying to trap you, and I'm not trying to game you so I can get your money. But I know I'm pregnant, and I don't have anybody else to turn to, so I need you to help me out. If I had the money, I would just go about my business. This shit is fucking with me. Loan me the money and I'll pay you back as soon as I'm able to. I'm not going to my family. Toni doesn't know and I don't want them to know about this. It's just between me and you, so you can walk away and nobody will think of you as the bad guy. So can you help me?"

"You sure you're pregnant?"

"Yes. I've been here before. I know my body."

I was standing by the hall window, my back toward Madison Ave and a million sky-high buildings. I asked her, "By me?"

J'nette cut her eyes at me and a vein popped up her forehead. She moved like she was about to double up her fists and bum-rush me, but she softened, let her shoulders slump. She dropped her face in her hand and whispered a frustrated "I don't know."

I blinked a million times. *"You don't know?"*

"I mean, I think so."

"How can you *not* know?"

The silence told me a lot about our relationship. Told me a lot about her dog-ass ways. That same silence sent me back to college, back to the University of Memphis, when I thought a countrified sista named Sabrina was the end all to be all. I thought me and her would be married by now. She'd fucked me over the same way, had left me lonely, damn near bankrupt, and brokenhearted. Had me chipping in on her rent while somebody else was slipping his key inside her lock.

J'nette said, "Could be."

I blinked, made my eyes soften, but my tone still burned with anger. "Why didn't you go to the other brotha with this?"

"Can't."

"Why?"

"Too complicated."

"Complicated?"

"Very."

"This is *fucked*. That's what's complicated."

"Walk away if you wanna. I won't blame you. I would."

I said, "I'll give you the money."

Her eyes were on her feet. Gazing down toward the sandy-colored tile. No matter how mad I got, it wasn't all her fault. She was just getting the bad end of it.

I asked, "You need me to go with you?"

"No." She twisted her lips as her forehead wrinkled. "I don't think I could stand to look at you afterward."

We stood in the hall, stalled in peace. Hard-core J'nette had been replaced by an innocent, fidgety child. With all the harshness, now she couldn't look at me without turning away.

"J'nette, why you act so hard all the time?"

"Can't help it." J'nette smirked and rubbed her nose. "That's my character. I'm a Bronx girl."

"Can I drop it by your office on Monday?"

"They laid me off Friday."

"*What?*"

"Let four of us go after lunch without notice."

"No notice?"

She shook her head. "Kicked me out. Right before Christmas. I'm broke because I had already spent all my money buying presents. And I had just paid my rent. So I gotta figure out what I'm gonna do to keep a roof over my head after the holidays."

"Why didn't you let me know?"

"And what were you gonna do?"

I shrugged. Didn't know why I asked her that question.

She said, "You and me ain't all that."

I nodded.

"That's why I came over to your place in the middle of the night all tore up. I needed somebody to talk to."

"Why didn't you talk then?"

"Because of the way you looked at me when you saw me."

"What did you expect, a red carpet?"

She hunched her shoulders. "I wanted to be held. I was so lonely. I'm not good at saying shit like that."

I wrote her a check. She gave me a hug.

"Jay, I'm sorry shit ended up like this."

Her head was in my chest, her nose stuffed up. I let her go, but I didn't look at her. Right now I couldn't stand to see what might be my unborn child's dying spark in her eyes. Maybe she felt the same way, because she moved across the hallway, turned her back to me, folded her arms, wiped her eyes with the back of her left hand. The check was in her right.

"Don't look at me," she said. "I'll keep you posted."

"Promise?"

"Just go. Thanks."

"If you need me, call."

"Go. Stop playing the concerned role."

Like a vagabond, I trudged back on the elevator, choked on my own soul when I spoke a raspy, "Look, J'nette—"

She turned around and almost snapped, "Don't call me. I'll be all right."

Silence became golden. The elevator door rattled closed. Shut us off into separate lives. Left me with an image of J'nette shuddering with a three-hundred-dollar check clenched in one hand and stubborn tears seeping from her bloodshot eyes.

It hurt to the bone. If it wasn't for us sexing, we could've been friends. Great friends who could've grown into a loving relationship once we understood each other a little better.

Right now she claimed there was a life stirring inside of her that might be stamped with my genetic code. And if she was being honest, that life wouldn't ever see a sliver of daylight. Wouldn't make it to its first breath. Maybe that was why my throat got tight and eyes watered up a bit. Why I bit my lip and kept slapping my gloves across my hand with each thought. Took a few deep breaths. Rubbed my eyes and wondered. Tried to make myself decent enough to march around the edges of Central Park, move on toward 110th Street, and head for the funk and noise and beggars and street musicians hustling for their next meal down in the bowels of the subway.

J'nette could be leaving with part of me. I thought about that a lot more, with more intensity when I made it to the lobby and saw the playground built into the complex's ground floor. That was why Solomon liked this building, because it gave his little boy a nice place to play when he came to visit. He loved his son.

I stood right across the street from Caanan Second Baptist Church and wondered if J'nette was holding on to a boy or a girl. J'nette could be leaving with part of what Momma gave me to pass on and keep what she'd created alive for years to come. That made me feel downhearted. Made my stride to the subway entrance slower than molasses in Alaska. Aside from all the jokes and the sarcasm, I'm human too. But too much had happened for us to just be friends.

6 Jordan Greene

Monday morning. My Walkman was tuned to 98.7. Isaac Hayes was warming up the airwaves with some classic soul on KISS-FM. I exited the subway where the E train stopped. Or started. Depended on which way I was going. Once again, it amazed me how so many people could be crammed shoulder to shoulder and nobody talked. Nobody looked at each other.

I shuffled through the crowd and climbed up into the falling snow. Isaac was taking advantage of his job and playing his own version of the tune "By the Time I Get to Phoenix."

By nine A.M. I was inside CompSci's smoky-black glass edifice, a building that looked newer and more stylish than most of the old-style brick and concrete structures rising high in the city. CompSci's en vogueness faced New Jersey and had a view of the World Trade Center and the Hudson River.

I dusted the snow off my shoulders, strolled into my office, then tossed my gloves, overcoat, soft leather attaché, and scarf across the brown swivel chair in front of my PC. It was warm so I took off my dark-blue blazer before sitting in my leather seat that faced the Malcom X picture on my wall.

Then I called downstairs and asked to speak to J'nette Barrett. One of her friends told me she'd been laid off. Just checking. I hate being played like a game show.

I was going to throw my overcoat onto the hook on the back of my office door, but I slowed down when I saw a few strands of scarlet hair were stuck on the black wool. Then something else broke that new train of thought, slowed me down a little more. Mark Yamamoto, one of the guys who works on my software team, stuck his head in my doorway. Mark's thirty-five, six feet tall, dark hair, clean shaven, dark-suited.

After he said hello, he giraffed his neck toward me, lowered his voice, and said, "You hear?"

"What's the word?"

He told me two people on our floor were laid off Friday. One of the middle managers and a lead programmer were given their walking papers. The manager had been here twenty-seven years; the lead programmer had come in from Microsoft two years ago. Bad career move.

Mark spoke over a nervous chuckle. "When I didn't see you Friday evening, I thought they'd gotten you too."

I shook my head, spoke over a job-secure grin. "Left early."

Our expressions changed to solemn looks. He left.

I was still holding my coat. Two strands of curly red hair were hanging on to the collar, like a memory that wouldn't let go. I fought the urge, then put the coat to my nose. Inhaled. The faint odor of Passion seeped from the lapel. I didn't know if that keepsake was left over from when I'd held Kimberly, or when I'd hugged J'nette. I dropped the long red hairs into the black trash can. Dropped the hairs, but hung on to the mental memento.

A plump, middle-aged, strawberry blonde in a flowered, ankle-length dress stuck her head into my office. Edna. She used to be our group secretary, but she was transferred to another manager down the hallway. Nobody else really cared for her, but we got along. I never went by her cubicle, but she'd always come and chit-chat with me a few times a week. Always smiled when she saw me.

Edna said, "Want to do lunch today?"

"Sure. I'll meet you in the cafeteria at noon."

She said, "Twelve-thirty's better."

"No problem."

"See you then."

She left.

My hands were busy, grabbing what I needed for the staff meeting we had at the top of the week. Weird thoughts and visions started galloping through my mind. Feelings that made my loins tingle and heat up. With my eyes open, I saw the curves of Kimberly's shoulders, the shape of her breasts, tasted the wine mixed with her saliva, heard her octaves of satisfaction when I was dancing inside of her, felt her on top of me, witnessed her shadow bumping and grinding on the wall, moving me from agony to ecstasy. My breathing was as thick as Aunt Jemima syrup. I'd started the weekend freezing, but she'd set me on fire in a matter of hours. Had taken me from fantasy to rapture. Had damaged my mind too. Damn. I wished I hadn't said a word to Solomon about what had happened. Momma used to tell us that if you told one person your secret, it wasn't a secret anymore. The word was out, so my business might be community property. I should've kept my late-night river crossing between me and the bedpost. Anger bubbled inside. My insides burned with scandal. I wanted to lie, but the kisses hadn't died. I felt a buzz. Some sort of a natural high. Trying not to think about her was only making me think about her that much more.

I stood in the window, watched snow fall from an overcast sky and put a one-inch frosting on the Big Apple, moved my tongue over my lips, tried to lick myself the way she'd savored me.

Behind me, people passed by laughing and talking loud as hell. I snapped out of the trance, put some pep in my step, threw some glide in my stride, and checked my voice mail. My brother Darrell had called Friday evening. His tone was bad news. All he said was that it was urgent—which meant he wanted me to dig into my pockets for some financial relief—and he didn't leave any details. Calling long distance, then not leaving a message defeats the purpose of the answering machine. He'd have to wait until I had a bulletproof mood.

Solomon had called and left me a message when he got in at six this morning. Seemed like he made it to work before the janitor showed up. He was an early bird who always chased the worm. I called him back. Less than a minute later, he was standing in my office, in a Brooks Brothers suit, sipping on a cup of coffee.

He yawned and closed my door when he walked in. "What the hell went down between you and J'nette?"

"Nothing." I shrugged. "Whu'sup with the hard face?"

"First, you left all of a sudden. She ran after you. When J'nette finally came back, she went straight into the bathroom and wouldn't come out. Zoe had to go in and sit with her for a while. Toni was mad as hell, calling you all kinds of names."

"We had some unfinished business and had to talk."

"I ain't no Sherlock." He sat down in my swivel chair, smoothed out his moustache. "But everybody figured that when she broke her neck chasing you out into the hallway. Now, stop talking in code."

"What did J'nette say?"

"Nothing. She was as evasive then as your butt is now."

I sat on the edge of my desk, told him what went down. With each word, with every gesture, my mind ping-ponged between two places. Kimberly. J'nette. Both mental spaces echoed with different flavors of regret. My words were on J'nette, but the corner of my mind that had been invaded by Kimberly snagged my thoughts. My imagination was filled and my cup was running over. My tongue was still grooving on its own, kissing a red-headed memory. My eyes tried to picture her, wondered what she felt for me. Wondered what she felt when she felt me.

Solomon was yakking, dogging out J'nette. My mind drifted, led my eyes to the right wall, strayed to the photos of strong black men who were keeping their eyes on me. Everybody was staring me down. Watching my every move.

Solomon's country ass got so loud I had to shush him a few times. He snapped, "*She's pregnant?* How far along?"

"Couple of months. She wanted me to give her three hundred."

"Three hundred damn dollars?"

I sighed, nodded.

He shook his head, sipped coffee. "You give it to her?"

"Yeah."

"Why you do some *stupid* shit like that?"

I rubbed my eyes, but I didn't say anything.

"Man," he choked, "she's probably lying her ass off. She's gotta be running a ghetto game, telling every man she's been with she's pregnant, and collecting three hundred dollars left and right. Hell, I bet she got another three hundred from the brotha she brought up to my place with her."

I told him how upset she was in the hallway. How she cried.

Solomon chuckled, shook his head. "Jordan, Erica Kane cries twelve hundred times a day, that don't mean she pregnant."

"Solomon—"

"Kick back and relax, 'cause I ain't through. Don't you think it's strange that the second she gets laid off, she comes crying to you that she's knocked up and needs you to dig *deep-deep-deep* in your pockets for some of your money?"

"Solomon—"

"Where's her money at? She's been working here for six months, still living with her momma and daddy, and don't have three hundred dollars saved up? What kinda crap is that?"

"Solomon—"

"Hell, she could've gotten an advance off a credit card."

"Solomon!"

"What?"

I nodded at the golden clock on my wall. "Almost time for my Monday morning status meeting."

"Who gives a shit? If you dropped dead right now, you know what? They'd still have a meeting." He stopped raging, crumpled up his coffee cup, shot it into the garbage, then stretched, scowled, and yawned again. "When was the last time you'd even seen or been with her before she called you up begging for dollars?"

"I get the point. Get your feet off my desk."

He didn't move his feet. He said, "Cancel that check."

We were interrupted when somebody tapped on my door. It

was another one of the people who worked under me, stopping by to make sure the meeting was still on before he went to the lab. Under his blond hair and beach-boy smile, he had that same insecure look darkening his blue eyes, that hope-I'm-not-next expression a lot of people in the company were wearing.

When he left, I changed the subject, asked Solomon, "Anybody in your office get laid off?"

"Our cutbacks won't hit until this Thursday. Work's slow, and I've gotta let two people go. I sho' hate to do it."

We said a few more things; then we adjourned the black caucus. He yawned and stretched again, then headed back downstairs to Systems.

I'd grabbed some change to get a cup of coffee, was about to leave, but my eyes went to Martin Luther King, Jr.'s, matted photo. A picture of him being held prisoner, sitting in a white man's jail. A photo in black and white. In solitary. His face lowered, no smiles on his round face. I stared at the reproduction of the man that had a dream and wanted to hear freedom ring.

By now Kimberly and Eric had made up. She'd packed up and moved back to her side of the tracks, back to her own artistic community. Her business card was in my wallet. A wallet that was three hundred dollars thinner. I stared at the phone for a few seconds. Felt fire running through my spine. I should give her a courtesy call, make sure Eric didn't lose his mind after I left. Hate to find out she got beat down. But what happened on their side of the tracks wasn't my concern.

Jordan, now this one is the first colonial capital of Ghana.

Wasn't that one of the big slave trading posts?

Yep. Sure was. And this seaport is Takoradi. Okay now, what's this one?

Oh, that's Qumasi. Heartland of the Ashanti empire.

Business was business, so I could put on my professional tone, dial her digits and make sure she was going to sell me one of her works. Yeah, I could do that. Business is business. Kimberly Chavers had talent and skills that couldn't be denied. She had pounds of potential. Might blow up one day and her work could have some serious value. Since I had a chance, I'd be a fool not to get in on the ground floor. If the chance was still there, it was time to take advantage of the opportunity. In the long run, I just might make back the three hundred dollars I'd lost gambling on the affections of J'nette.

That burning Kimberly had created was spreading. I'd tasted her intelligence from head to toe; she'd done the same with me.

When I picked up the phone, I raised my eyes, stood face-to-face with my framed photo of a man formerly known as Malcolm Little. He had red hair, goatee, glasses, and was brandishing his own charismatic smile. Malcolm and Martin weren't the only 11-x-14 photos I had on display. Matted prints of Coltrane and Miles Davis decorated the same plain-white walls. But this morning, it felt like Malcolm was panting fire and frowning down on me. Even though he was grinning, his eyes were jabbing at me like he thought I was about to buy a pair of ugly-ass Bruno Magli shoes and lease a white Bronco.

I'd be lying if I said that Kimberly's work wasn't great, but she didn't have the patent on talent; there were a million and one places in Harlem to buy black art. Black art created with the hands and eyes and hearts of black people. Not made from our blood, sweat, and tears. I put the phone down.

Around one, Edna and I were still in the cafeteria, finishing up the fruit salads we'd had for lunch, talking about the layoffs. At the next table, a couple of brothers were making steel-toed small talk about the old-but-not-forgotten O.J. fiasco. Small minds never seemed to stray far from what was unimportant. Their gestures were exaggerated, and the emptier the room got, the clearer their voices became.

Heavyset tapped his Bible and said, ". . . cultural reciprocation for the sins of the father. That's why he ain't guilty."

"Or as James Brown put it, The Big Payback!" The lanky brotha with the short Afro laughed like he was a GED-bred genius.

"O.J.'d better borrow from Rodney King to pay them people off."

Heavyset high-fived Afro.

They were talking about Geronimo Pratt getting his freedom when they picked up their trays and laughed away.

Edna looked at me. Turned her scowl into a warm smile.

She said, "You're nice, Jordan."

"Thank you," I said. "You're nice, too."

"You know why I like you?"

"No." I grinned and waited for a joke. "Why?"

Lines grew in her face. She dipped her voice into a whisper, like she was giving me her deepest, darkest secret. "Because you're not like *them*. You're nice."

My smile erased itself. "Excuse me?"

"You don't act like the others."

"The others? The other, what?"

She pursed her lips, widened her eyes, and nodded at the empty table where the janitors had been sitting. *"Them."*

My mind spiraled. When my head cleared, I sat back in my chair and picked up my freshly served reality check. I'd been eating lunch, hanging out with her for almost three years, and that was how she saw me. A potty-trained version of *them*.

I leaned close to her face. "I am *them*."

Her hands covered her mouth; her pale skin reddened. She understood. I held up the back of my hand and reassured her that my skin tone wasn't fading like Michael Jackson's. She stumbled over her words, tried to apologize for putting the sheet over her head in public. She was stuttering. I headed for the elevator.

When I got back to my office, a dozen yellow roses were on my desk. From Kimberly. That explained why everybody in the hallway was smiling at me when I hopped off the elevator looking like a frown come to life. I had a thirty-minute-old message from her too. I crashed in my seat, smelled a couple of the flowers, couldn't decide if I should blush or hang on to my grimace, stared at the wall, questioned if I'd overreacted at Kimberly's apartment, and pondered the same thing about what I'd just done downstairs, looking at the matted photos of the brothers watching over me.

I saw Edna getting off the elevator. Her blue eyes collided with my brown ones. She lowered her head, wobbled toward her cubicle, then turned around and hurried back on the elevator.

Again I smelled the bouquet. A woman had never sent me an arrangement before. Now I understood the power of the flower.

They softened up my feelings, and, yep, I understood the true power of the rose. I understood why men gave them, and why most women softened up like warm butter when they received them. It had to work the other way around, because it was working on me.

Damn, it was working.

I took out Kimberly's business card, tapped it against my forehead about a hundred times before I dialed her digits.

A little pep was in my tone when I thanked her for the yellow roses. I said, "I was thinking about you right before I got them."

Kimberly's voice smiled. "You thought me up."

"What?"

"You thought about me and I sent you flowers and called. You thought me up."

"How did you get my work number?"

"Easy." Her voice was perky, like nothing good or bad had ever happened between us. She said, "I called the CompSci operator, asked for the man called SmooVe."

We laughed.

She said, "I hope you don't mind."

"You get the prize for originality, daring, and audacity."

"Is that a good thing?"

"Today it is."

"Well, I didn't know what you thought."

"About?"

"I hoped you didn't think that I picked up guys in cabs and, you know. I guess what I'm trying to say is that I like you and I would like to see you again. I mean, maybe we could still go somewhere together and get cappuccino or something. Maybe we could pick up some tickets in Times Square and catch a play."

This had been a rough day. Actually, a rough season. I smiled at her warm words, at the way she sweetly offered to kick it with me. On an overcast day like today, it took away some of life's chill to be given a few lines of dialogue filled with sunshine. I tried to not be so easy, tried to weigh down my own enthusiasm, but her perky voice carried some serious affection.

I asked, "Are you nervous?"

"No, just unsure. I've never gone after any man before."

"You going after me?"

"Maybe." She sang that word. "I wanted to make sure you made it home okay. And I wanted to apologize for, eh, you know."

Kimberly said that after I left, she left Eric in the hall. Begging. Claimed she didn't even like him enough to be a friend.

I said, "But, you used to like him?"

"Until I got to know him. You know how people are on their best behavior when you first meet them, then later you see the real them with the phony mask of kindness taken off?"

"I can relate." I thought about J'nette. She was damn sweet for a while.

Kimberly flirted. "I hope you didn't think I was too freaky." She sounded embarrassed. "It'd been months since I did it."

"What about you and Eric?"

"I told you, stopped seeing him a while ago."

"Other people?"

"I date every now and then. I'm not dead, you know."

"And nothing for months?"

She laughed. "That's the difference between men and women."

"What?"

"When women say *dating*, we mean we're going out on a date with somebody. For men, dating and fucking mean the same thing."

Intrigue took over. I'd never met any woman who was so free.

She continued, "I've been feeling real bad about what happened, and I haven't had but a couple of minutes sleep. I'll understand if you don't want to hang out."

"Got a pen to write down my number?"

Her voice had a wider, broader smile when she giggled. "Yeah. I don't know how you do this to me."

"What?"

"Make me grin and blush and stuff. Nobody would believe I ever acted like this with anybody. Sending a man flowers."

We flirted for about an hour, then made plans to see each other later. When we hung up, my manager walked in wearing his standard IBM look. He looked like a tall, heavyset, pot-bellied Ross Perot with style. Dark suit. White shirt. Power tie.

I stood and shook his hand, "Afternoon, Rodger."

"Greene," Rodger said. He was clinging to a beige folder. Made me wonder if he was holding my layoff notice. He nodded at my yellow roses, didn't come close to sharing a smile, then said, "I need to see you in my office."

When we got into his corner office, he motioned for me to close the door behind myself. I did, then sat in one of the two black-leather office chairs facing him and all the certificates and awards he'd been given over his many years at the company.

He glanced at the beige folder. "You have a good weekend?"

I chuckled. "It was a week too short."

He didn't laugh. Just raised his eyes to mine. His voice and posture shifted from casual to business. So did mine.

He leaned forward and said, "This is off the record."

I answered with an unsure "Okay."

"We have a potential problem I want to avoid."

"Okay, shoot."

"It's a reported violation of the company's ethics policy. You understand in light of recent troubles, all accusations have to be investigated, regardless."

I shifted in my seat, then leaned forward and put my elbows on his desk. My instinct said be assertive, whatever was happening. My eyes tracked his movements. Attacked whatever Rodger was hemming-and-hawing about. I asked, "What's going on?"

"Edna just filed a grievance concerning you with Ethics."

"What?" My face did more contortions than Jim Carrey had ever done. "Edna Riordan filed a grievance against me?"

He nodded, stayed poker-faced, stared at me like he was reading my reaction. My final response was a sideways look of confusion. He raised a hand and said, "It hasn't come upstairs yet. But my wife told me Edna just stormed out of their department."

"What kind of a complaint?"

"An hour ago she marched downstairs and alleged that you made racial slurs at her while she was eating in the cafeteria."

"You're kidding?"

He slid me a reproduced copy of the charges. Edna claimed she made a harmless comment about workers not bussing their trays from the cafeteria table, then I insulted her with racial slurs. After I read the copy, Rodger kindly took the lies from me, tore them in half, then stuck them into the document shredder—or word de-processor as we called it—next to his desk. He destroyed the unprofessional link between him and his wife, Sarah. No one could prove they passed information and kept each other informed.

He sighed, like it pained him to speak, then asked, "Did you?"

"No, that's flipped around. She made a racial slur to *me* and I let her know I was offended."

"At times, she has been outspoken. And a pain. Which was why I transferred her to Jack's department."

"At this point, what do you recommend I do?"

"Would you consider apologizing to put this to sleep?"

"I didn't do anything I should apologize for."

"I know. But Ethics has to investigate all complaints. Especially those that if left unanswered could fuel lawsuits. Lawsuits aggravate the stockholders and that hurts company standing, public and private."

"Lawsuits? This can't be serious, right?"

"It's not, but it is at the same time. We're thirty percent overstaffed and they're looking for any excuse to lay off, especially since a lot of the old timers refuse to take the golden handshake. I'm not saying this would be the reason, but it could be a determining factor down the road."

I chuckled, kept my attitude light. "You mean an excuse."

"Exactly. My viewpoint is, I don't want them to be able to have any counterpoints or bullshit, excuse my French—"

"French excused."

"—reasons for moving my staff. It's already hard enough for me to justify not downsizing at a faster rate, especially with dwindling workloads."

"What about my performance?"

"It's excellent. Above average."

"Then I don't see a problem. I could just transfer to another division."

"But there are several people who might be displaced, people who have excellent records, and know there aren't any positions with the company."

Everybody knew CompSci had a hiring freeze, both inner and outer company. They were letting positions fall open and reassigning tasks within the group. Experienced people were being laid off and work was being shared among those left behind.

Right now I'd give all of this crap up for a summer breeze and a chance to dance in an open field filled with four-leaf clovers and dragonflies. All that and a friendly glass of lemonade.

I said, "Will NAFTA help the company?"

He hunched his shoulders, then shook his head. "Doubt it."

I sat back in my chair and interlocked my fingers with my pointer finger stuck in my chin. "Okay, cut to the chase. What does that have to do with me?"

"CompSci wants to demote a few managers to lower job titles so they can keep them with the company until everything is smoothed out."

"Politics."

"This entire arena is political. They're looking at numbers, not people. It's getting real thick and scary. So many people are looking for work, it's a buyer's market. Companies are getting ruthless. My job's on the line just like everybody else's. But until I'm gone, I'm still looking out for my people."

"You've been here over thirty years."

He smiled and pointed at the golden CompSci pin on his tie clip. "Thirty-one. I was working here when computers had vacuum tubes. And they'll have to drag me out kicking and screaming. Since Sarah and I are taking care of four of the grandchildren, we need all the money we can get."

I tried to make myself relax and be as positive as Rodger Phelps. But then again, he had nothing on the line. No chaos echoed with his footsteps. No anguish in his heartbeats. The best I could do was smile and say, "Thanks for the heads up."

"It might be nothing. I wanted you to know, just in case."

"I appreciate it, Rodger."

My boss nodded. Gloom clouded his dark eyes.

When I stood, Rodger rose to his feet, leaned forward, shook my hand, and said, "We didn't have this conversation."

7 Jordan Greene

By eight P.M., Kimberly was at my place carrying a pink flowered overnight bag. She bounced in wearing wide-legged jeans, pastel sweater, boots, and a navy-style coat. The tam on her head and dangling earmuffs made her look rebellious and artistic.

Her hair was in braids, tied together at the end. That hairdo jarred me, made my blood feel like a river of water flowing down into a stream of discomfort. I'd seen a lot of non-black women jocking the sistas' hairstyles. And every time a white woman sported something ethnic, I'd heard the sistas' whispers, been privy to the back-handed compliments and sometimes straight-up negative comments on everything from hairstyles to Kente outfits to the dance called the Moonwalk, groaning and wondering if African-Americans would ever have anything that the other races didn't steal, imitate, or try to duplicate without giving credit where credit was due. Yep. Sistas would rage about white women ripping their fashions off, all while their cocoa-complected frames were draped in Levi's and Anne Klein. The brothas wearing the Tommy Hilfiger shirts and Nike gear would do the same.

Kimberly dropped her bag in the living room, then followed me into the kitchen. I was boiling vegetarian ravioli I'd bought at Price Club, adding I Can't Believe It's Not Butter and garlic sauce to my twenty-minute creation.

"Needs more garlic," Kimberly said, then asked, "What does your weekend look like, SmooVe?"

"Me and Solomon might go hang at Birdland."

"That's on Twenty-eighth, right?"

"Yep. Between Seventh and Eighth Avenues."

"I've been there a few times. Kinikki and I used to drop in at

Bentley's, but now the crowd's so young and they pack 'em in so tight, that place is a fire hazard."

I nodded. "It does get packed."

"Everybody in there looked under seventeen years old. I felt like I was there to baby-sit all those delinquents. But it is flattering when somebody that young buys you a drink and asks for your phone number."

I laughed along with her.

I said, "Me and Solomon don't do much of the hip-hop scene. And if we did, it'd be on the weekend, but it seems like everybody throws down on the weekday, and that doesn't fit my schedule."

"Solomon. Let's see, that's your friend who's closer than a brother, right?"

"You got it. What did you have in mind for the weekend?"

One of her girlfriends, Sharon, was supposed to fly out to Los Angeles for the weekend, but Sharon's Fortune 500 husband needed to fly to Cabo San Lucas on business, and wanted his wife with him. Sharon was giving the L.A. tickets away.

Kimberly asked, "Ever been to L.A.?"

"Nope."

"We used to live about an hour away from L.A. in Sunnymead."

"Where's Sunnymead?"

"Deep in the desert. Middle of nowhere. Mom-Mom used to hate it because they didn't even have a mall."

"Mom-Mom?"

"That's what I call my mother."

"What does she call you?"

"Kim-Kim."

We laughed.

I said, "What do you call your pops?"

Her half of the laughter died when she said, "Dad."

"You haven't talked much about him."

She shrugged. "He's a jerk. He doesn't listen to women. End of discussion. We're estranged."

"How long has it been like that?"

"Since I was born."

"I didn't know your folks weren't together."

"They're together." The youthful timbre in her words faded; what was left behind stiffened. She cleared her throat and said, "They're still happily married. Very. It's me and him who are estranged. Him and Mom-Mom are still hubby and wife."

"When was the last time you saw them?"

"Thanksgiving. I bit the bullet and went back there for four days. And for four days, me and my mother's husband didn't share two words."

I switched subjects, asked, "So what's up with Los Angeles?"

"Sharon called this afternoon and offered me the tickets."

"How much does she want for them?"

"Free."

I echoed, "Free?"

"She can afford it, no problem. Well, she wants me to donate a piece of art and make an appearance at a black-tie benefit she's chairing for some AIDS organization when I get back. I was thinking about asking you to escort me. If you're not busy."

I nodded. Didn't commit one way or the other.

Kimberly was still talking. "It'll be part vacation, part business because I need to go by a few shops on the West Coast and self-promote. So if you're game, we can fly first class to L.A., rent a car, and whatever."

"You sure are a free spirit."

She laughed.

And in between her chuckles, I thought about it. Thought about the pros and cons; the whys and why nots.

Inside, I did have a serious emptiness. An emotional void. And this time of year, a void was definitely intolerable. Maybe loneliness was gravitating to loneliness. I wanted to ask her what the hell we were doing, where this whatever that had started all of a sudden might be headed, but it would be too premature. Today was today, and tomorrow would be tomorrow. Sometimes grasping words sounded desperate, or expecting, and ruined a damn good thing. Let it ride.

Late Friday night, after a five-hour ride through the clouds, I smelled the laid-back attitude of Los Angeles as the plane landed. The dry, salty odor of the Pacific met us as we hustled through the thoroughfare toward the hotel shuttles. From coast to coast, from sea level to thirty-thousand feet, having Kimberly on my arm was making me notice all kinds of things, especially the mixed couples. Right now, those commingled relationships were loud as hell.

We were at baggage claim. My eyes were on the people, scanning to see who was watching me. Peeking at the black people who didn't give me an ounce of eye contact.

"Every now and then you sound real southern." Kimberly said that to get my attention. She snapped another picture of me with her 35mm and smiled. "Last night I almost died when you said you were *hooongry*. Not hungry, *hooongry*."

At the Pacific Shore Hotel in Santa Monica, we unpacked. One side of the dresser was filled with her stuff, the other with mine. Her side with makeup, Crest, blow dryer, Frizz-Ease, and other girly stuff. The other side had my Nexxus products, Colgate with baking soda, Magic Shave, condoms laced with spermicide, and Ambi.

The next morning we showered and hit the streets. Stopped long enough to ask strangers to take a couple of pictures of us with Kimberly's camera. Yesterday I was shivering, trudging through snowflakes. Now, palm trees and people in shorts and on rollerblades made it feel like we'd landed in another season. I kept my excitement in check. Momma always told us, "Don't never act like we ain't never been nowhere before. 'Specially front of white folks."

I wonder how she'd feel if she could see me now.

We ate on the promenade, bought a map, and figured out how to get to Melrose Boulevard—which was a *very* watered down version of New York's Greenwich Village. We stopped at a gallery long enough to network. We saw everything. People with hair dyed three un-matching colors. Bodies with pierced tongues, nose and nipple rings, tattoos on top of tattoos—shit we didn't have to leave New York to see. People like that lined the streets of NoHo and SoHo and the East Village. The only difference was that on the West Coast they had better tans.

We stopped at Condomania. While I was checking out the variety of flavored condoms, tickler condoms, and crazy condoms with shapes of little animals, a dark sister with long permed hair and a mulatto sister with short, wavy, golden hair sashayed in. They saw me holding Kimberly's hand, picking out protection for my erection. The mulatto sister shook her head, made a funky sound, turned her face from me. The dark sister moved away. Kimberly didn't see anything. She hadn't noticed the glares or jeers from JFK to LAX. I'd seen them all. Every scoff made my stomach knot.

Kimberly strolled to the back of the store to find some raunchy gag presents for her girlfriends. The mulatto sista drifted into my comfort zone, then snapped loud enough for me to hear, "He needs to check himself. All on that whigger."

Damn, I hadn't heard that insult in a while. Hadn't ever heard that disrespect spat in my direction. Whigger meant white nigger, somebody white trying to act negro. A fake, a fraud, a cultural thief.

My constitution felt heavy, but I refused to stare at my feet. Dark-brown eyes to light-brown eyes, I glared right at the bitch. First she grimaced and growled like it was feeding time at the zoo, then she laughed and shook her head like what she saw was pathetic. The same thing me and my friends and family used to do when we saw a Mandingo on the arms of a Miss Daisy. Only now it was different because all of it was bull's-eyed at me. I couldn't duck or dodge any of the scowls.

The diss grabbed my neck tighter than a lyncher's noose. Her sour eyes shouted that I was a bonafide sell-out, Uncle Tom, wannabe, house-nigger roaming the streets not so incog-negroe.

Something must've been etched in my face because when Kimberly swayed back over to my side and took my hand, her smile switched gears. She asked, "What's wrong?"

"Nothing. Just a little jet lag."

"Want to go back to the room? We can just hang out later on the promenade by the hotel. The concierge said there are a few places to shoot pool, some dance clubs, and a plethora of places to pig out near the hotel."

"No, I'm cool."

"SmooVe?"

I winked. She winked too.

The dark sista eased into our space. Her chocolate-coated top gums showed, exposed clear braces. She said a quick "Hi."

Kimberly smiled. "Hi."

Anger boiled in the pit of my stomach. My hands were clammy.

The girl said, "I just wanted to apologize for my friend."

Before anybody could say anything, she'd walked off. Rushed out the front door chastising her sneering, half-white friend.

Kimberly asked, "What was that all about?"

I shook my head and mumbled, "Nothing."

"You know them?"

I shook my head again.

"What did her friend do?" Kimberly's voice changed back into the business tone she had when I first met her in the cab, back to when we were strangers. She asked a rough, "What happened?"

I shook my head. "Nothing worth talking about. Let it go."

Kimberly's chest rose with her harsh breath. She stared in the direction of the sistas, then back at me. Without a word, she paid for her gifts and headed toward the door.

She didn't look back when she snapped out a firm "Ready?"

Before I could answer, she was out the door.

I massaged my temples. I should've stayed in New York. Should've waited for another cab.

All the way back to the hotel my only friend was silence. And silence was all I heard. Radio off, attitude on. Not a solitary word was spoken, muttered, or mumbled on the forty-minute drive from Hollywood back to Santa Monica. Nothing was said while we took the stuff we'd bought out of the car. Her hot spirit had gone cold. Kimberly didn't even glance in my direction or get close enough to hold my hand while we walked from crowded underground parking to the busy hotel lobby. With her bag bouncing off her leg, she moved fast enough to walk a country mile in a New York minute. But Kimberly's face perked up and grinned when she spoke to the shoeshine man we passed by. Then her shoulders tightened and the ice princess returned. Her lips were pursed on the elevator, her eyes on her hands the entire time.

I finally asked, "Are you okay?"

She raised her eyes to mine, then lowered them, "Yep."

The elevator stopped on our floor. She stepped off the vertical carriage before the doors opened all the way, sashayed ahead, and rustled the electronic pass key out of her purse.

When we got into the room, she grabbed a bag and went into the bathroom. Sounded like she stumbled and shrieked.

I yelled, "You okay?"

No answer.

When she came back out, she'd changed into sweats. No words. More anger.

"Where are you going?" I was taking off my Timberland boots and jean shirt. I know she heard me, but I had to ask her again.

She tied her braids back and said, "Running."

At the door, she put her hand on the handle and held it.

I said, "Kimberly."

We stared for a moment. No smiles. A very uncomfortable gaze. Her tension galloped over and smacked me in the face, hurt almost as much as the sista's words had clawed my neck. Kimberly came back in and sat on the bed next to me.

She whispered, "Jordan?"

I sat up. "Yeah?"

She exhaled, said a soft, "Don't do that."

"What?"

She put her hand up to the side of my face and kissed me, then said an unmistakable, "Don't discount what I ask you and please don't lie to me. Don't ignore me like that, okay?"

"Okay."

"That's what my father used to do. It hurts me."

Again, I apologized.

She asked me what had happened.

We looked at each other, knowingly.

I told her what went down, how I felt the scenario. It felt weird sharing those kinds of feelings, maybe even popping the lid on a few cultural secrets with her. I tried not to make my words seem evasive, but I didn't want to sound harsh. Wanted to keep my shield up and be stronger than strong. The way she scowled, the incident troubled her more than it had agitated me.

Her brow crinkled. She put her hand on mine. I gazed at her skin and mine. She asked an almost embarrassed, "Have you ever dated somebody who wasn't African-American?"

"Nope."

Her eyes fell on our hands, on our skin. The only parts that were close to being the same hue were the palms. Kimberly wasn't blonde haired. Wasn't blue eyed. Wasn't a pale, Oklahoma Caucasian. I've known a few "sistas" who had less of a natural tan than Kimberly. I've met jet-black sistas who wore sky-blue contacts and acted more European than Princess Diana. And so far as going insane in the mane, Jada Pinkett, Mary J. Blige, Faith Evans, and about eight million sistas had dyed their hair platinum. I wondered if white people ever complained or got riled about that kind of shit, when things that were considered white were snatched up by black people.

She said, "If I make you uneasy, we can just call airline reservations and go back to New York. No harm, no foul."

"No. It's not you." I paused. "Well, to be honest, it's me. This is new. I'm not accustomed to this kind of dating."

"What *kind* of dating? What, you don't usually date women?"

We laughed a little. Very little.

I said, "You know what I meant. I'm not used to this kinda difference. Not like you are."

A moment or two went by.

Kimberly finally said, "What makes you think I'm used to it?"

"Aren't you?"

"No."

"You've lived all over. C'mon, you even lived in Africa."

She shook her head. "Nope. Stayed celibate. Didn't *date*."

"Am I the first brother you've dated?"

"Yep." Her voice lowered. "You sure are. Surprised?"

"Guess I misread you."

She stifled what she was about to say, then admitted, "I thought you were used to it and, I dunno, assumed you liked cute . . ." She sighed out a fake laugh. "Liked red-haired artists."

"Artist? Were you going to say white women?"

"Jordan"—she was getting upset—"why should any of that matter? We're just two adults having fun. Right?"

I backed off. "Right."

"White's a color. I'm a person, a human being, not painted."

"My bad. Well, I'm black and I'm proud."

"No shit? You're *black*? Gee, I never noticed."

"What kind of European are you?"

"My mother is German and Irish." She swallowed, sulked, toyed with her hair, asked, "You have a problem with who I am?"

"Well, I've never been attracted to anybody but sistas."

She paused. "Oh. I see. Guess I'm not your type."

"No." My mouth felt like it had been stuffed with cotton. "What I'm saying is I'm very attracted to you too."

Kimberly tsked. "Then what's the problem?"

My answer was a shallow shrug. I'd never felt so black in my life. So many things were on my mind. I don't think I could handle looking at people and seeing a cross burning in their eyes.

A moment passed before I asked, "What do your friends think?"

She nibbled her lips. "Don't know. Didn't tell them."

"Who does Sharon think you're here with?"

"She didn't ask."

"Are you ashamed?"

She grinned. "Cautious. But I'm like that, regardless. And it's not because you're African-American. I don't share my business with anyone. Outside of that, I make my own rules and set my own standards."

"I noticed."

"You should too. Most of society's rules are racist."

I agreed. "That's because we live in a racist society."

"And it's more racist for some than it is for others. Try being a woman for fifteen minutes."

"I'll take the zero on that test."

We were treading in a sea of confusion.

I asked, "Why did you invite me to come with you?"

She shrugged. "I like you, SmooVe. I want to spend some time with you and get to know you. Thought we might have fun. That's the only reason I need. That's what matters to me."

Outside of the obvious, we were opposite in every way. Artist. Engineer. Conservative dresser. Trendy dresser. Yet everytime I glanced at her I felt a tingle. Warmth. Electricity.

She asked, "Are you cold?"

"Little."

She bounced over to the wall and adjusted the temperature, stretched, yawned, then scooted up on the bed with me.

She said a solid, "If we're going to be together, even if it's as friends and not as lovers anymore, we can't run every time some bitch says something."

She spat that venom out like she'd said that many times. Her hostile tone reminded me of my bitter brother, Darrell. Reminded me of the times when I was growing up and we fought with the white boys from the other side of the tracks.

I agreed. "True that."

"Her attitude and a buck-fifty will get her on the subway."

"You're getting hot under the collar."

"Jordan, remember I told you I grew up in all those places? Remember I told you my parents lived in Oakland for a while?"

"Yeah."

She paused, stared at her flesh. "Well, in the neighborhood my family was in, the people didn't care too much for me. Didn't care too much for us, actually. Those two years we were there were the *worst* in my life. Everybody was very cruel to me. That's part of the reason I don't care too much for my daddy."

"What did he do?"

"Nothing. When I told him what people were doing, the names the people called me, how they chased me home from school, he didn't do anything."

Her body was warm. Felt like she was getting upset to the point of becoming insane, then her disposition became a little easier. A lot brighter.

Kimberly pulled her hair back from her face and touched her forehead. "Jordan, look right here. See that line?"

She showed me an old scar. It was almost gone, shaped like an imperfect, upside-down L. I asked, "What happened?"

"Some black girls chased me home from school, called me names, knocked me off my bike. I fell on my face, had to get fifteen stitches."

"I hadn't noticed it. Your skin heals pretty well."

"Just because you can't see the scar"—her voice almost died— "doesn't mean it's healed."

Kimberly covered her face with her hair, hid the scar, closed her eyes, and hummed the same Rachelle Ferrell song she'd hummed the first evening we'd sat and talked. Rubbed her hand over my chest, squirmed, and hummed. She rolled over, crawled on top of me, kissed me for a while, tried to tongue and grind and rub away her torment, then sighed, rolled over to my side and yawned.

Kimberly's tone was sweet, womanly. "SmooVe, hold me."

My arms pulled her warmth into mine, but I was nodding off.

She said, "One more thing before it becomes a problem."

"What?"

"Toilet seat down."

"I'll think about it."

"You made me so mad I almost fell in."

"Look behind you before you back it up."

"Down."

"Up."

"Down, down, *down*." She ribbed me in the side and gave me another kiss. A couple of minutes later, she was breathing hard, her head resting on my back.

"Up."

"Down. I've got your plane ticket."

"I'll try to remember to put it down."

"And I'll try to remember where I put your ticket."

8 Jordan Greene

Two hours later, I had hopped out of the shower and was on the suite's sofa, windows open so I could see the Ferris wheel, merry-go-round, and other rides down on the pier. The Pacific Ocean was slamming against the shores.

I was on the phone, making a call I'd been reluctant to make. "Whu'sup? I got the message you called."

"This you?"

"Yeah, it's me. Whu'sup?"

"Nigga, 'bout time you called back. Hold on a minute," my brother Darrell said, then dropped the phone on what sounded like a hard countertop. His radio was blasting Nat King Cole singing "The Christmas Song." It faded out and WDIA overlapped its call letters. I was just about to hang up and call back, because I thought he had forgotten about me, when I heard a toilet flush. It flushed again. And again. Darrell turned off the radio.

He picked up the phone, belched, then asked, "Where you at?"

"Behind that preposition."

"Which part of New Yawk is that?"

"Darrell—never mind. I'm in Santa Monica."

"California?"

"Yeah."

"You done moved again?"

"Nope. Me and a friend came out for a few days."

"Friend? One of them New Yawk women?"

"Uh, yeah."

"I bet she a red-bone, huh?"

Red-bone meant light-skinned. I hesitated. "You know it."

"Shit, I need to come up to New Yawk and scoop me up one. Where she at?"

"Who?"

"Red-bone."

"Downstairs in the gym on the StairMaster."

"See you living large. Must be nice."

"Darrell, this is long distance. Who died?"

"First off, I was hoping you was all right."

"I'm cool."

"That and I need some help."

"Knew it." I groaned. "What's wrong now?"

"Reggie. Your brother got us in a bind."

"Damn." I wanted to choke on my own breath. "How bad?"

"Sitting down with your wallet open?"

Reggie had called Darrell a couple of weeks ago from the blood bank. He was trying to get paid, but they wouldn't let him because he'd been down earlier in the week. Darrell said by the time he made it to him, Reggie was acting anxious. Twitches. Spasms.

Tremors. No coordination. Half-dressed in the cold. Reggie said he was living "here and there. Wherever." Darrell was going to take him to the hospital, but Reggie said he just needed to lay up a couple of days and get himself straight. When Reggie got back to Darrell's place, Darrell got him to take a shower, eat some left-overs, then sleep. Reggie crashed for two days straight. On the third day, when Darrell got home from work, Reggie was gone. So was the twenty-six-inch TV. So was Darrell's good coat. Pants, shirt, sweaters, tennis shoes. VCR. Credit cards. About a hundred dollars in cash Darrell had hidden in a sock drawer. By the time Darrell called in his cards, they'd been charged up with eight hundred dollars worth of stuff.

He said, "To top it off, some young niggas came knocking on my door a couple of times in the last three days looking for Reggie."

"You call the police?"

"Police? I'll call my gun before I dial nine-eleven."

Darrell said the brothas had been sitting outside, stalking. So now, Darrell said he was carrying his peace-maker with him even if he was just going to take out the trash.

"What were they talking about?"

"Those young-ass punks tried to bust my balls, acting all hard and half crazy and shit, claimed that Reggie owed them some back money for some merchandise."

"What kind of merchandise?"

"You already know."

The hotel door opened and Kimberly came in with a beige hotel towel around her neck. Her wavy hair was tied back with one of those soft, woman-hair-things. We grinned and finger waved.

She whispered a surprised, "Still talking to your brother?"

I nodded a frustrated yeah.

She smiled and kept moving toward the bathroom. My eyes were on her frame, checking out that womanly walk she does so well. The back of her purple sweatsuit was soaked with sweat, especially at the crack of her butt.

I patted my stomach. Pinched my sides.

I asked Darrell, "How much they say he owe them?"

"Niggas said three hundred fifty. I don't thank he owed 'em that much. But they looked like they meaned business. I wasn't scared of 'em, but I didn't want 'em to get to Reggie before I could find out where he ran off to. I ran by the ready-teller and gave it to 'em. Just in case, you know."

"Three hundred fifty?"

"That was my rent and food and gas money."

"Okay."

"So, I'm gonna need your help."

Life was tight for me too. But you had to do what you had to do. Regardless. Every time we did this shit, we said it was the last time. We put our feet down firm. Then the next time came along and we were doing it again. Last time, it cost me four hundred to keep them from finding Reggie down south in Hernando floating facedown in the Mississippi River.

I tried to cut to the chase. "What you need?"

"I called around and thank I'm gonna be able to just tell the credit-card folks that my cards was stolen, and that'll be the end of that. I'll do that, so long as I don't get, uh, Reggie don't get in trouble with them."

"All right."

"But I'm gonna need some money to stay on track. I just started at FedEx a couple of months ago, and I'm almost about to make my probation—"

"How much?"

"Just the rent money." Darrell let out a pissed-off groan. "I'll have to wear my goddamn work coat every goddamn day. Good thang I had that on. Send me what you can. I don't want to set you back. Ain't no need of everybody being broke."

"Let me see what I got."

"Don't leave me hangin' on this, all right?"

"Okay."

"Send me a bag of them good-ass New Yawk bagels. I hear they supposed to be the best in the country."

"No problem."

The age-old irritation in our voices bloomed and seasoned the rest of the conversation. People think that just because you live in

New York, your finances must be the best and you have it made in the shade. New York is expensive; you have to make a middle-class salary just so you can afford to live in the sections that don't have rats the size of cats.

Once we'd made a date for me to send him a money order or a cashier's check, we hung up without wishing each other a brotherly Merry Christmas or Happy New Year.

I had four more messages. All from J'nette. Damn damn damn. Felt like I was living in a season of No Justice, No Peace.

All the first message said was, "I need to see you." The next three were rude, accused me of dodging her calls.

Kimberly was getting out her shampoo, getting ready to do her head, and she'd said she wanted to re-do her nails, so that would buy me some free time. A second after she closed the bathroom door, the shower came on. I picked up the passkey and slipped out the door, went downstairs to the pay phone.

The first thing J'nette said was, "I didn't go."

"Well," I said and did my damndest to not sound worried. I wondered why she kept calling me instead of the brotha behind curtain number two. "What're you going to do?"

"I want to get it over with Tuesday."

"How's about Wednesday?"

"Why not Tuesday?"

"I'm out of town."

"Where?"

"Memphis."

Her voice trembled. "I want you to go with me because I don't want to bring nobody else into this. I'm going to a place by Northern and Astoria Boulevards."

"That's close to Shea Stadium."

"It's in that direction, yeah."

"Why are you coming all the way to Queens?"

"Because I don't want to run into any scandalous people from Jersey. It's supposed to be a small family planning clinic."

A moment passed before I said a broke down, "Okay."

"I want to stay at your house Tuesday. So I can get there early and get it over with. We need to get this over with."

I almost said *Hell, no!* but she was right; we needed to get this out of the way. My eyes were on the elevator, hoping Kimberly didn't happen to come down for any reason.

I told J'nette, "All right. I'll call you back tomorrow."

By the time I got back up to the room, Kimberly had turned off the lights and lit candles. One was on the dresser in front of the mirror. Another was on the dining table. The curtains were open and gave a starry view toward the beach and the ocean.

She'd blow-dried her hair, made her mane straight. Her hair was long and hung down her back, inches below where her bra strap would've been. Her perfume and a burning vanilla incense spiced the suite. On the radio, the blue digital lights read 91.7, and Norman Brown jazz was filling the room, doing the rest. Her pouty lips were red, shining. This was a different woman. In her eyes, I saw her asking for approval. I nodded, grinned. Then I saw her temperature rising. She stood up and let her white Victoria show parts of her secrets.

With a smile, she invited me to her playground.

As I walked over to her, she tilted her head.

9 Jordan Greene

Solomon pulled his five-year-old Celica out and chug-a-lugged from borough to borough to meet us at JFK on Monday evening. He'd fought through traffic and was standing at the gate grinning up a storm when we got off the plane. Zoe's engagement ring was in his hand and he wanted me to see it ASAP, wanted to know what I thought. When I called him from LAX five hours ago, I had barked at him that it was too soon for him to even be thinking about getting married again. He snapped and chastised that I'd flown to L.A. with a "peckerwood" I'd met in a cab.

That killed my argument.

Honestly, I didn't know what he'd think when we got off the plane. Solomon twisted his face, nodded a couple of times. They spoke, shook hands. Two seconds later, he was rambling about Zoe and showing off the marquis.

I said, "Have you and Zoe talked about jumping the broom?"

Kimberly interjected, "That is a *beautiful* ring."

Solomon smiled at Kimberly, moved closer. "Think so?"

"She'll love it. May I look at it?"

While we fought through the international crowd and shuffled downstairs toward baggage claim, Solomon ignored me. Kimberly forgot about me. Underneath that avant-garde exterior and that I-can-hang-in-a-man's-world attitude she boasted, she was still a woman. Kimberly was excited, talking fast, asking him about the potential marriage proposal. They talked. I lagged behind.

It wasn't until we got to the parking lot, Kimberly had gotten in the car, and we were jamming our luggage in the trunk, that Solomon leaned close and asked me about J'nette.

Solomon asked, "How far along is she?"

"I'm not sure." I handed him four dollars to pay for ten minutes of parking. I asked, "Your woman say anything about it?"

"Put your wallet away. You know your money ain't no good with me." He lowered his voice a little, like an old southern black talking about one of the church members. "As far as I know, they don't have a clue she's knocked up."

I closed his trunk. We stood there blowing air from our mouths, shaking heads. Solomon was sharing my anxiety. That's what friends are for. That's why we're closer than brothers.

He adjusted his scarf and asked, "Why you taking her?"

"Trying to be a friend. Somebody's got to be responsible."

Last night I kept having the same dream about J'nette plopping out a baby. Only this time, J'nette and the baby had Edward Scissorhand claws. That struggle evolved into a nightmare about Reggie. We were in a room filled with fire. He was walking about ten feet in front of me, and no matter how hard I ran, I couldn't catch him. I screamed his name, ran to beat his stroll, but I couldn't reach him. When I grazed his shoulder, he stopped, jerked to face me, and he had J'nette's face on his chunky and chocolate-colored body. J'nette was laughing her ass off.

We dropped Kimberly off. Solomon dropped me off. Solomon stayed about five minutes. Then he left me to my thoughts.

I called J'nette, made sure she still had the money I'd given her, then told her she could come over around nine. I talked to Kimberly around seven and told her I was going to sleep early. She had planned on staying up late to work on an oil painting for some European magazine I had never heard of. First thing in the morning she was going running early with one of her girlfriends.

J'nette showed up an hour early, a little before eight. By nine, I'd left her in the living room watching TV, showered, and crawled into bed. Minutes later, she turned up the heat, undressed herself to the bone, and tried to climb on me. I eased her frame off mine, pushed her away, asked her to get some sleep so we could get up early in the morning and take care of this.

She looked offended. Told me I was insensitive.

She was still trying to run her mental game. So, she played the mad game, which I didn't really care about at this point. J'nette went back into the living room and turned the TV up real loud. Had it on that stupid Physic Friends program. *Loud.* It might sound cold-blooded, but I couldn't wait to get her out of my place, down to the clinic, and out of my life. Every time I thought our business was done, either she called or showed up to irritate my ass.

She came into the bedroom long enough to grab some covers and say that she was going to make a pallet on the living room floor. Then she turned the television's volume up, started surfing through one-hundred-plus cable channels. I heard CNN go by at least three times. I yanked the pillow off my head, went into the bathroom, hopped in the shower, soaped up, then remembered I'd already showered.

It was almost two in the A.M.

When I came out of the bathroom, J'nette was in my green cotton robe, standing in the bedroom with a dresser drawer halfway open. She jumped. Stepped away from the dresser.

I asked, "What're you doing?"

She flippantly held up her hand and rattled her jewelry, then snapped, "I was making sure I got all my stuff I left over here last time. That's all."

She closed the dresser hard enough for the mirror to shake, then headed back toward the living room. The television finally cut off. I thanked God for small miracles.

Peaceful hours went by. We both woke up cringing at each other, looking like we'd been sipping cold coffee laced with fresh manure. After we got dressed, I walked into the living room, and her overnight bag was flopped on top of my off-white sofa. The bag was new, but had a filthy bottom. I picked it up and put it on the carpet. Before I could take two steps toward the kitchen, J'nette stormed into the living room. She looked down at her bag, then shot daggers at me.

J'nette snapped, "Why you throw my bag on the floor?"

Her lips were tight. All of this was throwing me. Yesterday, she'd sounded cool, plus she'd looked so human the last time I'd seen her.

I said, "I didn't throw your bag on the floor."

"How did it get on the floor?"

"I took it off the sofa and *put* it on the floor."

"You didn't have to throw it off your funky little sofa."

"I didn't *throw* your bag."

"I heard it all the way in the bathroom."

A beat later, we were having a stupid argument, shouting back and forth about her stupid bag. I tried to stay calm, tried to explain that I put it on the floor because I didn't want stains on my sofa. Made sense to me. But the more I tried to throw light on the issue, the darker it became. It got out of hand when I yelled for her to quit bitching. She howled and wanted to know who I was calling a bitch. After I took a breath, lowered my tone, and nicely told her I didn't call her a bitch, but said she was bitching, she flipped out and screamed that if I said she was bitching, then I had to be calling her a bitch, because only a bitch bitches.

Her voice was echoing off the walls when I walked away.

J'nette blew up. She followed me from room to room, hollered in my damn ear, stepped on the back of my heels, bumped, pushed me around, shoved, shoved, shoved.

I made fists, stepped up on her, gave her a cold, defiant, Wesley Snipes-ish sounding "I've had enough of your shit."

She doubled her fists and barked, "I wish you would."

It was a no-win situation. She was on the last nerve of my last nerve and I just wanted her to shut up. The Montel Williams sensitive man approach only worked with an Oprah Winfrey sensible woman.

She turned around mid-sentence and stomped into the bathroom, slammed and locked the door. I was tempted to weld it shut and build a brick wall in front of it. But I stepped outside to suck up a breath of fresh air and clear my head before it exploded like the World Trade Center. My feet kept moving, led me on a therapeutic walk to the corner and back. It was about thirty degrees, a decent wind chill factor, but I was too pissed to feel my fingertips ache. Too mad to notice a beautiful sunrise was in the making. Boiling blood kept me warm.

When I stepped back inside, her nasty-ass luggage was back on my sofa. Shredded photos were scattered all over the floor and coffee table. When I picked them up, I thought she had torn up pictures of me and her, but they were mutilated pictures of me and Kimberly. Ones we'd just taken in Los Angeles and had One Hour Photo Matted on the promenade on the West Coast. J'nette had rifled through my dresser, found the pictures. That was what she was doing last night when I showered. She was tiptoeing around, snooping through my belongings the way panhandlers rifled through trash. Her ruthless, crooked face was standing in the bedroom door with her arms folded under her breasts, tapping one foot in sync with her rotating neck. I *hated* it when sisters did that snake shit.

She snarled and stepped to me. "Thought you were in Memphis?"

"What's your problem?"

"I guess Memphis has a damn Hollywood sign, huh?"

Kimberly's camera had put a digital date and time on all the pictures. No need to deny. No need to alibi. It hit the fan. Hard and loud.

She screamed about me being a dog: while she was going through hell, I'd flown to California to be with some "white-ass bitch." She assumed Kimberly lived in L.A. That was cool by me.

She switched emotional gears and said she wasn't going to get an abortion. When she lost her mind, the first thing I did was remind her, "You don't even know who you're pregnant by."

I shouldn't have said that. She flew her teary-eyed butt into the kitchen and grabbed a cutlery knife, came back slicing and jabbing at me with a fervor. Without a thought, I did the manly thing and ran my ass off. She chased, made threats. I ended up playing Zorro and swinging a golden lamp at her from the other side of my water bed. She wouldn't budge, stood solid between me and the door.

Then she acted like she was going to stab my waterbed. Somehow we got to wrestling with the knife. I took it away. Well, I didn't actually take it away—she threw it down and I dove and snatched it up before she went for it again. Now, I had the knife, but she kept on socking and pounding my chest.

Then she freaked me out. She stopped hitting me. Started crying. At first I thought she was trying to trick me, but her legs wobbled, and she collapsed down to the floor, fell with the ease of a pillow in flight. A second later, I sat down.

She rubbed her eyes and said, "I'm scared."

"Scared?"

She nodded. "Scared as fuck."

J'nette said she didn't believe in abortion, but she didn't believe in having a baby without it having a daddy. I asked her why didn't she talk to the other guy.

She said, "It's the twelfth hour. Don't matter now."

I didn't take it beyond that. I figured the other man must be married. Maybe homeboy wasn't a brotha and she didn't want anybody to know. Even though they dogged out brothas, sistas jocked and flocked to Italians and Puerto Ricans left and right.

"I don't want to go through that again," she said. "I've already been through this shit three times and after this time the doctor said I might not be able to have any children."

My mouth dropped open while she played with her cuticles and continued telling me how she might not be able to carry full term because of her weakened reproductive system. He thought this surgery would pretty much put the lid on her chances to have her own kids. She lost me when she started whimpering, getting medical and whining about weak walls, crap like that.

"Jordan," she said my name soft and easy, like I was her best friend. "If I have the baby, would you let me put it on your insurance, so that way I can take care of it until I get back on my feet?"

"You mean, say that the baby is mine?"

"Yeah. But I won't put your name on the birth certificate and I'll sign papers that say you're not the father."

She said it like she was asking for change for a dollar. Guilt was a huge emotion, but stupidity was something else. I barely lied on my taxes. I wouldn't lie about something like this. I had to say what made sense to me.

I rubbed the bridge of my sweaty nose and let out my gentlest "We can't do that. If it's mine, yeah, I'll do the right thing. If it's not, then, I'm sorry. It wouldn't be right. For me, for you, for the baby, for whoever the baby's daddy is. That's the kind of shit that'll come back to haunt all of—"

She struggled to her feet, marched away from me, and grabbed her purse. "C'mon. We're going to be late for my appointment."

Minutes later, we'd walked down to the Waldbaum's grocery store, found a yellow cab, and were heading toward Northern Boulevard. She was glued to her side. I was glued to mine. It felt like we were trying to prevent catching a disease from each other. I couldn't believe I'd ever touched her in a loving way.

For a while I put my attention on everything except for what was inside the cab; when we were caught at a light, I stared at a Channel 9 News billboard pumping up Ernie, Brenda, Storm, and Russ as the news team at ten P.M. When I sniffled and brought my eyes down from the skies long enough to get a Kleenex out of my pocket, I lost my wind and almost freaked out. Kimberly and a tall, svelte sista ran into the intersection, dashed by right in front of us. Kimberly's breath steamed out of her mouth with her stride. If she'd glanced to her right, she would've gazed dead in my eyes. If J'nette had stopped pushing her cuticles back and looked up, she would've seen Kimberly. Redhead and her friend kept moving. In New York, you don't peep inside cars. Thank God. Both were in pastel sweats, jogging and so busy talking they didn't even notice my cab.

Before we got to the clinic, I said, "You don't have to."

J'nette snapped, "I don't have a job. I can't get another job if

I'm black, a woman, and pregnant. And if I did have the baby, child care costs too damn much. And if I'm not working, what the fuck am I supposed to do? I'm pregnant. I just got laid off. I'm not going on the county for nobody. Hell, I'll be damned if I go AFDC. Once people get on that shit they get caught up and don't ever get off."

The cab driver looked in the rearview and said, "Excuse me? You want to go the AFDC? Where is that?"

"No noooo no!" J'nette said. "Nobody's talking to you. Keep your eyes on the road."

The driver raised his gloved hand. "So sorry."

I asked, "You want to maybe talk to a counselor first?"

"Jay, I'm pregnant. Not crazy."

After I walked her through all the frantic right-to-lifers who spit-screamed and threatened us by shoving blown-up photos of aborted babies in our faces, J'nette was even more shaken. I was just as disturbed. Pro-lifers had killed a doctor down in Florida. Had blown up another place. A doctor in Kansas was gunned down. Somebody went on a kamikaze mission and tried to drive a propane truck into the mouth of a clinic. These fools meant business and would do a Kevorkian on you in a heartbeat.

We'd gotten out of the cab in front of a short, chunky Puerto Rican woman who had a five-foot poster: ONE DEAD, ONE WOUNDED. A heavyset, bearded brotha semi-blocked us with a bright red sign: A BABY WITH POTENTIAL, NOT A POTENTIAL BABY. Me and the brotha glanced at each other. Since he didn't have a uterus, I wondered what the fuck he was doing out here.

We slowed our charge when J'nette stumbled on uneven sidewalk. A gust of wind blew us to the side. Pushed us together.

I coughed out, "You okay?"

Her voice cracked, but nothing audible came out. She gripped my hand so tight I thought she'd torn off a finger. My teeth clenched with the pain and a chill ran up my body. J'nette lowered her head and sped up her stride. I did the same.

While I sat with her in a place filled with regretful faces, she struggled to fill out the forms. Her hands were too shaky. I took the clipboard from her and filled in the blanks for her.

I asked, "What's your middle initial?"

She said, "L."

"What does that stand for?"

"Lynnette."

I said, "J'nette Lynnette?"

"Yep."

Any other time I would've laughed, but today I didn't think much would be funny.

She stared at her hands. "What's yours?"

"Jordan is my middle name. My first name is Elijah."

She wiped her face. "I never knew that."

For a few words, we sounded like friends. Were pleasant toward each other the way we were when we first met. She remained stiff-faced and told me she would be okay, then said she wanted me to meet her down the street at McDonald's in a couple of hours. She didn't ask me to leave; she told me to go.

After I stumbled out in the wind, I wondered what she was going through. The off-white walls and the stone-faced receptionist made the place read like a house of horrors. It wasn't so easy for me to sit it out over an Egg McMuffin and McCoffee.

I went around the corner and Western Union'd four hundred dollars to Darrell, then called and left him a message to let me know when he picked it up. Shit. Three hundred dollars to J'nette. Four hundred to Darrell. And I spent another three hundred in L.A. Kimberly had the plane tickets and hotel room taken care of, so I'd paid for the food and the rental car. Based on the balance in my check book, I'll be eating soup for the next three months. I had a few savings bonds stashed in my safety deposit box, dollars I'd been saving up for a rainy day. Right now, it was storming like a big dog.

A little over two hours later, J'nette came back out. She fought a strong breeze that blew her hair every which-a-way as she crossed the street and headed toward Mickey D's. I was worried and, even though I was glad she had finally come out, I was scared to face her. Ashamed. She looked alert, but moved much slower than her normal pace. A spiritless stride. I didn't know what to say, and from her expression and the hollowness of her words, she didn't want anything said to her. Especially by me.

We hailed a cab. The moment we got in, she stared at me with how-can-a-man-be-so-cruel? eyes. I felt her glare, saw some of its fiery glow in my peripheral. The heat made me glance her way.

She said a cold-blooded, "Happy?"

Her word chilled me. I didn't answer. I just pulled off my gloves and sent my eyes the other way, toward the coldness in the streets. She loosened her gray overcoat, rubbed her eyes.

I asked, "Want to relax at my place?"

She stared out the other window, wiped her nose.

I said, "Well, you want me to ride back to Jersey with you?"

She lamented, moved like she was in mourning, wrung her hands over and over.

When she did open her mouth, she told the driver to stop at the subway. At Roosevelt Avenue station. As the cab slowed, she leaned over and jammed a folded note into my pocket. It was one of the yellow fact pamphlets from the clinic's lobby. She had scribbled a message on the back in red ink. She hopped out and closed the door. Headed through traffic and people, moved in the direction of Zaika Restaurant and Sweets, toward the row of shops under the metal and concrete bridge. A few steps later, she turned around and stared at me. Her mouth opened, her lips and tongue started to form some words, but she didn't say anything.

I opened my door and stood in the wind, waited to see what she wanted to do. J'nette walked back toward me. Fought to get her purse open. She tussled out a small wrapped present and sat it on top of the cab. Slid it from her side to mine. She made a brief hand gesture at the green, sparkling Christmas paper decorated with a tiny golden bow.

Again, she tried to say something. My throat lumped. Palms were sweating inside my gloves. We didn't share a sound, not even when the cab driver blew his horn and screamed for me to either get in or out.

After J'nette awkwardly fingered her hair, in between short breaths, she dropped her head and wiped her eyes then gradually disappeared into the hustle of the nonchalant crowd. Went through the opening that led downstairs to the subway. She didn't feel enough to turn back; I didn't feel compelled to chase her.

I wondered about me. Wondered why life had to be like this.

I opened the box and looked inside. The bud of one dead red rose. Then I read the shaky handwriting on the note:

Jay,
Good-bye and forever stay out of touch. Oh, yes, I forgot to tell you. Kimberly called. We had a nice little talk. Merry fucking Christmas.

J'nette

10 Jordan Greene

By the time I made it home, Kimberly had called. Her voice was obstinate; the message said, "Call me when you get a minute."

I didn't. With an all-night fight, then J'nette dropping dead roses, I'd suffered enough battle scars for one day.

Darrell had called too. He had picked up the money. No doubt we wouldn't talk until the next bad times rolled around.

Solomon came over around three. He still had his putt-putt out and we drove to Rockefeller Center, shopped a bit, checked out the huge Christmas tree. Solomon took photos of the tree, then we went by his place for a few, long enough for him to take a few more snapshots when we were down at the Lenox Avenue, Saint Nicholas Avenue vendors in Harlem. After we played off brother after brother trying to peddle us bootleg movies, CDs, and tapes, Solomon took a picture of the Malcolm X street sign. All the snapshots were for his parents. His folks got off on photos of New York. Loved to brag to the neighbors about how their son from Pine Bluff was living large. I wanted to double back by the Garment District, but it got too late and hunger pains kicked in.

By eight, we were back at my place, chewing on leftover pork chops. Solomon started examining that ring, pacing room to room like a foolish dreamer in search of his own silver lining, clearing his throat, wiping his wet palms on his sweats.

By nine, we were sitting around the living room eating gourmet microwave popcorn and watching an old black and white movie starring a very young Eartha Kitt, Sammy Davis, Jr., and the dude who played Grandfather Huxtable on "The Cosby Show." I'd been wanting to see that movie for almost two years, but always missed it for one reason or the other.

My place was tossed from where J'nette had tornadoed her way from wall to wall at the crack of dawn. *PC*, *GQ*, and *EM* magazines were scattered on the semi-dusty endtable. The screen on the big-screen TV needed to be hit with some Windex; so did Mom's picture and the little African-American jazz band statuettes in the entertainment center. Other magazines were still on the floor, scattered on the carpet where J'nette had left them.

The smoke detector started humming. Before I could race into the kitchen, the foul odor had drifted down the hall. Solomon had accidentally programmed the microwave on 30:00 instead of on 3:00. The popcorn had been fried. Solomon was standing in the middle of the lingering smoke, hand-fanning the fumes.

After that, I still couldn't catch two minutes of the movie without him opening his mouth. Solomon was preoccupied with Zoe and that damn ring. All day long, everything we'd talked about had led back to Zoe. When we finally fanned most of the smoke out and sat back down, Solomon pissed me off because he kept opening and closing the stupid engagement ring case. Each time it clicked open, he'd suck his bottom lip. When it clacked closed, he'd sigh. He'd already asked me what I thought about that piece of the rock at least twenty times in the last ten minutes.

"Come on now," he slid the ring under my nose, "tell the truth. Don't put me on. What you think about it?"

"Solomon"—my eyes were still on the TV—"it's cool."

"Sho' nuff?"

"Yeah, it's smooVe."

I was tired of looking at the damn thing, and the click clacking on the case was surfing on the tip of my last nerve.

But Solomon was my southern-fried homeboy, my best friend, counselor, and friendly ATM who charged no interest. We're two fish out of southern bayous trying to swim in a big northern pond.

What bothered me about him and about Zoe was the fact he

wanted her so bad. Too bad. To the point of obsession. Way beyond the few months and fewer nights they'd shared together.

Maybe I was jealous because I'd never wanted anybody that bad. Hadn't wanted to greet a million sunrises with anybody that badly. Hadn't wanted to sample anybody's fruits until the sweetness was gone. Maybe I was feeling the blues because no honey-flavored woman had ever wanted me in a way of forever.

Zoe had already dumped two brothas this year. J'nette had told me that much. Both were lawyers. She had a pattern. And from what J'nette used to say about her, since Zoe's divorce, her spirit had been restless.

Solomon kept emphasizing he was thirty-two. A very settled, southern thirty-two, which comes out to be about a mental forty. And he kept complaining that he was tired of chasing the shadows of non-productive relationships. Tired of running after sistas who claimed they wanted a good brotha, but when they met one, didn't know what to do because they were too busy running mind games. Too busy putting a good-intentioned brotha on hold while they chased the brothas who were dogging them out.

And he said Zoe's a young thirty and claimed to be tired of being chased by a bunch of Mr. Do-Wrongs, brothas who claimed to want everything and offered anything, but in reality only wanted one thing and gave up nothing.

I asked, "So you and Zoe have talked about marriage."

"From a philosophical point of view."

"And?"

"Both of us are family oriented. So we believe in what it stands for, or since times have changed, what it used to and still should stand for."

"Solomon, there's a gap as wide as the Grand Canyon separating the ideological-philosophical from the truths of an undeniable reality."

"Chill out and stop using big words."

I rephrased and emphasized what I said, "Talk is cheap. Action speaks louder than words."

He gazed at the ring like it was the remedy to his misery. That was how I used to look at J'nette up until a few weeks ago. Weeks that zoomed by like a lifetime. Now the search was on again. We were all hunting something. It seemed like the simpler it was, the harder it was to reach.

I asked, "What're you thinking?"

"Nothing ventured, nothing gained."

Solomon went to the bathroom, then sang his way into the kitchen and poured his third glass of Kool-Aid. The movie was in full swing. I had a moment of silence, so I kicked back and enjoyed the bad-ass scene where Eartha Kitt and Sammy Davis, Jr., danced a throw-down number together.

My southern-fried buddy came back in and plunked the case down in front of me. Solomon put his feet on the coffee table and crossed them at the ankles. I frowned at him.

"Get your feet off my furniture."

He smiled. "Hush your mouth."

He had a short-man, power complex. He didn't have his shoes on anyway. We were both just sitting around in dark blue sweats being lazy, nervous, and pitiful. Solomon grabbed a handful of popcorn and started talking with his mouth full, yacking like we were in the middle of a conversation, "Me and little Sierra got along pretty good. Real good. We went to Chuck E. Cheese. She loves me to death."

It took me a second to remember that Sierra was Zoe's little girl. I huffed, "You only saw the kid once."

He smiled. "Twice."

"But it was the same day, right?"

He wrung his hands. "Yeah."

"Like I said, *once*. And *all* children love you at Chuck E. Cheese. It wasn't you; it was the talking bears."

"But you know how it is when something feels right?"

"Afraid not. How?"

He touched his chest and smiled as he held his heart. He tried to express his feelings in words, but I guess what he felt couldn't be expressed with a noun and a verb. First, his face cringed like he was digging down to the depths of his soul to emphasize the emotion, then he smiled, his face lit up, and he grunted out a passionate, "UNnnununumMmMmmmmpHHHH!"

We laughed.

Guess I'd finally realized something that was right in my face.

In his face. He was in love. Not just in love, but in *love*. I'd been taking his situation for granted, because I know how brothers mask-out anything resembling a real emotion. My own problems were in my eyes and I hadn't been listening to the truth behind his playful words. He wasn't just chasing a woman, he was chasing *the* woman. Solomon was always in control, and I'd never seen him broadcast any shade of doubt, so the insecure face he'd been sporting was new to me.

Solomon's my best friend and I'd best act like his. The threads of my mismanaged life were snapping all around me, but sometimes what was happening to me just wasn't that important. My bed had been made.

I turned the television off, clicked on the brass light on the endtable, picked up the ring, and looked at it, with detail. When I made an impressed sound, Solomon cackled, slapped his leg twice, smiled at his small victory, then slid over closer to me.

I said, "This looks expensive."

"Wanna see the certificate of authenticity?"

He'd snapped it out and stuck it in my face before I could answer. And it was appraised at a *grip*.

I groaned. "Solomon, considering what you make, and taking into consideration the two-month's-salary standard-guideline thing that women say a man is supposed to follow, you ran out and spent three times what you had to."

"Jay," he raised his palms to the sky. "What price can you put on what you feel, especially when what you felt feels real?"

"Damn, this is the bomb." I couldn't help but smile. "She seen it?"

He lit up. "Not yet. I'm gonna drop it on her Christmas."

"In front of her family?"

"Naw." He pulled his top lip. "Just me and her. I don't wanna be tacky and pressure her. And I don't want to get shame-faced. I mean, it's just an engagement thing. I wouldn't mind, but she don't have to run off and buy a wedding dress the next morning, unless she wants to. I want her to know I'm serious about her and I want to work toward something solid, with her pretty smile at my side."

"What about the kids?"

"Me, her, my little man, DaReus, and her daughter, Sierra,

could be real solid. I wish she was DaReus's mother. It'd be a helluva lot easier."

"Your ex-wife tripping?"

"Like you wouldn't believe. No matter how much money I send her, she wants more. I'm sending a hundred dollars a month *more* than I'm supposed to, plus I still send her money when DaReus stays with me, and she still wants more."

"Damn."

"Child support can be a motherfucker, even for a good daddy."

All the glee he had for Zoe vanished. Watching his pang made me feel like the best decision I'd made was telling J'nette I wouldn't let her use my insurance. Wouldn't let her use me. Once you started paying, you never stopped.

I told him, "She must want you back."

"If she hadn't been fucking 'round," he said, then flipped his hand and made a *tsk* sound, "she'd still have me. The only reason I stay cordial with her ass is because of my little man."

"If Zoe says no, does she get to keep the ring?"

"You gone crazy?"

"Just wanted to make sure you wasn't."

My phone rang. Like I'd done three times, I let it roll over to my answering machine. Four more calls came in, back to back.

Solomon chuckled. "Want me to get it?"

I grabbed a handful of popcorn. "Machine'll get it."

Solomon laid back on the sofa and crossed his legs. "Somebody is hunting you down."

A couple of minutes later, my stomach grumbled and I jumped up to make a potty call. I was rolling off the two-ply when my doorbell rang. Before I could crack the door and yell to tell Solomon to see who the midnight caller was before he opened it, I heard voices. I messed around in the bathroom, sprayed some air-freshener, and brushed my teeth just to blow time and let the smell die.

I was coming down the hall rubbing lotion on my hands. Kimberly and the sista I'd seen her running with were in my living room, standing in front of the entertainment center. Solomon had them cornered, showing them that ring.

Kimberly pulled off her Giants baseball cap and smiled. Some. I smiled back. Some.

I thought she'd cut her hair, but it was in a braid, tucked inside her jacket, making her hair look boy-short. She didn't have on any makeup, her face had windburns, so she looked twenty. For the first time, without her pointing it out, I noticed the faded scar on her head.

Kimberly's grin waned. She rocked side to side, opened and closed her leather coat. She said, "Did you get my message?"

I nodded. The last of my smile faded.

Her friend sent me a crooked grin, parted her soup-cooler lips and interrupted the awkward moment of silence. "So, you are the one who's taking up me friend's time?"

She was taller than me, Solomon came up to her breast, and she had Nigerian features, a Jamaican accent, smooth skin. She unsnapped her black parka, loosened her red scarf, then took her baseball cap off and let her shoulder-length braids fall free.

I made my face grin. "I'm Jordan. You must be Sharon."

She walked over and gave me a firm business handshake. "Sharon is our other friend. My name is Kinikki Cameron."

"Kah-knee-key?"

"Yes. That was pretty good."

"Kinikki. Nice to meet you, Kinikki." I said her name twice. Repeat it twice, stored for life.

"I'm an artist, just like Kimberly."

Solomon jumped in, "Y'all rest your coats for a while."

Kimberly shook her head. "We're only stopping for a minute."

Kinikki and Kimberly shared a conspiratorial glance, then Kimberly molded her lips up into a happy face, eased her six-foot friend out of the way, gave me a slight hug, got close enough to whisper into my ear, "Are you avoiding me for some reason?"

I matched her smile and whispered, "Nope."

Kinikki laughed. "You two cut dat out now. Enough time for dat hanky-panky later. Jordan, do you have anything to drink?"

"Kool-Aid. Pepsi. Wine."

Kinikki said an immediate, "Wine will be fine."

Kimberly followed me into the kitchen. I poured a glass of wine and Kimberly took it into the living room and came right back. While she strolled, she massaged the back of her neck.

She gestured toward the kitchen table. We sat down. She crossed her legs. Strummed her fingers across the glass top. The tips of her french-manicured nails made a continuous roll of taps. I sipped my Kool-Aid, and when I put the glass down, she picked it up, took a few swallows. When she put the glass back down, it had chocolate lipstick on the rim. She looked at me. I sat back, took in some wind, let it go, rolled one thumb over the other.

She tilted her head, then said, "You've got dandruff."

"My scalp's dry."

"Get some moisturizer. You're *flaking*." Kimberly stopped her drumming, scratched her head, then asked, "Who's J'nette?"

She sounded jealous. Maybe she was wondering how she could compete with a sista.

I cleared my throat, wriggled. "You talked to her?"

"Don't do that."

"What?"

She leaned, touched my hand. "Don't answer my question with a question."

"Is that why you came over? To ask me that?"

"Actually, it was Kinikki's idea. After I left you a message, and you didn't have the decency to return my call, I wasn't going to bother with it. Or you anymore, after the things your friend said. But Kinikki, well, she thinks I like you too much and thinks I should hear what you have to say about it before I write you off as another bad choice."

"Do you?"

"Do I what?"

"Like me too much?"

"I'm here. You tell me. Do I?"

"Don't answer my question with a question."

Kimberly didn't smile. Her face stayed firm. She brought her hand to the bridge of her nose. "Who is this J'nette who answered your phone last night?"

With clenched hands, I told her. I didn't have a choice because I didn't know or have any way of finding out what version of this jacked-up scenario J'nette had told Kimberly. Her face, her eyes, nothing about her well-controlled body gave me any clue. I didn't know how bad I should feel about what was happening, or what had happened. Me and Kimberly had met and ended up in this whatever we were in so fast, I hadn't had time to cleanse the residual of the last relationship from the bottom of my hiking boots. Kimberly had a way of watching me when I talked, made me think she could recognize a lie by the shape of my mouth. It didn't matter; I didn't have any lies to tell.

Kimberly blew disgusted air. "Did you make her go?"

"She wanted to go. She asked me for the money."

With her hands on the table, she fidgeted in her chair and asked in her distant business tone, "Was it yours?"

I sighed, licked my lips, and shrugged. "I don't know."

"Jordan, the shit you're saying doesn't make sense."

"It's the truth."

"Sounds like bullshit. Then why did you give her the money? Why did you let her spend the night?"

"It was more convenient. I mean, I don't know."

She crossed her arms. "Are you still sleeping with her?"

"No."

"Seeing her?"

"No."

We slid the chairs back, then stood. Before she took a step, Kimberly said a jarring, "You know what else is fucked up? This morning, I saw you two in the cab."

There was nothing I could say.

She stayed two steps ahead of me, buttoned up her coat, tugged her mitts back on, then stuck her hands in her pockets.

Solomon was on the sofa, still showing the ring to Kinikki.

Kinikki looked at Kimberly and sang an unsure "Ready?"

Kimberly said a plain "Yep. We're finished."

Kimberly was damn near in a sprinter's position, her hands balled up, her head tilted forward. Solomon was still in his own world. He glanced at his watch and decided he was going to head home too. Kimberly asked him to drop her off at home and to drop Kinikki off at the subway. They said they'd give him a few bucks, money they would've given a taxi, but he refused. He was more than happy to oblige. Southern hospitality. Told them he was going the same way and it wouldn't be any inconvenience.

Kimberly silently walked out first, then Solomon, then Kinikki. My eyes were stuck on Kimberly's sway, glued to her style of dress. In my few years, I'd never met anybody like her. Never knew anybody so complete. She was open, and a mystery at the same time. A mystery who was moving on without looking back. I didn't know her well enough to earn any heartbreak, but I felt it anyway. I already knew I'd miss her for a while. A long while. Didn't matter. I'd learned a long time ago that all things come to an end. Especially the good things. So, for me heartbreak was as expected as sunrise and as comfortable as worn shoes. Melancholy moments leading to long minutes of mental madness was nothing new.

Kimberly eased into the backseat of Solomon's ride, faced forward, didn't glance back. I felt stupid standing out in the dark, lingering in the cold without shoes on, waiting for nothing, so I mumbled a general good-bye to the gentle breeze and shuffled back down to my fortress of solitude.

Back inside, I picked up my *Times*, strolled around in my own quiet, turned off the lights in the living room, clicked on some vintage Charlie Parker, went in the kitchen to microwave a cup of water for my herbal tea.

All of my movements were slower than molasses. Anxiety was thickening my blood, weighing me down, making me feel ancient. Hell, I was born old. It's like that when you're drowned with responsibilities the moment you slip out of your momma's womb.

The door bell rang. It was Kimberly. She was standing underneath the gentle radiance of my yellow porch light, eyes closed, arms folded tight. Whistling an incensed version of "Jingle Bells."

I asked, "Whu'sup?"

"Was it yours?"

"I didn't know."

"What does that mean?"

"She didn't know."

Kimberly turned away and let her breath steam away from her face. Then she put her eyes back on mine. "Should we keep seeing each other or should I go home?"

"What do you want?"

"Don't answer my question with a question."

"Stop asking so many questions."

"Stop being so secretive."

"Stop being sarcastic."

"Stop pissing me off."

She turned around and waved good-bye to Kinikki, who was standing outside of Solomon's car. They pulled away.

Kimberly blew a stream of air, said, "You gonna let me in? I'm cold."

"You mind unfolding your arms?"

She dropped her arms to her sides.

I stepped back.

She walked in, unbuttoned her coat, kissed the side of my face, my lips, gave me a hug.

She took my hand and said, "C'mon."

"Where we going?"

"To wash your hair. It's as flaky as you are."

"That wasn't funny."

"I wasn't trying to be."

"Don't start."

"Don't make me."

"Are you one of those women who has to have the last word?"

"Yes."

11 Jordan Greene

Solomon called me screaming at the top of his lungs. Zoe was just as loud. On Christmas morning, he'd given Zoe a framed picture, a swank golden frame that recorded messages. Solomon held it up to his end of the phone and played what he'd recorded: *"My dearest Zoe. You're the woman of my dreams. I want to dedicate my life to loving you and building something real together for us, the children we have, and the unborn ones I think about every time I see you. Ain't no—I mean, there is no other woman for me and I know I'm the man for you. If you open up the back of this here picture frame, you'll find a ring that represents my feelings for you, for me, for Sierra, for DaReus, for all of us. The gold symbolizes how precious you are. The diamond means that what I feel for you is forever. The unending circle symbolizes the same forever I want from you. Will you marry me?"*

He said that Zoe broke into tears, shouted, and accepted before the message had finished. Zoe was still in the background, screeching like she had been attacked by the Holy Ghost.

It was six in the A.M. They'd been up all night; I'd been asleep for three hours, because I'd partied for a bit, hung out with Kimberly at the club called Shadow. I yawned, then cackled a rough, "Congratulations!"

"Wake up, Negro! I want you to be the best man."

"What about your brothers?"

In the background Zoe screamed how much she loved her man.

Solomon shouted, "*We* are brothers. They can be ushers or something."

He asked where Kimberly was.

Redhead was at my side, under my flannel sheets, cuddled next to me, breathing lightly.

He chuckled, "She keeping your yuletide warm?"

"You know it."

"What y'all up to today?"

I told Solomon that Kimberly was going to be with me all day. We were going to exchange Christmas presents when we finally woke up in the afternoon. Then cook a small meal, do nothing, stay warm, and watch game after game. But tomorrow afternoon she'd be doing her traditional thing and hooking up with Kinikki and going out to Long Island to Sharon's. Last year they packed up their satin pajamas and got together at Kimberly's place; this year it was Sharon's turn to host their little joy luck club. Kimberly said the girls always kicked the men to the curb and got together the day after Christmas, sipped brandy, and exchanged presents.

Solomon said, "So, she ain't gonna be able to kick it with us tomorrow for Kwanzaa."

Kimberly stirred. Her eyes opened for half a second.

I whispered to Solomon, "Hold on."

I ran my fingers through Kimberly's hair, lightly touched her face, around her lips. She stirred again, smiled a little, looked so young and innocent. I felt my insides warming up with a feeling of good. I kissed the side of her face then slipped out of bed, headed for the kitchen so I wouldn't wake her. The apartment was damn cold on my naked body so I grabbed my housecoat and put my slippers on as I left the bedroom.

I turned the burners on the stove on to make some instant heat, then sat at the kitchen table and finally answered Solomon, "Nope. She won't be hanging with us in the Collard Greens Projects tomorrow."

"Too bad. I wanted Zoe to meet her. I told Zoe how cool Kimberly is."

"What Zoe say?"

"She rolled her eyes."

We laughed.

I wondered if Kimberly wasn't busy tomorrow, whether or not I would stroll by Marcus Garvey Memorial Park with her smiling, us standing hand in hand. I enjoyed what we had, looked forward to the next phase, but I didn't know if I was ready to put on a colorful dashiki and Ray Bans, pump my fists, step in the doors of Black Books Plus, and buy books on black empowerment with Redhead peeking over my shoulder. I already knew that all day tomorrow Solomon and Zoe would be snuggled and blushing from ear to ear, her ring sparkling like a beacon of happiness.

But that was them.

If Kimberly was available, I wondered if I could stand with my buddy and his fiancée on one side and Kimberly at the other.

I hated the hypocritical feeling I was feeling. It was as thick as cold oatmeal.

I mean, I'd rented a tux and gone to Sharon's AIDS benefit a few days ago, had been around all of Kimberly's friends, people she introduced me to without hesitation or reservation.

But in my world, she'd only met Solomon. She knew about everybody else, but I hadn't dragged her along for a face-to-face. None of the sistas I associated with had ever heard me mention

Kimberly's name. But they knew. J'nette had spread the word the moment she cried her way home from the clinic.

Solomon said that they were planning an "impromptu" engagement party on New Year's Eve at his place, wanted anybody who had ever come to one of his world-famous card parties to stop by and celebrate his newfound dream. I told him that I wasn't going. I didn't want to show up and decrease the peace. It wouldn't do the world any good to have me, Kimberly, and J'nette breathing the same air. When jealousy and alcohol mixed, a brotha never knew what might jump off.

"Look, Jay," Solomon said. "J'nette is Zoe's friend, true enough, but you *my* friend and this is *my* house. I pay the rent here. J'nette don't like the scenario, she can walk her ignorant ass out."

"I just don't want no shit."

"They don't start no shit, then it won't be no shit. I got your back, all day, all night. You know that."

He wouldn't let it go, or take no for an answer.

The first person I saw when we walked in, all smiles and grins, was Toni. She was in a green velvet dress, golden jewelry, holding on to her Puerto Rican boyfriend. Disgust lived in her eyes. She didn't like to see me breathing. She came over, didn't say shit to me, but introduced herself to Kimberly, then asked Kimberly who she was and what she did, smiled when Kimberly shook her hand. Toni adjusted her cleavage and hurried back to her beau-of-the-night.

About twenty people were moving in and out of the apartment, so no matter where I went, somebody was there with a drink in their hand. I was ready for attitude from the regulars when I strolled in with Kimberly, but the way she looked in her golden, wide-legged pant suit and her wavy hair hanging over her shoulders and down her back, not a damn thing could be said, especially by the women sporting the fake locks. But just because I didn't hear anything negative, didn't mean it wasn't there. I knew the routine: black folks loved to talk about you when you left the room. Solomon's neighbor, Yasmean, was there. Without a date. She sported a tight red dress with *super* cleavage, and her shoulders lost some of their sultriness, her posture rang a loud disappointment when I showed up holding Kimberly's hand. After Yasmean had a couple of drinks, she jumped friendly with a brother who dangled a mistletoe over her head. After they shared a two-minute kiss, she stayed up under him the rest of the night. I don't think the brotha ever saw her face because his eyes were glued to her cleavage, and his tongue was hanging down to her breasts. Yasmean had so much cleavage that if she jumped up one good time, one of those suckers would pop out like toast.

I'd be lying if I said I wasn't kinda leery about dancing with Kimberly, because I'd always been skittish about dancing with white folks. They were too unpredictable. Some of them went to aerobics and thought they'd learned some moves. Kimberly danced real nice, surprised me with a strong rhythm, a sexy softness to her moves. And her groove wasn't repetitive or orchestrated. She went with the music.

Solomon cut in for a dance and I headed for the kitchen with our empty champagne glasses. Toni stood in my face when I went to freshen up our drinks. She said nothing for a moment. But the way her tongue was jammed up in the front part of her lip, I knew harsh words were only a breath away.

I said, "How's your twin bookend doing?"

She barked, told me J'nette had packed up and moved back to D.C. Then she gazed me up and down, "Get out of my face and go back in there with that Bambi."

"Excuse me?"

"Ain't no excuse for a brother like you."

"You getting loud with me, Miss Antoinette Barrett?"

Toni stepped closer. "You had the nerve to bring that white girl up in here. You ain't about shit."

I smiled. "Happy New Year to you too."

Toni started hand-combing her hair, dragged her fingernails through her mane from forehead to neck, just like J'nette always did. Same egg, same habits. Sometimes they were so much alike, I couldn't tell where one of them ended and the other one began.

Back in the living room, since the windows didn't have any blinds, all the skyscrapers across the land lit up the island called

Manhattan. Central Park was covered with snow and looked like a winter wonderland. Solomon was leading the crowd and cha-cha-ing with Kimberly. Zoe was talking and laughing with Yasmean, both in evening gowns, holding a drink in one hand while they girl-fanned the other. Kimberly winked at me. I gave her the rapid tongue. She laughed, kept on dancing.

At midnight, I slid a golden ankle bracelet into her hand, whispered, "Happy birthday."

She smiled. "You shouldn't have."

"Like?"

She whispered, "Definitely."

"Good."

"I don't know why, but I'm crazy about you. And I'm not the type who gets crazy about anybody. If that's not okay, let me know, then my resolution will be to back off and punt."

"Cut that out!" Solomon yelled. He had pulled Zoe out on the floor and was slow dancing like it was a mating call for all.

"Happy New Year everybody!" Zoe grinned ear to ear and held up her new ring. Smiled harder than hard.

I wondered if I'd ever be happy that way. They looked and acted like they were a family already. I looked at Kimberly and wondered if she would be part of the solution or another problem.

Solomon gyrated his woman; she shrieked and ran away. It looked funny because he was so short and moved so quick.

"I like this." Kimberly kissed me. "Your friends are fun."

"You think so?"

"Solomon looks so happy."

"Yep." I nodded. Some jealousy cruised my veins. I said, "That he does."

"Is your ex here?"

"Nope. Her twin sister is."

"Is she the one in the emerald dress?"

"Yep."

Kimberly lost some of her smile, shook her head once or twice. She said, "She's attractive."

I didn't say anything. I matched Kimberly's coolness.

Kimberly continued, "And to be honest, she's the worst."

"She bother you?"

"Nope. Just reminds me of when I was growing up. She needs to grow up. Some people can't accept what they consider different. Even if it's not."

"Somebody say something?"

"Nope. Negative energy wipes out insincere smiles. Like I said"—Kimberly pushed her lips up into a blooming smile—"she reminds me of the girls I grew up with."

"Back in Oakland?"

"Yep. Out in Oaktown, as they called it."

"This kind of party bother you?"

"I'm with you, not them. You're a good dancer."

"Thanks. You too."

She raised a brow, smirked. "You sound surprised."

"Some."

"Guess you thought I'd start doing that side to side thing that Eddie Murphy joked about."

"You know it."

"Puh-leeze."

We shared a laugh. A very hard laugh. Rubbed cheeks.

Toni was across the room, watching. She was smiling, but I knew that was a well-disguised frown. Knowing her, she'd already run to a phone and dialed J'nette's number down in D.C.

Forget them.

Then for a moment I wondered who I'd be with next New Year's. I've never spent two New Year'ses with the same woman. Never made it from birthday to birthday with the same soul. As a matter of fact, I've only had a couple of relationships that made it through three consecutive seasons.

I thought about my own family. My brothers. Wondered where they were spending the first moments of a new year. Who they had their arms around, who was holding them, cheek to cheek. If there was any such thing as a New Year's wish, I'd wish we were closer, mentally. Wished we owned the same kind of brotherhood I shared with Solomon. I wanted my brother Darrell to get over the pain. Wanted my brother Reggie to have a safe life. I didn't have the slightest idea if they were happy, how life was treating them. They knew even less about me.

Solomon came over, gave me a two-armed, man-to-man

hug. He said an emotional, a heartfelt, "Happy New Year, my brother."

"Happy New Year, my brother."

Then I hugged Kimberly. Told her happy birthday again. Hugged her long and strong. Held on and didn't let go.

It seemed like all eyes were on me.

Kimberly whispered a naughty "You know what I want?"

I grinned. "What?"

"A thick slice of New York cheesecake. I'm craving."

We both laughed a little.

I asked, "Know where you can get some of that cheesecake?"

"My place. Second shelf of the fridge next to a nice bottle of Spumante with our names written all over it."

"Let me go get our coats."

"It'll be there. Let's finish our dance. Hold me close."

I did. She held me closer.

When the music faded, we shared a gaze. She looked as delicate as a snowflake, and just as unique. In her eyes were friendship, and a twinkle of seriousness that made me shiver. Whenever her eyes met mine, it felt like all of her attitude, all that crap that a woman picks up from struggling in a man's world, all of that dissipated. She became vulnerable. Her femininity shined through. She stared at me with the soft eyes of a gentlewoman. Soft, trusting, and longing. And that eye-to-eye makes me weak for her, softens me up, takes away the edge, and makes me feel like a man. Allows me to feel the way a man is supposed to feel. She doesn't have to speak what's in her heart for me to know that she has some feelings for me. Some decent feelings. And I had the same for her. Couldn't take my eyes off her. Couldn't pull my heart away if I tried.

Kimberly smiled at her bracelet, kissed the side of my face, then whispered over her champagne-spiced breath, "SmooVe?"

"Yeah?"

"Are we *dating* tonight?"

"You decide."

part two

Ghosts Hanging from My Trees

12 Kimberly Chavers

Jordan makes me feel warm. That feeling thrives deep inside me. He's attentive. Very much in focus with me. He's not controlling. He's giving. Encouraging. Understanding and not intimidated by me or my ambitions. And I met him in a cab.

Most of the time, he holds my hand when we walk. He didn't do that too much at first, but now he does. On his own. Not all of the time, but enough for it to be appreciated, not so much that it's irritating and feels like he's clinging. If I take his hand he doesn't act like he wants it back.

If I'm at his place relaxing, which I sometimes do to get a change of scenery and to get away from my phone's constant ringing, he stops working on his computer whatever stuff to come over and kiss me and bestow that hug he always gives me. A couple of times during the week he calls me just to ask me how my days are going, and when I tell him, he listens. Not only does he listen to what I say, he remembers little details. His voice always rings soft and pleasant when he talks to me, almost as if he has created a special tone, a new flavor just for me. I feel like I matter to him. He considers me. I know, because this morning as we showered, while he washed my back, he whispered it into my ear. He watches me be a woman. He sees me first thing in the morning and still tells me I'm pretty.

Oh, we argue, but we always make up. Sometimes I start a little—what would I call it?—a love-spat, just so we can jazz it up. I know it's wrong, but I like the playful game. And when we heat it up, most of the time he lets me have the last word. Most of the time.

One thing we argue about is the damn toilet seat. My pet peeve. Enough said. Another thing is that he's such a man and thinks I take too long to get dressed. Too long to do my hair. I'm worth the wait. How do I know? Because even though he complains, he waits. And when he sees me sashay out of the bathroom with my face done, he smiles, his eyes get that look, and he can't keep his hands off me. I rest my case. I do take too long, but it's because I'm a habitual procrastinator and am always getting wherever I need to be five minutes after I need to be there. I inherited that trait from Mom-Mom. It's in the genes.

He eats off my plate, which I don't like people to do, but he'll do it anyway. That's how he tries to start something. He pisses me off because he doesn't eat right, bad diet, so he gets sick easy. You know, colds, the flu. Stuff like that. I've got him in the habit of jogging with me a couple of times a week. On those days I run slower and not as far because he's not a runner. It's the togetherness that matters. And exercise stimulates your carnal appetite. Well, mine anyway.

I find myself thinking about him a lot. Too much. If I see a man with a nice suit or outfit on, the first thing I think is how much better it would look on Jordan. When he wears a suit, he stands like he should grace the covers of GQ.

I'm in love and it's scaring the shit out of me.

I hadn't seen or talked to him too many times over the last week and a half because I fell into a deep groove working on a painting. One of those days I broke free and we went to Times Square to hang out. On the way we decided to catch a play, and as we left the subway and hiked upstairs from the Times Square 42nd Street station, we passed the Disney Store and I noticed a jewelry store I had been yearning to stop by. It had a big sign with that sweet–sour four letter word, SALE. Even though I can't afford to buy anything, I had to at least go see what they had so I'd know what I couldn't afford. I dragged him through traffic and across Seventh Avenue, not because he was reluctant, but because he was more interested in seeing Geraldo Rivera and his camera crew taping on the streets. I could care less about the Southern Baptist people boycotting Disney. So I pulled him along. Plus I just walk faster than Jordan does. He laughed when I pulled him with me, then he pulled me to make me slow down. He's a joy. Jordan's naïve in so many ways, mostly about the rudeness of New York. He thinks that if he's nice, people will be nice in return. I keep telling him, this is New York. New set of rules. In New York, rude is nice. Nice is offensive.

He's more mellow. Maybe because he's southern. I grew up in San Antonio for a while, but all of that niceness left me a long time ago. But all those things are what I enjoy about him. Him and that little southern twang-slang accent he tries to hide. It comes and goes, creeps out every now and then. Especially when he gets excited. Or around Solomon. Put them together, and ten minutes later they sound like an episode of "Hee Haw."

While I gazed at each piece of jewelry on display, Jordan stood next to me and held my hand. He has a way of slowly rubbing his flesh up and down mine that makes me, you know, get that loving feeling. It tingles and I let him do it as long as he wants. The rubbing.

The East Indian man waiting on us asked, "Would you care to look at the engagement rings on sale?"

I rubbed the back of my neck and tried not to cringe. It felt like my face had an idiotic smile. He annoyed me because of his rude assumption. And usually if you meet a man, and that subject comes up without them initiating it, they get an attitude, think you are trying to trap them and douse their freedom with the cold water of commitment. Some, not all. But still, most men. And some women. Myself included. More women than you'd believe. Every person with a uterus isn't in search of a white picket fence, a Volvo station wagon, and two-point-five children waiting to be carpooled to school.

But Jordan didn't flinch. Before I could interject a negative, Jordan rubbed my hand and said a smooVe "Sure. Let's peep a few."

I had started clearing my throat and tugging at my ear. My heart began to pound and my palms sweated. And I don't usually sweat. He patiently contemplated each ring and helped me try them on. He asked me what I thought. Even though a couple of them were so well crafted and had stones that made my heart murmur, I kept saying I didn't like any. Made a fake face of hate at the ones I really cared for. I deliberately gave a different lie about each. Didn't like the stone, didn't like the band.

I changed the subject and decided I wanted to go catch a matinee. As we sat in the theater, it occurred to me I was in a relationship. I mean a real relationship. Not another fly-by-night affair. Not another fling-thing that expires in sixty to one hundred and twenty days.

It might sound juvenile, but I actually had a *boyfriend*.

When I first met SmooVe, I'll have to be honest and say I thought it was going to be a one-niter with a fine-ass man from down south. After it was *so good*, I thought it would be a two-timer, then back to my life of distance and celibacy. Then I thought, what the hell, and figured I'd extend my fantasy, something positive I deserved, and take him to L.A. for a sex-filled weekend before I went back to my regular life. Then he was cool, so I said he'd be a nice someone to spend the holidays with sipping cocoa and watching the bombardment of Christmas movies.

But the magical moments kept going. I kept calling him, asking him out. He kept calling me, asking me out. The next thing I knew I had a drawer at his place. A drawer filled with enough clothes that if I wanted to spend the night, I didn't have to take any. And he had a left a couple of suits at my place.

What I felt started growing. Nice and easy. Like a foundation was being put down a day at a time.

Then he asked me if I wanted to start saving to go to the Bahamas for next Christmas. The notion flew right by me, because I didn't think much of it. I didn't take his words seriously because men have been known to make promises they never intended to keep. And time had a way of breaking promises. But the idea of the hopeful event, the remembrance of him asking with such a desire, well, it made me tremble with just as much yearning.

Okay, now we were sitting in the musical *Bring In 'Da Noise, Bring In 'Da Funk*, and Jordan leaned close to me and broke my never-ending thoughts when he whispered, "What's wrong?"

I smiled. "Nothing."

"You like the performance?"

"Definitely. The tap dancing is awesome."

For almost two hours, I trembled. Not because of the show's performance. Not because of the Bahamas. But Christmas was months away, so Jordan planned to be in my life for a while. It would be our second Christmas. He considered me in his plans. I mean, you wish for something like that, for a man like him to wander into your life, but when it seems like it's actually happening, it scares you down to your cuticles.

To be honest, even though I sort of liked him from the moment he shivered his runny nose into my life, and I guess I sort of went after him, sort of let things get this far and this deep, I hadn't planned on being with him this long. To tell the truth, most of my relationships only last about six months before they go sour for one reason or another. Maybe what's bothering me is that after making him confess to me—I've never lied, but I've never told him the truth about my situation.

He only knows Kimberly. Not Kim.

I don't know how to tell him any of my personal problems, my secrets, and that frightens me. I've told him *almost* everything about me. Almost all of the surface stuff. Just enough to make him comfortable. I never tell all, because in the past, people have used it against me. People are like that by nature. Most of the people I've trusted, anyway. It's not that I intentionally hid it from him, it just wasn't heavy in the front of my mind. It wasn't any of his business. It shouldn't be, I keep telling myself it's not, and to wait a little longer, but still, I want to tell him. Especially if he's going to be around. Especially since it feels like I want him to be around.

We stood on the curb after the show. Jordan joked as another empty cab drove by him. "Why don't you hail the cab, then I'll do like we did last time."

I laughed. "Jump in and act like we just met, then you start kissing and rubbing all over me?"

"Yeah. That'll freak the driver out."

"Okay. But keep your hands where I can see them."

"Make me."

Then I was going to tell him as soon as I got back from showing my work in San Francisco, but he met me at the airport. More like surprised me at the airport. I had been thinking of how to tell him. I had been trying to find the right words to use to explain why I had neglected to tell him a few things. The hardest one, the one that could be the least forgiven, is that I'm married. I've been married for a long time.

As I walked through JFK preoccupied with this thought, he stepped out of nowhere with a dozen yellow roses. We'd always given each other yellow roses; a symbol of our growing friendship to go along with our undying passion.

The following week I planned to unburden myself, wanted to tell him about all the misleading things I'd said. I was supposed to meet him at my house at three, but he didn't show. Around five, I received a call from Solomon telling me Jordan was in the hospital. Solomon said I didn't need to come down, it wasn't serious, but I was on the way to the emergency room before I had hung up. Jordan had almost passed out running. His asthma started acting up and he was being macho and trying to run through the wheezing. It only made it harder for him to breathe and the Primatine tablets they bought on the way home didn't do a bit of good. When I asked him why he did something that stupid, he said that he was training so he could run a 10K with me. At my pace. I was mad, but I couldn't stay mad when he said that. He'd hurt himself considering me. He fell asleep and I sat in his hospital room and watched him for three hours before he woke up. They gave him oxygen, put the mask over his face. That scared me. I tried not to cry, but I couldn't help it. And I never cry in front of anybody. Ever. No matter what pain I had, I never wanted to come across as a weak, whining woman. That was the way I grew up. Wanting to cry with nobody to defend my tears. So I went into the ladies' room until I was all cried out. I love him and I felt like I'd almost lost him.

"Hey," Jordan said. His voice was coarse, dry.

I held water to his face. "How you feel, knucklehead?"

He grinned and tried to sit up. "Better."

I smiled a little. "I'm mad at you, you know that, don't you?"

"Figured you would be."

We held hands as he recuperated.

That was weeks ago. And I think about it all the time.

How do I sit in his face, maybe go to lunch with him and say, "SmooVe, buy the way, I'm married, but it slipped my mind. Could you pass the Grey Poupon?"

I don't want to lose him because of my lie. But telling the truth about that would mean I'd have to be open and honest about other things.

To kill my mental madness, I was ready to admit my wrongs, but I had to have wine to wash down some of my anxiety. Last night we were sitting around, drinking Chablis. I was on my second glass. I usually stopped at one, but I hoped being a little inebriated would help the truth flow. I'd become comfortable with my thoughts, the moment was right, then the damn phone rang and messed the first line that would've led to my confession. I answered and the voice at the other end thought he had the wrong number.

"Yeah," he said with a southern accent. "Elijah at home?"

"Sorry, nobody lives here by that name."

Whoever it was hung up and called back. This time he asked for Jordan. And as soon as he did, I remembered that Elijah was Jordan's first name. It was his oldest brother, Darrell. Jordan talked about thirty minutes, and I fidgeted the entire time. Kept thinking that I could've told what needed to be told by now.

When he hung up, he told me what had happened. His other brother Reggie's dad had died and no one knew where Reggie was. Jordan had no idea. Darrell had even less of a clue. Reggie did drugs a lot and disappeared from time to time, but never for more than a couple of weeks.

Watching his anguish, my problem seemed so small. Very inappropriate.

Jordan asked me if I wanted to tag along to Memphis for a few days. He grinned like everything was fine, but the pain was in his eyes and resonated in his every word when he said he had to make sure everything was okay. Said he needed to find Reggie, had to see for himself. I told him I would love to go, but I had some work to do, convinced him that he should go ahead, and call me if he needed me to come down.

He told me, "I'll always need you."

His words, the honest way he spoke his passion surprised me.

Tomorrow he's flying back home to Memphis, but tonight I'll comfort him. My secrets can wait. They'll have to.

13 Kimberly Chavers

"May I speak to Miss Kimberly Chavers?"

"Speaking."

It was eight o'clock, the sun was going down on my world, and I'd just made it home from Greenwich Village. I'd struggled from subway to bus to taxi, lugged my shopping bags up three flights of dusty stairs, and was about to rest my sack of photography, art books, and supplies I'd bought at Rizzoli's, over in SoHo on West Broadway. I'd wandered around and busted my monthly budget and spent too much. I always did when I used shopping as therapy.

I was really excited because I'd sold three paintings out of Clair's gallery this week. And one of the buyers wanted to commission me to do a family painting. Plus, a trendy magazine was paying me too much money to contribute to their winter edition. So financially I'm on the road to being secure. For a little while anyway. At least none of my bills are behind like they were a year ago.

"Good, I'm glad I caught you."

"Who's calling?"

I had been about to pick up the phone to call Jordan at his brother's apartment in Memphis, but it rang before my hand reached the receiver. I'd answered quickly and sexily, because I hoped it was him. It wasn't.

"This is Brent Perkins."

"I'm sorry," I said and scratched my nose. "Brent Perkins?"

"From the agency."

"Oh." I remembered. "Hello, Mr. Perkins."

"I've got some good news for you . . ."

During Jordan's absence I had been trying to take care of my little problem. At first I tried to find my estranged and deranged husband myself, but I realized I didn't have the foggiest idea how to find him. It has been almost seven years. Both of his parents have died; his sister has moved from San Antonio—or maybe she has given up the lesbian life, married and has a new last name.

"... we found Peter Oliver Stenson. He's living in San Luis Obispo, California."

"Where's that?"

"Between Los Angeles and San Francisco. Midway between."

So, I'd gone to the phone book, called several agencies, and went with The Brent Perkins Agency, but not until after I called the BBB and found out they had a good rating. I always did that before I committed my money. I found some old documents that had Pete's, I mean Peter's, Social Security number on them, and that was all he needed to get started running some stuff through his computer network thing.

Years have wafted by. I'm still married. Fuck.

"He's head chef over at a seaside restaurant a few miles out at Morrow Bay. At least that's what his W-2 stated. Made a little over 40K last year. No children. Married, filing separately. Guess he's been paying major penalties and much higher taxes."

And I'd been suffering with the same penalties and the same higher taxes because of a stupid mistake I'd never corrected. Double fuck. No, quadruple fuck. He's filing married? After all these years? Shit.

"Hello, are you still there, Miss Chavers?"

"Yes, I'm here."

"I asked if you wanted his phone number and address?"

This should be a piece of cake. I mean, I've been living alone since I escaped from Texas, and I've stepped up to the plate, confronted and conquered many complex things in my life. I've fought off a mugger on the nasty and noisy E train; I've completed more 10K charity runs than I can remember; I've lived by myself in foreign countries that oppressed women's rights; day after day, I've struggled and supported myself in a competitive, creative field; I've set my own standards of excellence. I've made my own rules to define who I am.

Then why do I feel so helpless? Why am I nervous? I haven't committed a crime. Where is this guilt coming from ... ?

"Miss Chavers?"

My secret was in my face. I could smell it. For the longest time I've ignored it. Wished it forgotten. Now it's rubbing the rejected memory against my flesh . . .

"Do you want the information you requested?"

Using the voice of a private investigator to reveal itself. You confront me; I confront you. Time to kill it and bury it.

"Yes, give me the number and the address."

"Hello, may I speak to Peter Stenson?"

"Yeah, this is Pete. Who am I talking to?"

"Peter," I released a long sigh. "This is Kimberly."

"Kimberly who?"

"Your wife."

There was a long pause. I heard his voice, and time shifted in a bad way. A very bad way. The memories that had settled had been stirred, and the odor from the past had been resurrected.

"Kimberly? Well, surprise, *surprise,* surprise."

His dry delivery sent a chill down my spine. His voice sounded the same, yet so very different. Age. Time. I never thought I would hear it again, and honestly, I'd hoped I would never have to.

We were both from military families and met when both families were stationed at Lackland AFB, close to San Antonio, Texas. It was easy for us to become interested in each other because we were about the same age and there weren't many others in our juvenile bracket at the time. Thrown together by circumstance. Young. Rebellious.

"Yes, Peter. Kimberly Chavers. How are you?"

"Chavers? Shouldn't that be Mrs. Kimberly Stenson?"

"No. I'm back to who I was, Kimberly Chavers."

"Oh really, now."

"Yes, really."

We thought we were in love, but we were just following our genitals. Bluntly, sex was new and daring and adult to us, so it was easy to confuse the sensation of being horny for more than it really was.

"How'd you find me?"

We wanted to get married so we could be together all of the

time. Our parents disapproved, but we didn't care. We thought we were grown, adults, smarter than everybody who was old-fashioned. In our ignorance, we figured that our parents didn't know what they were talking about. So we got married anyway. We knew we were soulmates. Too bad only one of us had a soul, and the other only wanted to mate.

"I went through a detective agency."

The loving man-boy I married had quickly turned into a tyrant.

"An agency?" He laughed. "You used an agency to find me?"

A ruler who demanded to know why *his* one-bedroom apartment wasn't clean, why *his* dinner wasn't ready. A king who didn't want his queen to work and wouldn't give up the money unless it was for something to benefit him. He would call to verify that I was where I said I would be. Smothering. He didn't want me to express my artistic side. Buying canvas and painting supplies was silly, he'd said. A waste of time and a waste of his money. His money. He wanted me to settle for working part-time at Dairy Queen. And besides, he said, only men were great painters. He didn't want me to go to college, and he refused to buy me books and other materials if I did go. Control was his middle name. He wanted a mindless woman. A slave who would be waiting for him every evening with open arms and spread legs. Wrong.

"Yeah. I used your Social Security number to find you."

So I walked out. Married a little over a year. We'd stopped sleeping together on a regular basis months before that. And until this moment, we have never spoken to each other since that day he came home and I was packed and gone, left with no forwarding address. Started from scratch.

"Oh, really? Well, what's up?"

As soon as I left him, and had made love to someone else who gave me the same feeling—actually better, because I had my first orgasm and found out how selfish Peter was in more ways than I'd realized—I knew what I felt wasn't love, just youthful stupidity. That and the need to get out of my parents' house.

"You still there? Kimberly? You there?"

This was really hard, because it was going too fast. I had had a plan. First I would make small talk, How have you been? What you been doing? How's your sister? Things I really didn't give a shit about to break the ice. But he was so abrupt and it took me off guard. So many things that I hadn't thought about and had avoided for so long had come home to roost.

Be abrupt.

"Did you ever file for a divorce?"

Stay calm. Don't let him bother you. Don't get upset.

"No. Why would I?"

Great. Strike two. I was hoping that maybe, just maybe, he had been granted a no-fault divorce in absentia.

"That must mean you've met somebody and want to get married."

"What?"

He repeated himself, even though I heard him the first time. Awkward.

"Yes. I've met somebody. But that's beside the point," I said and allowed my professional alter ego to take over. "It's stupid that neither of us has made an effort to rectify this matter. It's been too many years. Too many."

"What do you want to do? Since you called me, I'm quite sure you have some suggestions."

"I can arrange for my lawyer to draw up the necessary papers for a no-fault. Are you in agreement?"

"Is this lawyer friend the guy you're going to marry?"

"No, and it's totally irrelevant who he is. We just need to concentrate on getting this no-fault divorce worked out."

"Why do you keep emphasizing no-fault?"

"Because that's the type of paperwork we will be filing."

"Why don't you do it yourself? It would be a lot cheaper than using an attorney. They sell over-the-counter divorce kits at damn near every drugstore in town."

"Because I let my attorneys handle all of my legal matters. I like for things to be done properly."

"Since you're making sure it's done properly, I assume you're paying for it, right? Since it's no-fault of mine that we're not still together."

Asshole. Whatever it takes to get you off the phone and out of my life. "Yes, I'll pay for it."

"Where are you?"

None of your business. I exhaled. "East Coast."

"Could you be a little more vague? The East Coast spreads from Canada to Florida. If I wanted to hunt you down I would've done it by now, don't you think? You called me, remember."

"Buffalo, New York."

"So what are you doing for a living?"

"Same thing I was proving I could do when we were in Texas."

"Still painting stuff?"

"Yes." Already I was agitated. "I'm a visual artist if that's what you mean."

"How are you supporting yourself in the meantime?"

I told myself, Stay calm. I wish Jordan was here; wish I had told him about this when we first met, then this wouldn't be bothering me so much. Intense. Stay calm.

"My work supports me. I'm getting by."

"I remember when—"

"Either I'll call you or my attorney will contact you as soon as the papers are drawn up. His name is Tony Laird."

"Okay."

"Like we agreed, I'll pay for the dissolution, so I'm assuming your full cooperation in this, Peter. This is a simple no-fault. No property. No children. Is there anything you'd need to know? Any information?"

"Yeah."

He didn't say anything for a few seconds. I said, "Well?"

He chuckled. "Do you look as good as you did—"

"I'll be in contact, Peter."

"Can I have your number?"

"No. I'll be in contact." I said it as politely as I could, without sounding rattled, so I wouldn't make the situation worse. I hung up the phone.

He hadn't changed. And what was worse, he'd brought out the angry part of me I thought I had washed away in the river of time. But for some people, time isn't a river; it's a cesspool. Now I was treading in the part of my life I thought was dead.

I have never disliked anyone as much as I did Peter. I correct myself, as I *do* Peter. Never, anyone.

This was going to be trouble. He was going to be trouble.

I immediately called my attorney and left a detailed message with his service, hoping that by setting this in motion now, finding out what had to be done, it could finally be killed and cremated. The only regrettable thing was it wouldn't be overnight. I wanted it done two yesterdays ago.

I was sitting on top of my kitchen counter, looking out the window at flourishing green trees and the clear sunny sky, debating whether I should heat some leftovers or something or take a leisurely stroll down the street for a veggie pizza and enjoy the weather, when the phone rang. I smiled because I thought it might be Jordan. Him or my attorney calling me back. Either way, I'd be happy.

I yielded a giddy "Hello. Is that you, SmooVe?"

"Nope."

"Who's calling?"

"You don't live in Buffalo."

"Peter?" I gasped.

"You live in Queens. I see you're still a liar."

I slipped off the top of the counter and almost stumbled into the refrigerator. The surprise at hearing his voice, at him being at the opposite end of the line without me calling him, left me breathless and speechless. Now my room felt distorted. Contorted and unsettled. Every peaceful thought inside of my head evaporated and was kicked out and replaced with the anxiety and paranoia from my lie being exposed, of the possibility that he was close to me and was watching.

I rushed to the window, searched toward the Bell Atlantic pay phone across the street. Not a person in sight. Not even a plane flying overhead toward LaGuardia Airport.

I snapped, "Where'd you get my number?"

"You gave it to me."

"Don't lie."

"You should follow your own advice."

I didn't know what to say. I had hung up from talking to him less than ten minutes ago. I tried to think of whom he might have or could have called in those few minutes. My parents? No, he didn't know where they were. Directory assistance? Impossible.

Maybe I told him myself, but no, I know I said Buffalo. He just said I said Buffalo.

"Peter," I spoke as calmly as I could, "how did you get my number?"

"Lower your voice," he said nonchalantly. "Like I said, Kimberly, you gave it to me yourself. I have caller ID. You called me, it displayed your number. So, babe, you gave it to me."

"BFD," I huffed. Big Fucking Deal. "What makes you think I'm in Queens?"

"I called information and told them your area code and prefix, asked them. They said it wasn't a Buffalo number. Queens."

"So?"

"So I called back to see what's really going on?"

"I told you why I called. It's divorce time. My treat."

"I don't get it. Why'd you hire somebody to find me, call me out of the blue, and then lie to me?"

"Well, you don't need to know where I live."

"Even if you told me, how could I find you? Aren't there about two billion people in New York? What did you think I'd do, hop on a plane and then drive around until I found you? I didn't bother you about finding me, did I? No doubt, since you hired somebody, you must have tons of info on me."

"That's irrelevant," I said and realized how defensive I sounded. "I called for one reason only."

"You sure you didn't call just because you were thinking about me?" he whispered.

"I told you why I called."

"Lighten up." He laughed curtly. "It was a joke."

"Still, you didn't have to call back. My lawyer will call you. Hopefully he will be able to accelerate the process, since you are in agreement."

"That's what I said, wasn't it? And that was the reason I called you back. I wasn't calling to start some shit."

"Excuse me?"

"Since you want it done so quickly, and you want to *accelerate the process*, and I'm going to be flying out to New Jersey tomorrow for business—"

"You're flying to New Jersey?" I said.

"Yeah. I'll be coming into Newark. We got a couple of East Coast restaurants opening and since I'm the head chef, I facilitate all the training programs, make sure they cook and serve in our style."

"In Jersey?"

"New Jersey. I'll be in Hoboken. Is that far from you?"

"How long are you going to be here—I mean there?"

"Three, four days. Depends on the size of the class and how quick they are."

"Oh." I felt a little awkward comfort in knowing his visit wouldn't be too long. But he was right. New York was big and even if he had my number he probably couldn't find me. But my emotions were creeping to the edge. Why did he bother me? After all these years, why was I rattled by him? He didn't do it all by himself, but he helped wreck my self-esteem once and it took me a long time to get it back. It took me too long to find me.

He said, "And we could sign whatever needs to be signed and get it notarized or whatever and that should take care of that. Maybe we could go catch a cup of java and talk old times."

"Thank you, no. You could just go by my attorney's office and have it taken care of."

He fell silent for a moment, then lowered his voice: "Why are you so afraid to see me, Kimbo? I'll be in your area and you can't find the time for a little conversation with your husband?"

"I'm not afraid and my name is Kimberly, please."

"Whatever." He puffed. "Kim, whatever . . ."

"Kimberly."

"All right, *Kimberly*."

"Thank you."

"Whatever is wrong with you right now, it wasn't me that caused it, all right? I haven't seen you in God knows how many years. When you left me, I let it be, didn't I?"

"You didn't have a choice."

"I never changed the locks. I waited a long time for you to come back, and it took me a longer time to accept that you weren't coming back. But I still left you an open door."

"I didn't need . . . wait, wait, wait. Pete, no, I will not have this discussion of the past. It's behind us, so let it be."

"Why so bitter? The last thing I said to you was that I hoped you'd be happy. If you are, I had nothing to do with it. If you aren't, I had nothing to do with it, all right? You left without a good-bye. I've always wanted to know one thing. Why? Is this because of you and your father—"

I cut him off, "My attorney will call you."

"Fuck it," he snapped, then slammed down the phone.

I let the phone bounce on the counter top. Cursed it. Head felt light, like I was dazed. Numbed with disbelief that I could be traced so easily. Bastard technology. He was going to be in New Fucking Jersey. Too close for comfort. I was agitated, too high-strung. This should be simple, basic. Damn divorces happened every three or four minutes all around the world.

Then my head throbbed. When it pulsed, the thin scar on my forehead hurt the most, felt tight. I massaged where the skin had been torn. Remembered walking home from school, carrying a dented bicycle, with blood running down my face, on my white blouse, my blue skirt, and my black patent leather shoes. Remembered sitting in an emergency room getting my face sewn back together. Felt the past once again. It never goes away. Never.

Outside was sunny, birds were flying overhead, I heard people talking, heard the sound of a car struggling to start, but it felt like it was raining. In my mind, clouds were moving in. I hadn't felt like this in years. That hurtful feeling was creeping back. I thought it was gone, but it was just numb.

Even the phone was crazed; it lost its mind, started repeating the programmed message, yelling at me, howling that if I would like to make a call, please hang up. They even knew when my stupid phone was off the hook.

No privacy; no secrets.

When the phone began screaming that crazy sound, wailing in psychotic tones, I slapped the receiver back in its cradle. Then it rang again. I winced, reached for it, thought it might be Peter calling back, then reneged and let the answering machine screen the call. It was Jordan, telling me everything was fine and he missed me. I put my hand on the receiver and almost picked it up, but changed my mind. Even though I missed him, I didn't think now would be such a good time to talk. My mind was too distracted, upset. I'd think more about it as I took a walk.

Fresh air, veggie pizza, and a bottle of Evian.

Yeah, that's what I'd do.

14 Kimberly Chavers

After a restless night and my morning stress-run, I hurried to meet Kinikki and Sharon for lunch at an always-crowded, *en vogue* spot on Hudson. A chic place where everything was outrageously over-priced. Kinikki and I would have settled for the five-dollar lunch special at a French bakery café like Au Bon Pain, but it was Sharon's turn to pick the meeting and eating spot, and she always went overboard. We always have to dress up, and I spend at least thirty dollars whenever she chooses the eatery.

I liked Kinikki head to toe. I loved her ways. Kinikki was born in Montego Bay and had a strong Jamaican accent. Whatever she talked about, each word carried the passion of her convictions. I met her and Sharon almost six years ago at a small gallery in the Village where Kinikki and I both had works on display.

Kinikki is an underrated genius. She flatters me, tells me the same, so we're good for each other's ego. Artists need ego boosters to offset the jealous and untalented critics.

Kinikki's best friend to both Sharon and me. Even though Sharon and I spend a lot of time gossiping on the phone, and she gave me tickets to Los Angeles and paid for the four-star hotel suite as a birthday present, Sharon and I are more like personable associates. Close enough to do favors for each other at the drop of a hat. Close enough for her not to hide her secrets from me. Close enough for me to lie to her husband about her whereabouts. But not close enough for me to share my dirty laundry.

Sharon's five-foot-three, but always wears three-inch heels. She's slightly overweight, sexy, raspy-voiced, dirty blonde, and transplanted from California's San Fernando Valley. Her husband's a too-skinny, filthy rich investor who has given her the pleasant option of working or not, so she's opted to spend a lot of her time doing charity work mostly on the behalf of galleries, and organizing benefits. That was in between doing lunch with whoever was available. Usually, it was either me or Kinikki. Seldom both. So, today was a special day for all of us.

Kinikki had Chinese eyes and a pleasant, naturally smiling face, with flawless skin. When we got out, she usually wears some form of Kente cloth clothing and a petite hat over her waist-length braids. To me, she's comical because she perpetually flashes her hands in New York, Italian style, and raves non-stop about her devoted husband. About how he bought her this or that, took her here or there, mostly after she'd bitched his ears off.

She'd only been with two men in her life. The first was her Italian art professor when she was a senior at NYU, the second was her Jamaican husband, Jamal. Kinikki always claims she's a genius between the sheets. If you asked, she'd tell you all about the art of Kama Sutra and convince you that she invented and copyrighted the act through the Library of Congress. I never told her, but I'd used the ice-cube fantasy she'd told me about on Jordan the first time we made love.

"Dat golden outfit looks perfect on you," Kinikki said. "Those buttons are *it*."

"Thank you," I replied. "I love your blouse."

"I wish I had your figure." Sharon pointed at me and spoke with a mouth full of lobster. "I'd wear more than a pantsuit. You look good in every ef'n thing. I'd die to have your calves."

"Really?" I grinned. "I'm comfortable."

Kinikki laughed. "Sharon would be parading around in something too tight, too revealing, and too expensive."

"Damn straight!" Sharon smiled at Kinikki. "Like that blasphemous mini-skirt you're parading your fanny around in. Something that's easy to put on and quick to slip off."

"Dat's the way Jamal likes it."

Sharon asked, "Aren't you going to finish your shrimp?"

"No." I pushed back my plate. "No appetite."

"Today, no diet." Kinikki pulled my plate over to her side. "Waste not, want not."

"You both eat like cows and don't gain an ounce." Sharon sneered. "I smell bread, I gain ten pounds. I hate the both of you."

Sharon always wore too-expensive business suits, usually a derivation of power-red, and openly boasted to us of her latest sexual infidelities. Her conquests. How she seduced men by tricking them into thinking they had seduced her, then played the guilty role and stopped returning their phone calls after a few sexcapades. She hated when they started to act like they were becoming attached, or whipped, but she loved it when they begged. She'd give a man one try at pleasing her. If he failed by being too brief or too selfish or too gentle, she'd pretend she didn't know him if they ever happened to meet again. She claimed that once she went to a hotel with an action-movie star, and as soon as he pulled down his pants and exposed his "elementary, frivolous, malnourished penis," she laughed her way home to her husband.

Sharon's thirty-seven. Her husband's fifteen years older. And by her standards, he was virtually impotent, only wanting to have sporadic bedroom and bedtime escapades. She loved daylight and obscure places. The more obscure, the better the orgasm. Even with her wildness, she'd never leave her husband. He loved her, and she needed some consistency in her life. And she needed it from him.

Kinikki groaned like she was on her death bed. She always made that attention-grabbing noise when she wanted somebody to ask her what was wrong, so she could soak in the spotlight and talk about what she wanted to gossip about. Since Sharon was too busy looking around at each table to play along, I went ahead and asked, "What's wrong?"

"Jamal wants to have a blasted baby." Kinikki frowned as she took the final bite of her halibut before sipping her wine.

I smiled. "Really?"

"What'd you tell him, dear heart?" Sharon asked in between peeping at the waiters, especially the buffed golden boy with the crew cut, sporting the too-tight pants.

"I told him to go right ahead!" Kinikki laughed, then mimicked him masturbating. "Call me when you're done!"

"Why not?" I said. "You've been married five years."

"Six beautiful years," Kinikki interjected and threw her hand up in a dramatic way.

I reminded her, "You're thirty-two."

"Twenty-nine," she swiftly corrected.

"Wait a minute. We celebrated your twenty-ninth birthday three years ago," Sharon said as she smiled flirtatiously at somebody.

"And it'll be my twenty-ninth again dis year."

Sharon chuckled. "And I guess next year'll be your twenty-eighth."

"Dat's the wisest thing that's ever come from your face."

Sharon gave her the middle finger. "And I love you too."

We laughed, then I asked Kinikki, "Well?"

She sampled her wine and gave a devilish grin. She stuck two fingers up to her head, made them look like horns. "Maybe I'll forget to take my pills for the next couple of weeks and see what *accidentally* happens."

"It'll happen." I smiled. "And if it doesn't, you'll have a helluva lotta fun practicing."

Kinikki growled and licked her lips. "When you're perfect, you don't need practice."

"Good for you. But practice makes perfect." Sharon sounded wishful, yet sarcastic. She then turned to me. "How's Jordan?"

"Fine. He had to go back home. He had a death in his family."

Kinikki said, "Back to Florida?"

"Memphis." I felt like we were worlds apart. "Tennessee."

I told her that Jordan's stepfather had died.

"That's awful," Sharon said. "Give him my condolences."

"So," Kinikki said, "when are you two going to get married?"

"Why do you always ask mc that?"

"I see the way he looks at you, dat's why."

"We don't talk about stuff like that." I shadowed my guilt with a Disneyland-sized smiled. "I miss him."

"That's sweet," Sharon said. "How's he in bed? Is he still attentive or has he turned into a hit-and-run accident?"

I blushed my answer; then we all laughed.

"I'm happy for you." Kinikki smiled. "Consistency is always a factor."

"That's most of the time." I giggled. "He's a man and has those moments where he can't seem to get it right."

"Like he's in a wretched drive-through?" Sharon asked.

"No." My breath shortened when I imagined Jordan's arms around me. Felt feather kisses on my face. I fantasized him moving inside of me right then. Felt him shivering and warming the words that bloomed from my heart. "He's never been that much in a hurry."

"Oh, God!" Kinikki groaned, then flipped her hands. "Like dat bastard Eric you used to see. I don't understand what you ever saw in him."

"Don't remind me and don't mess up my day."

Kinikki asked Sharon, "How's Todd?"

"Fine," Sharon mumbled and lazily tapped the end of her fork on her plate. "He's in Vermont closing a deal. Todd is just fine. Too fine. *Damn* fine."

Sharon's focus was beyond us. She cunningly leaned a little closer, then whispered, "I don't want to sound stupid, but are black men really better in bed?"

Kinikki's mouth dropped to her plate. I was speechless too. Kinikki and I gazed at Sharon's anxious face and laughed so hard we almost choked. Lost all of our composure, then sipped our wine until we found it again.

Kinikki and I peeped around to see who Sharon was admiring. An African-American man with a slightly receding hairline, square chin, very thin moustache, and a strong, dignified look was smiling at her. He nodded his head toward Sharon, grinned, then pointed at the vacant chair across from him.

Sharon prodded, "Ladies, will one of you answer my question?"

Kinikki answered with a straight-faced "You'll have to judge dat for yourself. Utopia for one is Erebus for another."

Sharon playfully snapped, "Stop speaking in tongues."

I glanced toward him and asked, "Wasn't he with a woman when we walked in?"

"*Was,*" Sharon whispered. "Now he's going to meet a lady."

Sharon picked up our ticket, blithely announced lunch was on her, snapped her fingers, summoned one of the waiters to pull her chair out, then eased from the table and straightened her jacket.

She yielded a potent "Time for dessert."

I said, "Be careful."

Kinikki said, "Condom."

Sharon winked. "It's not that kind of party."

I repeated, "Be careful."

"Always."

Then with the grace of a movie star, she sashayed over to the table with her blushing, newfound curiosity. He stood and pulled a chair out for her. His smile wouldn't quit.

Kinikki asked, "No time to go over to the billiard place on Mulberry and play a few games? I need to get even wit you from the last time you put a spanking on me."

"Not today. I've got some trouble to take care of."

"What is wrong?"

"I need to call my attorney."

"You're not in trouble are you?" Kinikki's smile collapsed.

After she swore it wouldn't spread, I told her my problem. And she was more understanding than I could have imagined, so I opened up and exposed everything—almost everything. I told her about the detective, about Peter calling me back, about him upsetting me by asking how did I look, about him scaring me when he asked if I missed him, about a lot of our past. I needed to vent, I needed to hear how it sounded out loud. Wanted to see her reaction so I could gauge what Jordan's might be when I dropped this bomb. But most of all, I was happy that she didn't wave my troubles off as being insignificant or foolish. She was just as concerned about me and Jordan. Especially since she liked me with him. She thinks we're good for each other.

Kinikki's the type who wanted everybody else to be happy. Still, she thought it inconceivable that her strong, independent friend who was so gutsy with co-workers and boisterous with art dealers would be so vulnerable and delicate in relationships.

"It's not just a relationship," I said. "It's *the* relationship. So that makes a big difference."

"You didn't lie."

"I wasn't straight either."

"I'm quite sure he has a few skeletons in his closet. All men do. Don't forget about him and dat girl."

"That was before us. Even though I didn't like the situation, I can't fault him for that."

"You'll be the same old Kimberly, it's just a legal thing."

"Why am I afraid?" I asked myself aloud.

"Why didn't you tell him at first?"

"One, he never really asked, not directly anyway, and it's never been something I've bragged about. Plus, my soon to be ex was no one I was proud of. And two—"

"Three."

"And three, I never thought this would go this far, our relationship. It's so intense, but in a casual, pleasant sorta way. You know what I mean?"

"But he hasn't asked you to marry him?"

"No, not yet. We looked at some nice engagement rings."

"Looking at rings is just looking at rings."

"I know, I know. But either way, I need to get this cleared up. This has become the most important thing on my mind."

"And from the way he is when I see him with you, I think you are the most important thing on his."

I smiled at Kinikki. Smiled at a true friend and thought before I said, "May I ask you a question, and get the truth?"

"Always."

"Why are you so unmoved by Jordan and me?"

"What do you mean?"

"I mean," I paused because the words were heavy in my throat, the pain I'd seen in Jordan's eyes when some African-Americans ignored him when he was with me, "by the black–white thing."

She laughed a little. "Because I'm not American. That's this country's hang-up. I don't subscribe to that doctrine."

My beeper vibrated and I pulled it out of my coat pocket. My attorney had put in his office number, followed by 911.

As we were walking to the phone, we saw Sharon and her fascination getting into a cab. Her dark-skinned friend held the door open for her as she succulently slid inside.

Kinikki said, "He's in for the dessert of his life."

I said, "Waldorf-Astoria?"

"Yep," Kinikki shook her head. "She's a four-star whore."

"Better her than us. She can afford it."

We laughed and gossiped while we headed for the pay phone inside the ladies room. Kinikki touched up her makeup while I phoned Mr. Laird. Tony's voice sounded sturdy and monotonic, probably because after forty years in the break-up business, a divorce was commonplace. He joked that he had a gray hair for each client he'd represented successfully, and he'd lost a hair for each case that he lost. In other words, he had a full head of gray hair. He didn't sound surprised to find out I had been married. Tony sounded rushed, but not impatient. He'd called Peter, and Peter would be in his office tomorrow.

Tony said, "Right after he talks to his own attorney."

"Why does he want to talk to his attorney? It's a simple procedure. I sign, he signs and it's on the way, right?"

"Bluntly, it sounds like he thinks he might be entitled to some monetary compensation and he wants to make sure everything is properly done to his satisfaction."

"What?"

"Don't worry. He's trying some legal tactics that'll only delay the procedure."

"Damn. How long will it take?"

"Six months." He coughed. "Minimal."

I almost dropped the damn phone. "Six months? Six fucking months. Tony, that's half a goddam year."

My head became crammed with all sorts of thoughts; everything around me—cars, multiple conversations in about three different languages—seemed so loud that the world became muffled.

"You can speed it up, legally," Tony said, "but it'll cost."

After a few breaths I reluctantly asked, "Much?"

"Much."

"Kimberly?" Kinikki put her hand on my shoulder. "Are you okay?"

I nodded to her. She slipped her thin arm around me as I continued babbling to Tony. "Six months? No way to speed it up?" I realized that I had just asked him that.

"Six months is standard. Unless you fly out of the country and get a quickie."

"What's his damn problem? I haven't talked to him in years. He should be grateful I'm paying for it."

"He feels he might be entitled to some of your past and future earnings due to the fact that he claims he helped finance you in the early stages of your career and you, in turn, abandoned him without cause. That your current success was dependent on him providing the initial financial foundation."

"That's bull."

"He claims he paid for your education."

"That's bullshit and he knows it."

I reminded Tony that we had been separated for almost seven years. *Much* longer than we were together. And we didn't have property. No children. He assured me we had some leverage there.

"Don't worry," Tony said nonchalantly. He chewed on something. "It'll only delay the procedure."

"And cost more money?"

"Yes," Tony said. "And cost more money. More paperwork, more procedures, more time, more money. Sorry, but that's the game. Nothing in this world is free. Not even freedom."

part three

Family Reunion

15 Jordan Greene

A massive stroke killed Reggie's daddy three days ago. Reggie's my middle brother, older than me by almost ten months. Momma broke up with Reggie's daddy six months before Reggie was born, then met my daddy while she was still carrying her load. Anyway, Reggie's old man didn't have any insurance. Outside of an uncashed Social Security check, the only money the man had left to his name was found underneath his mattress, which was chump change. Not a dime left in a savings account. Just a stack of bills waiting to be paid.

So Reggie's daddy's family was out in North Memphis, near Chelsea and Hollywood Street in Goodwill Village, taking up a collection and pooling together to get a decent casket and pay for the funeral. All of that was what Darrell heard from one of the relatives. The neighbors and the local church would probably make up the difference. Southern people were like that in an emergency. Like an African village coming together in crisis.

Darrell hadn't found Reggie. Hadn't seen or heard from him since the last time he'd been ripped off by his sibling. I hoped Reggie wasn't doing the same thieving from everybody he staggered across. If he had ripped off the wrong brotha, that could've been his last con. He'd been MIA for months. Nobody had heard his voice, not a soul had even seen him in passing. That's why I was fretting and fidgeting in the heat. And that was why I'd been passive about Darrell's remarks about Kimberly. If Kimberly hadn't answered the phone, he wouldn't know. But north to south, the word was out.

When Kimberly handed me the phone, Darrell barked, "Tell me that wasn't a damn white woman answering your phone."

I cleared my throat. "Yeah."

"Who she?"

"What's up?"

"At least tell me you picked up a hooker."

"That was my girlfriend. Kimberly."

"She white?"

"Right."

Anger, irritation, and disappointment were on his face when he picked me up at Memphis' airport. He shoved his calloused hands deep into the pockets of his stiff and starched Levi's, growled, frowned, shook his head, then snapped, "Sistas ain't good enough for your ass no more? Or you done got beyonds that?"

Southern accents twanged out over the P.A. system. I kept moving, adjusted my garment bag on my shoulder.

He kept on snarling, "White folks ain't nothing but trouble. And black folks messing around with white folks like that ain't right. Why you have to get into some foul shit like that?"

"Darrell, right now Reggie is the problem of the day."

He popped me in the back of my head.

I ignored him and asked, "Where did you park?"

"Outside."

"Let's go. I'm tired."

He drove, deep in thought. Looked worried. I knew he was worried, because he was scratching the circular birthmark on the back of his thick neck. Darrell's complexion is dark brown, so the circular, beige spot stood out. He always tried to pretend he could handle whatever was dished out. Did the same thing when his wife walked out on him, when she took their baby and vanished. In the true spirit of the African warrior, he tried to remain strong.

I was just trying to survive the Memphis heat and stickiness while we rode in his air-conditionless cheap-mobile. Two minutes with him and I missed the crowds and piss smell of the subway.

Darrell moaned. "You done lost your fucking mind."

We left Memphis Intenational Airport not talking to each other. Darrell hopped on I-240 westbound, cursed when he realized he was riding on empty, then got right back off the interstate. He stopped at the Exxon at Elvis Presley Boulevard and Brooks Road long enough to put in five dollars worth of gas.

I stared at the Luby's restaurant across the street. My mouth watered, stomach growled. I was so stressed I hadn't eaten.

Darrell didn't signal when he screeched out of the lot onto Elvis Presley Boulevard. He turned so hard I was slung into the door. He drove worse than a New York cab driver with diarrhea. He zoomed through two lights right after they'd turned red, which definitely wouldn't work in NY, because the instant the other side turned green, they were off and running like the Indy 500.

"What, you thank the grass greener on the other side?"

I didn't answer. Tried to find something to dab the sweat off my face with. All he had in his glove compartment were white-turning-brown napkins from KFC.

"A white bitch, huh?"

"Darrell." I was ready to slap him. "Her name is Kimberly."

"I hope this bull ain't serious. I hope you just doing something like the other brothers and trying to get your rent paid."

I almost snapped. That pissed me off to the tenth power. I rolled thumb over thumb. Had to remember who I was dealing with. Black, white, yellow, or brown, all women were bitches to him, waiting to be used. All except our mother. His tone always softened and echoed respect when he talked about Lucille Greene. When he said bitch, it didn't ring like he was being evil. It was just that in his small brain and narrow mind, that was a synonym for female. Guess I should've FedEx'd him a thesaurus for Christmas. He was ragging on me to camouflage the real issues. Hiding that hopeless feeling we shared.

Darrell grumbled, "One of my brother's drugged out, the other one running after white women. Momma gotta be turning over in her grave."

I cleared my throat. "Any idea where Reggie is?"

"Look at you, dressed all preppy and shit. Clean cut. You look funny without your moustache. What kinda shirt's that?"

"Polo. You know where Reggie is?"

"Wearing a shirt with a white man on a horse, huh?"

"I never looked that close."

"Maybe you should open your eyes."

"I'll take that as a compliment."

"It ain't." Darrell finally said, "I ain't got no idea where Reggie's at. Might have to swang through his old stomping grounds to see if anybody seen him. I called the police station here and in Mississippi and West Memphis to find out if he was locked up, then called John Gaston and Methodist to see if any unclaimed bodies had turned up since last December."

"And?"

"Nothing. But that don't mean nothing, though. He could be sleeping in an unmarked grave."

"Darrell, kill the negative attitude."

"Tell me I'm lying."

I couldn't. That dose of reality hurt more than I'd ever show. Right now wasn't the time or place to let emotions run free. Had to stay cool, calm, and collected about the head.

Darrell lit a cigarette. When he sat it in the ashtray, I grabbed it, flipped it out the window. That was my way of getting revenge. He wasn't supposed to smoke because of his asthma; I shouldn't be sucking up the cancer secondhand because of mine. My recent flare-up scared the hell out of me. I hadn't had an episode since I was seventeen. Thought I'd outgrown it. The wheezing, the pain that came when my chest locked up, begging for a teaspoon of air, couldn't speak—I didn't want to go there again.

He balled his fist up and snapped, "What's your problem?"

"Quit smoking."

"I did. Until I heard you was sleeping with the enemy."

"Darrell, you ain't about shit."

He'd been smoking quite a bit. I knew that the second he picked me up because his teeth were wearing another coat of smoker's stain. Especially the chipped one in the front. And the car reeked like we were riding inside the butt of a cigarette. The worn seats had a million tiny, circular burn holes.

Darrell said, "Nigger, don't make me shoot you."

"Stop saying nigger."

"Nigger, nigger, nigger. Somebody has to remind your ass."

He popped his last Kool Filter King out of the pack, threw the empty pack into the backseat, stuck the tumor-stick into his mouth. When he fired it up, he cut his eyes at me. I feigned like I was distracted by the very nicely framed sister in the blue jean

mini-skirt and peach halter top—take away two points because of
her super-duper basket-weave and flip-flop house shoes—then I
stretched and yawned. When I brought my hand down, I snatched
it out of his mouth. By the time he'd cursed and reached for me,
I'd thrown it out the window. The fool socked my shoulder, slob-
bered at the edge of his mouth, called me every name under the
sun, red neck peckerwood lover leading the way.

Then he bobbed his head and laughed. "You kinda quick."

I turned on the radio that didn't work, then clicked it back off.
"Because I quit smoking in high school."

"That's your problem. Hungry?"

"As hell. You buying?"

"Pokey, you the big money grip living high off the hog."

We laughed. I hadn't heard my nickname in a while.

"Cool by me, Pokey," Darrell said. "Cool by me. I'll spring for it."

We were cruising Elvis Presley Boulevard, coming up on Grace-
land. Darrell checked his rearview, then made an illegal U-turn
right in front of the King's white iron gate decorated with all the
musical notes. I peeped over at Overdose-ville and tried to read
some of the graffiti on the outside wall. Writings left by people
who wanted others to know that they were there before them.
Down in Whitehaven (which is now nicknamed Blackhaven), a
line of dedicated white people were out front reaching from the
white gates south for about one hundred feet. The sun was beating
down on the tops of their heads and I know they had to be funked
up by the tenacious heat and humidity. It was hot enough to make
your Right Guard fall right off. Since the King had croaked on his
porcelain throne, I'd seen lines of cars with tags from Florida to
Canada to Washington to California. Still-believing tourists who
didn't know any better. Elvis was deader than Hoffa and they
didn't get the memo.

"Ain't that some shit?" Darrell sucked his teeth, then shook his
head. "Paying seventeen dollars to look at the grave of a fat, dead
hillbilly."

"Lighten up, all right?"

"Oh, after he ripped black people off and said a nigger couldn't
do nothing but shine his shoes, you defending him too?"

"Just getting tired of your mouth."

Darrell screeched another U-turn. A couple of portly Caucasian women, modeling blue-light-special short sets, yelped and grabbed their children. Everybody in front of Humpty Dumpty's wall jumped to attention and frowned at us. Panic filled their eyes. Darrell laughed for the next two blocks. So did I.

16 Jordan Greene

"You still partaking of that swine, huh?"

I downed a corner of my blueberry pancakes, then crunched the bacon loud enough to irritate Darrell.

He shook his head, talked with a mouth full of scrambled eggs loaded with hot sauce, "What's Bambi's name? Thelma or Louise?"

"Kimberly Denise Chavers."

He took a swig of orange juice and nodded. "I know why you didn't bring her down in this neck of the woods."

"Why?"

"Jim Crow."

I don't know why he thought he was so damn wise. He had three failed marriages under his belt. The last two women he married I never met. They were divorced before the rice hit the ground.

"Kimberly. Yep, she white all right. White-ass name."

"Darrell, quit tripping."

"What happened to fine-ass Sabrina? Now, that bitch was bad. Had a ass that wouldn't quit."

Sabrina. Like that name didn't sound white. Thanks to the heartbreak from Sabrina, when I left the University of Memphis, instead of working at FedEx, I fled the South and moved to New York. Sabrina was the first woman I dated when I came to Memphis from my Brownsville hamlet. A thick sister, fresh out of high school, sporting a waistline that gave her backside a nice southern appeal. We made eye contact and shared a smile at freshman orientation. Dated from that day to the middle of my senior year.

Dated until I stopped by her off-campus apartment one day, used
my key to get in, walked into the bedroom, and . . .

"A brotha named Bobby happened to Sabrina."

He nodded. "If you was laying the pipe right—"

I snapped, "Shut up, all right?"

"Kiss my black ass."

"Your pug nose is in the way."

"You a asshole."

"And you're the whole ass. I don't give partial credit."

Darrell choked on his pancakes on that corny one-liner. Whatever he was chewing shot out of his nose.

"Darrell, you all right?"

"That was funny!" He laughed and wiped his eyes. " 'I don't
give partial credit.' Man, I gotta remember that."

We sat in the IHOP on Airways and talked. I told him about
Kimberly. He listened. No matter how positive I made her sound,
he wasn't thrilled. Not because she was white, but because she
wasn't black. Like him, I held my ground and remained strong on
the outside. Darrell is three years older than Reggie, almost four
years older than me, and acted more like a father than a brother.
That came from having to be the man of a household that housed
no steady male role model. Which was part of the reason we were
so distant. He was too opinionated and I hated being pushed
around, verbally or otherwise.

"Got a white woman."

I motioned for him to lower his voice in this crowded, southern
atmosphere. "I'm dating a woman who happens to be white."

"What's the difference?"

"If you have to ask, you'll never know."

"Just for that, you pay for the food."

I said, "Thought you were paying."

Darrell huffed, "That's what you get for thinking."

I finished my coffee and gave him a twenty to cover the fourteen dollar bill. Darrell went to pay the bill, then came back to get
me. I asked him for my damn change; he ignored me and kept
moving toward the front door. I had to dig back into my wallet for
the two dollar tip.

By the time I caught up, Darrell had a new pack of Kools and

had flirted the stout girl behind the cash register into giving him
her phone number. She had a pretty face, and was blushing so
hard I saw her upper gold-star tooth.

"This is my baby brother, Pokey. I mean, uh, Elijah. I mean, ah,
Jordan."

"Pokey," I said. "Call me Pokey."

"Pokey, this is Traci."

I nodded, spoke, but she was too busy checking out Darrell's
broad shoulders and sixteen inch arms to even share a courtesy
glance with me.

She blinked out of her trance, stopped being enthralled long
enough to say a hopeful, "Y'all from around here?"

Darrell said, "I live in South Memphis."

She smiled. "Really?"

"Pokey here live up in New Yawk."

"New York? I always wanted to go up there." Traci made herself look busy by organizing the register. "So, Darrell, are you
really going to take me to the movies, or you just running off at
the mouth?"

Darrell smiled, but he kept his upper lip over his chipped tooth.
"Sunday evening. Serious as a heart attack."

That would be right after the funeral. He might as well take her
to the service. She could catch a front-row seat, get some buttered
popcorn, red hots, a large Pepsi, maybe some pork rinds.

She peeped left to right then said, "I don't mean to cut y'all
off, but I gotta get back to work before my supervisor starts to
trippin'."

I said, "Nice to meet you, Traci."

"You too, Pookey."

"Pokey, not Pookey."

"I'm sorry." She blushed. "Pokey."

Darrell winked like he was the mack of the year. "Sunday, five
o'clock. I'll be on time, rain or shine."

"You don't have to wait until then to call me."

Darrell smiled like he was in like Flynn, then asked, "What
time you get off?"

" 'Round four. I leave here and pick up my little girl and get
home around four-thirty."

"Maybe I'll holler at you around five."

"Sounds good."

He sounded like a pimp. She blushed, liked what she heard. Whatever turned him on from dusk to dawn. Their eyes were devouring each other.

Outside, Darrell said, "You see the ass on that girl?"

"I saw thunder thighs, if that's what you're talking about."

He popped me in the back of my head. I shoved him.

We rode in silence for what felt like a long time, then stopped at a light at Third Street and Belz. A shopping center and fast food joints were at every intersection. We were in the heart of working-class South Memphis, the Harlem of the south, about a half mile from Darrell's place. He lit up a cigarette. He took a long draw, held the cigarette, studied it methodically.

He shook his head and mumbled, "This is another one of their ways of killing us off."

"I don't see a gun being held to your head."

"Same gun that got you chasing their women."

Silence sent my thoughts back to why I was here. Back to Reggie. I rolled thumb over thumb, cleared my throat, fidgeted in my puddle of sweat. Thoughts got worse by the second. Humidity and silence only made the anxiety grow.

Darrell was gripping the steering wheel, chewing his lip.

I said, "Darrell . . ."

"I know." Sadness and fear showed in his face. "Gotta find Reggie. Gotta find Reggie."

Darrell zoomed up Third Street. We headed north.

17 Jordan Greene

I was dreaming.

Kimberly was in my arms. I was gently stroking my hands up and down her naked back, barely touching her skin. We were in a dark room, but luminosity rested on her happy face. Soft lighting came from above and below at the same time, fell on the bed in a perfect circle. Covers were rumpled around us. She smiled, laughed, scooted closer, and I tried to kiss her sweaty neck, but she moved away and tickled me. The moment I caught her and untangled the sheets, I pulled her scarlet mane from her eyes so I could see and enjoy all of her face, then tasted her tongue, gave her a lot of baby kisses, walked my tongue around to her earlobes. Kimberly opened her mouth, licked her lips.

aaaahhhhahhhhaaaooooohhoooohaaoaaaaaoohaahaoaoahaaaa

I eased around and began running my tongue around the curvature of her face. Tasted the edge of her lips.

creeeek . . . blam . . . creeeek . . . blam . . . blakity . . . blam . . .

I woke up. It was midnight dark. I was confused. Dazed.

creeeek . . . creek . . . blam . . . blakity . . . blam . . . creek . . .

Loud noises. Somebody was screaming like a fire engine. Sounded like somebody was breaking into my apartment. I jumped up to grab my lamp, but a pain in my side made me stumble. I hit my shin on the edge of something hard. A glass coffee table.

creekittity . . . creekittity . . . creekittity . . . cree . . .

The table tilted and a stack of *Jet* and *Ebony* magazines spilled on the floor. Then I fell. The carpet hid my *thud*. More pain. I bit my lip, muffled my scream. Something wasn't right. I didn't have carpet this thick . . .

creeeeek . . . creek . . . creeeee . . . creeeek . . . creee . . .

I wasn't at home. My damn shin ached like it had been cracked. I adjusted to the pain, cleared my head, heard mumbles and giggles in the darkness. The pain in my back grew. I took short breaths, grabbed the edge of the couch, and pulled myself back on the sofa. It creaked. I adjusted so a spring would stop stabbing me in my back. Then I heard Darrell's voice. His bedroom door opened and a soft light hit the hallway wall. I quit rustling around and pretended to be asleep. I left my eyes cracked just enough so I could see out.

A moment later, somebody walked out. It was Traci, the waitress Darrell met earlier that day. She stepped into the hall and the night-light revealed she was very nude and sweaty. Her panting was louder than the central air. She pulled her braids back from her face, hand-fanned herself, ran each of her hands across her sweaty breasts, licked her fingers, twisted her neck, then opened a door and walked into the closet. After realizing what she'd done, she giggled, exited the closet, then went through the adjoining door, the bathroom. The toilet seat dropped into the feminine position. Body fluids trickled.

Darrell staggered out of the bedroom wearing worn-out boxers, puffing on the last of a Filter King. He scratched between his legs, did the same to his butt, and headed toward the kitchen.

The toilet flushed. Traci came out of the bathroom. She saw me see her then she hurried down the hallway, back into the bedroom. My eyes closed. Darrell long pooted. My eyes opened. He was pouring a glass of something.

"Man," Darrell said, sounding winded. "That girl's wild."

I nodded off.

"Pokey?"

It was a struggle, but I opened my eyes. Darrell was standing over me, dressed in jean shorts and a wrinkled T-shirt, holding a glass of water and more pain pills. That meant four to six hours had passed since I dozed. The magazines had been neatly placed back on the table.

Darrell sat on the edge of the sofa and extended his hand. "Here, time to take two mo'."

The curtains were drawn, but it was still too bright. The sun must've been high in the sky. My eyes struggled to find some focus. Traci stepped out of his bedroom, adjusted her waitress uniform, and bounced into the bathroom, singing a tune by Chico DeBarge.

Darrell held my shoulder. I had to struggle to sit up. The pain wasn't as bad as I thought it would be, but the pills were sucking the consciousness out of me. I moved too fast and a sharp pain came, then short spasms. I moaned, made a noise like the ones I'd heard through the night, but more constipated than sexual.

"Chill, take it slow, Pokey."

I made an okay sound.

"You sure you don't wanna go to the emergency room?"

I made a no-thank-you-I'll-be-cool sound.

I popped both chalky-tasting tablets into my dry mouth at the same time, washed them down with tap water. The cold water hurt my dried-out throat when I swallowed. I eased back down, shifted around and got comfortable. Darrell adjusted and fluffed the pillow under my head, pulled the cover over me. I pulled the cover back down. It was too goddam warm.

"I'm dropping Traci off at work. I'll be right back . . ."

My eyes lost focus, changed to fuzziness.

I tried to remember what all happened yesterday. My heart pumped hard when some of it came back, then faded. I started thinking about us looking for Reggie. The ordeal.

18 Jordan Greene

Yesterday, Darrell had made a stop near LeMoyne Owen College, not too far from where slaves were buried in a common grave, not too far from where I heard that the first black millionaire was buried. Darrell caught up with one of Reggie's old friends. He was hanging out at a liquor store near McLemone and Mississippi. An area that's not one of Memphis' tourist attractions. He hadn't seen Reggie in months either, but he gave Darrell some information about a female Reggie used to do business with.

"Where we going?"

"Reggie used to do business with a strawberry. Wanda."

"Strawberry?"

"Fucks for drugs."

"I already knew what it meant."

He spat. "Glad you ain't lost touch with the vernacular."

"Define vernacular."

"Fuck you." Darrell spat again. "Dude said Reggie wasn't sleeping with her. She was either a double-D—"

I said a sarcastic, "Double-D means drug-dealer."

"Shut up. She just knew where to get the stuff at."

I wiped my face. "So where we going?"

"Poplar and Ayers."

"Shit."

The projects. A strip of urbaness better known as Dixie Homes. That wasn't a good place to be looking for somebody, especially somebody you didn't know, even if you were black and they were black. The only color that mattered was green. Money-green paper with pictures of dead presidents.

Don't get me wrong. We grew up in the projects too. But these were different projects. So, we could be considered different tribes. These were my people, but they weren't my people.

The section of buildings at Ayers was closed down, boarded up, probably condemned. Darrell turned left on Pauline and whipped into the first vacant parking space. A couple of brothers were under a shade tree hitting a forty ounce. Both looked under twenty-one, dressed hip-hop, bright colors, striped T-shirts, too much gold. One had a shoulder-length Jheri-Curl; the other sported a nappy, seven-inch flat-top fade. Two extinct hairstyles, living and breathing, in stereotype heaven. But the stereotypes had to come from somewhere, so this must've been one of the birthplaces.

The moment we wiped the sweat from our brows and got out of the car, the brothers bobbed their heads and flashed sideways peace signs. Darrell returned a straight-up peace sign. I nodded, then headed away from the spectators, toward the red-bricked, two-story apartments.

Darrell called out, "Hold on, Pokey."

He popped the trunk and rambled through some stuff. When he closed it, he had put on a wrinkled, long-sleeve denim shirt.

I asked, "You cold or crazy?"

Darrell grinned. "Nope. Neither."

He headed toward the tree, said, "Whuddup, fellows?"

Jheri-Curl said loud and clear, "Ain't nothing up but the cost of living. Nothing going on but the rent."

"What up with you, G?" Flat-Top asked Darrell.

"I'm looking for Wanda. You know where she live at?"

Jheri downed the last six ounces of the forty, belched, spat, then said, "Who you and what she to you?"

Darrell said, "We trying to catch up with our brother and we wanna know if he's over or if she's seen him."

"Like I said, who you, G?" Jheri talked out of the side of his mouth, sounded irritated. "We don't know you from Adam."

I kicked back and let ignorance communicate the best it could. All of this noise bothered me, but I didn't let it show.

Darrell said a smooVe "Darrell Greene."

"And why you bring a narc?" Jheri flippantly asked.

Clean shaven, wearing 501s, a Polo shirt, dark shades, short stylish haircut. Looking for a druggie. I fit the profile.

I chuckled, pointed at Darrell's car, then let out a little louder laugh of solidarity, "In a cheap-ass Hyundai?"

Jheri and Flat laughed. Darrell didn't.

Jheri spoke to his buddy. "I guess a real narc wouldn't be riding round in a tired Rodney King–mobile, huh?"

Flat held up his empty forty-ounce. "Whatcha gonna do for us? This America, you don't get somethin' for nothin', G."

Darrell reached into his back pocket and pulled out a few singles—my singles—and held them up. "You know Wanda?"

They sprung up off the ground, grinning like it was Christmas morning. Jheri grabbed the money and counted it. While Jheri was running off at the mouth, asking for a few more dollars, Flat snatched the money out of Jheri's hand and pointed east. "Second building, downstairs, left apartment, the one with the raggedy screen door, homey. Her name on the mailbox. I just saw her walk in a few minutes ago."

"Damn, we coulda held out for mo' money, K.C. You don't know shit about negotiating."

They bolted to the parking lot, ran like Batman and Robin, then jumped into a faded blue Monte Carlo with shiny rims. Flat-Top cranked the car; one of Tupac's songs thumped from the speakers. They screeched away like we didn't exist.

We read the dented beige mailbox to find the apartment. The name Wanda McClain was scribbled on the outside in green ink. We could've saved our money. Darrell opened the broken screen and knocked on the splintered wooden door.

A female yelled from the back of the house. "Who is it?"

"Darrell. I'm looking for Wanda. She home?"

There was a moment of silence. The voice from the other side of the door said, "I don't know nobody named Darrell."

He frowned at me, shrugged. I shrugged back at him.

Darrell stalled, made a confused face like he was in Final Jeopardy.

"We're friends of K.C.," I blurted out.

"Put your face up to the peephole," she said. When we did, she said, "Hold on for a minute."

She walked away from the door. A minute later, we heard the front door being unlocked. Darrell gave me the thumbs up. When the door opened, a blast of cold air was thrown in my face, along with a spoiled odor, like old hamburger meat. A cappuccino-colored female about my height was standing there dressed in red, sagging, ripped baggy jeans, and a faded black, gold, and green T-shirt that showed Malcom X's face and read: BY ANY MEANS NECESSARY. Her long auburn hair with black roots had a side of dandruff and dangled in her face. Pimples were on her shiny forehead. A ghetto beauty. On the thin side, with Somalian features. I always looked at black people and tried to relate them back to Africa.

Her skeptical eyes met my apprehensive gaze.

She didn't smile and gave a cold "What up?"

Darrell said, "We looking for Reggie."

"Reggie?" She scowled. "Reggie who?"

Darrell said, "Reggie Greene. You know him, right?"

She scratched her scalp.

Darrell asked, "Do you know where Reggie is?"

She glared at me. Then back at Darrell. She rumbled, "Thought you were friends with K.C."

"We just finished talking to them," Darrell said. His tone was impatient. "They said you might know where Reggie at."

"I'm tired of you bastards coming around here looking for Reggie. He ain't here, don't live here, won't be here, so tell your friends to stop coming by here with this bullshit, all right?"

She tried to slam the door, but Darrell blocked it with his hand. It made a loud thud. They were like rude versus rude.

"Wait, I'm his brother from across town," Darrell said as quick as he could. That was also his version of an apology.

"First, you with K.C., now you somebody named Reggie's brother."

Wanda struggled to close the door, but Darrell had leverage.

I said, "No, really, straight-up, he's our brother. Did he ever mention his brother from New York?"

She didn't let go, but she eased off pushing the door and stared at me. Made me wonder what she was thinking.

"Are you a narc?"

She checked me out head to toe.

I said, "I'm his brother. Darrell is his brother too."

For a second, I thought her eyes flickered, said she didn't see enough in common for us to even be second cousins. But the fire in her peepers went away, changed to normal brown eyes.

"All right. I guess I can trust you," she said with a slight smile. I adjusted my shirt. Smiled back. She released her grip on the door, yawned, and motioned for me to come in. I was stepping through her door when Darrell lost his mind, mumbled something with the word *bitch* smack dab in the middle. I grimaced back to tell him to knock the ignorance off until we left.

Looking back was my first mistake.

Crackkkk.

A sudden sharp pain in my stomach . . .

Thummmbphh.

. . . then in my shoulder. Somebody hit me with something. The next thing I knew I was falling and the wooden floor caught my face. In between pants and grunts, I found a few teaspoons of air. After tears cleared from my eyes, I raised my head. Wanda was over me gripping a Louisville slugger. My eyes watered up again; tears blocked the little vision I had left. In between moans and groans, I used one hand to shield my head while my feet pushed me away from the overlapping noise.

Something broke.

My eyes cleared long enough for me to see Wanda was on one end of the bat and Darrell had the other. Then my eyes clogged up again. There was a wicked scuffle. Somebody crashed on top of me, felt like they were thrown and landed on me. It had to be Wanda. She was light and her wild hair slapped across my face. The back of her head . . .

whhummppp

. . . bumped the bridge of my nose. That hurt like hell and watered my eyes more. She was jerked up and tossed. I know that because her entire body rose and flew away at the same time.

"Pokey!" Darrell screamed. "You all right, man?"

"Do I look all right?"

I wiped my tears on my sleeves. Opened my eyes. Wanda had one knee on her plastic-covered light-green sofa, huffing and puffing under a tacky picture of dogs playing poker. She had the bat in a cocked, ready position. Mad, scared, wide-eyed, totally fixed on Darrell. I saw why. Darrell was holding a shiny black revolver. She faked like she was going to swing at him. He raised it. She reconsidered. Wanda sat back and dropped the bat across her lap, but she didn't take her hand off the handle. Either she was crazy or didn't get the concept of paper-scissors-rock. Her eyes welled up, but she didn't cry.

"Why y'all always fucking with me?"

"Get up, Pokey," Darrell yelled, over her cries.

I moaned, shifted my weight, collapsed back down.

"What the fuck do y'all want?"

Darrell screamed, "Shut up!"

"Take what you want and get out. I ain't got no money, I ain't got no drugs. I'm straight, now leave me alone."

"Wanda, we don't want any money. We're just looking for our brother," I said the best I could through the pain.

I pulled myself back into a corner next to the door, so I didn't leave my back open. Some of my warrior instinct came back a little too late. I struggled my wallet from my back pocket, pulled out my driver's license, slung it across the room. It landed on the sofa by Wanda. Darrell jumped over me to the front door to see if anyone was coming after all the commotion.

Wanda asked, "What's this for?"

"My ID. I'm Jordan Greene, Reggie Greene's brother."

She looked at the picture. Her lips moved and she mumbled when she read. When she finished she walked over, bobbing her head the entire way, then slammed the license in my face.

"Why the hell y'all come pushing your way up in my house? Why you men always have to push women around? Push me around? Sometime you ought to try asking instead of taking."

Darrell dug into his pocket and took out a Kool. He tapped it twice before he slid it into his mouth.

"*No smoking.*"

Darrell growled, "What?"

"Are you deaf and stupid?" Wanda snapped with supremacy. "I said *no smoking* in *my* house. I know it ain't much, but you're gonna have to *respect me* in my house."

Darrell looked at me, then frowned back to her. He chuckled like she was no big deal, then said, "All right."

"Y'all need some *home* training." Wanda said that to Darrell. She pulled her hair back from her face, took a couple of deep breaths, and made a "Whew" sound.

Darrell had dropped his gun to his side, but he kept his eyes on her. She scowled deep into my eyes like she was contemplating jumping off into my shit. Not a drop of respect.

I shifted positions, moaned like an old man.

Her voice softened, "You all right, Narc?"

"No."

"Good, you stupid bastard. Serves your black ass right," Wanda said, with a twisted expression swelling in her face.

I turned my head. Made her invisible.

She asked, "What's Reggie's middle name?"

Darrell distorted his face and asked, "What?"

"I said," she repeated, "what's Reggie's middle name?"

"Michael," Darrell said. "Reginald Michael Greene."

She turned to me. "Where was he born?"

"Brownsville."

Back to Darrell. "What hospital?"

"At home," Darrell answered, his voice more comfortable this time. "All of us was born at home."

Back to me. "When's his birthday?"

I looked at Darrell. He looked at me.

I shrugged. "End of May, beginning of June."

Darrell interjected, "Ain't it in August?"

She shook her head, then ran her fingers through her hair.

"June fifteenth. He's a Gemini. One week from Cancer. His birthday was just last month. Y'all some pitiful brothers. I bet y'all don't ever send him a present or call, right, Narc?"

Darrell asked, "What you to Reggie?"

"Something you two ain't. A friend."

That verbal slap caused silence. I looked at Darrell; he looked at me; then we both looked away from each other. She walked around the room for a moment, thinking. Then she picked up the slugger and stepped over me to put it behind the front door. She glared at Darrell. They were saying something in the silence, a warriors' truce, I hoped. We remained quiet.

Wanda walked into the back bedroom and came back shaking a large bottle of Tylenol 500s. She softball pitched it and it hit me on my nose, the same damn spot she'd fallen on. That pissed me off, but I acted like it didn't faze me.

She said, "You gonna need these, Narc."

I tried to sound like an angry Denzel Washington. "Yeah, thanks a lot for hitting me in the stomach."

"Your lucky day. I was aiming at your head."

She walked into the kitchen and came back with a glass of ice water in a scratchy mason jar. She downed half in a couple of hard swallows, then handed the rest to me. I popped three Tylenols and washed them down so they could catch up with the pain. The coldness of the water hurt my throat and I choked. She ignored me. She straightened her clothes, then her furniture. Darrell tried to help, but she gave him a glower that made him stay away. But knowing him, he didn't want to help anyway. If you asked him, no matter who made the mess, cleaning up was a woman's job.

When Wanda was done, she stood in front of Darrell. Toe to toe. Her head almost reached his shoulder.

She asked, "You got a ride?"

Darrell nodded. "I'm driving, yeah."

"Put your pop gun up. We going for a ride."

Darrell asked, "Where we going to?"

"I know somebody who might know where he at." She chuckled. "A fucking twenty-two. Piece of shit. Get a nine."

Darrell stuck the gun up under his denim shirt, stuck out his sweaty hand and helped me up. Again I moaned like an old man.

"Pokey," Darrell said, "does it hurt?"

"Only when I breathe."

"Then hold your breath," Wanda said. Very cold and defiant.

19 Jordan Greene

Wanda had Darrell stop around the corner from her apartment. She took us to some more run-down apartments behind a pawn-shop on Exchange Avenue, then made us wait in the car while she ran inside to talk to somebody unseen and unheard. In the mean-time, a flock of rough brothas were sitting around, gawking at us like either we were lepers, or they were mad about their SAT scores.

She bounced back into the car, armpits dank, and said, "I found out where he might be holed up at."

At the same time, me and Darrell asked, "Where?"

She used her fingertips to wipe some sweat from her forehead, pulled her hair back, then sighed. "Drive."

I grumbled, "I hope it ain't a freaking crack house."

She cringed like she'd lost her last marble, then sighed again, sat back, and commanded, "If it is, you don't wanna go?"

Darrell made a pissed-off sound. "Just gimme the fucking directions."

She shook her head. "I'll show you where he at."

Darrell shifted like he was ready to slap her.

I touched Darrell's shoulder to calm him, groaned because it hurt to move, then asked Wanda, "Why do you have to show us?"

" 'Cause these people won't let you in if I ain't there."

"Who are these people?"

She ignored me.

I blew air. "Are these drug people?"

Again, she didn't answer. That was all I needed to know.

Sunlight was changing to dark. I was in the backseat, quietly marinating. Wanda was giving directions, talking only when we had to turn right or left, keeping the upper hand.

The pain in my side wasn't too bad now, not since I'd found a comfortable position. We drove along MLK Expressway. An hour later, we got off I-40, made two rights, a left, and then headed up Highway 179. We drove that two lane road toward Whiteville. Trailer homes, cotton fields, John Deere farm machinery were on both sides of the highway. As we passed Harmony Baptist Church I saw a sign that read, DILIGENCE IS THE MOTHER OF GOOD FORTUNE.

Wanda looked out her window. "This car registered?"

Darrell said, "Yeah."

Wanda was fanning her right hand in the humid winds. She said, "Who to?"

Darrell answered, "Me. Why?"

Wanda continued playing. "Because Johnny Law—"

I mumbled a surprised, "The police?"

"—been jocking us for the last ten minutes."

I looked back.

"Stupid!" Wanda growled through her teeth. "What the hell you do that for?"

I looked because I didn't trust her. We were passing Virginia's Beauty Shop, Tanning Bed, & Grocery and two State Troopers were in a car, tailgating us. One was on the radio.

Wanda remained calm. "Where your gun at?"

Darrell's eyes were straight ahead. "Tucked in my back."

Wanda eased over, pretended she was kissing Darrell, stole his gun from his waist, dropped it on the floor. On my feet.

"Darrell, your breath stanks. Quit smoking." She pretended to nibble on Darrell's ear. "Narc, kick the gun under the seat."

I kicked the gun through the old fast food sacks and hamburger wrappers and empty cigarette cartons, used my feet to slide the gun under Wanda's side, so I could blame it on her if we had to, then crammed junk food bags on top, stuffed the opening with a cigarette carton. Adrenaline was flowing like the Nile. Fear covered my pain. Wanda moved back to her original position and slyly peeked in her side-view mirror.

"Any second," Wanda mumbled, grinned, and masqueraded like she was having big fun. "We're gonna get pulled over."

"Why?" I complained and fanned myself. "We're not speeding."

Darrell blew up. " 'Cause we niggers, Pokey. Riding three-deep in the boondocks."

I growled out our childhood mantra, "I'm not a nigger, I'm a Negro. When I become a nigger I'll let you know."

Wanda lost her mind. "Narc, why don't you just shut the fuck up. Stupid. You sure you Reggie's brother?"

Bright lights, loud siren. More fear, less pain.

Darrell slowed and pulled over toward the gritty right shoulder. He said, "Well, Pokey, you so damn good with white folks, let's see how you handle this."

Wanda asked, "How he good with white folks?"

"He moved to New York, lost his mind, and hooked up with a damn white woman. All them *fine* sisters up there, and he had to get something with blond hair and blue eyes."

My tone was louder, more defensive than I intended, "Red hair and hazel eyes."

Darrell spat, "And she still white as a cracker."

Wanda jumped in, frowned like she had a mouth filled with castor oil, "Your brother sleeping with a Wilma?"

Darrell nodded. "She got that punk letting her answer his phone all times of the night."

I countered, "She's a woman who happens to be white."

"Well ain't you the corny one." That was Wanda. "I'm not surprised. Damn oreo."

"Go to hell."

"Oreo. Your jungle fever–looking ass."

"Leave my brother alone," Darrell spoke real low. "I know your tacky ass ain't trying to start nothing."

"And what you gonna do, pull out your gun and shoot me? Both of y'all can kiss my—"

Bright lights from big flashlights beamed in from both sides at the same time. The police were already out of their car and on top of us. Darrell kept his hands on the steering wheel. Wanda's hands were in plain sight. It hurt, but I sat up so it wouldn't look like I was trying to hide. Kept my hands in my lap. We didn't leave any excuses for an accident.

It looked like a gun, sorry I killed him dead like that. Let's go get a doughnut.

With my peripheral vision, I caught a glimpse of the officer to our right. His gun holster was unstrapped. The ritual began.

"License and registration, please," the officer to the left snapped out.

Darrell asked, "Is there a problem, Officer?"

"Not yet." The officer to the right spat. He was about my age and looked like he had something to prove.

We remained quiet. Didn't even wipe the globs of sweat from our faces. We knew the routine. It was dark and we were in the boondocks. Speak when spoken to.

The officer to the right gave Darrell the stone-face, humphed, and said, "You from Memphis?"

"Yeah," Darrell said. He'd never say "Yes, sir" to him.

"What y'all doing all the way out here?"

I was about to ask if it was against the law for black people to ride from point A to point B without needing a pass from the big man at the plantation, but Wanda grinned and spoke up, "He's taking me to a friend's house."

The officer to the right said, "Your friend got a name?"

Wanda paused before she said, "Veronica Giovanni."

I didn't believe her. From the raised brows, I don't think Johnny Law did either. Their looks made the temperature shoot up twenty degrees. The humidity doubled.

Officer to the left handed Darrell back his paperwork. "You been drinking?"

"No."

"You sure?" Officer to the right sounded stern. His face twitched like he'd been having a bad day.

Darrell's voice was calm. "Yes."

"Your pupils look dilated. Step out of the car, please."

Officer to the left escorted Darrell to the curb. Made him do the finger to the nose bit. Officer to the right shined his flashlight down and read Wanda's X T-shirt. His lips moved when he read, "By Any Means Necessary." Air jetted from his nostril. Lines popped into his pale forehead.

He spat, gave us no southern comfort when he bobbed his head and grinned, "Let me see some ID for the both of you. *Now.*"

Darrell was walking a straight line like he was auditioning for the black circus. I slowly leaned sideways to get my driver's license from my back pocket. When I bent over, a sharp pain struck. I let out a low moan.

Officer to the right asked, "What's wrong with you, fellow?"

I said, "I hurt myself playing baseball."

Wanda chuckled.

His expression was somewhere in between offended and confused. Then he let out a short laugh. He checked out Wanda's I.D., handed it back, then read mine. His eyes lit up.

He sounded excited. "You from New York?"

His new attitude caught me off guard. I was so used to telling people up north that I was from Memphis, that I almost shook my head.

"Yeah," I nodded. "I live in Queens."

"I've always wanted to take my wife to New York!" Officer to the left turned to Officer to the right, who was talking to Darrell, "Rick, this here fellow's from New York City!"

"No shit." He spat to the ground. He wasn't enthused.

"Look at his driver's license. It's a good picture too! Looks just like him. Ours don't come out this good, do they?"

Andy Griffith and Barney Fife began questioning me.

Been to the Statue of Liberty?

Yes.

How was it?

Nice, big. You can see the entire city from there.

What else've you done?

We went down on Broadway . . .

You been to some of those plays?

Yes. *Miss Saigon. Porgy and Bess. Phantom. Cats.*

Question. Answer. Question. Answer. Laughter. Dumb question. Answer. Question. Answer. Stupid question. Laughter. Vague answer. Question. Answer. Laughter.

"Well, y'all take it easy!" and "Drive carefully!" was said when they headed back to their police car. They left Darrell on the curb. They forgot about him. Darrell slowly walked back to our car, eyes fixed on the officers, and got in real slow, eased his butt on the seat like he had hemorrhoids.

The officers made a U-turn, kicked up some trash. A minute passed and Darrell hadn't moved, hadn't blinked his eyes.

Wanda turned around and looked at me. "Yep. You good with white people. Oreo."

"I like *Narc* better."

"Whatever."

Wanda gave a curt laugh. Darrell slammed the door, turned the key to start the car, and that made a grinding noise because he hadn't turned the engine off. We were free. They didn't search the car, and that was all that mattered to me. Darrell just sat there, both hands gripping the steering wheel, mumbling. Then after a few seconds, it became loud enough to be heard, ". . . Tawana Brawley, Latasha Harlins, Yusef Hawkins, Rodney King, Malice Greene. Why *they* always fucking with us? Motherfuckers just mess with us because they can. Always *fucking* over us! Playing with our lives. Always *stepping* on us, *stepping* on our dreams, our families, us. *Making* me walk and tap dance like some *puppet*, pulling the strings and making me *dance*."

Darrell shoved the door open and jumped back out of the car, then slammed the door. Wanda looked back at me. My eyes were on Darrell. He marched down the road, moved like he was being driven by demons, then after about forty yards, his head dropped, and his shoulders were damn near dragging the gravel.

"What's his trip? Ain't he never been pulled over before?'

"Can you drive a stick?"

"Yeah, I can drive a stick. My momma didn't raise no fools. You not gonna leave your brother, are—"

"No. Jump over and just follow him down the road. Follow him. Let him walk it off."

"What's his trip?" she asked again as she slid over.

Darrell's first wife, back when he was eighteen, used to work at an upscale restaurant in downtown Memphis, overlooking the Mississippi River. She was a cook or something. Yeah, a cook, because Darrell said that she said only white folks had the good jobs up front with the customers—waiter, waitress, cashier. All the African-Americans—I think we were Afro-Americans, maybe Negroes then—had the jobs in the back out of sight: bus boys, dishwashers, cooks, fixing food and cleaning up after white folks, he said.

His wife, Stephanie, was a very pretty woman. Petite and quiet. But she could be vicious when provoked. He loved her fire. That was one thing me and Darrell had in common; we loved women with fire, which was why I'd found J'nette so damn appealing. But if you play with fire long enough, you'll get burned. Anyway, Darrell and Stephanie had been married a little over a year, had been blessed with a beautiful, hyper, one-year-old daughter, Jasmine. One night after Stephanie had cleaned up the kitchen, one of the waiters assaulted her. She reported it and they treated her like she was a criminal.

Did you like it?

Everyone knows how fast and loose you young colored women are.

The process ripped everybody apart. She couldn't look Darrell in the face because of how *they* made her feel.

Maybe it was my fault. I was too friendly, I led him on. . . . Darrell couldn't come to touch her in that way, because she had been violated. *They* had done it to him. *They* stole his family. *They* messed up his life. *They.* The waiter didn't even get fired. She did. Everything got bad at Darrell's home. Stephanie left, took Jasmine, and has never called Darrell since.

I told Wanda, "Nothing. Everything. Just follow him, keep him in sight. If he stops walking, stop driving. Keep your distance and let him have some space."

"Can't we just wait for him to come back?"

Darrell was walking, letting headlights from our car be the sun on his back. I looked out the window. Saw the darkness in the woods. Thought about burning crosses. Thought about the term people used to use, "strange fruit." That was what they called brothers they found hanging in trees. Strange fruit. Felt a different kind of reality, one that made my sweat run cold. One that made me have doubts about the scarlet-haired woman I'd left in Jackson Heights. But those doubts were shadowed by what came from my heart. I wondered if that discomfort would ever go away.

Wanda repeated herself, "*Narc,* why can't we wait for that fool to come back. Let his ass walk by himself."

I said, "Not out here. Different tribes."

"What the hell are you talking about now?"

"Nothing."

Wanda shook her head.

Almost two miles later, we were still crawling at a snail's pace. My thoughts were scattered between what's right and what's wrong. If we *couldn't* trust whites, and we *didn't* trust blacks, whom did we trust? Always so close to death from both sides of the fence.

A car passed with its bright lights on, interrupting my day-dream. Then darkness. Mr. Heat was still sitting on top of us. And he brought along his woman, Miss Humidity. Wanda smacked her left arm, killed a mosquito. We were both sweating. Me, more because of the pain. I could tell she was getting fed up with Darrell because every now and then she'd start mumbling about how immature he was acting. She was right, to a degree. Darrell was starting to work my last nerve's last nerve.

Somebody was musty, probably me. My twelve-hour deodorant was deader than that mosquito Wanda had clobbered.

I popped two dry Tylenols, because when the excitement died down, my new friend, Mr. Pain, returned, stronger than before. It was too quiet. Silence was wrecking my nerves, so I decided to make some conversation. I needed to keep my cool. The only thing me and Wanda had in common was the fact that we knew Reggie. That, and Darrell was pissing off both of us.

"I hope Darrell's all right by the time we get to Reggie."

She cleared her throat. "How come?"

"I don't think I can deal with Darrell's attitude and Reggie's grief at the same time."

Wanda stared at me in the rearview mirror. One eyebrow went up, slow and easy. Her face crinkled, like she was contemplating. She asked, "Why would Reggie have grief?"

I was in the middle of nowhere, sweating like crazy, in the backseat of a tired-ass Rodney King–mobile, throbbing in pain, popping Tylenols like they were going out of style. And I know these stupid pills were going to make me constipated.

I said, "Reggie's dad died—"

"*Died?*"

"Yeah. We need to get Reggie to the funeral—"

"When his daddy pass?"

"Earlier this week."

The car jerked to a halt. Wanda reached back and clocked me with a flurry of punches. All closed fists. She was almost in the backseat on top of me, screaming something about me and Darrell being no good and selfish. I couldn't hear what she was yelling because she'd slapped the side of my face and my ears were ringing. That really reminded me of my momma. I tried to twist away, but the pain gripped me in the side, had me trapped. She stopped beating me and turned her back. Mumbled. My fists doubled and I wanted to hit her, smack her wicked butt upside the back of the head, but I reneged because she might hit me again.

I yelled, "What's wrong with you?"

She jumped out of the car and dashed to Darrell, screaming obscenities all the way. Darrell waved her off, kept moving like she was nothing. She hit him in the jaw, closed fisted.

That was when I choked out, "Fuck!"

They were swinging at each other, but nobody landed a blow. It had to be the heat. This was a bad dream. Everything was falling apart, going crazy in the heat. Had to be the heat.

Darrell backed off, raised his hands in truce, then stepped to her and started to say something. Before he could complete the sentence, she kicked him in the nuts so hard it hurt me.

I frowned and said, "Owww-oww-oww-ch."

He bent over, like he had a choice, and Wanda leaped on top of him, closed fisted punching, before he even hit the ground. She fought like she grew up in a girls' home. I struggled to get out of the car, did my best, but I couldn't fine the damn release thing to let the front seat up. By the time I did, Darrell was grimacing and limping, following Wanda back to the car. Wanda was flinging her arms and screaming at nobody and at everybody at the same time. When Wanda got to the driver's side, Darrell was ten feet behind. She started doing the rotating-neck-snake-thing that made my flesh crawl. And she was viciously pointing at Darrell. I was more afraid of her than I was of the police. And they had guns. Hell, I had a gun at my feet and I was still too scared to pick it up.

Wanda yapped, "Don't give a damn about you and whatever

your hang-up is. This ain't no goddam *white man*! Family should overrule that *crap*. Your brother's daddy died, that's what's important, but you out here *tripping* off some bull. This is about Reggie. Your family. Whatever your trip is, stick it straight up your butt and quit buggin'. Understand?"

Darrell wiped himself down, spat, and walked to the passenger side and got in. Wanda got in on the driver's side and slammed her door so hard it scared away the birds sitting on the telephone wire over us. Wanda was crying.

Darrell snapped, "Don't ever hit me again."

Wanda matched his tone, "Don't give me a reason to."

Wanda started the car.

Darrell reached for a cigarette.

Wanda looked at Darrell. "No smoking."

"It's my car."

"I'm driving."

Darrell lit the cigarette anyway, then sat back and spat out of his window. "Like I said, it's my goddam car."

Wanda snapped on her seat belt, screeched off, speed-raced about thirty yards, then slammed on the brakes. Darrell flew into the dashboard, coughed, and spat the cigarette into his lap. The sudden jerk threw me into the back of Darrell's seat, made my side hurt so bad I almost peed in my pants.

Wanda looked evil again. "Like I said, no smoking."

"*Crazy bitch!*" Darrell screamed. He was shifting around and struggling to find the cigarette that was burning in his lap.

"You call me a bitch one more time, that's your black ass."

"Fuck you. Bitch."

"Leave her alone, Darrell."

"I don't need your help, punk-ass Narc."

"Kick her ass, Darrell."

"Shut the fuck up, Pokey."

"Fuck you, Darrell."

We rode in silence for the next ten minutes. Sweat had glued my shirt to my back. I was sitting in a better position, so I wasn't hurting so bad now. Quiet. This time, I learned to appreciate the silence. All I heard was the tires melting against the scorching pavement, and occasionally the sounds of locusts singing love songs in the trees. A few crickets.

Wanda slowed down and turned left down a tree-lined dirt road. The road came up so fast, if it were just me and Darrell, we would've passed right by without seeing it. Rocks and earth crumbled under the tires. A long cloud of dust flew behind us. The dirt road made me think of where we grew up, of our mom, who'd gone on to a better place. She'd been gone almost eleven years. Eleven years that went by too quickly.

"Darrell! Reggie! Pokey! Time for supper!"

"Okay, Ma!"

"We on dah way!"

"Yes'm!"

At the second entry, Wanda pulled into the driveway of a big, farm-type house. A place with a serious spread. Acres that held the funk of livestock in the air. That and the aroma of fresh fruit, probably plum and fig trees. A june bug flew by and committed suicide into the windshield. More pain and death.

Then I wondered who the hell Wanda was to be taking us anywhere? She wasn't rational, not even by a crazy man's standards. What if she was setting us up? Darrell said she was a strawberry. And a berry would do anything for a taste of money. Anything. And she had made us stop at a rough-looking place before she led us all the way out to No Man's Land. Had made us wait in the car. She could've been calling ahead to set us up. Maybe Reggie had done something else since the last time. Maybe stole some stuff from the wrong people, ripped off one of these crazy people, somebody crazier than Wanda, and this nighttime, backwoods set-up was the payback.

My nerves were blowing up. Darrell was so mad he was quiet. With us all in the car, I couldn't get his attention without tipping off Wanda. I cleared my throat a few times; he didn't look back. Wanda glanced my way, rolled her eyes.

This wasn't cool. I was trapped in the backseat. In pain. There wasn't much I could do if something was about to go down.

I spoke up, "Wanda, come clean."

She blew air and mumbled a bitter, "What?"

"Exactly what are you to Reggie?"

She cleared her throat, wiped the tears and sweat from her face. "I'm his wife."

2 0   J o r d a n   G r e e n e

Wanda parked in the middle of the circular driveway. Darrell was still shut down, but he helped me get out. We walked slowly because that was the best I could do. I took short breaths.

The front doors were like those huge double doors on the TV show "Dallas." Pure white, made of good wood. I don't know the type because I didn't know a damn thing about wood.

Wanda pushed an intercom buzzer. She hadn't given us any eye contact since she claimed to be my brother's wife.

"Who is it?" a female voice asked.

She cleared her throat. "Wanda Greene."

Darrell and I looked at each other when she said that.

Darrell asked, "Why does your mailbox say McClain?"

Wanda shrugged. "I ain't changed it yet."

A minute later, the door opened and a petite black female, about thirty, was standing there with a big smile on her face. A thin, fair-skinned brother with wavy hair was behind her.

"Veronica!" Wanda smiled. "How are you!"

"Wanda!" Veronica grinned. They let out a pair of high-pitched squeals and did the huggy-kissy girl ritual. Wanda pulled Veronica closer to where we were standing.

"Veronica, these are Reginald's brothers. This one over here is Jordan. He flew all the way in from New York to see him, *girl*! Jordan, this is Doctor Veronica Giovanni."

Wanda had changed. She called me by my name and it sounded funny when it rolled off her countrified tongue.

Wanda pointed at Darrell. "And the big one's Darrell."

He smiled. "Evening, nice to meet you, Sister Giovanni."

"Please, call me Veronica."

She pulled the other guy standing behind her up to the door.

"This is my fiancé, Terry Wallace. Terry, these are Reggie's people. You've met his wife, and these are his brothers."

We all exchanged greetings. Veronica put her arm through Terry's arm, hugged him.

"Is it okay to visit Reggie?" Wanda bit her lip. "His brother came in from New York and I didn't get a chance to call first."

Veronica waved her hand. "It's fine. If anybody asks, I'll tell them you called ahead. This time."

Wanda smiled. "It won't happen again."

"I'm sure of that. He's working out back."

"Good." Wanda gave a big smile. "Thanks, Veronica."

Terry and Veronica started up the spiral stairs. Darrell turned and set free a final wish-that-was-mine look at Veronica's butt while she ascended. He shook his head, ran his hand across his crotch.

Wanda led us down a long hallway toward the kitchen. I found a stride that minimized pain and maximized speed. Since I wasn't in New York, I didn't have to break my neck moving, so I took it easy and stared at everything. There was very little furniture and what they had was modest. Awards, plaques, and group pictures were on the wall. The place was very organized. A couple of people, around my age, were reading parts of the *Wall Street Journal*. Two middle-agers were playing dominoes. I'd never seen bones played without hostility. Three teenagers were gathered in a room we passed, watching a movie, *U.S. Marshals*. I heard Wesley Snipes' voice pleading with Tommy Lee Jones.

In the kitchen, a lovely, middle-aged black woman was cooking, while a spunky, teenaged white female cut up vegetables and put them next to the shucked corn. I stole a carrot slice when I passed. They smiled at me. The young girl laughed and softball threw me another carrot slice. I caught it and nodded.

Quite a few people were here, and not one looked related to another. It wasn't noisy. Controlled.

Then I realized where we were: a halfway house.

Chickens clucked past us while we hiked up a trail wide enough for two people to stroll side by side. Wanda was in front; I stayed abreast of Darrell. We passed a small stable yard holding two horses and a Shetland pony. One of the horses crapped while it walked. Such talent.

We hiked up to a small garden with several rows of vegetables in bloom. Small labels on tiny sticks identified what was planted where. A series of ten-foot poles supported a stream of lights.

Somebody was at the end, crouched down in the dirt, working the earth with bare fingers. A wicker basket half-filled with ripe tomatoes was at his side.

Wanda smiled, broke out running like Flo Jo, yelled, "Baybeeeee! Hey, baybeeee!"

He jumped up, startled. It was Reggie. Wanda ran the rest of the way, gave him a big hug, kissed his dirty face.

Wanda bounced up and down. "Hey, baby!"

"Woman, you scared the mess out of me!"

He returned the hugs and kisses. Reggie's hands slid down her back, squeezed her little buttocks. In the next heartbeat, he picked her up and twirled her around. They didn't notice us. Reggie looked different. Thinner. Down from two hundred plus to about my size and weight, one seventy something. The last time I saw him, he had a full beard and a nappy Afro, looked like Linc from "The Mod Squad." Now his hair had been texturized and pulled back into a ponytail. He looked chic, like a stylish country boy dressed in overalls. His sweat glistened under the lights, made him look like a fresh, chocolate-glazed doughnut. They stopped laughing and spinning with Wanda facing us.

Reggie laughed in a happy, baritone voice. "How you get here? I thought our car broke down."

Wanda's face changed. Like she remembered who she came with and why we were here. She glanced around Reggie. Pointed. Reggie turned around. He strained, glared in my eyes.

He said, "Elijah?"

I paused, stared, then said, "Hey, Fathead."

His eyes drifted to Darrell. He squinted. His laughter had died when he saw me. Now the smile left his face.

"Darrell?"

"What's up, nigger?"

Reggie rushed over and hugged me. That hurt my ribs, but I

didn't give in to the pain. He did the same to Darrell. We've never hugged each other. Never touched with open hands.

Reggie pulled Wanda closer to his right side. She was tame with him. Had switched from tigress to pussycat. Wanda was rocking on her right heel. Reggie took a deep breath, then looked at me, at Wanda, at Darrell.

Reggie cleared his throat. "Who died?"

Reggie shared a room with the men who were downstairs playing dominoes. I sat on the bed that had the Asian calendar on the wall over it. Reggie was on the edge of his bed with Wanda snuggled behind him on her knees, knuckle-massaging his shoulders. Darrell lingered by the window, shifting constantly. Darrell was still mad about getting kicked in the nuts. He'd been silent since we came upstairs. Life was better when he was quiet.

Reggie sounded ashamed, overjoyed, and relieved when he talked. "Been out here in Whiteville about five months. I hit rock bottom. I'd wake up and had no idea where I was or how I got there or where I was going. Wanda had just left here. She was here at Doctor Giovanni's program for 'round seven months—"

Wanda corrected, "Eight."

"Right, eight. I went by to buy some stuff, and she started preaching to me about how wrong I was about what I was doing. She told me I was, y'know, contributing to the genocide of our people, of all people, which was the last thang I wanted to hear from her. She said I didn't respect myself, so I cussed her out and left. I kept thanking about the thangs she said. I started dreaming about what she said. I mean, I was unhappy. I been that way since Mom died."

"Yeah," I said. "I've felt the same way." My own confession surprised me.

"I mean y'all, if you don't mind my saying so, Mom always thought so much of you two. Especially you, Jordan."

I shook my head. "She loved us the same, you know that."

"She loved us all, but not the same. She expected more out of you. I'm not jealous, that's just a fact." He coughed, then rubbed his eyes with the back of his hands. "I went back to Wanda's. Apologized . . ."

"You *never* apologized." Wanda pushed him upside the head, then kissed him where she pushed him.

Reggie grinned. "I'm sorry. You 'cept my apology?"

Wanda matched his happy face and said, "Yeah."

"Why didn't you call somebody or something, nigger?" Darrell said abruptly. That came out of nowhere, like he'd been saving it up. "Got us running all around town looking for your ass."

Reggie cleared his throat, then stood. He spoke slow and deliberate. "First off, I'm not a nigger. Darrell, I'm your brother. If *nigger* is a state of mind, I now live in a different country. I thank it's time for you to move, too."

Reggie sat back down. Slow and deliberate.

Darrell had a twisted look on his face. Straight-up shocked. Darrell looked at me. I almost laughed. He was the only one left in Niggerville.

Reggie spoke in a real soft voice where we had to practically strain to hear him. "I didn't call because I've gotta do this on my own. I've been a failure all my life. If I started this and couldn't hang, nobody would haveta know."

"I'd know," Wanda said, "and you ain't dropping out. You my man and whatever it takes, we gonna do. I made it and you gonna make it."

Darrell asked, "What about your daddy's funeral?"

"Can't make it. I don't mean to be cold-blooded, but I'm committed to staying here for the duration. No matter what happens out there, I'm staying in here. I make no contact with the outside world till I'm straight. Until they say I'm straight. Tell them to understand, or at least try to, ah'right? Can't do nothing for the dead no way."

"You only gonna have one daddy, baby," Wanda said. "Think about it, 'cause I don't want you to have no regrets."

"He was a father, not a daddy," Reggie said, starting to sound bitter. "Last time I saw him, he put me out of his house. He told me he disowned me. I went to him—"

Reggie started to shake, and the suddenness made me uncomfortable. He ran his hand across his head and almost broke loose the ponytail. Wanda rubbed his back. She was going to cry. Then

Reggie pulled himself together. Wanda did the same. It was like, whatever he did, she did too.

"I went to him for help. I told him I wanted him to help me, you know, to get offa the mess I was on, y'know. He cussed me out, told me to get the hell out. I was leaving. I really was. I wasn't mad. I was hurt inside, but I knew I'd hurt a lot of people, that was on me. My fault. So I wasn't mad at him. Wasn't even gonna sweat it, y'know. I understood, 'cause I brought it on myself. I was just gonna go. Then he said he wasn't sure I was his child anyway. 'The bitch was fucking everybody.' "

Me and Darrell let out some mean-sounding gasps, looked at each other, then back to Reggie.

He nodded. "That's what he said. Kept saying it."

Reggie and his dad look exactly alike. Same height, shade of blackness, eyes, grade of hair.

Reggie said, "All I remember is, I grabbed him, started hitting him. I wanted to beat him down, bad, y'know. I coulda killed him. I wanted to. Y'know how we ain't never let nobody, man or woman, say nothing bad about Momma. After all she did."

"Let it go, baby," Wanda cried. "Please? Baby . . . okay?"

Everybody quieted. This was awkward for all of us. Darrell was pissed, and next thing I knew he reached for a cigarette. But he looked at Wanda and put it back in his shirt pocket. For a moment, I felt like I wanted a smoke my damn self. For a moment.

Reggie finally held his head up. "He filed charges, assault and battery, I think."

"And the police was coming by looking for him." Wanda said, "I told'm he left me and I don't know where he was at. That's the real reason I ain't changed my mailbox."

"I'll deal with that after I get out." Reggie stood up. "But I gotta do what's important to me first."

Wanda sat back and watched Reggie the way a mother watched a troubled child. He glanced back at her and smiled. Then she smiled. They winked at each other.

Reggie looked at the clock over his roommate's bed and smiled. "I don't mean to cut your visit short, but I got a ten o'clock curfew. House rules. It's a little after nine and I still haf'ta finish my chores before I shower up."

"Maybe I'll stop back by before I fly to New York."

"No. See me after I get out. Nothing personal, ah'right?"

"I understand."

"Maybe I'll come up there to see how you living. Look like you living large."

"Ah'right." I mimicked Reggie's tone. Reggie laughed, then walked to Darrell and gave him a hug.

Darrell jumped into the middle of the pleasant conversation. "Oh, by the way. Did you know your little brother got a white woman?"

Again, everybody silenced. I let out a long breath.

Reggie's face was blank. He asked, "You happy, Elijah?"

My face was blank too. I wanted to sound enthusiastic about how she made me feel, but I kept it low-key and said, "Yeah."

"Cool." Reggie smiled. "That's all that matters. But still, be careful, ah'right? Don't forget."

"I won't forget. Can't."

A worn Bible lay on Reggie's dresser. The bookmark was half-way through. Next to that was a small photo of our mother, lodged in the corner of an 8-x-10 framed photo. He had a photo of himself standing outside with the multi-ethnic group I'd seen downstairs.

"Ain't that a bitch," Darrell said. "Momma probably turning over in her grave listening to this shit."

Reggie pushed Darrell. "I love you, Brother. But you need to lighten up."

Darrell cursed Reggie, laughed, and pushed him. Darrell was laughing, but his tone was serious as a heart attack. "You owe me. Where's my coat? My damn TV? That's what I came here to get."

"I'll tighten everybody up when I get on my feet." Reggie pushed Darrell, just like we did when we were growing up, play fighting. "And stop cussing so much. Me and Wanda don't cuss."

Me and Darrell shot each other a look, then we frowned at Wanda, then shared an expression with Reggie. Reggie stared at Wanda. Her eyes dipped to her feet and she made a confused face.

Reggie asked, "Wanda?"

"Just a little bit, baybeeee." She held her thumb and pointing finger close together to quantify her vulgarity.

We all started laughing, including Darrell. A dull pain hit my ribs, causing me to moan out, "Arrrgh."

We told Reggie what had happened. How she'd hit me with a bat, then sent a foot deep into Darrell's crotch.

"Your woman is wicked," Darrell said with a straight face. He was massaging his groin. "If she your wife, control her."

Reggie shook his head. "She ain't as mean as she was."

Laughter came from everybody but Darrell. He was talking about Wanda, but a new anger was engraved in his face, had made a vein sprout in his forehead. A similar vein was throbbing in my neck.

Reggie went over to a cherrywood dresser, opened the bottom drawer, took out a small bottle, threw it to me.

I asked, "What's this?"

"Roboxin, a muscle relaxer. It might make you a little sleepy, though. It knocked me out solid. I hurt my back fooling with one of them dang horses a coupla months ago, and this is what Dr. Giovanni give me."

We headed to the car. With his hand on Reggie's shoulder, Darrell asked, "You sure about the funeral?"

Reggie replied a solid "Yep. A hundred percent. Dead can't do nothing for the living and the living can't do nothing for the dead."

Wanda eased in between and hugged Reggie. Gave him tender kisses. Me and Darrell headed to the car, gave them privacy. At the car, Darrell lost his humor. Me too. Darrell was opening and closing his hands. Sweat was on the tip of his nose. I was doing the same move, sweating the same way.

"Good thang Reggie's dad passed away," Darrell said in a harsh whisper. "Damn good thang."

"Why's that?"

" 'Cause I'd have to kill his ass. Lord knows I'd have to kill that motherfucker."

"Only if I didn't get to him first."

21 Jordan Greene

I woke up and looked at the clock. Almost eleven in the A.M. Some sweat on my neck. Very little pain in my side. I went back to sleep and dreamt of nothing. A peaceful nothing.

I slept until one. When I finally woke up, I was drenched in sweat because Darrell had the air set at about seventy-five and the severe summer heat made that supposed comfort null and void. My side wasn't hurting too bad, reduced to a dull, bearable isolated throb, but it was stiff. My shin ached, and for a few moments I couldn't remember why, then I saw the coffee table. I stretched and yawned, stumbled across the room and dropped the setting to about sixty, then took a cool shower and dressed in jean shorts and a T-shirt.

I called Kimberly. She wasn't home, so I left a flirty message letting her know everything was fine and to call me back if she wasn't too busy working or running in and out of Manhattan.

Solomon wasn't home either, but I left him a brother-to-brother message. I hadn't seen or talked to him since he rode with me down to this jewelry shop in Times Square. I was browsing engagement rings and thinking about Kimberly. It was a ring she looked at and said she didn't like. Her mouth couldn't cover the truth that bugged out in her eyes when she saw it. I had sort of wanted to talk to Darrell about my possibly getting engaged, but I didn't need his opinion.

Darrell's place wasn't filthy. And even though the masculine black-gray color scheme worked, all of his furniture was either worn or secondhand, tattered, so no matter how clean the place got, it wouldn't look too much better. In comparison to me, he has never been concerned with material things. I guess part of me was making up for growing up without. Overcompensating. Payback from tattered hand-me-downs. Now I had a load of suits I didn't wear. Subscriptions to trendy magazines I didn't read. I've changed furniture in my place, just because. A couple of times I moved for the same reason.

Even with the firm roots our mother planted, sometimes I felt unstable, no foundation. Maybe because, even with a loving, caring, attentive, protective mother in the house, we'd never had a consistent, solid father figure. I'd like to think that it didn't bother or affect me, but the reality of it is that it left a void, a space, a yearning that couldn't and wouldn't be filled by anything. At least nothing or anybody I was aware of.

I felt a gap of unknowing, a feeling that when I look back at my family tree only one side will be fruitful, the other pruned. An unbalanced fruit tree, wobbling, made unstable by the slightest ripple in the current. It would seem that knowing and accepting would make shit like this more bearable. But it didn't. You wore it, but it never became fashionable. You just became used to the pain. You ignored the consistent suffering.

22 Jordan Greene

By the time we picked Wanda up, she'd French-braided her hair and slipped on above-the-knee jean shorts and a big Martin Luther King T-shirt. I crawled in the back seat and we headed out on I-40 East to Highway 59. We made an hour drive to Brownsville to take flowers to Mom's grave. While we drove, Reggie's father, our former stepdad, was being eulogized. Minutes later, his remains would be routed to their final resting place. All of us avoided talking about Reggie's incident with his father. We'd buried that too.

I asked Wanda, "What kind of work you do?"

"Right now, I'm hunting for a job." She asked Darrell, "How long you been working at Fed?"

He smiled. "A little while."

"Can you get Fred Smith to drop me one of them applications?"

"What kinda job you want?"

"I'll mop the nasty floors, scrub and wax the planes. Hell, I'll fly the packages from here to Nashville on the back of Tweety Bird and ride back butt-naked on the face of the Road Runner. Don't matter. Money is money is money."

I used to sort in the hub back when I was in college. My senior year. I asked Darrell if they had any of those positions open.

"Sorting?" Wanda smirked. "What's that? The laundry room?"

"Naw, mail." Darrell laughed. "Packages and boxes."

Her face softened. "I want to be able to go into the grocery store and pay for my food without having to use food stamps."

Darrell's car was equipped with old-fashioned, four-fifty air conditioning. Let down four windows, go fifty miles an hour. Torturous, muggy heat blasted into the car across our faces every minute of the ride.

We took a straight shot out on 1-40 East, toward Wolfchase Galleria, Lakeland, and Loosahatchie River. Slowly, but surely, we went toward the place we used to call home sweet home, fanning ourselves when the torrid breeze was too much to bear. After being up north in a loud and wild city where my people used to flee for freedom, New York made my old southern stomping grounds look like a very small town. The madness in Times Square made these roads seem so thin, so tame and untraveled.

After we cruised by Somerville and twenty-four country miles snailed by with us having some back and forth lazy chitchat. A McDonald's, KFC, and Dairy Queen popped up at the Brownsville exit. Kimberly said she used to work at one of those DQ's down in San Antonio. I used to think food there was heaven on earth. Back when I was growing up, getting to eat away from home was a treat that was better than heaven.

Wanda said, "We gonna get something to eat?"

I said, "My stomach's growling too."

Darrell said, "My belly does that, locks up and growls like a bear everytime I think about you laying up with that white woman."

Wanda said, "Give it a rest. Damn. You worse than a woman. With that attitude you got, you probably ain't even got a woman."

Darrell said, "Shut up."

Wanda laughed. "I'm family, bro-in-law. You can't shut me up."

I interjected, "Children, be nice."

Wanda continued, "And I ain't got no money, so Narc. . . ."

I said, "I got you covered."

She said, "Thanks. Find a Piggly Wiggly so I can get a soda or something."

Darrell said, "We'll get some grub when we get to town."

My big brother kept his Rodney King-mobile rolling steady on Anderson. Took me into the heart of a déjà vu. A wonderful déjà vu. There was no Apollo or billboards polluting and blocking the skyline, no people shoving, no sea of yellow cabs, no entrances to subway stations along the way. A-frame houses. Wooden swings swaying gently. Soft and warm winds. Huge front yards. A Kingdom Hall and a couple of Baptist churches announced that this was religious territory.

Darrell slowed and pulled to the side of the road.

I said, "Why we stopping?"

Wanda said, "We have to."

I jumped a bit, felt a twinge in my side when I looked behind us and said, "It ain't the police again, is it?"

He said, "Naw, fool. Funeral procession coming down the way. Right in front of you."

Wanda chipped in, "How you gonna miss that long line of cars on a two lane highway, Narc?"

I relaxed, chuckled, said, "Yeah, we do have to stop, don't we."

Darrell looked at me in the rearview mirror, said, "They don't pull over and respect the dead where you living at now?"

I shook my head. "Not really."

Wanda said, "You lying."

I added, "Most of the time they don't respect the living, let alone the dead. Up there dead people are about as useful as paperweights."

Wanda humphed, shifted a bit, then said, "I don't thank I wanna visit no place like that."

In both directions, car after car came to a halt on the right side of the road. Several men were working at an auto shop, slaving in the heat and repairing cars, but when they saw the headlights from all of the cars in the funeral, all conversation ceased mid-sentence, every one of them stood straight as they could, took off their greasy baseball caps, and watched whoever was inside that black hearse make their last ride through town.

It was so quiet I could hear grass bending in the breeze.

Compared to the tranquil place I was sitting, New York was an alarm clock that never stopped clanging.

After the last car in the procession drove by, we pulled out in order, blended with the light flow of traffic, and moved on.

I was missing Kimberly. Missing her like crazy. Longing for her smell, her voice, to taste her tongue, to hear her laugh.

Cows and horses were on the sidelines pigging out on all-natural snacks in the meadows. More cotton fields.

I asked Wanda, "You ever picked cotton?"

"Nope. I thank my momma did though."

A moment passed. I asked, "Where is she?"

Darrell said, "Who?"

I said, "I was talking to Wanda."

She said, "Who?"

I answered, "Your momma."

"She passed a long time ago." Her happy voice faded to a soft mumble. "When I was in elementary school."

Another damp moment passed. I asked Wanda, "You got more family out here?"

She shifted, but she didn't answer.

Shotgun houses, barns were along the side of the highway. Worn from years of neglect, and in need of tearing down, but every one of those walls could tell a million stories. Could tell about the evolution of a people. Could let us know how far we'd come, could remind us how far we had to go.

Wanda said, "Narc, why you get so quiet all of a sudden?"

I smiled. "Thinking."

Darrell said, "Me too. I feel you back there, Pokey."

I nodded. "I feel you too, big bro."

Darrell took the highway to Main Street, busted an easy going left.

Wanda cackled and shouted, "Oh, check it out, check it out, check it out."

Darrell said, "What?"

She fanned herself and laughed. "Y'all got clothing stores, a movie theatre. *Yee-hah. Well, doggie.* Mini-mall, a library, beauty and flower shops, and a small bookstore."

I said, "Knock it off."

We were passing the county jail and Wanda kept on ragging on my birth grounds, "*Good-googity-moo.* Brownsville is coming, coming, coming up. If it get's any better, it might be up there with Mayberry RFD."

All of us laughed at her sarcasm. Threw some laughter into the air.

Wanda said, "I'm hungry y'all. My head's starting to hurt. Feed me 'fore I get mad and hurt somebody."

Home was still green as ever. More people had bricked their country castles. After living shoulder to shoulder in New York, I'd forgotten how much property came with a house. Much had changed. Old buildings had been torn down, nothing built in their places, leaving empty spaces looking like a mouth with some of its teeth yanked out. Buildings had been thrown together in other parts of the city, parts that used to be open pastures. Supermarkets. Convenience stores. Gas stations. Mini-malls.

Where I used to know everybody in town, I didn't recognize anybody. But still everybody we passed made eye contact and waved, followed by a healthy "Good mornin'."

There weren't any impatient drivers blowing their horns and extending the middle finger of love. Everyone did a few miles under the speed limit. No one zoomed by us. I had to readjust my mental barometer. For a while I wouldn't have to worry about muggers, car-jackers, terrorists.

We stopped at a little mom and pop–type fish market. Me and Darrell snacked on some frog legs and crawdads. Wanda ate catfish and spaghetti. We rubbed our ice-cold sodas across our foreheads and chests. We were at a splintering picnic table, under a huge shade tree that housed empty locust shells, pigging out and fighting a losing battle with greedy mosquitoes. One mosquito was so fat it could barely fly. Too heavy for takeoff. Wanda swatted the greedy bastard with her tennis shoe.

Darrell asked, "Where you from?"

"Memphis," Wanda said. "Born at John Gaston like most black folks."

"At least y'all could afford to be born in a hospital," Darrell joked. "We just sorta popped out, I guess."

A couple of elderly men passed, walking slowly down the dirt road on the opposite side of the intersection. One had a wooden walking stick to aid him in his stooped but steady stride. The other was in coveralls and had what looked like a bluish handkerchief he used to wipe the top of his bald head and his face as he strolled. Both stopped at the same time, raised their arms, and waved. I looked around. There was no one else out here. I stood and waved. They smiled, stopped waving, and moved on. Black men distributing peace down to another generation.

A wave of happiness rolled through my body.

I was at home. Back where the foundation of me was built. Right now, New York didn't exist in my mind. In my life. There was no job. No subway to race for. No apartment in Jackson Heights on White Oak. No Kimberly waiting for me with open arms.

She was the only thing I missed.

"I never been out this way." Wanda sipped on her cream soda. "Far as I go is to the racetrack, and that's right across the West Memphis/Arkansas Bridge."

Darrell said, "Don't tell me you ain't never been down on the riverboat to gamble?"

Wanda shook her head. "I ain't got no way to get down to Tunica. And if I did, that's stupid. I ain't going in no casino and lose the little money I ain't got."

I asked, "What people do in Memphis?"

Again Wanda shrugged, said, "Some folks go to First Friday's when they have it at the Peabody or the Crown. I ain't into that. I kinda want to go to the Pink Palace and see that slave ship they got down there. Start doing stuff like going to the Orpheum and seeing plays. One day, I will. Me and Reggie gonna be going to all of that kinda stuff."

I said, "You haven't been to the Orpheum?"

She shook her head, then a little smile came up in the corner of her lips. "My momma took me to movies when it was the Malco. A long, long time ago. When I was in elementary. I still remember that she bought me popcorn. But no, I ain't been since it changed to a theater for plays and stuff."

I asked, "Why haven't you been anywhere?"

Wanda shrugged. "Don't know. Can't afford it, for one. And if I could, I don't wanna go places by myself, for two. Maybe because I don't know nobody anywhere else. Everybody I know lives close by. Everybody I know's either on drugs, or trying to get off drugs. I avoid the ones that's on drugs and don't want to get off and I still don't trust the ones that's trying to get off 'cause they think they too good at running game. But I been there and I can see right through it."

At Oakwood Historical Cemetery, there were a considerable amount of weeds around Mom's tilted headstone. We yanked out what we could by hand. Wanda had some sewing scissors in her purse and she used those. I had soap and water and some SOS pads in a bucket and tried to scrub the thickened mildew off the marker.

"What was she like?" Wanda softly asked. She ran her fingers across the lettering. "Reggie loved her with all his heart."

"She was a petite lady with a big heart and a strong spirit who more than anything wanted her family to stay together," I said without hesitation. "Her three bad-ass boys."

"We would've gotten along real good." Wanda smiled.

I shook my head. "Last thing we'd need was both of you in the house at the same time."

"She loved her nappy-headed boys," Darrell said. "Made sure we had what we needed. She was good. There twenty-four seven."

Wanda repeated, "Twenty-four seven."

Darrell threw in, "We grew up just north of here. North Mc-Clemore Avenue and Thomas Street."

Then Wanda started crying, and it scared me. It wasn't a gradual cry. The gates burst open. A wail that started so fast I didn't know what to do. Wanda dropped her purse and walked back toward the car. I followed. Darrell was on my heels, but I waved him to wait and let me go alone.

When I got to the car, I put my arm around Wanda's thin frame. She squeezed me real tight and struggled for control.

"I told myself I wasn't gonna cry."

"That's okay," I said. "What's wrong?"

Wanda wiped her face. "I lost my baby last year."

"Lost?"

"They took my baby."

"I didn't know you had a baby."

"I have a girl. Niara Amiri." She wiped her face on Martin Luther King and smiled. "They took her from me because I was, you know, sprung. They sent this trifling sister and this white man out to my house because they said one of my neighbors turned me in for neglect, and the next thing I knew, the courts took her and gave her to her lyin' daddy. He had a lawyer and I didn't, so they fucked me over when I got to court. Gave him full custody and took away my visitation rights. Then he moved to some part of Texas. I think they in Dallas. They won't tell me where she is or let me talk to her or nothing. I'm straight now, and they don't care. I'm doing all the things I need to do to get her back. I ain't slipping, but it's so slow, and it's so hard, and I get so lonely and I hate that she's growing up with some other woman she probably calling Momma. Getting all big without me. I missed her birthday two weeks ago. It hurts the most at night, because it's quiet. Too quiet. And she's not running around the house, you know, yanking stuff off the dresser or, you know, just doing little kid stuff. I miss her. I miss combing her hair and dressing her up. She's probably talking and I don't even know what her voice sounds like."

"I didn't know. I'm sorry."

Wanda wiped her face on my T-shirt. "And Reggie's gonna be gone for another two, three weeks. Might be longer than that. The stupid car broke down and I can't afford to get it fixed for a while so I can't go nowhere. I need reliable transportation to go look for a job. And if, I mean, *when* I get a job, I need a way to get to work. Catch twenty-two. I just got too much time on my hands to think about what ain't right with me. I'm trying not to be angry, but I am. I try not to cry, but I do."

"You're family." I gave her a hug. "We'll help."

"Did I just curse?"

"I thank so." I realized my home dialect was slipping back.

She said a frustrated, "Sorry."

We walked back to the grave. Darrell had wandered off a few yards, smoking. He saw us and dropped his cigarette in a bare spot, stomped it out.

"What's going on?" Darrell asked.

"Nothing but the rent," Wanda yelled. She grabbed the scrub brush and began cleaning the marker. "Nothing but the rent."

We fell silent, made ourselves busy with our weed pulling and scrubbing. A few minutes later, Darrell walked away, meandering in the direction of the train tracks on the back side of the cemetery, lighting another cigarette while he looked for our maternal grandparents' graves.

"Thanks," Wanda whispered. "You all right for a narc."

"You're welcome. I think."

After we finished, we said a brief prayer, then stopped at a service station to wash our hands and gas up.

We cruised back into Memphis and rode down Beale Street, parked, walked and looked at the newness that was only new to me. I hadn't been back since Beale had been refurbished. Back when I left the University of Memphis, once I boarded that plane and flew to New York, I thought I'd never come back this way again. It's not that I didn't want to, I just didn't think I'd have the opportunity to. The streets were cobblestoned. The artistic neon signs in front of the buildings gave it a New Orleans, Bourbon Street, Mardi Gras atmosphere. The sun was going down. That gave us some relief from the direct heat. All we had to deal with was the everlasting humidity. It was too early for any entertainment, but not too early for touring.

"If you get a chance, go to Joyce Cobb's place," Wanda said and peeped in the window. "Or BB's club across the street. They be jumping on the weekend. I saw Wendy Moten at Joyce Cobb's. Sister got it going on. She straight."

I kept thinking about how Wanda knew and felt so passionately about the basics of life, but hadn't been anywhere. Geographically speaking. You could buy an education, but you couldn't buy common sense. She had plenty of that. Wanda's paid a high price for her master's degree on the streets. There wasn't a scholarship to finance her through the school of hard knocks.

We were so different, but we're still two sides of the same coin. Two shades of the same color black. Maybe the same shade. I'd been gone too long from where I came from. She needed to get away before it did her in. I think I'd started to forget where I'd come from; she couldn't help but remember.

part four

Secrets

23 Kimberly Chavers

"Kimberly, Peter. I'm still in New Jersey. Before I stop by your attorney, I want to meet with you to talk over the divorce. I would like to get a chance to see your face. If you want to stop running. I've already left two messages, this is the last one. I wish you'd stop this game you're playing."

Against my better judgment, when I got the last irritating message, I decided to call Peter. But I had to call Tony first and get some professional advice. I was surprised that he was in his office at 10 A.M. In his typical poised manner, Tony said it was up to me. As long as I didn't sign anything, it couldn't hurt for me to get a feel for where Peter was coming from. With that in mind, I reluctantly agreed to meet Peter at Starbucks, which is a very public spot on Astor Place in the Village. I couldn't believe I was even talking to that fool again, let alone going to see him.

I groaned in exasperation. It felt like my yesterdays had rushed and caught up with me and become my stressful today. The things I had struggled to forget, the things I had put aside and behind me, had suddenly become as clear and as painful now as they were then.

Before I could get dressed and pull my T-shirt on, the phone rang again. It was my mother. I loved her to death and admired her down to her last strand of royal red hair, but talking to her ran my blood pressure up. She always had a hidden agenda that she'd eventually get around to bringing up. And that was the last thing I needed to entertain right now.

Why did it seem like everybody who was against me, all the people who didn't understand or listen to me, were showing up back to back?

I opened my glass closet door to look for my pantsuit and forced out a sweet "Hi, Mom-Mom."

She had that usual worried sound in her voice. A sound which came from her thinking about me too much. "How are you doing, Kim-Kim?"

"What's wrong now?"

"Nothing's wrong," she said and perked up her tender voice. Mom-Mom always sounded so timid. "We just haven't heard from you since Christmas. You on your cordless phone?"

"I called a few times."

"We didn't get a message."

"I didn't leave one."

She asked, again, "You on that cordless?"

"Yeah." I pulled the antenna all the way out to kill some of the static. It didn't really help, so I pushed the button on the receiver and made it switch to one of the other channels for a better reception. I said, "Mom-Mom? Better?"

"Much."

With the clacking of pots and pans, then the rattling of plates, the echo of water running, I knew she was standing over the double sink washing dishes. Probably glancing out toward Puget Sound while she listened to classical music. She had me on the speaker phone, which meant Daddy wasn't home. I asked, "You and Daddy ever get around to opening the presents I sent you?"

"Yes. You know we did. The silk blouse was lovely. The slacks were nice, too. Next time, get a size twelve. I'm down from a fourteen."

"Diet?"

"Yes. And water aerobics at the Y. Tuesdays and Thursdays."

"That's good." I paused, then tried not to have an attitude when I cleared my throat and asked, "Dad like his present?"

"It was nice." Mom-Mom paused too. "He uses the camera all the time."

"Did you open the Nikon, or did he open it?"

"I opened it."

I paused. "You tell him it was from me?"

"Yes," she forced out. "Kim-Kim, don't start."

"Why doesn't Daddy ever open anything I send him? Why doesn't he ever call to let me know if he likes it or not?"

"He likes it. He likes it a lot."

"Then why won't he call?"

"Because both of you are just alike. Stubborn and bull-headed. You're too much alike. That's why you don't get along."

"It's because he's—" I started, then made a soft growling sound and closed my eyes. "You know how he is."

"Why don't you ever try to talk to him?"

"When I did, he didn't listen. Communication is a two-way street. Whenever I tried to tell him what was bothering me or what was wrong he never—"

"Kim-Kim," she said in her mother tone, the one that used to send me to my room or put me on punishment for what felt like forever. And I knew this was what the phone call was about. It was about the same thing the last call and the call before that were about. The distance between me and my daddy. About me and my mother's husband not getting along. He doesn't understand me and I don't see things his way. We don't feel the need to wear each other down with negative conversation, so we don't talk. His mind still ticked in the "Donna Reed," "Father Knows Best" era, and he thought men should be in control and women had their place. He acted like I was some sort of rebel just because I didn't bite my tongue or buckle under when he pissed me off. I told him, in plain English, that I wasn't in the military, so he didn't outrank me. Whenever I have called him, no matter what my opinion was, no matter what my view was, it seemed like he was playing devil's advocate. He doesn't listen, just runs off his stone-engraved opinion like he was giving orders to a bunch of troops. But Mom-Mom was always playing the middle-person and stepping in, trying to pull us closer together.

"You could call him. He misses you."

"Why won't he tell me, then? When I call, all he does is hand the phone to you. That irks me. Dag. Why does he do that?"

"You'll have to ask him. Why don't you come back to Seattle for a while?"

"I hate Seattle. I hate the nasty weather and I hate the people."

"Your relatives are here."

Mom-Mom was talking about her side of the family. "They're nastier than the weather."

"Kimberly, don't start. I just wanted to hear my favorite artist's voice." Again, she paused. "Why don't you call your father?"

"Because we always have the same argument. He always manages to bring up the fact that I don't get along with his side of the family."

"You don't get along with anyone."

"Hush your face."

We laughed. That brought down the tension a few notches.

I rubbed my hand across my arm, touched a few of my clay-hued freckles, then said, "None of them like me. You know how they treated me. Like I had some kind of disease or something. Like I was a leper."

"I don't want to argue with you. How are your finances?"

"Fine."

"If you need some money—"

"No, I'm fine. If things get tight again, I'll let you know. And I'll pay you back the money I borrowed last year."

"No. The money was a gift. Why don't you get a smaller place?"

"I've got too much stuff."

"Put some in storage."

"In New York? No way."

We turned the conversation away from family stuff and started talking about the soaps. Wanting the old Bo back on "One Life to Live" was our main topic. We were giggling and yacking like two girlfriends who missed each other. I loved it when we chit-chatted like that. I loved Mom-Mom so much. I loved my daddy too, but it wasn't on the same level. Maybe because we never opened up and had the same type of honest dialogue. And the moment he opened his mouth, I did have a tendency to expect the worst and get defensive.

I told Mom-Mom about the magazines I'd done some work for, then let her know I'd been doing much better, selling more work for higher prices out of Clair's shop.

"Clair's? Isn't that your boyfriend's sister?"

"Me and Eric broke up last year. And Clair's his stepsister. They don't get along."

"Good. I didn't care for his voice. No character. He rubbed me the wrong way."

"Oh, now you tell me. What kind of mother are you?"

"I did tell you."

"When?"

"Remember when I told you if you brought him home to visit I'd put you in separate rooms?"

We laughed. I told her that Jordan and I were going to the Bahamas, and that a few weeks ago Jordan and I had gone to Planet Hollywood to the premiere of Bon Jovi's 45-minute video/movie, that we'd met Bruce Willis, Demi Moore, and the Italian actress Annabelle what's-her-face. I couldn't remember her last name, and Mom-Mom was trying to remember who she was. Mom-Mom was a movie buff.

She asked, "What movie was Annabelle in?"

I said, "*Jungle Fever*. What's funny?"

"*Jungle Fever*. You could've starred in that one."

We laughed.

I let the laughter fade before I said a solemn "Guess what?"

I told her that I'd finally contacted Peter. Told her how I'd found him, where he was living. Let her know I was going to meet him so we could talk, maybe sign the papers and get this divorce underway. Mom-Mom talked about how she'd divorced her first husband, then met Daddy the night she was out celebrating it being finalized. Eight months later she was married again. We talked about that for a few minutes. Her tone was that of my overprotective mother again.

She asked, "Why does Peter have to come all the way out there?"

"He was going to be out here anyway. It's a lucky coincidence."

"Lucky? Strange, yes. But I wouldn't think that it was lucky. Be careful."

"Okay, Mom-Mom."

Before she hung up, Mom-Mom said in a soft and caring voice, "Call your father. He'll be back home from Canada tomorrow."

I softened too. I asked, "Fishing?"

"Yes." Her voice smiled. Then she sang, "We're not getting any younger, you know."

She always said that to make me feel bad. It did. With a word, she could make me feel good or bad, be quiet or babble. I mimicked a childish, "Okay, Mom-Mom."

I caught a taxi to the subway, rode the E train to the Lexington Avenue station, transferred to the six, and got off at Union Square. Where I was going was at the next stop, Astor Place, but I had to make sure this coincidence wasn't some sort of setup. I walked the rest of the way. I wanted to see him before he saw me. Plus I had to stop by Barnes & Noble to meet with my protector. After talking to Mom-Mom, I felt it would be best if I had Kinikki come out from her Upper West Side brownstone and meet me down here at the bookseller, then trek over with me. I had a bad feeling, and I didn't want to journey into this meeting alone.

Kinikki was over thirty minutes late. By the time we made it to Starbucks, I hoped Peter would have given up, left Manhattan, and headed for anybody's airport. I was late and I didn't care.

Even though the place was half-filled with customers—half of them college-aged couples who were touching and feeling each other as they stood in line, and a couple of same-sex couples who were doing the same—my soon-to-be ex-husband was the first person I saw through the tinted glass window. He was in the window at a wooden table. I felt nothing when I saw him. I looked right through my own reflection into his face, and I almost didn't recognize him with the thinning hairline and full beard. He looked like a difference version of himself. He looked nicer, better with the years, but I didn't let my eyes show I noticed. Anything positive would be a weakness. Plus, I knew how he was. I maintained my hard business eyes. He checked his watch then dropped the *Village Voice* he was reading and adjusted his wire-rim glasses as the door opened. He was at a table under a ceiling fan, legs crossed, with a cup of coffee and the last of what looked like a blueberry muffin in front of him. Jeans. Sandals. Ugly Hawaiian shirt people in Hawaii wouldn't wear. I wouldn't even blow my nose on that hideous creation. People in New York wore just about anything, but he was stretching the limits of creativity. I know he didn't recognize me at first because I'm at least thirty pounds lighter than I was back then. I don't walk with my eyes held down anymore. Thanks to my dermatologist, my skin had cleared up. Plus, the last time he saw me my hair was dyed an awful, sooty black and styled in a tomboyish page boy. A hairstyle he picked out for me. Back in that life, I'd barely seen the inside of a beauty shop, dressed plain, lived very homely. Now, I felt funky. The mood I was in wasn't the best, so I'd dressed in oversized ripped jeans, an oversized T-shirt with a picture of a hip-hop Bugs Bunny and Tazmanian Devil on the front and back. My cross-trainers weren't laced. Kinikki had on a red and white Nike sweatsuit, the jacket wrapped around her waist.

A lot of work was being done outside of the coffee shop, and a scaffolding as wide as the twenty feet of sidewalk was overhead and shadowed us, but Peter twitched when his eyes recognized me. My insides bubbled. He was staring at the braids in my hair. He stood. I pulled off my shades and put them into my purse.

He had the nerve to smile like he was happy to see me. "Kimberly."

"Peter," I said as plain as I could.

This was a bad déja vù. Without a word, Kinikki swayed past the counter and went over to the only empty table on the other side of the room. We'd already talked about what I wanted her to do. I wanted her in the room, but I didn't want her right up under me to hear my business, especially if it became too ugly. Or too specific.

This coffee shop was peaceful. People weren't loud and the acoustics helped the conversations carry. No band played music to drown out wandering words. I would've asked him to step outside near the entrance to the subway and talk, but it was still too muggy. The air felt like a dragon's breath. And with all the exhaust coming from the vehicles, it smelled just as deadly. I needed to feel the cool air on my sweaty forehead. And besides, I didn't want any of the curious people I knew to pass by and see me with him, maybe stop on their way out of the subway for an eye-opening introduction.

His freckled face wore a huge surprise at the different me he saw. He said, "You want to talk here or go somewhere else?"

"Here's fine," I said, and opened my purse to take out my wallet. The overwhelming aroma of the pastries made my stomach rumble. I hadn't eaten since breakfast and I was getting a hunger headache. "Why did you want to meet with me first?"

"Want me to get you something to drink? Maybe a muffin?"

"I can afford it."

His eyes were creepy-crawling all over me. I felt his eyeballs on my skin when I went to the counter and bought two heated blueberry muffins. At first I thought I might be worried about nothing, but when I turned around, he was staring at me. Not smiling, just staring and bobbing his head. I ignored him.

I placed a square butter substitute on each saucer, then took one to Kinikki, just to reassure Peter I wasn't alone.

When I sat back down, he stopped frowning at Kinikki long enough to ask me, "Who's your friend?"

"A *friend*." I nibbled my muffin, used my pacing to show him how insignificant he was. "Now, what's this crap you told my attorney? That you think I might owe you some money for your investment in my career?"

"Don't act like you don't know."

"Don't act like I do."

"When you ran off, you took the money out of the savings account and used it to start this whatever you're doing."

"Are you speaking in reference to my career?"

"Okay. Career."

"I withdrew less than half of the money. Not even a third."

"Six thousand dollars."

"I earned it. You made me quit my job at Dairy Queen. You wouldn't let me work and I wasn't going to stay trapped—*wait*. I'm not going to have this argument."

Peter crossed his legs and readjusted his heavy, six-foot frame so he could lean forward. I leaned away and took another bite of my muffin. The muffins here were great. Made with real blueberries and were a dream, especially with the butter. But I couldn't even taste it. I was going through emotions while going through the motions. I glanced at his left hand. At least the won't-let-go bastard wasn't still wearing the wedding band he'd bought for himself.

He grinned. "How was Africa?"

I slyly looked over at Kinikki. She was watching me and nibbling her muffin. She mouthed some words, asked if I was okay; I ran my fingernails over my braids and sent her a brief nod.

This time he laughed it out. "How was Africa?"

"Who told you I went to Africa?"

"Grapevine. Was it a secret?"

"Not the point. That was after I finished college. How did you know? Have you been in contact with my family?"

"Nope. I ran into one of your cousins in San Francisco."

"Who?"

"Mark."

I stopped chewing. "Mark Chavers?"

"Yep. He told me after you left whatever college you went to in Seattle, you sold everything, packed up, and ran to Africa."

"I didn't run. I visited."

"Heard you were in Ethiopia for a while." Peter asked, "You find what you were looking for? How did they treat you? Evidently they had some influence on you."

"Influence? What do you mean by that?"

"Your hairstyle, your clothes, your choice of friends. Looks like you're having some sort of identity crisis."

I snapped, but kept my voice low. "Are you going to sign the fucking papers or not?"

He laughed.

I said, "I paid for my own education."

"With the money you stole. You owe. I want my money back."

"It was a joint account. We were married."

"Were?" He fingered his empty ring finger. Rubbed it like he thought that mini-shackle that people call a ring was still there. He said, "Legally, we still are."

"Physically *were*. Psychologically *never* were."

I think he almost sulked. He uncrossed his legs, crossed them again, then sipped his coffee. Tried to look so in control. But I understood men; they always try to maintain a facade of being harder than iron, stronger than stone, but they're more fragile than a rose.

His voice had stiffened when he said, "You abandoned the marriage and embezzled the money."

"Is that what this nonsense is about?"

"It's not nonsense. You stole from me."

I shook my head. "You should've talked to a better attorney. There's nothing for you to take from me."

"Well, if you knew all that, why did you meet me?"

"Because I want this over ASAP so I can get on with my life. Peter, sign the damn papers."

"Under one condition."

"What?"

"Go to dinner with me."

"*What?*"

"Go out to dinner with me. Tomorrow. Me. You. And none of your friends glowering over my shoulder."

"Why are you playing this game?"

He sipped his drink. "Dinner and we'll call it even."

My beeper vibrated and stopped me from rattling off a series of four-letter words. I thought it might be Tony's office calling me to see how this was going. At first I thought it had a prefix code of 911 for emergency, but it had the area code 901. Memphis. And the same exchange 946 number Jordan had left on my answering machine. I still hadn't talked to him since he left and I couldn't call him right now. His calling made the urgency of this situation go off the scale.

I gulped air, felt like I was about to choke on all the love I had for a man called SmooVe, then let that feeling be my rock to shield me when my words snorted out. "I'll tell you what, you sign the preliminary papers, then I'll go to dinner with you."

"If I sign the papers, how do I know you'll go?"

"If I go to dinner first, how do I know you'll sign?"

He laughed.

I picked up my backpack-style purse, screeched my straight-backed chair across the tiled floor, and stood up. People looked. He sipped his drink. Kinikki gathered her belongings and stood up too.

"Leaving so soon?" He tapped his watch. "You've only been here ten minutes. We have a lot of catching up to do."

"Sign the papers. Have Tony call me to confirm. Then we'll meet for a *business* dinner. Otherwise, have a good life."

I walked off.

"Kimberly." That was Kinikki calling my name. She caught up with me. "Slow down before you trip on something."

"Is he watching me?"

Kinikki peeped back, then said, "Definitely. Hard and long."

"Bastard. I see his reflection gawking at me."

I didn't go downstairs to the subway, because I didn't want to take a chance of having him follow me. I flagged down a taxi and decided to ride a few streets and get on a train somewhere else. Inside the cab, Kinikki had an expression of surprise on her face. I knew what she meant, but I didn't ask and she didn't say. When she finally parted her lips and let a few words out, I cut her off and said, "Thanks for coming down with me."

"So." Kinikki pulled her warm-up top from around her waist and laid it across her lap. "Dat was your husband from way back when, huh?"

"Yeah."

"Interesting."

"That was it."

"Married."

"Unfortunately."

"Just when I think I know you"—she bobbed her head—"I find out more 'bout you. You are more complex than I would've imagined. More colorful than all of your paintings combined. I have never seen you behave in such a wretched fashion."

"Forgive me."

"Forgiven."

"And keep this between us. Damn, that fucker pisses me off."

"Watch your mouth. Girl, watch your mouth and hold your temper." Kinikki put her hand on top of mine. "Calm yourself down before your explode."

Kinikki bailed out at the subway. She wanted to get home in time to meet her husband for lunch. She was trying to meet hers, I was trying to delete mine.

"You getting out?" she asked.

I smiled a little. "No. But thanks for coming down."

She winked. "Dat's what friends are for. You be easy and call me if you need to talk."

"Okay."

"Call me even if you don't need to talk."

We laughed. Mine was nervous; hers was worried. She kissed my cheek and wiped away her lipstick. Her voice sounded like nothing but friendship as she told me it would be all right, which was damn easy for her to say because her house was always in order. Mine hadn't been correct in years.

I wasn't ready to go back home to nothing, so I went over on Park Avenue and got out at 46th. Went into the Bank of New York and deposited a check, withdrew a few dollars so I wouldn't be broke. Then I walked and walked, passed by trucks and cars and sucked up and choked on the exhaust from bus after bus. I was being assaulted by that New York heat that made the murder rate go up during the summer months. It was all over my sweaty, PMS-ridden body. A Mercedes-Benz dealer was across the six lanes of madness at East 56th, and I wished I could afford a nice C-class car with air. Wished I could afford to pay for the parking. And I was hungry. But I didn't want to stop to eat, so I grabbed a hot dog from a vendor and kept on walking and thinking.

My stomach cramped a little while I was at Raspberry Sport, looking at shoes. I'd walked all the way to 57th and Lexington. And after I tried on shoes for an hour and bought nothing, I went back out into the street and kept moving. Tried to sweat what I was experiencing out of my system. My anxiety and I had made it past the teenagers hanging out in front of P.S. 59 and were almost at the Queensboro Bridge before I flagged down another taxi.

I told the taxi driver to take me back toward Times Square. I'd do some shopping, catch a movie, anything that kept me from going home.

Three movies and a meal at Sbarro's passed before I headed home in the darkness. Everything was a blur because I was thinking about too much of nothing. I hiked up the three flights to my warm apartment, grabbed my cold bottle of Evian, opened the last of my M&Ms, and checked my answering machine. I had two messages from Peter. Bastard. Then to top the lunacy off, Eric had called. Punk. He said he saw me and Kinikki getting into a cab, and wanted to know if I wanted to meet him for some drinks. Before I could unfasten the top button on my sweat-rimmed jeans, the phone rang again. That pissed me off.

I snapped, "What?"

"Whu'sup? You on the phone?"

"Jordan? This you, SmooVe?"

"Yeah, it's me. Get my page this afternoon?"

"I left my beeper and I just walked in," I lied without hesitating, and felt the duplicities building, stacking on top of each other like straws on a camel's back. "What time is it?"

"Almost ten."

My clock said that it was ten P.M. too. And I knew Memphis was on a different time zone. From the way Jordan talked about Brownsville, it might even be in a different time.

I asked, "Where are you?"

"New York, baby."

My chest tightened and it felt like someone had drained all the oxygen from the room. "You're back home?"

"Yeah. I paged you when I was on the way to the airport in Memphis. I'm here. Want some company?"

I blinked, hesitated. Found some air. Heart palpitated like it had never done before. Yeah, that was nine hours ago when he paged me. I wanted to see him, would love to get caressed and pampered and licked up and down real bad, would love to play tantalizing love games with him until he couldn't stand it, but too much was going on inside my head. And I didn't want Peter calling back while Jordan was over here. Not before I found a way to tell him about my situation. On the other hand, I didn't know if I should tell him because I didn't know which way this was going.

I tugged one of my braids and bit my lip. "Can I come over there tomorrow? I need to finish up something I'm working on."

He paused. "Sure."

A lot of disappointment echoed through the phone before we hung up. That hurt. My body was in the middle of a serious emotional craving, especially since I knew Jordan was so close, but my mind didn't want to be bothered with anybody, regardless.

After I turned on the air and set it on high, I stripped down to my panties and threw my bra into a corner on top of the other three or four. I hadn't cleaned up around here in days because I'd been stressed and racing in and out of the city. Plus, I'd been spending so much time at Jordan's that I hadn't really been here long enough to take out a broom and a mop. Floors were starting to look dull. Dust had settled on everything. Fingerprints were on almost all of the glass. The plants needed water before they shriveled and died. But I'd get to all of that tomorrow. Maybe.

No, I'd do it tonight. Right now. I'd clean and think.

The phone rang again. It was Peter.

I sat up and asked a hostile, "What do you want?"

"Are we doing dinner?"

"This is blackmail."

"It's just dinner between old friends."

"We've never been friends."

"May I come by your place to pick you up?"

"No."

"How are we going to do this, Mrs. Stenson?"

"Chavers."

"It's your call."

I wanted to poke my eyes out and punish myself. I said, "Meet me."

"Where?"

"I'll let you know in the morning."

I hung up without saying bye. I didn't even know why I was doing this. I mean, Jordan and I were dating, and for what it was worth, that was all I could call it. Dating. We never said we loved each other. But in some ways we acted like it. So, if actions spoke louder than words, they were shouting it out every time he saw me, howling passion out every time I saw him. When I gazed at him, I felt my emotions churning in the bottom part of my stomach and warming me from the inside out. I wanted the love thing, but then again, I wasn't sure if it fit into my life right now.

Like Kinikki said, looking at rings was just *looking* at rings. Shopping and buying are two different things.

The phone rang again.

I snatched it off the receiver, said my calmest, "Why are you calling back, Peter?"

"You all right?"

"Jordan?"

"Yeah. Who's Peter?"

"An artist friend of mine and Kinikki. What're you doing?"

"You have time for dinner tomorrow?"

"Kinikki and I have some business in the Village tomorrow."

"Just checking." He paused, then I heard the disappointment in his voice when he said, "Call me when you get a minute."

"Sure."

We hung up. I picked up the broom and looked at my floors. Shit. Forget it. I dropped the broom, picked up the phone and called Jordan back.

I said, "Can I come over?"

He laughed, but it rang out like confusion and bewilderment.

I was hopping out of a cab before I knew it. When he opened the door, before I absorbed any of the coolness and floated into the fading potpourri smell of his place, he gave me a generous hug. Kissed me like he missed me.

He said, "I had a dream about you."

I smiled and dropped my overnight bag on the floor.

He covered my eyes. When I opened them, he was standing in front of me holding a colorful shopping bag with a picture of the Memphis Pyramid on its sides. He had a sackful of presents. A beautiful soft, light blue and gray sweatsuit from The University of Memphis. A cup and two T-shirts from Beale Street. A denim shirt from B.B. King's blues club. A card with a cartoon picture of a couple kissing. At the bottom he wrote, "For Kimberly, Just Because."

Inside, I started crying. Everything rushed in. Guilt was stomping on top of my rising mood swings. Jordan was trying to find out what was wrong when I hurried by him to the bathroom and closed the door. Put my back against the wall and baptized my head in my hands. My nose clogged, became stuffed with the mucus of sadness and anger, made me feel so silly.

"What's wrong?" he said from the other side.

My emotions had more strength than my resistance, pushed my thoughts out of my mouth and I said, "Love you."

Without hesitation, he said a warm "Love you too."

Oh, great. Damn. I hated that he had said those words. When you said those words, you had so much responsibility to live up to. There was too much going on in my mind. I should be at home working and I should be trying to clear up things between me and my dad and I should call and curse Peter out and I should tell Eric to stop dialing my number or I'll move my work from their gallery and I should make love to Jordan all night.

I said, "Will you hold me tonight?"

"You want me to?"

Don't ask me why, but I didn't like his answer. I was about to use the bathroom, but I looked down at the toilet seat. It was up. That irked me. I'd asked him over and over to be considerate, and still it had been up since December. How could he love me if he couldn't remember to leave the damn toilet seat down? It was a damn deathtrap. I know this is his apartment, and we don't live together, but that's not the point. I didn't appreciate it when I almost fell in and drowned. And how many times would I have to ask him to stop buying colored toilet paper? I had already politely told him to get plain white paper, or any damn paper without infectious dye in it. And of all things, he had bought a roll of cheap, thin one-ply that felt like fine-grade sandpaper. Cardboard was softer than the stuff he had bought. Plus, he never put the damn paper on the roller right, always put it on upside down. Toilet paper should pull over the top.

I pulled myself together, but my emotions clicked into high gear and I monsooned out of the bathroom, slid by him and his worried face, picked up my overnight bag, and headed for the door.

Jordan looked as confused as I felt.

"Jordan, I'll call you, okay?"

I was gone before he could answer.

24 Jordan Greene

Kimberly was great, but so was J'nette when I first met her. They all were. That's what I was thinking when I was on the way to the subway early in the A.M. Those thoughts drowned out the rattling of the train. I wasn't due back to work for two days, but after a restless night, I decided to go in and hunt down a moment of normalcy.

A little before seven-thirty, I found my buddy Solomon down in the cafeteria at a table by himself, yawning and munching on a bagel. I grabbed my own cup of coffee and chocolate twist doughnut. Even though eggs and bacon permeated the atmosphere, the building smelled like yesterday's air. The ventilation was malfunctioning. The air-conditioning was out of whack, so some floors were too cold and others were too warm. The cafeteria was freezing, but they had opened the side doors for a warm-air/cold-air exchange.

So far, nobody knew I'd come back early. I didn't have any paperwork to get done. No meetings to attend. Nothing to do but sit with my buddy and stew in my thoughts about Kimberly.

We sipped java and I told Solomon about all the crap that happened in Memphis—Wanda, Darrell, and Reggie.

Solomon laughed a little. "You get your side X-rayed?"

"It's not hurting. Most of the blow hit my stomach." I pinched myself. "I'm tightening up, but I guess I have a little ways to go."

White- and blue-collar employees filtered into the cafeteria, pushed through the turnstiles, grabbed fat Styrofoam cups of coffee and super-sweet doughnuts. Others were out on the patio, chain-smoking themselves conscious. Caffeine, nicotine, and sugar. Most would snap your head off if they didn't get a dose of all three. We all looked like professional addicts getting legal fixes.

Sometimes I wondered what was the difference between our legal-
ized drug problems and my brother Reggie's illegal substance
problem.

At first, I had wanted to vent to Solomon about Kimberly, because he had a way and always seemed to understand women better than I ever would, which was why he'd never had a problem
with them. Last night had me feeling uneasy, especially after she
didn't sound too happy to hear my voice, then called me Peter.

Our suit coats were draped on the backs of the two empty
chairs. Solomon had flipped his dark blue tie over his shoulder; I'd
done the same with mine.

After I lollygagged about Memphis, I figured I'd switch the conversation over to him, then work it back to me and Kimberly. I
asked, "Have you and Zoe set that date yet?"

"Nope." He sighed, then sat back and tongue-scratched the
roof of his mouth. He rubbed his eyes. Enthusiasm about Miss
Right was nowhere to be seen. Or heard. He opened his briefcase,
took out a plastic bottle with tiny red pills. Allergies were flar-
ing up.

I asked, "What's she waiting on?"

"I don't know. She's sorta hinting around about a spring
wedding, but she ain't made no kinda effort to do nothing." He
popped two pills, washed them down with coffee. "She hooked up
with her girlfriend and went down to D.C. for the weekend."

"For what?"

"Her and Toni went to see J'nette."

I stalled, waited for him to keep talking, but he didn't. I said,
"Haven't heard her name in a while."

"Get used to it. J'nette might be coming back."

I hadn't heard from J'nette since the cab ride from the abortion
clinic. Since she went through the family un-planning. And since
all the sistas knew about Kimberly, none of them had been friendly
with me. Cordial and abrupt in passing, but not friendly. They had
their girlfriend-thing going, where if J'nette was mad at me, all of
them wore the same angry face.

I asked, "Moving or visiting?"

"Moving back up with Toni. But she might be rooming with
Zoe until Toni finds a bigger place."

Wrinkle-faced, flowered dress–wearing Edna Riordian wobbled in. At the moment of eye contact, she huffed, turned, and left the cafeteria. Back in January, the first day I came back to work after the holiday break, the Ethics Committee had a couple of its reps call me into their second floor office for a little surprise meeting. They had a sista and a white guy "interview" me about some "concerns which had been brought to our attention." I guess they figured the sista would have more of a way and would be able to get more out of me. They let her do the talking while the white guy sat in silence and took notes, which was pointless and a waste of a good ninety minutes, because with no witnesses and no photos, it turned out to be my honest word against Edna's bodacious lies. Like the Michael Jackson scandal, minus the payoff.

We blended with the crowd, headed for the elevators. Solomon was off on a mental tangent. He kept touching his face, his moustache. A vein popped up and down in his forehead.

I nudged him, "Everything all right between you and Zoe?"

"Everything's straight up and down like six o'clock."

"Why the long face?"

He grinned. "Tired. My allergies are creeping up on me."

Solomon straightened his coat and broadened his smile. He was still fidgety, bouncing his case against one leg while his fingers strummed the other. Something deeper than what was living on the surface was bothering him. Women had a way of doing that to a man. They had a talent for wrecking rising spirits.

Kimberly had to be mad because I didn't take her to Memphis. I offered, she refused, but maybe she wanted me to push the issue, show her where she fit in my life.

At my desk, before I had a moment to flip through the week's "while you were out" notes, Rodger came in.

"Greene." He smiled and shook my hand. "You're back early."

"Made it back last night."

He smiled, but his mood wasn't happy. He said, "Did the funeral home receive the flowers we sent?"

I nodded. "They were beautiful."

He motioned toward his office and said, "Greene."

I followed him to his office. I thought he was going to say he knew I didn't go to the funeral, and my not going was another company violation. After we closed the door, he sat in his chair and twirled his Chinese balls in his hands. Rodger kept his voice low and told me CompSci had lost the last contract. After we were beat out by Boeing, management went into a frenzy, shuffling staff to save assets until they found the light of day.

But it was always dark at night.

Rodger slid me a chart, a corporate structure diagram with yesterday's date inked on the bottom. CONFIDENTIAL was stamped in the upper right corner. Somebody had advanced him the chart as a favor. This draft was the result of many days of midnight thinking and spelled out the interim solution.

My position and responsibilities were being transferred to another department. And I would have to charge my time to a burden account. A buffer account for inactivity during employment.

Which really didn't matter. He told me I'd be getting laid off in a few days. Rodger's position would be dissolved in less than a month. One of the higher-ups was demoting himself back down to our division, bumping Rodger out into the streets.

We sat in silence. Stared out at the city.

I said, "Thanks, Rodger."

He nodded. He had no words to give me.

Back at my office, I looked around at my territory. Malcolm's told-you-so smile, Martin in his cell, and everything else would be dropping from the walls. Sadness at the inevitable rose in my chest, but hey, it was my fault for getting too comfortable in the first place. I needed a change of pace and place anyway.

I called Kimberly. No answer. I checked my answering machine. No messages. I called Solomon, told him what was going down. His area had made it through this fiasco unaltered. After a few minutes of moping, then redoing my resume, I went to the lobby, picked up a *Post* and *Times*, flipped through the classifieds. Called a couple of contacts in New York, New Jersey, and Chicago to see if the fish were biting. Nothing today. But that didn't stop me from burning up the fax machine with my resume, didn't stop me from getting online and shipping my credentials across the Internet.

In the warm evening, I left the building, followed the stream of flitting employees. Solomon was leaving at the same time.

I asked, "Hungry?"

"Yeah. Let's go grub. My treat."

We bought a fistful of tokens to last us for a while, rode the subway for a few stops, got off, hiked down a side street loaded with nail shops, places to get hot bagels, and a group of Asians doing sketches of tourists for twenty dollars. Solomon was silent as we passed by Jacqueline Kennedy Onassis High School for International Careers. We stopped at the Near and Far Chinese restaurant. We were going to go to the Pig 'N Whistle, but that place was too crowded, and I was starving. Anxiety does that to a brother. I gobbled down shrimp-fried rice; Solomon had a combination plate and spent the whole time picking over it. For somebody who ran his mouth nonstop, he was damn quiet. Hadn't said two high-energy words since we left work. I guess he didn't know what to say. I'd even changed up the conversation, made it generic, talked about how it surprised me that high schools were stuck in the middle of blocks like the one we were on, right in the thick of things in Times Square and on Park Avenue. He didn't even nod. He was glancing out the window toward the tourists on a double-decker Premium Outlet Shopping bus.

Solomon hurried out about six, said he had to shoot home and meet Zoe because he had promised to take her to a movie.

He hopped on the subway and headed in the direction of Harlem; I went back down to the strip. Walked, blended with the people, and looked like I belonged. Since the mayor had gotten Disney to move one of its stores on the square, with places like the Times Square Brewery and about a million other better class shops on each block all taking the place of most of the XXX places, the city looked good. There were a few peep shows and nude girl places on the strip, but there weren't as many as ten years ago. No, today New York was a nice experience. Especially since the chill of winter wasn't nipping at my fingers. After I called Kimberly again and didn't get an answer, I flagged a cab to see if the driver would stop. It pulled over before I got my arm all the way up. I chuckled and waved it away. I did that trick three or four times before I went into Virgin Megastore and blew some more time, bought En Vogue's latest CD. There used to be four soul-filled sisters in their group, but there were only three of them now. I guess they'd been downsized too. Damn budget cuts are everywhere. That made me laugh hard as hell.

After I bought En Vogue, Wu Tang, and *The Best of John Coltrane*, I took the E train back to Jackson Heights. On the subway, I found a hard orange seat in a box filled with people who didn't speak or make eye contact. I was jerked when the train took off, jerked so hard I bumped shoulders with the people. The train was clattering and clacking down the tracks. I was thinking about those old black men down in Brownsville, men who stopped in the heat and spoke to me from a distance.

I spoke to a few people. They didn't speak back. I didn't care. I'd done my part.

As soon as I made it home, the phone rang. I was dancing because I had to pee real bad, but I answered the phone first, hoped it was Kimberly. It was Zoe. She was looking high and low for Solomon. She thought he was hanging out with me, so I didn't tell her any different. I was just watching his back.

She asked, "Has Solomon gotten there yet?"

"His allergies were acting up. He stopped to get some medicine."

She sounded worried: "Tell him to try that Dime-a stuff."

"All right."

"At lunch he told me you two were hooking up after work." She paused. Left an awkward space. Enough space for me to suffocate. She finally said, "He said he was going home with you."

"He's not here yet."

Another pause before she said, "Well, have him call me."

"Okay." Something else was on my mind. "Solomon told me you went down to D.C. for the weekend."

"Yeah. We brought J'nette back. Solomon didn't tell you?"

"He mentioned you went to D.C." It was my turn to leave an awkward space. "How's she doing?"

"You talked to her since she left Jersey?"

"Nope."

"She'll probably call you tonight."

"I didn't want her to call. I was just asking."

"All right," she said. Some animosity was in her tone. I didn't know if that attitude was directed at me, or if it was something she was banking for Solomon. Maybe she didn't want me dipping in J'nette's business. Zoe did a good job at keeping the strained friendships separate. She continued, "Tell Solomon to call his fiancée as soon as he steps a foot in your door."

When Zoe hung up, I dialed Solomon's home number. His answering machine kicked on, the beep kicked in, and I left a message: "Whu'sup? Man, Zoe just called over here looking for you. I was just covering your tracks and watching your back. Give me a ring as soon as—"

His answering machine cut off. Somebody picked up the phone. It was Zoe. Damn damn damn. She had called me from his house and was standing over the machine when the message played.

Zoe asked, "Why you have to watch his back and cover his tracks?"

25 Kimberly Chavers

Around lunchtime, I met Peter at Tony's Manhattan office and we signed the papers. After I signed another document saying that the divorce was my treat, which now should be damn minimal, he didn't give me any hassle. Actually, while we were in Tony's office, Peter was professional and polite. Now I was on a six-month countdown to sanity. Tonight I could talk to Jordan and tell him I was in the process of getting divorced, which sure in hell sounded better than still being married and separated.

Before the ink dried, Peter's attitude changed. He switched into a chummy-pally mode and put his hand on the shoulder of my blouse, felt obligated to remind me of my promise for dinner. I shifted, pushed his hand off me, then told him I'd meet him on 34th Street in front of Macy's. At eight P.M. Sharp. I let him know I'd wait until 8:01, then I was leaving by plane, train, or automobile.

Outside of Tony's office on Sixth Avenue, before I could stop a cab and leave him on the heat of the sidewalk, he called my name, "Kim."

I gritted my teeth and cut my eyes at him.

He smirked. "I mean, Kimberly."

I released a sigh of exasperation. "What?"

"Dress nice."

"Excuse me?"

"And leave the attitude on your doorstep."

"Excuse me?"

He repeated himself. I ignored his wink and grin, flipped him the bird, stepped away from him, and dove into my cab.

After I got home and thought about it, and especially since I had nothing to gain from going, I was tempted to stand Peter up. But I had a bad habit of fulfilling my promises, no matter what. I think I inherited that from my military-minded father. My sense of discipline and obligation. Besides, this might be painful, uncalled for, very uncomfortable, but it wouldn't kill me.

I showered, put on some Perry Ellis, dressed in my figure-boasting, magenta business suit, so I wouldn't display a single swatch of flesh, and a sleeveless white cotton blouse from The Gap. Washed my hair and put in Frizz Ease so it would be wavy. The suit was light, so I shouldn't get too warm. I wanted to look so *fine*, echo so much maturity, femininity, and splendor that Peter sat across from me and suffered for all the years gone by. Plus, when I left dinner, I was cabbing it straight to Jordan's to try to get a grip on the rest of my life. That's who I was dressing for. That's who I'd be undressing for, forever and a day.

I grabbed my purse, dropped in my can of pepper spray just in case Peter's wandering eyes turned into roaming fingers. I wished I had a stun gun or a harpoon or something.

Before I headed out to this last supper, I played back my messages. Jordan had called.

2 6 Kimberly Chavers

Hours had passed. Kimberly had been knocked unconscious. Her heated body felt the new bruises on her face from where she had been beaten and thrown on the gritty asphalt. At first she found peace inside the eerie silence. Then the noise came back. Screams were still inside her head. They wouldn't stop. Rage was there. Her mind was moving like a monsoon.

The sounds of the outside world stomped through her ears, snailed around her head, and blended with her slumber. A car's horn blowing. Voices came and went. Somebody was talking and laughing to somebody who was laughing and talking. Hard footsteps passed with a brisk rhythm—*clickity, clop, clickity, clop.*

A siren cried in the distance, grew louder as it got closer, then faded as it moved away again. Then, what terrified Kimberly came back. The painful moan crawling from inside of her. She felt hands on her throat. In her half-sleep, half-dream she thought she saw a shadow with its thin arms stretched out, its hands firm on her windpipe, tightening on her throat. She used her nails, clawed at the shadow's face. She couldn't reach it. The shadow's hair bounced. Her eyes widened; her insides were coming up. The shadow was strangling her.

Slowly, what felt like a cold death twisted into an unwelcome warmth and reminded her of a frustrating life. The numbness turned into a mean stiffness and harsh pain. She coughed herself awake. Wicked convulsions had taken over her body as she lay on the hard, piss-damp ground, on her back, choking on her own saliva. Killing herself.

She gagged, groaned, rolled from her back to her stomach, and pushed her aching arms between her face and the ground. After what felt like a lifetime of choking and puking out the fluids that kept splashing back into her face and fallen hair, Kimberly caught her breath and pulled the tangled hair back from her face and out of the rolling sweat. Under the half moon and motionless stars, under the Big Dipper and Orion, she felt the indentations from the debris-ridden ground. Tiny pebbles had stuck deep into her skin. The insides of her mouth felt ragged. Loose flesh hurt and tasted like something vulgar had moved inside, mated, and plastered its offspring from wall to wall.

Her lip felt tender, throbbed and hurt when she licked the edge of her mouth. Without a mirror, she could tell it had bubbled, swollen. She tongued across her teeth and licked the inside of her mouth. It tasted coarse, like copper. Blood. She tried to spit, but the blood, saliva, and sweat had mixed into something obscene and pasty.

She listened for noise, for any sound to let her know if she was alone, or being stood over for prey. She heard jingling, winced, then realized the noise came from the bracelets on her arm. She couldn't slow her breathing and her legs shook.

Kimberly managed to pull her bare feet back up under her body. She dragged herself over to the brick wall and tried to pull herself upright. Her eyes fought to adjust to the darkness, to the dim light from the high-rise buildings in the distance. She tried to arrange herself, to pull her ripped blouse back to a decent form. In her mind, she filtered through her jumbled thoughts.

Dizzy. Disoriented. She tried to remember who she was, and mumbled *Kimberly Kimberly Kimberly* like she was fighting to convince herself that Kimberly was who she was.

Visions of Oakland, San Antonio, Germany, San Bernadino, and Ethiopia went by. But she knew she was in New York. But was she in Upper Manhattan? Lower? The Village? Jackson Heights?

Her head throbbed when she raised it; she touched the spot in the back where it hurt the most. There, her hair had bunched and was sticking to the damp spot. Then she remembered being hit in the head. Falling. She wondered how much time had passed, how long she had been sprawled out, unconscious and vulnerable.

A warm breeze came. A sudden blast of air grabbed her skin, pulled her blouse. Her mind told her she was naked from the waist down. Then a sudden wave, a new fear from possibly having been raped ran over her dulled senses and horrified her fully awake. Her eyes widened; she scuffled around; thought she heard somebody near her; let out a short scream; then panicked when a hand clamped down over her mouth. Defenseless. Her pepper spray was in her purse, but where was her purse? With her free hand she reached to scratch the hand over her mouth. When she clawed the hand, it hurt her. The hand clasped over her mouth was her own.

She dropped to her knees and felt around the ground for her missing pants, but they were still on. Torn, but not ripped and shredded like she feared they might have been. Kimberly backed against what felt like a wall and ran her hands between her legs, touched and touched and touched herself. Her panties were on. Felt nothing that said anything had forced itself inside of her. For a moment, it gave her a different kind of relief. For a moment. Pain and dismay reminded her there was no relief.

After another second of fumbling, she realized one of her breasts had fallen loose from her satin bra. She thought it had happened during the struggle with Peter. She remembered him smiling, pissing her off, trying to touch her, wanting to kiss her, then her slapping him as hard as she could. She remembered walking off, leaving him sitting at the restaurant, him chasing her outside and down the streets. Down this alley.

Yards away, the sounds of late-night traffic, the echo of cars running over a loose manhole cover, the rudeness of horns blowing, all rushed by. For safety, she knew she needed to get away from this seclusion and out into the open brutality.

People walked by. None stared into the mouth of the darkness. The shallow backlight hid the faces and silhouetted two figures passing on the streets. She thought she saw the crown on the Statue of Liberty jutting up at her eye level. No matter how many times her eyes went in and out of focus, the top of the Statue of Liberty stayed right in her face. That made her blood chill, try to get a feeling for the ground. She hoped she wasn't up that high, walking on the edge of a building. *Am I on Ellis Island?* Then her ears came to life and she again heard street sounds, loud and clear. Streets that seemed miles away. Headlights passed a few feet away, kept moving. Kimberly heard hard steps . . . *click, click-op, click, click-op* . . . somebody was wearing cowboy boots, their faint conversation in Spanish. Then some laughter. Voices of girls. Young women. It sounded like something she should trust. Her mind told her she had no choice. Kimberly called out, a choppy, moaning cry for help. A sound that startled her because she sounded like a raspy-voiced foreigner. She had never heard her own voice with a pitch like that—pitiful and helpless with no strength.

She found her wind, tried to call out again. The figures slowed down, stopped their conversation, then sped away without a word. Of course. No sane citizen would follow a strange cry into the dark. In this land of cons and tricks, it would be too stupid.

Kimberly staggered another step, moved beyond the brick walls of warehouse-size buildings, edged away from the lofts toward the street lights and the sounds. She saw fire escapes clinging to the sides of almost every building, and again, she looked straight ahead and saw the crown from the Statue of Liberty, still there, rising between two red brick buildings, climbing up from the concrete. She moved toward the sunken Lady Liberty, made an anxious and panicky sojourn toward freedom, then tripped on something and fell. Fell too fast to catch herself. She landed on gritty asphalt, scarred her arm. More pain to her head. With squinted eyes, she looked back to see what she fell on. At first she thought it was one of the garbage bags that lined the street.

It wasn't.

It was Peter.

She clamped her hands over her mouth, muffled most of her screams.

Focused with her fear.

It was Peter.

Bright lights came out of nowhere, flashed straight into her eyes and blinded her.

She moved her hands and let her screams live.

Red and blue lights were rotating while people wearing badges walked back and forth inside the yellow do-not-cross tape, taking pictures and asking questions. Varick Street was roped off; traffic was being diverted. The sounds of scraping shoes moved back and forth; mumbles filled what was silence a few minutes ago.

Two ambulances came.

One rushed to Peter.

One of the attendants took Kimberly's hand. She staggered away from the darkness and sat in the street lights with a thick police blanket draped around her shoulders. They checked her injuries. Mild concussion. Mostly scratches and bruises.

She had a small knot in the back of her head. A busted lip. Her diamond earrings were gone. They looked into her mouth and said her teeth were fine. She thought, thank God. When they helped her on a gurney, she saw them with Peter. They had put him on another gurney, lifted him into the other ambulance and sped away. She thought she saw Peter look at her.

Kimberly wondered about this mess. What would she tell Jordan? What started out as a simple problem had snowballed. Peter was hurt. She was beat down. She'd have to call Jordan, and when he came to the hospital, explain, justify going to dinner with a husband nobody knew she had.

As they wheeled her from emergency room parking through the double doors, the overhead lights burned her eyes. The change from midnight-dark to noon-brightness came too suddenly. She wasn't ready for the transformation. She saw a pay phone, but before she could mumble her concerns, she'd been whipped down a hall of ailing people. One oversized woman was on another slim gurney—a bruised face with unmoving eyes.

Over two hundred people. Flurry and rattle sprouted from everywhere and blended in with the pages for Doctor this or Doctor that, people who were wanted here or there, stat. Voices in many other languages. A baby wailed a never-ending scream. An old man with blood coming from his foot cursed as he was wheeled by.

Somebody grunted, "Excuse me."

Somebody else snapped, "What the fuck happened to you?"

"You're blocking the aisle."

"Whose damn child is this?"

Somebody in a white uniform, with a plastic badge showing a

big smile, asked about insurance. After Kimberly told them that her parents still had her covered under one of their policies—one with full coverage for accidents and injuries—smiles came more often, service got better, and the questions became fewer.

When they asked if she had family to call, she wanted to contact Jordan, but cleaned her mind of the yearning and gave them Kinikki's number.

They called Kinikki.

Kinikki called Sharon.

She tried to relax in the long white hall with an I.V. in her arm. A river of time washed by and the next thing she knew, she was laid out on a different gurney under a hospital blanket and her head had been wrapped in gauze. The only way she knew the gurney was different was because the padding felt softer and one of the wheels squeaked when it moved. Her head hurt. Embarrassment had grown like a wild weed, but she was a lot calmer.

She didn't know when, because *her* internal clock wasn't working, but her friends had appeared out of nowhere. Kinikki was dressed in jeans and a Reggae Festival T-shirt. She held Kimberly's right hand, while Sharon stood close to her with a hand on Kimberly's left thigh. Kinikki was crying quiet tears and smiled when Kimberly opened her eyes. Sharon had put her glasses back on when she stopped crying. Kimberly was too tired, too hurt, too shamefaced, and all cried out. Plus, even now, she didn't want to start to blubber in front of friends and a hall full of sick and dying strangers.

"Are you okay?" Sharon asked, and dabbed her own eyes. "I mean, how are you feeling?"

"Don't make her talk," Kinikki said. "Let her rest. She's been through a lot."

When Kimberly cleared her dry throat, then opened her mouth to talk, Kinikki said, "Hush. Save your strength and don't be upset. Dat's what you must do. Plenty time for talk later."

The young officer who had driven into the parking lot and found the fiasco came over to see how Kimberly was doing. She nodded, moaned she was fine. The teenage Puerto Rican girls who had passed by the scene had become frightened by Kimberly's shrieks in the darkness, flagged down the police officer, and told them somebody was down by the ATM screaming for help. They didn't know if somebody had been attacked, or if it was a mugger/rapist trying to lure them. They were standing down the hall in the front of the curious and nonchalant hospital crowd, next to Kinikki and Sharon's husbands, Jamal and Todd. Both girls bit their fingernails, and looked at Kimberly. The young saviors waved. Kimberly smiled a thank-you the best she could.

Then they left. Disappeared like angels into the night.

When the police officer came back over to her, he first wanted to know if she was okay. His asking sounded more like a procedural, ice-breaking question than sheer concern. She nodded and groaned. It hurt when she moved her head. Kinikki and Sharon both moved to the side, then back toward their husbands. Kimberly closed her eyes. The officer spoke. With a soft investigative tone, he told her his name, then asked question after question as he scribbled. Even though she thought she had already told him, the officer again wanted to know her name. Then she realized it was a different officer with the same standard-issue police moustache.

She said, *Kimberly Denise Chavers.*

Kimberly Chavers, the artist?

Ah, eh, yes, that's, eh, me. I'm Kimberly.

I've seen your work in the Village.

Oh.

Were you acquainted with the man by the ATM?

Yes.

Was he the person who assaulted you, Miss Chavers?

He's my husband.

Oh. Based on what the young girls told us, we had assumed wrong. Then you are Mrs. Chavers?

No. Miss Kimberly Chavers. I use my maiden name. We're separated. We've been estranged for a while. For years.

Oh, I see. What was his name?

Peter Stenson, the third. How is he?

I'm sorry. I thought you had been informed. Then I regret to tell you Mister Stenson died two hours ago. He was D.O.A.

27 Kimberly Chavers

I heard the officer's voice saying, *Mister Stenson died Mister Stenson died.* It played over and over like a scratched record.

How did everything come to this? The last thing I remembered with any clarity, with any certainty, was procrastinating about getting dressed, then sitting on the edge of the bed playing back my answering machine and listening to Jordan's message. He sounded depressed, a little frustrated.

"Whu'sup, Kimberly? I don't mean to keep calling you, but I haven't heard from you since you stormed out of here. And I'm worried. Call me to let me know you're okay, all right? Could you do that for me before I put out a missing person's report?"

A grin grew on my face. I played it twice and absorbed his voice. I dressed, went to the door, headed out so I could make it down to 34th Street by eight, but as soon as the diminishing sunshine hit my face, my priorities became clear. I hiked back up the stairs, went back inside and straight to the phone. Before I left to go meet an unimportant Peter, I called my important Jordan back. I didn't know what to say, but I had to talk to him before I left. Maybe prepare him for what I wanted to talk to him about later.

I told him that I was about to step out to a business meeting. He asked if he could tag along, said we could have some fun. That made my throat tighten. My lie had me cornered.

"No, that's all right." I chuckled and stared at my French-manicured nails. "I wanted to apologize for last night. I'm just really stressed about a few things."

"Like?"

"Jordan," I said. "You said you love me."

"I know. You said you love me too."

"I did and I do."

"Right before you walked out on me. What kind of love is that to be giving a brotha?"

"Don't get evil on me," I snapped back at him because he sounded like he was pissed off. "Do you love me?"

"Yeah." Vulnerability had walked over his words. "Is that a problem? Or should I back off and punt?"

I laughed. "No."

"You know what that means, don't you?"

"What?"

"We're in love."

"Ha, ha," I said, and then we both laughed. I thought that maybe I was overreacting to everything going on in my life. But I was so, well how should I put it? I didn't share all of me with everybody. I saved some for Kimberly. Especially the parts that could be up for scrutiny. I sighed. "We need to talk."

"About?"

"You and me. About me in particular."

"What about you?"

"There are a few issues you haven't been exposed to."

"Like?"

"We spend a lot of time together and, you know. I'm in love with you. Damn, I keep saying that. I feel so vulnerable when I say that."

Jordan laughed. "Sounds more like you hate me."

"Stop teasing." I cleared my throat. "We need to talk."

"All right. I needed to talk to you about a few things too."

"Your brothers okay?"

"It's not about them."

"I can come over after my meeting." I felt myself smile. "If it's late, I'll wake you up."

"Knock hard."

"Okay."

I made it to 34th Street forty minutes late. Peter was still there, off to the side of all the pushing and shoving people, waiting in front of Macy's. He had on a light-green suit and tie. A petite, short-haired, African-American woman in jeans and a beautiful, orange-patterned blouse was smiling and flirting with him.

When I stopped near them, she frowned. The woman scowled at Peter, and when his smile told her he was waiting for me, she shook her head, made a *tsk* noise and said, "Oh. Now I see."

Peter asked, "See what?"

"You another one of *those* brothers."

Again, even though I wasn't with Peter in that sense, I was appalled. She didn't even know me and she talked around and about me like I was less than nothing. And it became obvious he had just met her while he was waiting for me.

"Even though she thinks she is," Peter said, smirking, and ran his hand across his wavy hair, "she's not white. She's a sister, just like you."

I said, "Peter, don't start with the idiocy."

"Why you brothers have to chase these white bitches?"

"I'm serious. She's not white." Peter winked at me. "She's black, like me and you."

Before I knew it, anxiety and anger had mixed, made me snap out, "Fuck you."

Peter laughed. "See? Told you. She just looks white. But deep down there's a little African Queen struggling to get out."

"Fuck you." I didn't know who I spouted my vulgarities to, but it didn't matter, because before I lost too much control, I had regained my composure. Before this situation got too indignant, before we got into one of those stupid New York street fights about nothing, I decided to let it go. The angry woman said a few more ignorant things, nothing kind, all slurs, nothing my ears hadn't suffered through over the years. Nothing that created a new level of being offended.

I hurried away and tried to flag down a cab. By the time I stopped one, before I got the door closed, Peter rushed in. Before the cab driver could say a word, I hopped out on the traffic side, made a few cars screech to a halt. Peter hopped out and chased me. I marched up the street in the middle of traffic. The cab driver hopped out and screamed curses at both of us. But I kept moving like a gazelle and hustled through traffic.

Drivers were blowing and cursing and flipping me off while I blew by them and cursed and flipped them off. These damn heels made it hard for me to strut too fast, or maneuver the way I wanted to without twisting my ankle. We were drawing too much attention. When I stepped back on the sidewalk, then did a tip-toe dance over the open grating so my three inch heels wouldn't make me stumble and fall, Peter was practically in my shoes.

"Away!" I snapped and flipped my hand at him. "Go away."

"We have a dinner date."

"Why did you say that bullshit to her, huh?"

"What?"

"You know. Don't play dumb."

"Kimberly, you're black."

"I'm not having that discussion."

"Your father's black."

"My father's mulatto. He's black, Indian, *and* white."

"That makes you black."

"My mother's Irish and German."

"And that makes you black."

I knew he was going to bring that up before he left. Like my father, Peter has never tried to understand me and what I felt. Even with a mulatto father, when we started moving from base to base, I was given a white culture. Daddy wasn't there when Mom-Mom delivered, and even though Mom-Mom told the doctors, they marked my birth certificate as Caucasian.

They deny it, but my father's side of the family was cruel to me. They were kind to each other, but I didn't fit in. For three years, starting when I was in the third grade, I had to put up with their inter-cultural racism and torture, had to live through their rivers of corrupt values and swim in their cesspools of shattered self-esteem. They loved to hit me because my arms would bruise. Seemed like I was always fighting my way home from school. Somebody always tried to take my lunch or my bicycle or whatever was left from the days before that hadn't already been taken. Then there were the names I'll never forget—Yellow Banana, Albino Coon, Ghost Nigger, Black Honky, Pale Face, White Nigger. Teasing was one thing, but those were personal attacks because I looked a little "different." When it came from strangers it was one thing. It hurt. But it pained like hell when the slurs came from your own family, when you were sitting across the Christmas table from your own family tree. They'd crack their little jokes, act like it was nothing, and when I turned beet red and showed any anger, they'd laugh and say I was overreacting.

I would get so nervous when I was around them I would urinate on myself. And the grown-ups thought that was funny. The embarrassment made me throw up. When the adults walked by, my own cousins would crowd me, get in my face, poke a finger in my forehead and whisper, so no one else could hear, "You ain't got no color. Tomorrow we gonna catch you and paint you so you look right."

That scared me. Hurt deeper than anybody could ever imagine. Day and night, they attacked my self-esteem. Mom-Mom made me use correct English, so everybody else mocked me and said I talked funny. So, to keep from being chastised, I didn't talk much.

And my father never took up for me and never made them quit. Never. When I went to him crying, he said, "Children will be children."

He never did a thing to help ease my pain or said anything to improve my self-love. Since his white father had abandoned his black mother, I don't think he felt obligated to defend me. It was almost as if he wanted the scorning to turn me black, make me more ethnic. I've lost any connection with him I could've ever had. He never said a thing to anybody, left me and my tears to Mom-Mom. Daddy didn't do a thing. Not even when I told him that his mother, my own grandmother, made silly jokes about me. In front of everybody, she'd call me Polka Dot. Zebra. Speckled. Grand-ma-ma Lorna called me Red-Kim. All of them called me Red-Kim. It may sound petty, but when you're a child, it hurts. You wear it and you *despise* it, but they continue to do it, because they *know* you despise it. It stays in your mind, because your mind stays with you. That was why I only sent flowers to Grand-ma-ma's funeral, then made up a lame excuse not to go. Her Zebra didn't want to see her, and I didn't need to see the rest of them.

On the outside, it may look wrong, it may sound bad. But to understand what it did to a person, it had to be you. You couldn't explain away the pain. And you didn't forget the words. The looks. The snickers. You never forgot the feelings of rejection. It hurt because of the way they said it. The way they talked down to me. The way they talked *at* me. It made me cry, and I hated seeing them. And since I didn't look like they wanted me to, like what they thought the people in their family should look like, I was the oddball. I was mistreated because my level of melanin wasn't acceptable. I read that because of interracial loving, there are at least fifty shades of black. I guess I wound up on the wrong end of the spectrum.

I went inside of me and searched for the positive. That was when I started becoming Kimberly the artist. I'd lock myself off by myself and create beautiful things. My work was my friend. My revenge was my success.

My older cousin Mark, who was the darkest of us all, was the worst. He tried to molest me and trick me by saying, "If you let me put my thing in you, you'll turn black."

I wanted acceptance so bad, wanted to be like them, I fell for it. And I kept looking at myself in the mirror all through the night to see if I had changed. Nothing, not a damn thing happened. Nothing, except Mark told all of his nasty little friends and they started hanging around the house like dogs in heat, running the same lie. "You just gotta get the right one."

For me to be such a "white girl" and different, they all wanted to sneak and get some of "the pinkness." They all wanted to break the skin. I told Mom-Mom what Mark had done, what he tried to make me let his friends do. She was upset. After Mom-Mom spoke with his mother, Mark stayed away from me.

They didn't understand why I didn't come around anymore. But when you weren't the one being attacked, you didn't remember. Bullies never remembered who they traumatized.

There was a period, right before I married Peter, when I told everybody I was black. After all, there was the "one-drop" rule. Or rumor. Or whatever. When I heard about the rule, I would sit around with pots of coffee and gallons of milk. Some days I would pour the coffee into the milk until the milk went away. Other days, I'd pour the milk into the coffee until the coffee disappeared. I'd put in three-fourths milk and one-fourth coffee and try to figure out if it tasted like milk mixed with coffee, or coffee mixed with milk. But either way, when I put in one drop, nothing changed. One drop of milk in coffee and it was still coffee. One drop of coffee in milk and it was still milk.

Yep, I was pretty fucked up in my head. Real vulnerable.

I met Peter in the middle of all of my confusion. At a time when I needed to be understood more than anything else. And since he was mulatto, he acted like he knew where I was coming from. And I do mean the man *acted*. He wasn't sincere. He just did or said what had to be done or said to get me to give up my virginity. What was left of it, anyway. And every time Peter introduced me to other black people, to his friends or family, he felt obligated to put out the flame in their eyes by being quick to explain that my father was mixed. At first he'd say *mixed*, later he'd just say, "Her father is a brother."

His mental stupidity was part of the reason he wanted me in the house and out of the public.

When I had had enough neglect and abuse, I left him and tried to make it on my own. Whenever I filled out a job application, or anything asking me what color or race or ethnicity I was, if I checked black or Negro, they always changed it, with either Wite-Out—that name's a joke in itself—or erased it, and wrote in Caucasian without asking. They assumed. I was tired of the hassle, needed my own money, didn't feel the need to explain who or *what* I was. And the way they glared, it was always a *what*, never a *who*?

When I went to Africa, I wasn't on a quest for anything. I didn't have to search for what I already knew. Without a doubt, I have drops of black running through my veins, and so I wanted to see the other side of my family tree. Alone. I'd sit and watch the Ethiopians and the beautiful people on the Ivory Coast. Then I'd look at me. Even though I had a couple of features which could be considered black, mainly in America, it wasn't enough to erase the rest, to make the other side defunct. Not enough coffee to make the milk go away. People in the motherland thought I was Italian, Scottish, Irish. Not once was I asked if I was a black American. Not once.

That made me sit around and wonder, why should I have to choose one background over the other? I probably had ancestors both on the Mayflower and on slave ships. Both slave owners and slaves. If I had the blood of slaves and slave-masters, I guess that meant I was supposed to hate myself. That wasn't going to happen.

And that was part, if not all of the reason my father and I weren't close. He couldn't understand why I didn't go to his mother's funeral. Why I couldn't go. My mother's side of the family always treated me nicely, not like I was some kind of a freak. They welcomed me, but they had that funny gaze in their eyes. They had accepted my father in their family, but they never loved him. They were just polite in his presence. And that hurt because of its hypocrisy. When Daddy received his orders and we traveled from base to base, we left them all behind. I was just Kimberly. Nobody's white girl. Nobody's Ghost. Nobody's Zebra.

Peter was still riding my heels. I felt all of those thoughts, relived each unwanted memory before I made it half a block. All the noises and people of New York had been shut out by dull recollections. Peter was huffing and puffing, trying to keep up. Which proved Californians were pussies, addicted to their cars, and couldn't handle the streets of New York.

"Okay." Peter was winded. He caught his breath, loosened his collar, brushed his beard. "Kim."

"Kimberly. My name is Kimberly."

"Okay, Kimberly. I'll say one more thing, then I'll drop it. White people don't have sickle-cell."

"I don't have sickle-cell."

"You have the trait."

I flipped him off. "Away."

A couple of blocks later I stopped walking, because Peter wasn't going to stop following. I was tired. Tired of getting nowhere too fast. Tired of running from a past that kept screaming out my name on the streets of New York.

I stopped and wiped the hair from my face. "Let's get this over with."

"Okay," Peter's tone was soft. "Kimberly, I'm sorry."

"No doubt."

"It's just that I haven't seen you in a long time. That's all. I've been wondering over the last few years how you were doing. This has been an open wound for me. I didn't know if you were okay, or if you needed help or anything. I knew you weren't in the best of shape when you left me. And besides, I've got a girlfriend.

We've been together for the last two years. Maybe after we get through this, I'll get married again."

"Then why the hell do you want to go to dinner with me?"

"Are we going?"

"Where's the girlfriend?"

"Back at the hotel."

"You left her in New Jersey?"

"No. California." He chuckled and dabbed his sweat. "San Luis Obispo. We work together."

He hadn't changed a bit. But at least he was letting her work.

I made him pay for the cab ride to the 300 block of Greenwich Street. At Toon's Restaurant, I ordered a small seafood salad and bass. Peter ordered pork and chicken mixed in noodles. Before the food came, I excused myself to the ladies room, then tipped to the pay phone near the entrance. I shadowed myself by the sports bar and called Jordan to tell him I would be there in a couple of hours.

Jordan asked, "Where are you?"

I told him. "Want me to bring you something?"

"Nah, I ate a couple of sandwiches."

"What are you doing?"

"I'm on the other line."

"Talking to?"

"Zoe."

"Why are you talking to Zoe?"

"Something's going bad between Solomon and Zoe and she wants to talk to me. I'll see you when you get here."

"Love you."

"Ditto."

"Oh, no. Don't do that *Ghost* stuff."

He laughed. "Love you."

All of a sudden, I started getting the hots for Jordan. Real bad, and real hot. I missed him. It was almost ten o'clock and I was having dinner with a moron. At this rate, I wouldn't be at Jordan's before midnight. I had to hurry this up. I needed a nice, decent *date* from Jordan. I had that love feeling turning circles in the middle of my stomach. He'd told me he loved me over the phone, and I wanted to hear it again, face to face. I wanted to see his eyes, watch how his mouth moved, and get close enough to lick his lips while he said it. I wanted to kiss and taste it as it rolled off the tip of his tongue. Then I wanted to hear it while we, you know, while we got wild and loose. But it was getting late and he had to go to work early, so I had to get a move on if I was going to get my groove on.

At the table, while I had my head down and we forced out hackneyed conversation over this last supper, I glanced up and was startled by Peter's staring face.

Peter gave me a slick smile, then abruptly asked, "Want to make love for old times' sake?"

"I'm sorry, what did you say?" I eased my fork down to my plate and figured I'd give him a chance to retract his inappropriate words.

"Remember how we used to go at it?"

"Go at what?"

"How we used to make love."

"Not really."

"I do."

"Good for you."

"So," he sipped his wine, "what do you say we cut the dinner short."

"And?"

"For one, you can stop playing hard to get."

"And?"

"Since this will be the last time we ever see each other, let's make love and end it the way we started it."

"I don't love you."

He half-smiled. "You look *so* good. Your hair. You've slimmed down."

I chuckled out some pity. "Yes, I have."

"You've firmed up. And if you don't mind me saying, you look nice. Real nice. I'm surprised and impressed."

"I see."

"And if you don't mind me continuing to be open and honest, I'd love to be inside of you for a night. I mean, after all," he grinned, "we are still married, right?"

"That we are."

"And let me tell you, I make love a lot better than I did back in them days."

I didn't bat an eye or let him know how much his comments had pissed me off. Like a rattlesnake, my eyes didn't stray from my target. He put his hand on my hand. Maybe he figured that since I didn't scream out my rejection, since my poker face didn't show the layers of disgust brewing in my stomach, I was being agreeable, had been seduced by his lust for something he should've treated right in the first place.

He scooted closer and I still didn't say a word. He didn't have a clue he was toying with me and a fast-rising Mother Nature. I just took another petite bite of my salad. His leg bumped my leg. I didn't squirm. His hand touched my leg. I didn't flinch. I just continued and chewed my slow bites and looked at him. When he caressed my thigh, I grinned and made like I was much too Zen for refusal. He smiled and leaned over to kiss me. Then he was as close as I wanted him. Closer than I needed him. I drew back and slapped the shit out of him and threw my half-full salad plate into his face as hard as I could. The delicate clear glass plate with the pretty designs clanged in the middle of his forehead, bounced across the floor, and broke into about ten big pieces and a thousand little ones. Peter cawed, grabbed his head, knocked the sticky salad leaves and croutons and baby shrimps off his face and slithered backward. The oily salad dressing had stained his suit. The entire room of well-dressed people shut up and gawked at us. I did like my girlfriend Sharon always did—genteelly picked up my napkin and dabbed the corners of my mouth. From any side of the room, I couldn't hear a fork clank against a plate. But I felt the eyes. And I didn't care in the least. Everybody had stopped eating to watch the show.

I sipped my wine, crossed my arms, sat back. I wanted to make sure this no-bullshit sneer on my face was the last he ever saw of me. A second later, I eased my chair back, grabbed my purse, and headed past the bar, out the door, and turned right at the TriBeCa Studio Deli. Headed down that narrow one-way street toward Varick so I could catch a taxi and get the hell away. A few feet later, right when I crossed the street and made it beyond the wooden doors of the bakery called Zeppole, Peter ran up behind me, hopped from the cobblestone street to the sidewalk, yelling, "Why did you do something crazy like that?"

"Bastard." I flipped him off. "Away."

"What's wrong with you?"

"Sorry. I guess my damn *black* side's coming out."

Again, I found myself walking down the dark streets with a stupid man following. This was getting to be the story of my life. I walked; they chased. Peter continued to curse me out as he tried to wipe down his stained suit. I just held up my middle finger to him. My stiff finger rang out louder than any of the ignorant, sexist bullshit he could stutter and say. Plus, what he said didn't matter because I didn't care. I didn't care about his words and I definitely didn't care about him. This time it was easier to walk because we were on a side street and it wasn't crowded. Peter followed. He shifted his tone and began apologizing for pissing me off.

A block later, an Asian man in a red jacket and black pants ran and caught up with us. Scared us both and made us jump. The man stopped his patent leather shoes right in between us, held out both of his arms, in a peaceful way, and slowed us down. He was our waiter from the restaurant. Peter had run out after me and hadn't paid the stupid bill. Then another man from the restaurant ran up, huffing and puffing, just in case the first one needed help. Peter didn't have any cash on him, at least not enough for the bill, because he was going to charge it. Bastard. So I ended up paying the bill, which was almost eighty damn dollars, tip included, because he was trying to woo me by buying a bottle of wine, and that left me less than enough to get back to Jordan's place. Peter said he'd pay me back as soon as we found an ATM. And we were going to go to the closest money-machine we could find right now so we could go our separate ways. I had a real man waiting for me and I was ready to end this asininity and find some real satisfaction and comfort.

Teddy's, the restaurant that had a replica of the crown of the Statue of Liberty built into its roof, was straight up the street. The next building was a bank. The ATM was on the far side, away from the streets. We walked around to the side with the broken lights and Peter was bitching as he got the money. While we were shouting back and forth, in the middle of our last pre-divorce argument, a white teenager and a black teenager leaped out of the shadows. They had been hiding and waiting for anybody to show up to use the ATM. I remembered all the television specials and news reports, about all the times I'd read about somebody getting robbed at an ATM. Realized how dumb I was to stop here, even if it would take less than a minute, but Peter had me so irritated I wasn't thinking. Wasn't acting. I was reacting. Reacting and rushing to get away from him forever.

The tall, wide, black teenager had a lot of earrings in both ears. He pulled back his dark, Tommy Hilfiger jacket and showed us the handle of his gun. He held out his hand. Before I could drop my purse and back up, Peter charged at him.

I screamed.

I tried to run, but my shoe twisted in the cracked pavement, the heel stuck and I slipped. The short, muscular, greasy-haired, white teenager pushed me and grabbed my chest like he wanted the same thing Peter had been begging for. He grabbed my breast, and I slapped his face so hard his head snapped back. We struggled and I dug my fingernails deep into his neck. He screamed and hit me in the mouth. I scratched him and didn't let go. We scuffled; I tried to trip him so I could run away, at least race back toward Varick Street and scream for help. But the bastard caught my arm and spun me quick and hard, threw me backward into the bank's wall. I hit the ground, fell near the parked cars, grabbed my head, felt thick, rough hands going over my body, snatching off my jewelry.

I didn't have enough strength in my right arm to keep my favorite golden bracelets from being pulled off. He struggled with the bracelets on my left arm, then stopped when I scratched him again. My purse was snatched from my arms. Jacket was taken. Shoes came off my feet. I heard Peter screaming. He was cursing and chasing the muggers. Dizziness rushed in. I fought to stay alert, but a thousand shivers, a coldness came over my body. I heard two or three popping sounds. Then a hard thud. Feet running away. Somebody moaned my name. In my benumbed state, I screamed my silent screams and passed out.

28 Jordan Greene

Zoe didn't buy my crippled answer for leaving that wild message on Solomon's answering machine. She said it sounded decrepit and deceptive, then kept talking the smooth and gentle way she does, spent her every breath reminding me that Solomon was supposed to be with me, and since he wasn't, then he was officially AWOL. She wouldn't let me get off the phone because she thought I knew where he was and I was going to call and let him know what was up. I couldn't let him know what was up if I didn't know what was up.

"Zoe," I said. "I have to use the bathroom."

"You've got a cordless, take the phone."

That had pretty much been the tone of the conversation since she picked up. I'd been flipping the channels and landed on NY1, the all-bad-news channel that had live reports from all five boroughs. A landlord in Brooklyn had hired twelve thugs to attack the tenants because of a dispute over money. Then a gangster had been arrested for beating somebody half to death with a car phone. Fifteen beaches were closed because of sewage spills. Manhattan had so much trash that they could fill the Empire State Building in a week. Nothing new on the news.

"Don't lie, Jay," Zoe lamented, then for the tenth time she wanted to know, "Is Solomon seeing somebody?"

"Solomon's not like that. He joined your church, didn't he?"

"So?"

"He switched from Baptist to Methodist just for you, and it's deep when a man changes religion for a woman."

My phone beeped and I put her on hold. It was Kimberly. Wherever she was, I heard soft Muzak playing in the background. She told me she'd be over in a couple of hours.

When I clicked back over, the first thing Zoe asked was if that was Solomon. I told her it was Kimberly. She groaned out a new attitude. Zoe had been complaining about Solomon, which was something she'd never done. Venting and letting her grievances be known. She claimed that it was Solomon who was putting off setting the wedding date, said she was ready to jump the broom when he asked her, she just wanted to have something small, informal, and inexpensive. She would've been happy with getting a cake from Make My Cakes on 110th and Lenox, crossing the boulevard to 111th and getting married on the steps of Canaan Second Baptist, then dashing across the street to Central Park and taking her photos at that spot on the tree-filled lawn that's packed with wedding parties from spring to fall. Something plain, simple, and local. The first time she married, she did it in the Bahamas, flew her entire family down, and spent way too much money on something that didn't last as long as the bills. Zoe hoped they'd get married before the summer was over so they could hurry up and get situated; she wanted to find child care for the children before the next term started.

It all sounded good to me, but she said Solomon told her he thought they should hold it off. He'd never told me that.

I said, "Maybe his ex is giving him a hard time. You know how sistas can get, especially when there are children involved."

"She was all right with it when I talked to her on the phone."

"You talked to her?"

"Yeah. For a hot minute. She called here one day and I answered the phone. Solomon was gone somewhere."

Zoe said Solomon's ex sounded like she wanted them to get married and take DaReus off her hands for a while, so she could be single and free and go run untamed in the streets.

A few minutes later, we started talking about work and I told her I was getting laid off. Mid-conversation, she asked, "Have you talked to J'nette?"

"No," I said. Zoe went silent. I thought she had been waiting for me to bring her name up, but I didn't. I asked a leading "Why?"

"So you still seeing that white girl?" Zoe asked. When she said *white*, it sounded descriptive, not racist. More of an adjective than an insult. I don't think she cared one way or the other. Anybody I dated after J'nette would never be her friend.

"Her name is Kimberly."

"The writer?"

"Artist. Yeah, I'm still seeing her. Why?"

Zoe said, "Well, let me put it like this. You need to talk to her."

"What do I need to talk to Kimberly about?"

"No. J'nette." Distress was in her voice. "You need to talk to her. Soon."

"Why?"

"She had your baby."

My mouth dropped open. If I didn't know better, I would have thought my heart stopped beating. I fell silent. Went numb.

I damn near shouted, "She did what and had a who?"

"Baby. J'nette had a baby. A little girl."

"When?"

"I guess you and her haven't been talking, huh?"

"Not at all."

"You sure?"

"Nobody said anything to me about a baby."

"Nobody knew. She didn't tell anybody. Didn't even tell Toni. So everybody's tripping."

Zoe said that back in December, J'nette had taken her savings and moved to D.C. with an old boyfriend. The one she walked out on when she came back to New York. Right before I met her. It wasn't his baby, because they hadn't been together for over a year, but he had told her he'd take care of her. She didn't want her baby to be born without a father, even if he was surrogate. He told her he still had a flame for her and wanted her back, pregnant or no. So she figured it was for the best. A couple of weeks ago, she found out he was seeing somebody else, actually walked in on them together, down-stroking in the front room at their place. She broke down and called Toni. And of course, motor-mouth Toni speed-dialed Zoe, and Zoe got big-ass Elaine on the three-way. Before the dial tone had faded, they were in a rental car heading south. They talked her into coming back. She didn't have any money, so she didn't have any choice. They didn't know anything until they rang the bell and J'nette opened the door with the baby in her arms. Breast-feeding and crying.

So, J'nette was back in town, staying at Zoe's place for a while because Toni lives in a claustrophobic apartment building that doesn't allow children.

Zoe said, "You're the father, right?"

"Hold on." I sat at the kitchen table and bent my head in between my legs and took deep breaths to keep from throwing up. I sat up and said, "You're joking, right?"

"Ever heard me tell a joke?"

"Now's a good time to start."

"No joke, Jay. Straight up, no joke."

For a moment we marinated in silence.

She said, "The baby looks just like her too."

"Great."

I told Zoe that J'nette said she didn't know who she was pregnant by. Zoe said J'nette was faithful to me; if J'nette was sleeping with somebody else, she would've known; they did damn near everything together. She knew all of J'nette's lovers. And the guys who were with them at Solomon's party were gay.

I tried to rationalize, "Then why did she tell me that?"

"She probably just told you what you wanted to hear. She's a lot more sensitive than she'd ever show you face to face. She's really a sister trying to get her life together, but shit keeps going wrong. She has too much pride to ask anybody to give her help when she's having a hard time."

"She said she didn't know."

"If she wasn't pregnant by you, she wouldn't have come to you in the first place."

Kimberly didn't show up by midnight. I grabbed some covers and camped out in the living room, just in case she popped up in the middle of the night. I woke up three minutes before my alarm went off. Kimberly wasn't here. I checked my front door for a note, just in case she had came by. No note. I called her house. No answer. I stopped by her place on the way to work. She wasn't there. Guess she didn't come home.

*   *   *

CompSci was dreary all morning. I had just gotten back to my desk from lunch, had begun sifting through my belongings to see what in my desk I wanted to keep, when I looked up and saw that Antoinette "Toni" Barrett had stepped into my office. J'nette's sister. She startled me. Stalking in silence. I didn't know when she walked in. Toni looked so much like J'nette that, for a second, I thought it was her.

Toni's jet black hair flowed in the same below-the-shoulders Cleopatra cut J'nette had before she axed hers off. Beige business suit and white chemise. Those mahogany Doublemint twins looked so much alike it was scary, but I think Toni was the oldest, because her face was narrower. Somebody told me the oldest twin always had the narrowest face because it paved the way through the birth canal. And J'nette's butt was a chicken wing smaller.

Toni cleared her throat, just like J'nette did before she got ready to talk trash. "Hello, Mister Greene."

"Miss Barrett." I stood up from my desk. "What brings you to my office?"

"Can we talk?"

I smiled. "I've got three minutes."

"Well, this might take a while. And it's very, very personal. Can we get together after you get off?"

"Can I ask what it's about?"

"Mister Greene," she said and her face turned into the same cold-hearted, no nonsense bitchy-bitch-bitch glower her sister used to dish out. She over-articulated each syllable. "Con-sid-er-ing the cir-cum-stances, I'm being as polite as I can. I already talked to Zoe and she told me she talked to you last night. So don't play the mind games."

I huffed. "You don't like me, do you?"

"I don't have to *like* you. Would it matter?"

"Nope. Just making conversation."

"What time are you getting off?"

"Five."

"I'll meet you in the lobby."

"For what?"

"All of us are going to TriBeCa." TriBeCa meant the Triangle Below Canal.

I said, "All of us?"

Toni nodded. "Zoe is going with us."

"Why do we have to go to TriBeCa?"

She said, "That's where my sister is."

I shrugged. "I'll try to make it. But don't wait."

"Don't make us have to come looking for you."

"Us?"

"Me, my sister, her baby, and the damn NYPD." Toni came in, walked up to my face. "I'm not letting you walk over her. I'll walk these halls and tell everybody I see how you dogged her and left her for a tired-ass white girl."

"Lower your voice, please, Miss Barrett," I said, firm. "Five o'clock. Lobby. Cool? Out my damn office. Bye. Adios."

She walked out.

Slow motion. My life started to move in slow motion.

We didn't go to TriBeCa, but ended up at Greenwich Avenue and West Twelfth, catty-corner from the Art Greenwich movie theatre, right above a flower shop named the Gay Rose. From my office to the subway, felt like I was trudging in leg irons, and I lived in moment after moment of regret and anticipation. And fear. All the way, it seemed like I was inside a bad dream. My world was out of focus, was covered with a layer of remorse that I was ready to confront and peel away.

The sky was bright, but inside my chest, the sun was going down. Stale, warm air kept me feeling moist. Garbage bags lined the sidewalks in front of the apartment buildings, businesses, and lofts, waiting for tomorrow's pickup. Multicultural people were going to and fro, heading into coffeehouses, stopping taxis, going inside movie theaters, restaurants.

Birds in a V-formation stopped flying and all landed on the edge of a building to rest. This overbearing heat had gotten to them too. Cars and taxis passed by, rode the narrow avenues with expertise, music bumping.

With Toni leading the way, we stopped in front of a red-brick building that looked more like a storage building than a tenement structure. Wrought iron rails led up to the light-blue arched glass doors that were chipped and rusty. She climbed the stairs to the buzzer. Toni asked, "Which number they at?"

Zoe said, "Elaine's place is number six."

They didn't make eye contact. None of us had since we left the coolness of CompSci.

We sat in a cramped warm apartment with slightly dirty white walls that, even though it was almost six in the evening, smelled like the remains of over-cooked breakfast sausage. Across from the front door on the wall was an enormous, framed picture of Joie Lee, Spike Lee's sister. On walls to both sides were huge pictures of Denzel as Malcolm X and Wesley Snipes in the movie *Sugar Hill*. Posters of Nia Long and Larenz Tate in *Love Jones*, and another of *Soul Food* were thumbtacked to a wall in the hallway.

I sat on a big purple bean bag, next to a stack of the *Village Voice*, facing the Jamaican restaurant across the street, making myself busy by flipping through some kind of a trade paper for wannabe actors and actresses. Several auditions for stage plays, television, and soap operas had been circled with a red ink pen. Zoe sat next to the tree-size house plant on the soft, azure-colored sofa, holding the last of a tall red plastic cup of water. Toni was in the kitchen whispering to Elaine, their tall heavyset friend with the big ass who used to work at CompSci in Employee Relations. She'd been laid off since February and was living off her unemployment and 401k until something came up.

Every now and then their eyes cut my way.

Elaine said J'nette and her baby stepped out right before we walked in and was surprised we didn't catch her on the elevator.

I picked up Elaine's phone so I could check my messages. The receiver was caked and smeared with brown-toned makeup and red lipstick. Smelled like many different brands of perfume.

Still no calls from Kimberly.

With a restless mind, I needed a little conversation, and Zoe was the friendliest of the bunch, if I could call what she'd been to me friendly, so I decided to try to talk to her.

I asked Zoe, "What time is J'nette supposed to get back?"

"Soon. Chill. You ain't got nothing to do."

"Why're we here? Is this where she's staying?"

Zoe hunched her shoulders and used the remote to flip through one hundred cable stations. "I don't know where she's staying now. Haven't talked to her today."

"I thought she was staying with you."

Zoe didn't answer.

Barefoot Elaine wobbled her wide, six-foot-plus frame up the thin hallway with the warped floors and handed me the cup of water I'd asked for almost ten minutes ago. She wore purple pants and a purple blouse, so she looked like a big Negro Barney.

She gave up a fake smile long enough to say, "Here you go, Jay."

"Thanks, 'Laine."

She headed back toward the kitchen.

I downed half of the cool water in one long swallow and sat the cup on the floor next to my briefcase, jacket, and tie. The silence, the hostility, the waiting was working the hell out of my nerves. I wanted to leave.

A minute later, the buzzer buzzed. Driven by the sound, me and Zoe watched the wall when it hummed. Elaine rushed back into the living room, made the water in my cup vibrate like a scene from *Jurassic Park*, and pushed a button on the intercom next to the front door.

She sang, "Who is it?"

"Solomon."

"Hey, man." Elaine perked up with an earnest smile. "I didn't know you were in the area."

"Zoe still over here by any chance?"

"Yeah. C'mon up."

"Is it all right to park out front?"

"You got an alarm on your car?"

"Naw."

"It's on you."

She pushed a black button on the fingerprinted beige box and it made another buzzing sound. This was cooler than cool. I needed some male reinforcement. It was starting to feel like I was in the middle of a male-bashing massacre, me being the male about to get bashed and massacred. Custer had better odds at his last stand.

Zoe grinned like a newlywed-to-be as she bounced up and sashayed to the door to let Solomon in. Her shoulder-length braids

swayed to and fro as she perked up. She met him in the hall and I
heard them laughing and talking. A few kisses. When they stepped
in, Solomon was dressed in plaid shorts and a Polo shirt, and Zoe's
lipstick was smeared on the side of his face. Zoe's new attitude,
her smiles threw me. In the blink of an eye, she'd changed. Toni
came into the room and stood in the doorway, arms folded.

She said a sweet "What's up, Solomon?"

"Nothing." He chuckled and nodded at Toni. "Hey, Jordan. I
didn't know you were chilling out up in here with the Joy Luck
Club."

Everybody laughed but me.

I tried to match his enthusiasm, "Whu'sup, Sol?"

Elaine called out, "Ask Solomon if he's thirsty."

Toni asked, "Thirsty? Want something to drink?"

"Whatcha got?"

Toni made a face. "Water and pineapple juice."

"Naw."

Toni passed by me, picked up the phone, and called somebody.
When Toni turned her back and started to gab and giggle and flirt
in Spanish, I let my eyes tell Solomon I needed to get away and
talk man to man, brother to brother, but he didn't see me because
Zoe's happy-go-lucky ass had already tugged him over to the sofa
next to her. He'd been recruited to the other side before I could
hand him a Help-Me-Bro-Man application.

Solomon said to Zoe, "You ready to roll?"

Zoe gently lay her head on his shoulder. He shared a broad grin
with me. Solomon cackled, "I swooped up to take Zoe back to my
place. You want me to run you home?"

"I'll let you know. Are you leaving now?"

Solomon started to rise and said, "Yeah."

Zoe held his arm. "Not yet."

She looked at me and tried to maintain her losing smile.

I got up. "Sol, let's step outside. Catch some fresh air."

Zoe cut me off, "Relax. We'll be leaving in a minute."

I sat back down. As soon as Toni hung up the phone, somebody
on the outside turned the doorknob. Then there were a few light
knocks on the door. My heart jumped with each thump. Zoe
bounced up and opened the door without checking the peephole.

J'nette walked in with a diaper bag over one shoulder and a sleeping baby in her arms. Zoe kissed J'nette on the cheek and smiled at the baby.

A baby.

It's amazing what one renegade sperm could do.

J'nette's hair had grown back out and she was wearing it in a cut just like Toni's, only a little shorter. Toni smiled her way in and took the baby. J'nette straightened out her baggy jean shorts and blue Howard University T-shirt. Outside of looking just a little bit fuller, and her breasts were rounder, more womanly, she didn't show any signs of having a baby.

J'nette gawked my way, saw me sitting on the bean bag, shifted a few times, snapped a look at Zoe, then did the same at Toni, then back at me. Her face slid from shock into a frown.

We stared for a moment. She said, "Hey, Jay."

"Hey, J'nette. Long time no see."

"Yeah," she said, wearing woe in her eyes, anguish that dropped a huge shadow over her face. "You heard, huh?"

My eyes were on the baby. "Yeah. They told me you had the baby."

"She had a which-a-what?" Solomon said, then his eyes doubled in size. "Hold on, now. That's your baby?"

In a scene that read like it had been rehearsed over and over, Zoe turned the television off; Elaine took the sleeping baby from Toni and headed toward the bedroom; Toni moved over and waited next to J'nette, held her hand; Zoe eased back to the sofa and sat next to her bewildered fiancé, bounced her leg while she held his hand; Elaine came back in without the baby and stood her big ass in front of the front door, blocking it like a bouncer.

J'nette regarded her twin, spoke softly, "Toni. Don't do this, please? It ain't all that. I can handle it."

"We need to clear this mess up so we can move on."

I shifted side to side on my bean bag, felt the tension flooding the room. All eyes were on me. When I looked over to Solomon for moral support, my glance was cut off when Zoe frowned at me. Solomon's mouth was still wide open.

"All right," Elaine said. She looked at me, then Zoe, then back to the twins. "J'nette, time to come correct. I told them what you told me."

In that instant, J'nette's eyes started to water, but instead of crying she flipped her hair back. Her sister held her tighter. J'nette glanced at Toni; her sister kissed her on the face. J'nette kissed her back; then her eyes floated toward Zoe. Zoe nodded with a little smile, sent a mental kiss, I suppose.

"J'nette," Elaine cleared her throat. "Is Jordan your baby's daddy?"

My heart was beating too hard, too fast inside of my throat. All I could do was follow my eyes to J'nette. I didn't see the point of this inquisition. We knew. The witch-hunt was over. J'nette raised her head, eased her eyes toward me. No smiles. Plenty of shame. I guess she remembered the last time we saw each other. At the clinic. The morning fight. Her wanting me to put the baby on my insurance and my refusal. The dead rose she left behind. Her spilling it all to Kimberly.

"J'nette," Elaine repeated a lot louder, a lot more intimidating, and again cleared her throat and pointed at me like she was Marsha Clark waving a bloody glove at O.J. "Is Jordan Demetrice's daddy? Yes or no."

J'nette looked at me, then at Elaine.

Toni stepped up to J'nette, got in her face and said, "Answer the question before I answer it for you, okay?"

Before I knew it, I spoke up, "I thought you weren't going to have the baby?"

J'nette said, "I didn't have a choice. I told you about my situation."

Elaine jumped in and took over, acted like she was the next Judge Judy. "Is what you told me the truth?"

"I wasn't lying." J'nette's tone rose, words cracked as her body quivered. She licked her lips. "I told you the truth. I swear to God on my grandmomma's grave. I'm not lying."

"It's all right," I said. "Don't lie."

J'nette's back straightened. She said, "All right. I won't lie."

All I could think of was that J'nette had been down in D.C., pregnant with my child, and hadn't made one phone call to let me know when she had the baby. And I was wondering how much it looked like me, how much like my momma, how much like my father. The man who died before we had a chance to hang out.

I asked, "How old is the baby?"

Nobody answered because nobody was paying me any attention. Zoe headed over to J'nette and gave her a hug. "It's okay. It's okay. Everything is going to be fine. Don't get upset."

J'nette said, "Keep it down. You might scare Demetrice."

I asked, "How old is the baby?"

J'nette said, "Don't worry, Jay. It's not your baby."

My eyes widened and my mouth fell open. "What?"

"It ain't your baby, Jay. I'm sorry. It ain't."

Solomon sat up on the edge of the sofa and ran his fingers through his beard as he stared at me. After J'nette's last bitter statement, his eyes were just as wide as mine. This scenario was a little too much for both of us and I could tell he was just as ready to get the hell out of here as I was.

The trio of women stood side by side, hand in hand. Looking like they were either going to start singing or swinging.

Elaine snapped, "Is Solomon the baby's daddy?"

Again, my eyes widened, bloomed like a rose. My mind told me that I didn't hear what I just heard. My gaze shot toward Solomon, but he didn't even flinch. He closed his eyes like he was waiting for the answer.

J'nette didn't hesitate. "Yes. That bastard is Demetrice's daddy."

Solomon opened his eyes and looked at Zoe's glare. She was standing now, in his face, eyes watering, shaking her head.

Zoe toyed with the engagement ring on her finger as she choked out, "C'mon, baby. Tell us she's lying, Solomon. I want to hear you say it to me. Say it in her face."

Solomon dropped his head into his hands. "Shit."

I snapped out, "You were sleeping with J'nette?"

Solomon said, "It's not what you think."

My eyes went to J'nette when I damn near shouted, "You were messing around with Solomon?"

Neither of them gave an answer, or a denial. Which, to me, sounded like a real loud *yes*. I don't know when, but I stood up, and I must've been rushing toward Solomon, because Elaine grabbed my arms from behind and led me over to her side of the room, closer to the front door. I was cursing, jerking, confused because it sounded like my best friend was the father of my ex-girlfriend's illegitimate child.

J'nette was disturbed when she said, "Don't wake up the baby."

They calmed me down. Some. My fists became open hands, but they felt like spears, as hard as a southern baseball bat.

Zoe stared at Solomon, asked, "Did you sleep with her?"

Again, Solomon was opening and closing his mouth. No answer.

"Nigga, answer the question! *Yes* or *no!*" Toni said and made a rugged move toward Solomon, but Elaine grabbed Toni's suit coat and pulled her back next to me. We collided like click-clacks, then I helped hold Toni too.

Elaine said, "No, Toni. We're doing this just like we said we was, all right? Ain't nobody gonna blow up in my house."

Toni, Elaine, and Zoe all looked like wild wolves. And I was ready to become their leader.

Solomon snapped, "J'nette, don't lie. That's Jordan's baby and y'all know it. Zoe, she's just trying to break up our engagement. She ain't happy, ain't got eye-water to cry with, ain't never been happy, ain't never gonna be happy, and don't want to see you happy."

Zoe stared J'nette dead in the face. Her voice cracked like a dry twig, "Did Solomon fuck you?"

J'nette's face puffed up, like a remembrance bloomed its way back into her life, and even the darkness of her skin couldn't blacken out her reddened shame as she started to cry. "Yeah. He did. He had sex with me."

"Did you come on to him?"

"Hell, no."

"Ever?"

"*Never.*"

Zoe asked, "Did he rape you?"

J'nette wiped her eyes and nodded. "Yeah. He"—she struggles with the word, then her eyes shot daggers at Solomon when she gnarled out—"he assaulted me. That bastard raped me."

"Assault? *What?* C'mon, J'nette. Don't lie." Solomon pleaded, then turned a shaky expression to everybody whose grating words were avalanching on him, "She wanted it. She came on to me!"

"You raped me, bastard, and you know it!"

Solomon yelled and jumped up, but didn't move close to anybody. "Why are you lying?"

"Bastard," J'nette snapped. *"I would never, ever, get with my friend's boyfriend. I don't even like your short ass like that."*

In the midst of her curses and tears, J'nette charged at Solomon, but Zoe and Toni held her back. It was loud. Screams of accusations and cries of denial came from everybody and the walls were tumbling down. It was brutal and sounded like a mini-riot had broken out. The window was up, so the sounds carried out into the streets and spread from Wall Street to Lenox Avenue.

Solomon yelled, "The bitch is lying."

I shuddered. It felt like the whole world quivered when he said that. The women's shoulders tightened, hands turned into fists, mouths fell. Before she could get all of her jewelry off, I grabbed Toni, but Elaine screamed like a wild animal, knocked a yellow lamp over, rushed at Solomon; he danced on the furniture, dashed to the far side of the room, couldn't get a clear path to the front door, huddled in a corner close to the kitchen. This time I grabbed Elaine and tried to hold her back, but she dragged me along like a robust mule yanking a thin plow through broken soil. Each yank made a small twinge come alive in my side; pain left over from my sojourn to Memphis.

The baby started to cry; J'nette ran by us into the bedroom.

It took Toni, Zoe, and myself almost three grueling minutes to unclamp Elaine's fat hands from around Solomon's narrow throat. All the while, she made death threats, twisted Solomon's neck, spat, slapped at his face, and barked, *"Who you calling a bitch?"*

For a moment, I wondered if Elaine was related to Wanda.

We tussled back and forth, knocked over everything that wasn't nailed down, and at this point, I didn't know if we were trying to save Solomon from Elaine, or Elaine from sending herself to a penal colony. We were all swearing so much it made it almost impossible to get a good grip on big-ass Elaine.

After he gagged and caught his breath, Solomon stopped kicking long enough to look around. Wide eyed. Solomon lay on the floor under the end table that was knocked over. The room thundered when Elaine stormed to the front door and snatched it open.

She snapped, "Get outta my goddam apartment."

Solomon pouted at Zoe. His face went from broods to whimpers to grimaces, then fell long, one of those sorry, can't-quite-make-the-tears-come-up, can-we-please-talk-about-this-alone expressions. Zoe dropped her head and shook it hard enough to make her braids dance. She turned her back to him and stiff-finger pointed to the door with much irreversibility.

My best friend, the man who was closer than a brother, his eyes never drifted my way.

Before he made it across the opening, before he was clear, Elaine gripped the door firm and slammed it hard. It bounced off the back of Solomon's heels. He grunted and stumbled out into the hall, fell into the wall face first. That had to hurt. Without a word, Elaine and Zoe headed back toward the crying baby.

A minute passed before I went to the window and saw Solomon's car pulling away from the curb.

I grabbed my coat and briefcase.

Before I made it to the door, J'nette hurried into the living room. Stared at me with non-blinking eyes of sorrow. It was too quiet. The baby must have gone to sleep.

I broke the stare party, nodded my farewell, and turned to leave. J'nette followed me. She touched my arm and asked, "Can I talk to you for a minute?"

After I caught a few breaths of warm air, it felt like reality had shifted again. The surreal feeling I had when I got to this neck of the woods was fading. Anger and other ill feelings had taken its place.

J'nette looked like she was coming out of a trance too. We stood in front of Elaine's building near the stoop, away from the few people who were outside, then crossed the street and stood in front of the Jamaican restaurant, next to the Bell Atlantic pay phone. Over and over, J'nette apologized. She claimed that one night after one of Solomon's card parties, she was too buzzed to go home, and he had told her she could crash in his spare bedroom. The one he had for little DaReus whenever he came up.

Which sounded cool because it was late night turning into early morning and she didn't want to walk to or ride the subway by herself. Besides, Solomon always offered room and board to whoever needed to crash.

And Zoe was there.

I wanted to know what night that was supposed to have happened, because I always walked her to the subway, and if she didn't come back to my place, I'd ride out to Jersey, spend the night and come home the next morning. She said I didn't come to that card party. We'd had an argument and I didn't show up.

They sat around, talked, and she fell asleep. When she woke up, her pants and panties were off. Solomon was on top of her, pushing himself inside of her and pumping, telling her that he knew she wanted it. J'nette's face winced, emanated fear. And his woman, her best friend Zoe, was dead asleep in the next room. Zoe had partied too hard too. J'nette said that she didn't know what to do, that she was scared. So she didn't do anything, just let him finish and hoped he didn't hurt her. Two minutes later, he walked right back out of the room, closed the door.

She grabbed her clothes and left.

Two weeks later, she missed her period.

She was telling me that Solomon had mistaken their playfulness, their being buddy-buddy and touchy-touchy for her wanting to get with him. Either that, or that was just the lame excuse he used to disrespect her. And me. She didn't know how to tell her friend, who was so in love, her boyfriend had raped her best friend right up under her nose. She didn't want to mess up their relationship, or my friendship with the brother. And she didn't think anybody would believe her side of the story, especially since she'd spent the night. And she had been friendly with him.

That was when our relationship went downhill. She thought she could act like it didn't happen, but it left her all messed up and confused. Her confusion grew along with the baby in her womb. She said she was going to tell me, tell everybody the same night she told me she was pregnant. But she backed down. Then she had thought about her condition. If she had another abortion, she'd never be able to have a child. And she wanted to be able to have a child more than anything.

She shrugged. "That's how my cards were dealt."

I said, "Catch-twenty-two. Damned if you do, damned if you don't."

"Yeah."

"What happened at the clinic?"

She fidgeted a bit before she told me. Said that when she stood in the abortion clinic, she grieved over all the bad decisions she'd made in her life because somebody else thought it was for the best. She stood and glared at the table of dissolution, and couldn't climb up, spread her legs, and give up what might have been her last hope.

She said, "I just couldn't. I'd rather have lost it trying to do what I thought was right."

J'nette said that with her heavy heart, she sat in the clinic's bathroom and one of the nurses consoled her for over an hour.

I asked, "How old's the baby?"

"Two months."

I threw my mind into a scientific mode and counted back. During our off and on relationship, we were off most of that month. But those months were ancient, hard to remember where I was and what I'd done. Shit, I couldn't even remember what I'd had for lunch today. Don't even know if I went to lunch.

"I should take a blood test," I offered, "just in case."

She shook her head. "You can if you want. But I know. I'm the mother. I know. I hadn't made love to you a couple of weeks before then, and I waited a while afterward. I wanted to make sure, you know, I didn't have a disease or something. It's his."

"What're you going to do?"

"Well, if I file charges like Zoe wants me to, and he goes to jail, I can't get any child support. My baby needs insurance. I don't know what to do. My life always seems to be in I-don't-know-what-to-do mode. But I'll do the one thing I can do. The only thing I've been doing."

"What's that?"

"Pray."

"Oh."

"When I left that place, I asked God every night to let me carry Demetrice full term. And she's healthy. I don't think He'll kick me to the curb now." We stood for a few awkward moments. Said nothing. Then, "You know what else?"

"What?"

"I was so in love with you."

"You never said."

"Didn't know how."

There was a long moment of quiet.

J'nette asked, "You still with Kimberly?"

I nodded. She sighed, then gave up something that resembled a shallow smile, the kind of expression a person has when they wished they could turn back the clock and do things over. Maybe not things, just one thing. One day. Or one night.

We shared a motionless moment that held a lot of memories and thoughts, maybe even shared visions of moments that could've been, but would never happen between us. Then that moment fled, went wherever used-up moments go.

She said, "We could've been good together."

Without saying good-bye, she dropped her head and walked back up the crooked concrete stairs at the front of Elaine's building and buzzed number six. We gazed at each other as she waited. No words, no expressions, no judgments. Just gazed. The door buzzed open and she disappeared without looking back again.

I trudged away, let twenty vacant cabs pass me by. Didn't have the strength to raise my arm long enough to hail one. And I didn't know where I was going. Needed to talk and think and talk to myself for a while.

Solomon was my best friend. He'd violated J'nette. That was all I could think of. I'd been closer to him, had done more for him than I had my own family. I found everything too hard to believe, even if it was staring me right in my face, even if I still had the scratches on my arm from where Elaine hurt me during the struggle.

Part of me wished J'nette had been pregnant by me, but that would only be to kill this other swelling heartache I felt from betrayal. Then I wouldn't have to mourn the death of a friendship. Wouldn't have to wonder why I was back-stabbed.

Solomon ate my food, drank my wine, danced to my music. Bastard even spent the night in my house, used my soap to wash his ass, and crapped in my toilet. It felt like everything I thought was real, wasn't at all.

With each step, I tried to keep my head up and my heart off my sleeve. All I could see was Solomon inside of J'nette. Changing my reality and destroying my peace of mind.

The pang in my gut sank another notch; over and over, I mumbled, "Short, midget, low-life son-of-a-bitch."

Part of me wanted to kill his ass. Another part wanted to sit down with him and hear his side of the story without all the screams and shouts. But, his words wouldn't change a damn thing. Not one damn thing.

When I passed by another Bell Atlantic pay phone, I slowed down long enough to loosen my collar and call Kimberly's place. Still no answer. Overnight she'd become aloof. And as far as I knew, she hadn't been home yet. And I've yet to hear of a late-night dinner that lasted almost twenty-four hours.

Seems like I'd been lured into another false feeling of security; what I thought was sugar was starting to smell like shit again.

Now I know how Zoe felt when she kept calling Solomon, trying to track him down and figure out where in the hell he was spending his time. I started to page Kimberly but I didn't.

I was trying to put my mind anywhere that would keep me from thinking of Solomon as a rapist. I was working on my own denial.

I dabbed my forehead and kept moving into the sultry air, stayed on the side of the street offering the most shade. But when the sun was going down, it didn't matter what side of the street you tried to find shelter on. Both would become dark.

29 Kimberly Chavers

The short nurse with the midwestern accent had just come into my private room, checked my head for the umpteenth time in umpteen hours, taken my vital statistics, then removed my un-touched hospital food tray.

I moaned with pain as I sat up on top of the rumpled covers of the firm bed in my short, striped NY Giants pajamas, my legs crossed at the ankles. This had been one helluva day. But thank God for friends. Sharon and her husband had gone to my apartment to make sure that whoever had stolen my purse didn't get my address off my ID, and simply use my keys to break in. My biggest fear is having my work stolen. Or destroyed. Sharon had a locksmith change the locks, then made sure all windows were secure. She'd packed some of my personal items, then left the stereo on talk radio to leave a constant stream of voices inside my space.

I shifted side to side, watched the wall television, flipped from NY1 to CBS to NBC to FOX, listened to the headlines, tried to floss my teeth over the pain in my stupid mouth, and hoped I didn't hear the stiff-backed reporters shout out my name, or see the media playing the crime scene for all of New York to enjoy over hot pastrami sandwiches. But crime was so bad, I knew everything didn't make the news. Violence was trivialized and ended up buried in the papers, printed after the produce section, crammed between the price of oranges going up and grapes going down. But I tried to be still, listened, just in case.

Like I said, I didn't eat any of the bland hospital food because an hour ago Sharon had run out to a restaurant and bought shrimp and fried calamari, then snuck it all up in her big iridescent bag. Kinikki left thirty minutes ago, right after all of us ate. She refused to leave until she was sure I had a filled stomach, a sane mind, and a few hands to hold until I drifted off to sleep. But it would be a while before I slept again. I didn't know if I ever would close my eyes and find peace again.

Now, Sharon was over in the corner, lingering in the eighth-floor window, checking her watch every other minute, peeping at her pager, glancing out the tinted glass at the lanes of bumper to bumper traffic creeping through the darkened city.

I asked, "How's it look out there?"

"There are just as many people on the sidewalk as there are cars on the streets. Nothing unusual."

I touched the knot on the back of my head. For a couple of

hours, my injury had left me blurry eyed, fuzzy brained, uncoordi-
nated, and unable to write down my own name. After they told me
Peter had died, I vomited for twenty minutes. Probably, inside the
tragedy, the funniest moment came when they told me that due to
my head injury they wanted to keep me awake, and Sharon
snapped, flailed her arms, and yelled, "Does it look like she wants
to take a damn siesta? This woman has been traumatized and
needs immediate attention. Who's in charge here?"

I had tried to tell her to calm down, but I couldn't mumble or
moan out a word in between Sharon's teary-eyed curses, frantic
babbles, and supreme finger snaps. But I managed to reach up and
touch Kinikki's arm, make a please-calm-her-down face, then
point at Sharon; Kinikki pulled Sharon to the side and told her to
"stop acting like a jackass," but it didn't help. Sharon got louder.
Three doctors and two nurses came at the same time.

Even though I objected, I finally agreed to let them keep me under observation while they made sure I didn't have signs of ex-
tradural hemorrhage. The last thing I needed was a stroke to mess
up the rest of my day. Sharon insisted that I let her keep track of
everything the hospital did, when and how long they took to do it,
just in case "we" needed to file a lawsuit.

Before I could answer her, Sharon had yanked a notepad out of
her purse and announced, "I'll document all improprieties committed by these imbeciles. My wonderful husband has a marvelous
attorney upstate that would have this hospital regretting any pec-
cadillos, and they'll be begging to settle out of court before the ink
dries."

Kinikki said, "Sharon, calm yourself down before you end up at
Bellevue."

Sharon said, "Kinikki? Go to hell."

"Send a limo."

They were snapping at each other and I was trying to remember what *peccadillo* meant.

The police questioned me. All I remembered was arguing with
Peter, moving toward the ATM so I could make sure he gave me
my money back, then waking up on the asphalt in pain. Everything in between was vague. Some of what had happened since
then wasn't too clear either. Shapes and screams, but nothing

solid, ran back and forth through my mind. No faces, no voices. Just shadows. Shadows that seemed to be everywhere when the lights were turned off.

By four A.M., NYPD had arrested the black teenager with all the earrings. That was what NYPD called and said. His face came back when the officer told me that. His face, and Peter struggling with him for pocket change. The police had dialed my pager and put in their direct line at the police station. He called back trying to find out what number they had paged, probably so he could find out the pager phone number and use it. Maybe sell it. While a female officer flirted with him, the police officers traced the call to his mother's Woodhaven home and were there in force within ten minutes. When they knocked on the door, he bumbled out butt-naked, his palms held to the sky. My charge cards and Peter's wallet were found in his bedroom. By sunrise, the police had the other guy. Yep. That's what the NYPD called and told me when I woke up. And it didn't make me feel better, not in the least.

My mind absorbed and accepted the reality of the situation, and the heat in my throat, the dampness that wouldn't leave my eyes, well, I guess I became overwhelmed with guilt and shame. I sat up and talked and cried and vented to Kinikki, sobbed that the whole fiasco was my fault. Kinikki reassured me that I wasn't to blame; somebody had mugged me.

While the consoling was going on, Sharon stepped to the side and did what she did best—coordinated and organized. Sharon had been on the phone, canceling my charge cards, closing my checking account, contacting my parents to get the insurance information. I had to convince Mom-Mom and Daddy that I wasn't about to die, spent all of thirty minutes calming Mom-Mom. Then when I finally got them off the line, Sharon got back on, called her travel agent and arranged for my parents to fly out from Seattle on the first morning flight. Then she called Peter's hotel and found out who they should contact at his job about the tragedy.

Sharon called Peter's job in San Luis Obispo and was put in contact with Peter's girlfriend. Peter *didn't* have a business trip to New Jersey. His girlfriend thought he was in Los Angeles, visiting friends for a few days.

Sharon used her poised business savvy and tried to keep Peter's woman from becoming too hysterical. She talked to her long enough to get Peter's sister's phone number in San Francisco. Peter's sister didn't have the slightest idea what to do, hadn't been in contact with Peter for ten years, and asked if I was going to take care of the arrangements.

Sharon answered an immediate "No. And due to lack of information about any holdings or partnerships he might have had, if any, anything done on this end would be slow and mishandled. But we will sign and fax anything you need."

As Sharon filed her nails, what she always did when she was a nervous wreck, she helped Peter's sister gather her senses and find out who to talk to so Peter's family could arrange for his body to be shipped west.

All the while, I listened in disbelief, then repeated the word that chilled me the most, "Body."

Peter was dead. One second he was disrespecting me and I was slapping him in the head with a salad bowl, the next, he was dead.

"Shit," I said as I rubbed my eyes. "What am I going to tell Jordan? This is fucked up. I'm a damn widow and he didn't even know I was married."

Sharon patted my hand. "Calm down before you have a seizure. I had an uncle who had one of those. Disgusting. One second we were all sitting at dinner talking, the next he was facedown, gurgling in his clam chowder."

"Sharon," that was Kinniki, snapping, "stop it with your dreaded stories. She don't need to be hearing all of dat right now." Kinikki turned to me, asked, "Where is Jordan?"

I said a worried "Haven't called him yet."

Sharon asked, "Why haven't you called? He should be here sitting in this chair holding your hand."

"Don't know what to say."

"First tell your man you love him," Kinikki said. "Then say the truth about dis situation. It's best you tell him than he picks up the *Times* and read about it."

I recited Jordan's phone number, moaned it by heart, and Sharon dialed. My hand trembled when Sharon handed me the ringing phone. The answering machine played the outgoing message. I prepared for the beep. I cleared my nervous throat and tried to sit up, "Boyfriend, this is your girlfriend. SmooVe, I've been in an accident. I was mugged, but I'm okay, so don't worry."

A couple of hours later, I had Sharon move the huge bouquet of flowers that Clair and Eric had sent to the room from the sink area to over near the double windows facing 168th. Just then, the door opened and my parents walked in. Holding hands. Mom-Mom and Daddy. George and Denise. Honestly, I felt a little sad when my plump, orange sundress–wearing mother smiled her worried smile. My insides felt swollen because I hated for my mother to worry, hated for her face to lose its sparkle and brilliance, because it upset me too. Since I was the only child left, Mom-Mom treated me like a baby. I knew why and that's why I didn't stop her. Even in my independence, I let my mother be a mother. She'd earned the right. I knew Mom-Mom had never really gotten over my older brother's dying. She wasn't supposed to get over it; that was her child. My brother. A brother I'd never know. But I always felt the connection between him and me, felt his spirit. So I grew up a skinny redheaded child who my mother did her best to protect. But, no matter how hard she tries, not even a mommy can do everything. Can't be everywhere at the same time.

"Hey, Red Head," I said and pushed the button to make the bed sit up.

She grinned a little. "Don't get up, Kim-Kim."

I loved the way she said Kim-Kim. When I was a child I asked her why she always said my name twice. She told me that it was because she loved me twice as much as anybody else ever could. That used to sound silly to me, but now when I think about it, it makes me want to cry with happiness.

I pouted, "I'm tired of lying down."

"Kim-Kim, relax and recover."

"I could do this at home."

Sharon was standing at the bathroom mirror brushing her hair. She cut in, "Your daughter is stubborn. She's had an argument with every nurse who has come in to render assistance."

Mom-Mom said, "Just like her father."

"Hey, Daddy." I smiled and reached out for a hug. "You guys have been gone awhile. I was getting worried. Where'd you go?"

Daddy said, "To the gift shop."

He gave me a small fuzzy brown teddy bear with a get-well card, then kissed my forehead, put his hand on the bed railing, stooped over to gaze deep in my eyes, stared like he was a doctor's doctor, searched like he could deduce if I was doing well or getting worse with just a glance of his stethoscopic eye. It was almost funny because I'd never seen him act like that. So sensitive and non-military. Almost like a father was supposed to act.

He wore an expression of anguish as he studied the swelling and scratches in my face. He asked, "Does it still hurt much?"

"Looks worse than it feels. My head feels like, I don't know, it hurts off and on. Depends on how I lie."

"Then do as your mother suggested and find yourself a comfortable position and stop moving around, young lady."

I sarcastically saluted him, did the same to Mom-Mom. After I had my Shirley Temple moment I then ran my hand over his salt-and-pepper hair. "I'm happy to see you, Daddy."

"I'm glad you're doing all right." He lowered his voice to a too-loud whisper. "Your mother cried practically all the way from Seattle to New York."

"I didn't boo-hoo as much as your father."

I paused for a second, waiting for a quick-witted denial, or a laugh from my father, and when there was none, when seriousness filled the air, I lowered my voice and asked, "You cried, Daddy?"

He winked and lowered his voice, "Something was in my eye."

Mom-Mom emphasized, "From Seattle to New York it was in his eye. He was showing anybody who would look the pictures of your art—he was more irritating than an Amway salesperson—and by the time we landed everybody thought they knew you. And he told them what had happened, over and over, had the flight attendant about to cry. Right, George?"

Daddy shushed Mom-Mom, then held my hand and stared at me. Stared like he was looking deep into a mirror. Or had drifted back in time. Then I saw that Mom-Mom had a funny expression. She tapped Sharon's shoulder, whispered in her ear, and they both headed toward the door. Before I could ask what the secret handshakes, whispers, and exchanged glances were all about, Mom-Mom said, "We'll be right back."

I asked, "Where you two going?"

She smiled worriedly. "We'll be right outside the door, by the nurses' station."

The door closed.

And I was alone with my father.

I couldn't remember the last time I'd been alone with him.

He fidgeted at my side, like he felt the same awkwardness. For a few seconds, nothing was said. I was waiting for some sort of bad news, so I half joked with a lip-quivering smile, said, "You're not going to tell me you're sick or something are you?"

"Not at all. Me and your mom are in perfect health."

"What's wrong?"

"I just wanted to let you know," he started, then held my hand for a while. Held it soft and gentle. He finally said, "You know I love you, don't you, Kim?"

I smiled. And as I nodded, my throat tightened, lips quivered a little more. I was about to become a basket case.

He continued, "I just wanted you to know that. We haven't gotten along too good over the years."

"I know."

"And I'd hate for something to happen to one of us and I didn't get a chance to tell my little girl how proud I am of her and all she's done. That's all."

My eyes watered. Some of the pang came because I remembered that Jordan had just flown back to Memphis because his stepfather had died. His brother's father. I was glad that wasn't my father resting eternally. My eyes were like leaky faucets, but Daddy's eyes watered a lot more than mine ever did. Like he had years of tears. Years of fears. I leaned up and squeezed my arms around him. "Love you too, Daddy. No matter what."

We stayed like that for a while. Holding each other.

His words choked, "It's been a long time since we hugged."

"I know," I said, trying to sound like the woman I am, but weeping like I was a little girl. A stubborn child. "I'm sorry. I'll come visit you. Maybe we can go fishing in Canada."

He rocked me. "Just call and talk to me sometimes."

"I'll do both."

"Kim, it's hard on me for me and you to be like this."

"I know. Me too. I'm sorry."

"You don't have to be. I should've been a better father to you. I was more of a provider than a daddy, I guess."

"You did all right. Aside from the black eyes and scarred arms, I turned out pretty good for a Chavers."

"I should've been there for you," he said, then paused like he had something heavy on his mind. I saw vivid recollections of the past in his face. Saw the ghosts hanging from his trees. He spoke a simple "I should've listened to your pain. I went through a lot of the same, you know."

"Never knew."

"I never talk about it." He nodded with his memories, slowly released his breath, then shrugged and touched his lips. "Kim-Kim—"

"Dad. Shush. It's okay. Hug your baby girl."

I grinned at him through my stuffy nose and stubborn tears, knew exactly what he was trying to say through his stubborn tears and stuffy nose. Underneath my little-girl smile, I wondered who'd been there for him when he was a child.

We sat for a few minutes and let the silence make us father and daughter. It was amazing how that same silence that once had put a wedge between us, now was making us friends.

I ran my hands over his hair again. Daddy's complexion is even lighter than mine, but his hair is curlier, especially when it's damp, and his features were more pronounced. Pronounced enough to leave no doubt.

I chuckled, "We done crying all over each other?"

He smiled. "For now. What about you?"

I said, "Enough already. This crying is making my head throb."

We laughed.

Daddy washed his face, smiled at my smile, then stuck his head out into the hall and called Mom-Mom and Sharon back into the room. When they eased inside, Mom-Mom was wringing her hands and pinching her flesh. Her face was blank with uncertainty. First she looked at my blushing grin and red-rimmed eyes, then at Daddy's smile and red eyes.

Mom-Mom smiled and said one word: "Good."

"Mom-Mom, you sure you guys don't want to stay at my place?"

"We'll come over and stay when you get out."

Sharon said, "I already put them up. Everything's paid for."

"Where?"

"The Mayflower." Sharon winked. "Top floor."

"If they stayed at my place it would be cheaper."

"Oh, hush and heal," Sharon said. "I've arranged for my driver to be available, so everything is fine. And your place is atrocious. When is the last time you swept your floors?"

"I've been busy. You know how I am when I'm working."

"Nothing short of trifling."

Mom-Mom said, "I can go over and clean for you."

"No, no, no." I couldn't stop smiling at my daddy. "I don't want you guys to be too far away."

Mom-Mom said, "There's a hotel only a block away."

Sharon scrunched her face. "It's overpriced, the rooms are the size of a breadbox, no room service, and it has cockroaches that look like Ed Koch."

"Really?" I slipped in some sarcasm when I asked, "How do you know?"

Sharon's face reddened, but she didn't answer me. She checked her watch, sighed out some high hopes, and folded her arms.

Mom-Mom continued, "And especially after what they did to you, and Peter, I don't want to walk these streets by myself. I saw on the news that almost all the kids in school own handguns."

I said, "They don't all own handguns."

Sharon interjected, "That's right. Some of those rug-rats own Uzis."

Mom-Mom shook her head, said, "Children are shooting each other in the classroom. Shooting teachers in the head. I don't know what this world is changing into, but it's not good. I don't understand why you live out here. This should be enough to make you want to move."

"Mom-Mom, it's not that bad. It's just a few kids who make all the rest look bad. There are some good people out here."

Sharon said, "Yeah, six-year-olds with enough hardware in their lunch pails to overthrow Iran, Iraq, and Harlem."

Everybody chuckled. I moaned.

"Let me tell you what's wrong with the children in America—"

Daddy was about to get too serious and hop up on his stump and start his usual diatribe.

"Sweetheart," Mom-Mom cut him off, "let your daughter rest."

I asked, "Are you tired, Sharon?"

Sharon checked her watch again, stretched and pulled at the hips of her green, pinstripe jumper. "I could use a horizontal nap to relieve some of this head-to-toe stress you've burdened me with."

Sharon's pager went off and she gave me a sideways glance, which meant she had a date with somebody other than her husband. That perked the social butterfly up. Yep. In a heartbeat, Sharon came to life, told my parents, "Your driver is downstairs, Mr. and Mrs. Chavers. She's the gorgeous and tall African-American lady wearing a black suit and accommodating attitude. Do take your time, and when you're ready, she'll be waiting. She'll take you to the Mayflower tonight, then she'll pick you up in the morning."

I asked, "How are you getting home?"

Sharon winked at me. "I'm making a drop by the Astoria to see a sickly friend. I'll arrange transportation from there."

I winked back. "Talk to you tomorrow."

Sharon grabbed her bag. "First thing."

"Thanks for everything."

"That's what friends are for." Sharon leaned, kissed my jaw, and whispered a raspy, "If anybody calls, tell them I went to Tiffany's to shop at a midnight special."

I lowered my voice, smirked. "Sharon?"

"What?"

"Condom."

"No other way," Sharon said. Then her tone went from jovial and anticipating to concerned and caring, "Are you going to be okay until morning? I can come back for a while after I get energized."

"Yeah. I'm not as jittery as I was this morning. I'm upset, but I'm better. My family is here. Go do your thing."

"First chance you get," Sharon spoke in an undertone, "get that stress taken care of yourself. Doctor's orders."

"Get your one-track mind out of here."

"I'll be back in time to check you out of this treacherous place. I would stay, but I don't care to sleep in buildings that have dead bodies in the basement."

"Thanks for reminding me."

"Rest. But, if you're up, page me in a couple of hours so I'll have an excuse to leave and go home to my hubby."

Sharon said her sweet good-byes to everybody, opened the wooden door wide enough for me to see the green tiled hallway. The corridor was pretty calm. No one would ever know that a little while ago I was downstairs in a bustling hall filled with complaining patients and overworked hospital staff.

My heart skipped a beat. As Sharon was sashaying out, Jordan stepped in. His damp, worried face led the way.

30 Jordan Greene

My emotions were running in full calisthenics but I felt some relief when I saw Sharon's smile. She hugged me and kept on going, moved like she was late. I hurried out of the Pine-Sol smelling halls into a fried-fish smelling room.

Kimberly's head was wrapped up in gauze, looking like a big white Afro. My eyes bucked. Her arms were scratched and bruised. Red medication to fight infection was spread over her skin. Parts of her face, especially her lip, were swollen, were black and blue with faint traces of dried blood. Kimberly was looking like she'd just gone twelve rounds with George Foreman.

Two other people were in the room, but I was in panic mode and wasn't ready to focus on them. I dropped my briefcase and hurried toward Kimberly; she tried to correct her posture. Nervousness was all over her rough face when she stared at the other people. My attention went to them too.

Kimberly said, "Jordan, these are my parents. Mom-Mom, Daddy, this is Jordan."

Her mother's hazel eyes were on my suit and briefcase. She asked, "Are you an attorney, or a friend of Peter's?"

Kimberly's face lost all of its worry lines and went into shock. Kimberly said, "Mom-Mom, this is the guy I'm dating."

Her mother said a strong "Oh. You're her boyfriend. She told me about you. Nice to meet you, Jordan."

My mind was playing tricks on me. Kimberly just said her pops was in the room, and I didn't see anybody but a middle-aged brotha standing by the window. The brotha with skin the color of butter moved across the room in two long strides and extended his hand, made strong, friendly eye contact.

"I'm George Chavers. I didn't catch your last name."

"Jordan Greene." My face twitched, came alive with spasms. He had Kimberly's last name. Most of my mind was on the subway and hadn't caught up with me yet. These were her parents. Both of them. I said, "Nice to meet you, Mr. Chavers."

"Likewise. I just wish it could've been under more favorable circumstances."

"As do I." Then I nodded. Two seconds later, I blinked.

Inside, I was in some serious shock. I would've thought it was a joke, but nobody was smiling, smirking, or denying. And he had her face. Same shape of the head, same full lips, same eyebrows. He was to handsome what she was to pretty, but the pretty outweighed the handsome. His face wore a distinguished roughness. Military hardness, I supposed.

The lady had Kimberly's hair, only with age and graying around the edges, short and tapered, a finer texture. Kimberly had the same hazel eyes as the lady. She stood and came over to me. "I'm Kimberly's mother. Denise Chavers."

Kimberly readjusted herself over and over, looked miserable.

We stared at each other for a moment.

I asked, "How are you feeling?"

She patted a spot for me to sit next to her. "I'm okay."

Her mother said, "She's not. She's trying to keep us from worrying."

Her mother began talking about Kimberly's being with Peter, and they were attacked, but she dropped discussing the details when Kimberly interrupted and said, "Not now, Mom-Mom."

Peter. The same name Kimberly had answered the phone with.

Kimberly said, "Mom-Mom, I haven't told him, yet."

I jumped in. "Told me what?"

"Maybe," her father said and touched her mother's shoulder, "maybe we should let Kim and her friend have some privacy."

Kim?

I missed most of what was going on because I was too busy comparing their features. If you mixed and matched George and Denise, you'd definitely come up with a Kimberly. She was them.

Her parents said they were going to go back to the hotel. Kimberly told her mother she would be all right for the night, but to call and give her their room number when they checked in.

The door clicked closed.

I looked at Kimberly and said, "Your father?"

"Yep." She smiled and groaned. "Mother too."

"Your *natural* father?"

"*Natural.*" She cleared her throat and frowned on my words. Kimberly took my fingers in both of her hands. My life felt overwhelmed with betrayal. Everybody was pissing on me from all angles. Secret after secret.

My soul ached because of the shape Kimberly was in, but if she wasn't caught up in whatever lie she was caught up in, I'd still be dancing in the dark. Just like if J'nette hadn't gotten pregnant that night, the secret would have been hers and Solomon's to keep. I could've still been with J'nette and never known. Zoe would've been Solomon's glowing wife and the stepmother of his child. All while he was the smiling stepfather of hers. Those were my thoughts on the way over here.

All of that was the sum of my anger now. What I was holding back, keeping submerged. But it was creeping, seeping through my pores. I took my hand back, followed the fresh smell to her flowers, read the card with yesterday's date. "Speedy recovery. With all our love. Eric."

She jumped in, "And Clair. If they were only from Eric I would've thrown them to the dogs. They don't mean anything."

My tone was low, deliberate, "Eric already knew you were in the hospital—"

"Clair told him. The only way she knew was because I was supposed to pick up some money from my work that's on consignment, so Kinniki called her to let her know, but Eric was in the shop, he answered, and—"

"And nobody called me?" My tone was razor sharp. She looked damned surprised when I said that. "You and Eric still have something going on?"

"No. I'm not like that and you know it."

"Your parents had time to fly all the way in from the other side of the country before I got a phone call. I was sitting around, waiting for you and—"

"Sharon made all the phone calls."

"How did Sharon find out?"

"I called her."

"You called your friend in Long Island first?"

"No, I called Kinikki and Kinikki called Sharon."

"But you couldn't tell them to call me?"

She didn't answer, not at first. Then she said, "Things were hectic and I wasn't thinking clearly."

"If you weren't thinking straight, then how did you manage to call Kinikki? *Why* did you have to call Kinniki? You told me she was who you were doing dinner with, right?"

"Jordan," she said curtly. She looked at me like she couldn't believe that we were having this conversation. An exasperated business tone had crept into her voice. "Don't get upset and don't upset me."

I matched her tone, "All I want to know is why didn't you call?"

"I couldn't."

"Why?"

"I didn't want to worry you." She scratched her arm and a tear rolled over cheek. "I'm all right."

A beat went by, then I said, "That was your natural father?"

She fidgeted, rubbed the back of her neck. "You already asked me that."

"I was talking to myself."

My eyes saw her in a different light. A much darker light. This was wacked. Instead of having a *Guess Who's Coming to Dinner?* experience, I'd been spending my time with the *Imitation of Life*.

"Jordan, would you stop gawking at me like that? You're making me nervous. Is that a problem? Does it matter?"

Staring out the window, I saw the reflection the night gave the shaded glass. Kimberly was still fidgeting. She winced like she wanted to cry, but didn't. I calmed myself, walked back over, and gave her a contrived kiss on the forehead, tried to see if, since I saw her in a new perspective, her flesh owned a new seasoning. I couldn't tell if it was salt or pepper. There was too much bitterness on my tongue to taste anything.

My mind drifted, went back to Solomon and J'nette.

My breathing slowed, heavied. My chest expanded. My shoulders moved up an inch with each inhale, down with each exhale. For a moment what was inside this hospital room didn't matter. My body felt heavy, carried a lot of torment. Kimberly's reflection was in my eyes, but no matter how I tried to block it out, I was having a vision of Solomon attacking J'nette.

I asked Kimberly, "What happened?"

"I was mugged." She said that like the answer was obvious and the question redundant. "They stole my purse and jewelry."

I almost asked her who stole her heritage, but I didn't. I blinked a few times, stared at her gauze Afro, tried to stay focused on what I should be focused on. She hemmed and hawed about the situation, and when I asked where she was when she was mugged, when I quizzed her about who she was with, she said a very elusive "Off Varick."

I already figured out that she wasn't with Kinikki, knew that because her mother was going on and on about somebody named Peter, but just to make sure this journey was heading toward the truth, I played along and asked if Kinikki was hurt.

She stopped her lip from quivering, cleared her throat, very lightly and ladylike, and confessed, "I was with somebody else."

I understood. There was no *business* meeting. There was a *somebody* else. "Was it this Peter guy?"

Her lip quivered; she rubbed her face. "Yeah."

"Was he hurt?"

Her head shook. Then her voice creaked, "He died."

"*Died?*" I repeated.

I wanted to know how did a *business* meeting turn into this. She blew her nose twice, then chatted in a roundabout way and explained to me about them meeting for dinner, going to get some money, then getting ambushed. Kimberly talked almost an hour nonstop. Married. And married to a brotha. She said that she didn't tell me she had been with Peter because she didn't want me to think she liked my skin color, and not me. She was trying to get a divorce. Ended up widowed. Part black. Mostly white. Definitely in love with me.

I wondered if any woman really knew what love was.

In the middle of this madness, she asked me how I felt about it, about us, about the Kimberly she was, about our future. When I didn't answer, she told me to stop staring at her like I was dissecting her facial traits. Like my eyes were scalpels operating on her heritage. I redirected my eyes. She asked me to please stop glowering at Eric's flowers.

She asked me not to be jealous over nothing, said that if flowers weren't from the right person they didn't mean a thing. I didn't have time to be jealous because I was too busy being real.

I didn't know what I felt. I already had too much on my mind, so much that I couldn't comprehend one decent feeling.

I wasn't who I was yesterday. It felt like I had nothing, not even the truth, and tomorrow I'd have even less. Even though I was the same on the outside, I was a different Jordan Greene on the inside. That meant we weren't the same Jordan and Kimberly.

"Were you sleeping with Peter?"

She looked hurt. "No. I wasn't."

My cold-blooded gaze told her I didn't believe her; she told me I didn't have to stay. I rose to kiss her bruised face, but she put her battered hand between us, stopped me with her scars.

Kimberly pointed at my briefcase.

My eyes told her I'd see her in my next lifetime.

Hers said the same.

I gathered my things and left another black woman in her bed of lies.

3 1 Jordan Greene

I felt the need to find something, only I didn't know what I was searching for. My mind slipped back to my high school values, back to when me, Darrell, and Reggie used to sit on Momma's back porch and wait for a cool summer breeze. I bought a pack of generic cigarettes from a street vendor down on Times Square, almost choked to death on the first one, threw the pack away. Then I stopped off for a couple of Lite beers at one of those XXX clubs where the naked women danced with golden tassels twirling on their breasts. Watched them grin ear to ear while they did carnal gymnastics from a silver hanging bar. After blowing almost thirty dollars on bad table dancing to loud music that couldn't drown out my thoughts, I wandered back out onto the street, cruised under street lights so bright they made everybody lose track of time. For a while I blended with the crowd of lost souls. Watched the hustlers hustle watches to the tourists who couldn't tell a real Rolex from a Timex from Malcolm X. Another was set up selling designer T-shirts, five dollars each. One of the shirts said: NO WHITE LADY, I DON'T WANT YOUR HANDBAG.

It was almost two A.M. in the city that never sleeps. A stagnant two A.M. And I was up at Central Park North, standing outside of Solomon's door, knocking and buzzing and yelling out his name. I had buzzed from downstairs, but he didn't buzz me up. But then again, I didn't expect him to. A young brotha I'd seen on the elevator a time or two let me breeze in the building on his coattail.

"Open the damn door, Sol," I said for the third or tenth time. I stood back in the well-lit, green carpeted hallway that smelled like it had a slight mildew stench. Water spots had left brown circles in the white ceiling. A leak. Corruption I had never noticed. I knocked again. "I know you're home."

The small round peephole darkened, meaning somebody inside was spying out. It lightened. Several locks clicked. The vertical burglar-bar was moved. The door finally opened, but he didn't move the thick safety chain so we could stand man to man.

I was very savage, spoke in my deepest southern drawl. "You ain't gonna let your homeboy in?"

"Look, man," Solomon uttered. "It's late."

"Talk to me, man to man."

"Don't start no shit, won't be no shit, all right?"

"Whu'sup, Sol?"

"What's up?" He said that like I should already know. He lowered his head, pretended he was tying up his housecoat. When he finally made eye contact, his thick voice faltered, his speech fluctuated between anger, shame, and fear. With his place unlit, his face could barely be seen because he'd cowered back a couple of long inches and lived in the shadows. But we stared.

"Why?" I asked. My eyes were swollen. I felt deflated. I was sweating, probably smelled worse than the Harlem River. "Why'd you do it?"

"She lied, man. She lied."

"Did she?"

A second passed. A second that felt like a month of bad dreams. He said, "Believe what you want. You know I ain't no damn rapist. If I did rape her, you know she woulda called the police."

"But you slept with her, right?"

"Jordan, think. Man, look. I dropped the hint and told you over and over she wasn't about nothing. I would've told you she was still offering me the goods, but you had broke up so I didn't see the point. J'nette is out for J'nette. She's just gold diggin'. Straight up gold diggin'."

I lowered my head, tried to shake away the madness and wake up from the dream I was living in.

Solomon said, "Hell, man, she asked me for the three hundred damn dollars the same night she asked you for it. Why the hell do you thing she was at my house acting like a fool?"

"You slept with her?"

"Yeah. More than once. It wasn't no damn *rape*. And it wasn't about nothing."

I paused. "Why?"

"C'mon, man. What difference does it make? You got your white woman, so why you trippin' off J'nette? You the one who said you didn't really like her, right? Stop walking both sides of the fence, black man."

I repeated, "White woman."

I chuckled like a man gone mad. Deep in my head, I heard all the people who'd said that. People from Darrell to Wanda to Solomon to Toni to strangers on the street. Blinked and saw how some people wouldn't speak to me because of Kimberly.

Then I focused on Solomon. Saw him fucking J'nette while I was at my apartment waiting for her to call. While she was my woman. Fucking her inside of the apartment I was facing right now. When I took a breath, odors overwhelmed me. I swear I could smell sex coming from inside of his cave. That smell had perfumed his body.

For a second I thought about trying to drop-kick the door open and break the chain, but I didn't see the point. Especially since I didn't know how to drop-kick a door. But I wanted to hear him say he'd fucked her. I couldn't go home until I heard him say it. I wanted him to look at me and say he went inside of J'nette. And he did. So I should go home. A second later I heard somebody tip-toe up in the shadows behind him. The sleepy voice sweetly asked who he was talking to. A very feminine voice I definitely recognized by its sultry smoothness.

He pushed the door up enough to hide me and my words, told her to chill and he'd be back to bed in a minute. After she giggled off into the darkness, Solomon cracked the door a little, but not as much as he had the first time.

After looking at me for a second, he asked, "Is that it?"

"Who?"

"Who what?"

"Who's that?"

"Just a friend," he lowered his voice. "Don't matter."

I shook my head. "You did me wrong. I wouldn't've done anything like that to you. *Never.* I respected you too much."

He didn't say anything. Didn't lower his head. Owned no shame. My not being able to see him, his hiding in the darkness pissed me the fuck off. Something inside of me snapped. Maybe it was the way he gazed through the shadows at me. Maybe it was the way he didn't tremble away from me. I backed up to the wall, then growled and charged and screamed and shouldered the door. Solomon grunted and bounced back. I backed up, kicked it flat-footed. It boomed; the chain broke; the door opened. Now there was nothing between us but a couple of feet of serene air. Space and opportunity. Solomon stumbled and jumped back, wide eyed, mouth open, grimacing like he'd just seen the grim reaper. Yas-mean was standing in the hall in a red Arkansas T-shirt, her mouth wide open. Exposed. When I growled into his place, Solomon screamed louder than Yasmean yelled. I saw her half-naked yellow skin. She wailed, flapped her arms, stumbled, and ran toward the back, screeched for Solomon to dial 911. He tried to make a break for the phone, but he tripped, lunged forward with his arms reach-ing every which-a-way, and crashed on his face. He groaned, grabbed his mouth and frowned up at me. My sneers rained down at him. Then I spat to my left. Turned and walked away from his begging eyes. I could've kicked his decrepit ass, but I didn't see the point. I just didn't see the point. Besides, he got the message.

As the elevator door rattled open, I heard Solomon's front door slam closed, caught the sounds of all the theft-proof locks being clicked on.

The elevator was going down and I kept thinking, kept hearing the sounds of him locking his doors. Lock, after lock, after lock. Maybe I should've had that kind of security, a nice crop of emo-tional locks to keep myself from being ripped off.

3 2 Jordan Greene

I wore a collarless white shirt and baggy jeans to work. Zoe called a few minutes after I made it in to talk and see how I was doing. She said she was fine, but the brittle texture of her voice told me she wasn't doing too well. Depression rode each syllable as she spoke. She said that she had gone by Solomon's office to have a few post-relationship words with him, but he'd called in sick today. I didn't say so, but he'd probably called in scared-to-death. She said she almost didn't come in herself because she didn't want to see his face, ever. That was the chance you took when you got your bread-n-butter at the same place.

Her voice smiled. "I'll stop by before you leave."

Throughout the morning people dropped by to wish me well. I noticed one thing about all of them. They all had that look of fear in their eyes that said their heads might be the next ones on the chopping block. And pity. But I knew in their hearts they also thought, "Better you than me."

I spent most of the morning going through an exit interview and check-out procedure: making sure I didn't have any valuable documents in my possession, verifying I didn't have any keys to the plantation's front door.

Then I sat in a meeting with twelve other people, a seminar about unemployment, explaining to the naïve how to roll over our 401k for a tax shelter, how to keep insurance going, about the benefits of a career search through the outplacement center on the first floor.

Rodger wanted to take me to lunch, and when he came by at noon, I told him I'd meet him in the lobby. I went to another department to handle my business.

I hopped off the elevator on Solomon's floor. Everybody in his area had either gone to an early lunch or were off working in a computer lab. I strolled into Solomon's office. Moved into his serenity. Closed the door. Locked it. Moved the pictures of his son away from his desk. Took Zoe's picture out of the frame on the top of his computer, put the photo in my pocket.

Then I kicked off my shoes and left them by his door. Opened all of his desk drawers, stood in a chair, and pissed all over the top of his desk, sprayed left to right to left. Made sure I hit inside the desk drawers. A nice, long piss I'd been saving since I woke up this morning. And the six cups of water I forced down about thirty minutes ago helped the river flow.

Even when you knew the difference between right and wrong, sometimes you just didn't give a fuck.

I powered on his computer, used the password "DAREUS" he had trusted me with and typed: Erase *.*

A message popped up:

This will erase all files.
Are you sure? (Y, N)

I wanted to type "DAMN RIGHT," but a simple "Y" was good enough to make the operating system happy. While everything deleted, I ran a magnet I had over his back-up disks.

At the door, I put on my shoes and glowered at his raining desk. Left, locked the room behind me so no one could get in.

Over lunch, Rodger slid me the names of three contacts.

I asked, "How soon are they expecting me to call?"

"Yesterday. I spoke with them while you were in Memphis."

We were at an outdoor Italian restaurant, eating thicker-than-thick New York pizza and sipping sodas.

He said, "All are in California."

"California?" I repeated.

"And they are *very* anxious to get their hands on you."

My mind pictured earthquakes, slow-moving Broncos, and racist audio tapes. Then again, the East had become a beast and wasn't my friend, so maybe I should make the best of a bad situation and head west. Make some new memories.

Put some miles between me and Solomon.

Leave a few states between me and sista Kimberly.

I asked him, "What do you have planned?"

He smiled. "Nobody in their right mind wants to hire anybody as old and with as many years as me. My asking price puts me out of the market. But with my investments, I'll survive."

Around three P.M., minutes after I got back from lunch, I let CompSci pay for a few long distance phone calls. After I left messages for all three West Coast companies, I called Darrell. He wasn't in. Then I called Wanda.

She shouted, "Hey, Narc!"

I moved the phone away from my ear and laughed. It was nice to hear a down-home inflection, even it was from a lunatic. I told Wanda I was getting laid off. She tried to cheer me up by telling me everybody has suffered at least one major setback in their lives, and she joked that she ought to know, because she'd had two. I just didn't expect three setbacks in just a few days. But Momma used to say everything, good or bad, happened in threes.

"Narc, even Melba Moore had to go on the county."

"She did?"

I'd been staring at my photo of Martin. The black-and-white picture of him being held prisoner in a white man's jail. In solitary. No smile. Waiting for freedom to ring.

Wanda was excited. "You didn't hear about that? Heard she was on welfare getting that check on the first and the fifteenth just like everybody else, and she used to be a millionaire."

"What happened to her?"

"Divorce. Married the wrong man or something."

Wanda said Reggie was doing fine and was so happy I had come to see him that he couldn't stop bragging to everybody at the rehab place about his brother from New York. He was touched that me and Darrell had dropped everything, put our lives on hold when we thought he needed us.

I said, "We're brothers. That's what brothers are supposed to do."

She and Reggie wanted to leave Memphis. Start over. Must've

been that season for leaving. What would hold them up would be that Wanda wanted to get her baby back first. At least to be able to talk to her child and get partial custody. She had been in contact with the social workers, writing letters, letting them know she was trying to build herself a safe environment. Looking for a fair second start.

In the meantime, she had lucked up on a job at Memphis's Southland Mall, a minimum wage gig. Wanda made it sound like it was the best thing going.

Zoe sashayed her bow legs and braids into my office when I was boxing up my things, taking Malcolm and Martin and Coltrane and Toni Braxton off my walls. Zoe had on a white T-shirt, jeans from 40 Acres, and a deep-red blazer.

Without my asking, she took off her jacket and started helping me pack while she talked. She yacked about everything—work, her child—everything except J'nette and Solomon. Uneasiness had her talking so long all I had to do was listen.

The engagement ring was off her finger. When she lifted a box, we both saw the emptiness on that hand at the same time, but neither of us said anything.

Zoe helped me carry everything downstairs to a cab. When she waved, wished me well, and turned to leave, she saw me struggling, dropping almost as much as I carried. She came back, picked up what I'd spilled, then hopped in the cab with me. As the cab pulled away, we looked at each other. She said, "You look like you need a friend."

"So do you."

We kicked back at my place and talked while I threw together some spicy baked chicken, brown rice, and vegetables. She stirred up the Kool-Aid and finally let loose what she had held back from nine to five. Her being hurt again.

She griped and growled out a nasty "Niggas and fleas. One spreads lies, both spread disease."

Just like I'd gone by Solomon's in the middle of the night in search of understanding, she had gone by J'nette's and tried to sit down and talk and make sense of why J'nette didn't tell anybody until now. Even though J'nette's words sounded sincere and made persuasive sense, Zoe still didn't understand. She didn't understand Solomon's contradictions, how he could get with J'nette in one silent breath and claim to love her in the next. She didn't understand J'nette's rationale for secrecy.

We sat on the floor and talked while an old Mikki Howard CD played low in the background. Zoe kept staring at the Africans-in-the-Village picture Kimberly had given me last Christmas. She walked over and ran her fingers over the oil painting's texture.

"That's beautiful," Zoe said. "Your place is nice. And you've got taste."

"Thanks."

She read the name on the print. "Kimberly Denise Chavers. She did that?"

"Yep."

"Wow. Bad. It looks real."

My voice was low, sarcastic, "A lot of things she does look real."

"That white girl can throw down."

White girl.

At some point after we ate, we stopped talking and let the sun go down on us. In the new twilight, Zoe slid over and kissed me. It came out of nowhere. And I surrendered myself to her, let her move closer. Shared my tongue with her. It didn't appeal to me on any great level, but it didn't offend me like it would've a few days ago. Part of me needed validation, wanted to be touched by more than a lie. Needed some physical contact. Like I said, I was different. And Zoe was different. I could see it. I felt it in her kisses.

Zoe unbuttoned my shirt, kissed my chest, unzipped my pants, kissed me again, took my hand, led me into my bedroom.

I pulled the covers back, sat on the bed. After she wiggled her jeans off, she reached to her purse and took out a condom. When she struggled to rip it open, that moment was all I needed to clear my head. I made her stop. Had to keep us from becoming what Solomon had proven himself to be. Had to keep Zoe from becoming what J'nette claimed she wasn't.

A wealth of tears ran from her eyes. Her lip quivered and shame invaded her eyes. She trembled and spoke in the tone of a wrecked soul, a desperate whisper, led by the inflection of a rup-tured heart, "I have to do this."

"Why?"

"I just have to. I have to put something on top of what he left behind. I want to cover it up."

"We can't."

"Let me. This way I know I won't go back."

I didn't let her use me. Wouldn't let her use herself. She asked me to hold her, and I broke down and gave her that much.

Lord knew, I needed to lay a new kind of icing on my misery, needed to frost my pain with something else too.

We sat up in the bed, relaxed next to each other like we were friends. The same kind of friends we had been for the last many months. I let her know that she didn't have to feel bad.

I was furious. "Rape or not—"

Zoe interrupted. "I'm not buying that rape shit."

"How could Solomon do some foul shit?"

She pulled the sheets up to her neck, hid her body, and said, "He didn't do it by himself."

A beat later, I said a pained "I was his best friend."

Zoe said a soft and gentle, a feathery "Just because you were his best friend, didn't mean he was yours. Just because I was his woman, didn't mean he was my man."

That was our last rationale. It didn't lessen the pain. Just gave it focus.

I told her about the pissed-off package I'd left drizzling on Solomon's desk.

She laughed. "That's *sick*. Way out of character for you."

"I snapped."

I let her know about Solomon and Yasmean.

She stopped laughing.

She gasped then shook her head. "I had a suspicion about her. She was always coming over, first one to get there, the last one to leave, all up in my face, giggling and smiling."

Zoe pulled her clothes back on and asked me about Kimberly. In our moments of secrecy, I told her everything. Which Zoe understood, all from Kimberly's point of view, because she'd been married and divorced. She said while she was in transition from marriage back to the single life, if she told a brotha she was still married, not yet divorced, he didn't take her seriously. Just wanted to get with her, then use her being married as an excuse to hit the road and search for single women.

I told her what Kimberly had said, how she'd cried over the mental anguish when she grew up.

Zoe said she understood Kimberly's childhood pain, but in a different way. From a different side of the tracks. Zoe was teased and ridiculed because of her darkness. She was always told she was too black. Was called Ju-Ju, Tar Baby, Sambo, Pygmy, and a hundred other disrespectful names she remembered all too well. Well enough to sound disgusted and angry again while we talked.

Zoe said, "Nobody can hurt black people like black people."

I could almost feel Kimberly's breath on my face when I said, "I know."

"Black people used to make me wish I was white. I was too black, too short, too fat, my hair was too damn nappy to do anybody any good." She held her heart. "And it hurt like hell. Made me want to crawl into a hole. Not everybody can put up with being teased."

We quieted for a second.

Then she covered her mouth and laughed, hard.

She said, "When I got married, I went to Chicago to meet my husband's grandmother, and the first words out of her mouth when she opened the door was"—Zoe switched her voice into an old, crabby woman's—" 'You couldn't find nobody lighter? Don't want no black-ass babies running around the house.' "

I laughed. "Damn. For real?"

"She didn't want him laying up with nobody that was darker than a paper bag."

I echoed, "The paper bag test."

"You heard of it too? Bitch actually grabbed a Kroger's *trash* bag out of the kitchen and held it up next to my face. Since I was darker than the bag, I wasn't good enough."

"She actually used it on you?"

"Damn right. And that heifer was darker than me!" She chuckled, but it wasn't a laugh. It was the same sound I'd made when I was standing outside of Solomon's apartment a few hours ago. "And after she did all that, right in our faces, the weak bastard I married didn't say a word in my defense. So, from that day, I knew it wasn't gonna last."

"That's unbelievable."

"It happened," she said and the laughter died. "It really happened. A few years ago I wasn't even looked at. Now brothers are crawling out of cracks and crevices."

Other than by white folks who hated everybody, I wasn't ridiculed or taunted or teased. My skin tone was a safe, middle-ground brown. I'd be lying if I didn't admit I was one of the ones who dished out the teasing every chance I got, did it to my own household tribe. Me and Darrell always ragged on Reggie, called him Skillet and Coal Man, when Momma wasn't close enough to whack us upside the head.

When I told her about Kimberly's being married and sneaking to get a divorce, and then about the assault, all she said about the drama of the day was, "I know it ain't right, but you'd have to be a woman to understand why she did what she did the way she did. How would you have reacted if she told you she went out and had married a brother?"

At first, I didn't answer.

"Don't take that much thinking, Jay."

I asked, "What do you mean?"

"You would've thought she was a white freak chasing brothers just like the rest of 'em, right?"

"I don't know."

"You know," she said. "And you know you know."

I still didn't answer.

Zoe said, "It's just messed up the way things turned out. She was caught in the middle of some serious gunfire and she's more concerned about you than she is about herself."

Some of my anger was at the fact that since Kimberly was part black, I guessed I wasn't as liberal-minded, not as free as I had thought. Just because I was with her didn't mean I thought it was okay when I saw other brothas or sistas with somebody white. But I'd stopped making negative comments. Maybe part of me thought I was proving something. She'd fooled me, and had let me be a fool all by myself. Another part was because of all the bullshit, all the jeers and sneers I'd tolerated since we had met.

I released a soft chortle of pity and said, "All she had to do to kill the madness was pump her fist and say a 'right on' or two."

"Like that would've made a difference."

"It should've."

"Well, I don't care what you say, she don't and won't ever look black to me. You can put Afro puffs on her head and make her dance the Cabbage Patch and sing 'Superfly' from dusk to dawn, she won't look black. Nobody at my engagement party thought she was a soul sister."

"Her father's a brotha."

"You said he was half-black."

"Yeah."

"If her daddy's a pumpkin-skin, then she's a quadroon or a quarteron, whatever they call it."

"She's a sista."

"*Whatever* she is," Zoe shrugged, let out a slow breath, sounded like she was tired of the subject, "that's her biz. We've all got some kind of problem. Everybody. All of us are looking for something."

I nodded. Made an unsure sound.

"Or trying to hold on to something," Zoe said, sounding like she was about to break down. She was kneading her fist deep into her thigh. "And some of us have nothing left. Starting from scratch."

"You okay?"

"No." Her voice cracked. "I'm tired of starting over."

I put my arm around her. She wiped her face, patted my arm, and kissed my hand. Again, I asked, "You all right?"

"Almost." She sniffled. "I just want to be okay when I pick my baby up from the sitter. She can tell when I'm upset. Then she gets upset. Then we both end up upset. I'll have to figure out what to tell her about Sol not coming around anymore."

We sat for a while, rocked back and forth.

I asked Zoe, "What're you thinking about?"

She shifted and looked at my face. "You really like that German, Irish, white, black, redheaded girl, don't you?"

Kimberly's artistry was on my wall. Two studio eight-by-tens of her also graced the walls. I said, "Yeah."

"I'm not into brothers and white women. Hell, I'm not even into brothers chasing light-skinned sisters just because they're light-skinned, but that's me. My baggage. If you care about who she is, and it's from the heart, and somebody says something to offend her, hold her hand. If they piss her off, hold her hand a little tighter. We all need somebody to hold our hand every now and then."

"That's pretty extreme for you."

"I know. And you ain't gonna tell nobody."

"I might."

"If you did, they wouldn't believe you."

We laughed.

Maybe Kimberly had been trying to find herself. Or maybe she'd found herself, and everybody else was too busy criticizing to notice. Ignoring the past and moving on. Reggie was trying to find and define himself. Wanda was doing the same. J'nette and Zoe would be in that same boat. One way or another, we were all trying to find ourselves. Some of us had to dig further and deeper and harder than the rest.

Zoe said she was ready to leave the Big Apple. Ready to take her little girl and disappear. She'd had enough of New York, and for her to get through this, she'd have to detach herself from everybody. Especially J'nette. It was too hard for her to look at that baby and not blame it for what happened.

"I'm giving Solomon his ring back."

"Don't," I damn near shouted. "Pawn it. Take a vacation or something. He messed up, not you."

She thought about it for a sec, then said, "If you insist."

"I insist. Go on a cruise."

"Europe sounds better."

"Do that, then."

"You want some'a the money?"

We both laughed at that. I said, "Nope."

"You just got laid off."

"I hope you don't think I worked all these years and didn't save. Even if I don't work for a year, maybe two, I'm cool."

She gave a cheery smile and I remembered I'd stolen her picture out of Solomon's office. I pulled it out of my briefcase and handed it to her. She studied it for a minute, then gave it back to me. She wanted me to keep it as a memento.

Zoe showered. While she put on some of my lotion and dressed, I showered. She waited in the living room while I dressed. Then I walked her to the subway. I'd offered to walk over to the bus stop and hop on the Q33, but she turned me down, said she was in the mood for a slow stroll in the warmth of the evening. Didn't seem like either of us had anywhere to go. Nowhere to hurry to. So a twenty-minute walk was just what the doctor ordered. Afterward it all seemed new. Maybe this kind of life was getting too old.

On the way down the stairs to the platform, Zoe said, "If I see you again, and I'm with the posse, and I don't speak, don't take it personal. I'll sneak you a wink."

"I'll look out for that wink."

"You're a nice brother. Deeper than I gave you credit for. You've got some morals. Some real values."

"I'm not from New York."

She laughed. "I almost kinda wish I'd met you first."

"Almost kinda?"

"Yeah." She tiptoed and kissed my cheek. "Almost kinda."

I kissed her cheek.

She said, "Thanks, Jay."

"What for?"

"For what you didn't do." She let out a sound of relief, blushed, then winked. "Sometimes the best revenge is when nobody knows you could've had it."

"Yeah." I gave a short nod. "You take care."

"You too."

She hopped on the G train and was gone to wherever she was going. She didn't say where she was fleeing to. I didn't ask. And it made me happy, if you could call the flicker of relief I felt happiness.

After I waved good-bye to a vanishing confidant, to a strong sista whose pained words took away a lot of my suffering, I headed up into the twilight, back to the streets.

Back to my new life.

33 Kimberly Chavers

My scarlet hair was frizzy, all in my face, smelled like copper, so I needed to wash and blow-dry the tangled mess ASAP. In my kitchen, I stood face to face with the black clock over my sink to see the time, but I couldn't read the numbers. It frustrated me because the more I strained my eyes, the more I saw gibberish.

With everything being so blurry, that made me jittery, and I felt like I had to hurry to get ready, so I stopped washing dishes and ran for the shower, started washing my hair and singing along with the shower radio. The music was loud, but I really couldn't hear. No matter how I strained, it was muffled.

I'd just rinsed the trail of soap off my back when I heard rattles coming from the front door. I clicked off the radio to listen. Even though I was sure it had to be locked, because I always locked it, I know I heard the front door creak open, then close. I would have written it off as some of the sound from the radio, tuned to HOT 97, but it was turned off. And with the bathroom door ajar, a draft pulled the dull gray shower curtain, made it dance. I turned off the shower. Stood still in the dark. Listened. Held my breath while my pulse raced.

At first there was nothing. Then whispers. Very un-feminine whispers, so I knew it wasn't Sharon and Kinikki dropping by without calling. Heavy footsteps came from all around me. Things scraped surfaces as they were moved. My space felt smaller. My chest tightened and I put my hands across my bare breasts. Then two voices came and went. Neither recognizable.

I eased out of the shower and cracked my bathroom door a little more, enough to hear the sounds of my stereo being dismantled. My television was being lifted. My works were being shifted, maybe even some of my canvas was being ripped. To make it to the phone, I'd have to dash across the living room door and pass whoever was in there. Naked, my only weapon would be a wet towel and dry screams. Naked. I was in the raw. When I reached for my towel to cover myself, I couldn't find it. It was gone.

I turned off the bathroom light, got back into the tub, and pulled the shower curtain back just enough to hide myself, but left enough for it to seem like nobody was in here. At least I hoped that was what would come across. I crammed near the faucet, moved my bare body tight against the wall. Then noises came from the bedroom, only feet away from where I was. My leg trembled more than I could control. Sweat drained over my wet skin.

Things in my bedroom were being tossed around and dragged into the living room. My art was yanked off the wall next to my bed. Footsteps came straight toward my hiding place. Stopped in front of the door. A few seconds of silence. Then the bathroom door swung open and bumped the wall. Whoever it was was big enough for his shadow to make the room go completely black.

For a long time, silence.

I held my breath, almost suffocated on my fear. The light clicked on and blinded me. He unzipped his pants, and I almost called out for help, but didn't know who I would be calling out to. The lid on the toilet seat went up. I heard his pants jingle loose change, then drop to his ankles. He sat down, talked to his friend, telling him what to take, what would fit in the truck, what paintings they could get rid of easily. His friend yelled that he'd found a gun in a dresser drawer. I wondered how it got there because I didn't own a gun. I hate guns. Maybe Jordan had left it for me in case something like this happened.

But Jordan wasn't in my life anymore. No more SmooVe times.

I tried to be still, tried not to breathe.

He grunted, strained, and did his business.

They had come back for me.

I stayed still.

Didn't breathe.

I felt him being still.

Matching my not breathing.

Then he yanked the shower curtain back, pulled it so hard all the plastic rings popped off and flew against the tile wall.

It was the white kid from the alley, the one who'd thrown me into the wall at the ATM. The one who hurt my head. First I understood that much. Then I remembered it all, recalled them attacking us. Remembered them shooting Peter. The mongrels weren't in jail. But I knew they were; the police reassured me. So, they'd broken out. Either that or they'd arrested the wrong people. Or they'd been released on a technicality.

We both jumped and screamed. My scream was fear, his was victory. I tried to get past him, but I slipped on the wetness of the shower floor. He stumbled back and flopped on the toilet. His hoodlum friend with all the earrings was yelling, running toward the bathroom. I heard several pops.

In the distance, Peter screamed. My scream was muffled.

I woke up and didn't know where I was. Light was coming in from a corner window, but it was still too dark.

"Kimberly, wake up."

I winced when I realized a man's hand was on my shoulders, shaking me. My vision focused. It was Jordan. He was on the edge of my hospital bed, calling my name, softly bringing me back to reality. He pulled me closer to him.

He whispered, "You're having a bad dream."

I mumbled and tried to pull free. "What're you doing here?"

"You want me to leave?"

"Yes."

"Too bad."

We stared for a moment. Then he apologized for the way he had behaved the day before.

I put my head on his chest, but it hurt because of the bump in the back of my head. He wiped the sweat off my face, talked me through my delirium, calmed me down. It was almost three in the morning. I didn't know when he came back or how long he'd been sitting there watching me suffer. The last thing I remembered was paging Sharon, then Mom-Mom and Daddy calling from their hotel to check up on me, then trying to get comfortable.

He asked me if I was in pain.

I asked, "How long are you going to be here?"

"Until you go back home."

We started talking. About the ordeal I'd been through. About me growing up the way I had.

He asked, "So, what are you?"

"What do you mean *what* am I?" Then elbowed him. "I'm not a *what*. I'm a human being."

"No, I mean what lineage. Are you African-American?"

"You saw my parents. What do you think?"

"Answer the question."

"Let's not get into this right now. Can we talk about something else for a few minutes?"

"You can't be red one day and pink the next."

"So, it was okay to date me if I'm white, but if I'm not, that changes everything?"

"I'm not saying that."

"Either way, I'm still the same Kimberly Denise Chavers."

That went on for about an hour. He had his point of view based on his experiences. I had my feelings based on who I was, based on the people who had given me life. Based on my rules.

The subject was finally set aside. For now.

Jordan had a lot on his mind, more than just me. He had other problems that my situation had magnified. My problems made his seem worse. He told me he received his layoff notice and might be leaving New York. Said he might be going toward the Pacific and working in California. That wasn't confirmed. If a job didn't come through, it would be too expensive to live here and he'd need to pay off his bills and readjust his finances as soon as possible, just in case. The thought of him not being around, of him having to go away and out of my life so fast hurt me more than the room's darkness would show.

He wasn't sure what he was going to do, but he didn't feel comfortable being without a job for the first time in his life.

I said, "You went straight from high school to college, worked two jobs, went to college year round, started working at CompSci two days after you graduated, maybe you should take some time off. You deserve it. You say you've always wanted to go places, this is your opportunity to have a few days off."

"Going on vacation won't put any money in my pocket."

I said, "No, but it will make your life richer. Give you a better view of the world."

I told him if he wanted, since my place was larger, he could move in with me to cut his expenses. It scared me when I offered him my space, because I never wanted to live with anybody who wasn't married to me. And I didn't want to get married, not ever again.

I said an unsure "You'd better take advantage of my offer before my medication wears off."

He touched my bruised face. "Are you going to be okay behind all of this?"

"Sharon is setting me up with a therapist."

"Why do you need a therapist?"

"So, you don't believe in therapy."

He shrugged. "I guess. I just don't know many people who had to go to therapy."

"I believe in seeing an expert when something is wrong." I patted his hand. "I want to make sure I'm okay. So I'll be doing that for a while. It's not like I'm crazy, I feel fine. I'm sad and feel like shit because of what happened, but you never know."

"Good."

"Now back to the question. You wanna move in with me for a while?"

"What's a while?"

"Until I kick you out."

Even though I didn't tell him, I had my own selfish reasons for wanting him with me. I didn't tell him, because like him, I guess I had that pride thing, but I still wanted us to work at being us. I wanted this hint of darkness to change into light.

I asked him, "What are you thinking about?"

"I was just thinking about how when I had my asthma attack, when I was laid up in the hospital and woke up, you were right there, looking all sad. You tried to turn your face so I couldn't see you cry. And now, we're back in the hospital."

"That we are."

"I should've been here the whole time."

"You're here now. That's all that matters."

He was concerned about my husband—I told him to stop calling Peter that—being killed and him sitting up on the hospital bed
with the new widow. He didn't call me a widow, but that was what
he meant. He asked me if that would be appropriate, especially
under the circumstances. I told him it would be up to us, not what
anybody else thought. Again, when I asked him if he needed me to
help him out, he yawned and said he'd think about it. Sometimes
pride needed a push.

I asked, "How long are you going to think about it?"

"How long do I have to think about it?"

"Don't answer my question with a question."

After that, his breathing heavied and he dozed off. I stayed
awake and away from the dark dreams. Lived a restless life sitting in
the dark, waiting for the sun to come up and destroy the shadows.

A nurse knocked on the door. She stuck her head in and saw I
was snuggled with Jordan. She smiled. I told her I was okay and
would buzz if I needed anything. She winked and left.

My eyes went wall to wall, searching for something to sketch
on. A pencil and paper were on the table. I eased out of the bed,
groaned my way over to get it, slipped back into the bed, and
started sketching Jordan's sleeping face.

I had stayed awake a lot of nights and painted my way through
my thoughts, through whatever troubled me. Sometimes I didn't
paint, just marveled at how day turned into night without a question, at how it slipped and changed without asking if I would mind
or be offended or if I needed the difference it brought. Sometimes
I would just patiently wait and absorb the transformation from
obscurity to the explicit. Sometimes I would sit in the night, and
wait in the blackness. Sometimes it got so dark, everything, every
familiar shape would fade and I didn't think there would ever
be light again. But I never had a fear I didn't handle. I didn't run
away from the night because I knew that darkness was temporary.
Sunrise always followed sunset always followed sunrise always
followed sunset. It was always like that and would always be
like that.

I was still thinking about Peter and felt like it was my fault. I
didn't know why I felt that way, but I did.

I needed to try to work it out in my mind. At least some of it.

Okay, so I took Peter to the ATM and I should have known better and watched my back because I know this city. I know its beauty and I know its dangers. He was the one who came out to dinner without any money. But he was going to charge the dinner on his credit card. He could've stayed behind and charged it if he hadn't been repugnant and chased me down the SoHo streets. Nobody told him to follow me. But I hit him in the head with a salad bowl and pissed him off. Maybe I overreacted. No. He earned that because he tried that stupid, disrespectful one-for-the-road routine. So I should have hit him with my bass dinner too. But *I* went to dinner with him. I could have just as well stood him up. But he kept calling and coerced me into going by using blackmail. Shit, I called him, so it was me who set this catastrophe in action. Wait, he called me back, lied about having a business in Jersey, then flew out here to harass me. He didn't have to come near the Atlantic Ocean. From the Pacific Ocean, he could've notarized and mailed or faxed whatever documents we needed to file a no-fault through Tony. It could have been simple, but he chose to complicate it. I married him. But he asked me to marry him.

"If he had never asked me to marry him," I mumbled, "I wouldn't be sitting up in this damn room with my head all fucked up. And he wouldn't be dead."

But still, I cried. I cried for Peter. Cried for me. Set free a few tears for his family. Cried for his fiancée who was waiting for his no-good ass to be boxed up in a block of ice. I'd have Sharon call FTD and send some flowers to Peter's family.

Jordan woke up a few minutes later. I didn't get much sketching done because I'd been crying off and on. Plus I was too fidgety. I'd been fighting sleep and shifting around. Running my fingers through his hair and playing with his ears so I could steal his attention. I was lonely and needed somebody to talk to. And I was jealous because he looked so at peace.

I pulled him up to me, kissed his morning breath, found a comfortable position, and pulled him between my legs so he could rest his head on my chest. He didn't like to kiss before he brushed his teeth, but I like to steal all the flavors, good or bad. I made him open his mouth so I could slide my tongue in.

He mumbled, "Stop."

"Give me."

He opened his mouth and slipped me the tongue. He reached to put his fingers in my hair, but I jerked and caught his hand. He'd forgotten about my injured head. He said, "Sorry."

I whispered an airy "Love you."

"Love you too. You okay?"

"Better since you came back."

He gave me a kiss that got better as he woke up.

I said, "I'm in the mood."

He chuckled, "What?"

I chuckled too. "C'mon, SmooVe. Love me down."

"Here?"

"Yes."

"You're delirious."

"Yes." I moaned and beckoned him toward me. "Just don't be rough. I'll lay on my stomach so I won't have that pressure on the back of my head. If we start rocking I could kill myself."

"What if somebody comes in?"

"I'll tell them I'm in pre-therapy."

"What about your parents?"

"Mom-Mom and Daddy won't be here until nine. And I don't get any more medicine until eight. You've got time."

"Not enough time."

"I don't want but a few slow minutes. And I do mean slow. You'll have to do most of the moving. Don't make any noise. Sometimes you get too loud. Don't make the bed squeak. Be SmooVe."

I started pulling off my bottoms.

He asked, "You're serious?"

"What do you think?"

"Don't answer my question—"

"—with a question. Will you come on?"

He stared at me for a moment to see if I was serious, looked at the bottoms I had in my hand, then stretched and said through his yawn, "Let me go pee first."

I sighed out my growing frustration, then kissed him. "And make sure you drop that damn toilet seat when you finish."

He went to the bathroom.

By the time he came back, I was sound asleep.
No bad dreams.

3 4 Jordan Greene

Kimberly kept having the nightmares. Even with her once-a-week
therapy, she'd wake up wide-eyed, shaking. That happened enough
for me to want to watch how she was sleeping, wake her up from
anything I thought might've been a nightmare. Most of the time
I'd wake up and she'd be sitting in front of her easel, creating. The
smell of fresh paint and soft jazz all through the night was something I was getting used to. Sometimes I'd crash on the futon and
watch how creations poured from her mind out through the little
brush she held so confidently in her fingers. A lot of times, I'd fall
asleep and not wake up until I felt her climbing on the futon with
me, pulling covers on top of us.

Days after I'd moved in with Kimberly, we were out in the Village doing a late Saturday breakfast, yukking it up at a crowded
sidewalk cafe with Kinikki and Sharon and their husbands. I'd just,
for the umpteen-hundredth time, played off that look of disgust
that a few bow-tie-wearing brothas slid over to me when they saw
me and Kimberly strolling hand in hand. That I'm-telling-the-
NAACP-to-revoke-your-membership scowl pissed me off to no
end, and I wanted to say something, but it deserved no response.
They didn't know me; didn't know Kimberly; didn't know us; so
it shouldn't matter.

But it did. I guess it always would.

Over the sidewalk meal, Kinikki announced that she was two
months' pregnant. We all applauded, then toasted.

Kimberly asked, sarcastically, "And how do you suppose that
happened to happen?"

Kinikki winked.

The women giggled and laughed.

All of us men shrugged and made I-don't-get-it faces.

Just as I raised a forkful of spinach omelette to my mouth, Toni, Elaine, and Zoe turned the corner and came teetering and ha-ha-ing through the crowd, steamrolling down the sidewalk in our direction. Elaine noticed me, huffed, slowed, mumbled something out the side of her face, and then they all changed their walking pace, snapped their eyes in my direction at the same moment. The laughter stopped and they loaded themselves with those hard, New York b-girl faces and passed by without a word. Toni had the strongest refusal to look in our direction. They were marching by on Kimberly's blind side. Kimberly and Sharon were deep in conversation, talking about planning a baby shower.

A few feet after they'd passed, Zoe slowed a bit, lost herself in the crowd long enough to peep back. She smiled a warm toothy smile, and winked a naughty wink. Waved hello. Or maybe it was bye-bye.

A couple of weekends later, me and Kimberly went to Shadow's about one A.M., just when things were starting to get jumping. When we walked in, Solomon was standing over near one of the bars. I hadn't seen him since the night I was at his place, ready to stomp him like a roach. That was almost three months ago, but that season seemed like yesterday. Before I could catch Kimberly's hand or turn her away, she had given a broad smile, waved him our way, and called his name. He saw her, saw me, turned his face, put down his drink and moved away from the woman he was talking with.

Kimberly asked, "What was that all about?"

"Nothing." I smiled. "I'll tell you later."

"No," she said. "Tell me now."

The phony smile faded from my face. I said, "He owes me three hundred dollars. That's all."

Maybe it was something in my eyes that gave her a better answer, but Kimberly never asked me anything after that.

Darrell surprised me. He sent me a money order for eight hundred dollars. And a note: "Pokey, just want to help you out the best I can. I saved this up and added some of my profit sharing to it. I know how expensive it gets up there. Let me know what else you need. I took Wanda out to see Reggie day before yesterday. That doctor got him a hook-up and it look like he going to get a job out in Phoenix, Arizona, driving a truck. He was glad to get that. He said to make sure you send him your address if you change it again, that way he can make sure you have his. Drop me a line and let me know you got this. Traci said hi. Don't be surprised if you call and she answers the phone. Peace. Darrell."

Another thing that made me smile even more was a postcard from Zoe. No address. It had a picture of the Martin Luther King Memorial on the front and a colorful Marcus Garvey postage stamp. The card had a postmark with a two-day-old date. Mailed from Atlanta. She had drawn a smiley face and wrote one word on the bottom in her friendly handwriting: *Thanks.*

Kimberly wanted to fly out to Los Angeles with me. I'd already done the phone interview with Dan L. Steel Computers Division, located right outside Los Angeles in Culver City, an upper-middle-class community. The face-to-face was just a formality.

All the way to JFK, as we rode down Woodhaven Boulevard through Elmhurst, Rego Park, across Jackie Robinson Parkway, and across Rockaway Boulevard, I could tell Kimberly had a lot on her mind. She'd been up all night before, in front of her easel, creating as the rain fell all over the city.

In the cab, the closer we got to the Howard Beach area and Jamaica Bay, the more she held on to her harrowed smile and gripped my hand.

She'd already hinted she hated the West Coast because it had no distinct seasons. She enjoyed the flavor, the colors of the East Coast. We had had a discussion about long distance relationships and she'd only said one thing—she didn't like them. No ifs, ands, or buts. Too inconvenient and too expensive. Her words were definite. I told her I had to work. I had to go where the fish were biting at my price.

So for the last few days, we'd had a lot of tension in the relationship. Both of us had been pretty snippy, then overly apologetic. We'd hardly touched for the last two weeks. Lovemaking was becoming obsolete. I'd had a constant migraine the last three days. It was just that after riding high and having my life flying in fifth gear, it was starting to feel like I'd shifted into neutral and I was grinding the clutch.

The rain was pounding down, drumming on the cab so hard we could barely see. I was daydreaming about past, present, and future. Thinking about how my life was this time last year; wondering how it would be this time next year.

Kimberly elbowed me and asked a simple "You love me?"

I said, "You know I do."

"How much?"

"Who can weigh love?" I said. She didn't crack a smile. A moment later, I asked her, "You love me?"

"Yep."

"How much?"

She smiled, kissed my cheek and said, "Too much to weigh."

Kimberly scooted closer to me and put her hand on my leg. I put my hand on hers. That was our first time touching all day.

Our red-eye flight was practically empty. Kimberly stayed quiet, stuffed her overnight bag into the overhead bin, grabbed a couple of pillows and blankets, sat back in her window seat, flipped her damp hair from her face, adjusted her skirt, then let out a very wounded sigh. She kept staring out the window, watching the rain pound the pavement. Her eyes were unhappy. Looked like she was ready to get off the plane and let me go on my own.

I stuffed my bag into a bin. "You okay, Kimberly?"

She snapped out of her trance, rubbed her nose. "Thinking."

"About?"

"Just thinking."

The flight attendant had just finished doing his all-American Easter speech about fastening the seat belts, and if you were on row twenty-something, you were the one crowned with the responsibility—even though we'd all be panicking and you probably had no training—for helping everybody else escape the burning plane if the pilot messed up, had too much Jack Daniel's, and took this puppy down at some place that didn't resemble an airport.

The flight attendant smiled his way by and made sure everybody was upright and buckled in, then went to his takeoff seat.

Kimberly unbuckled her seat belt, pulled up the arm rest separating us, leaned over and gave me a light kiss. When we finished, she reached into her purse and took out a small box. I reached for it and she pulled it back.

I asked, "What's wrong?"

"You know, if you get this job, and you will, then we're going to have to make a life-changing decision."

"And if I don't get it?"

"We're going to have to make a life-changing decision."

My eyes darted from her to the box.

She asked, "SmooVe, will you marry me?"

I searched her face for the teasing smile, but it wasn't there. She was so serious. I reached for the box, but she pulled it away from me, took it back to herself.

She asked a stiff "Well?"

I asked, "You bought an engagement ring?"

"Don't answer my question with a question." She sighed, then asked a softer, "Well?"

I smiled. "Yeah."

She took a deep breath and let out a long "Whew."

I touched her hand. "You all right?"

Before I could get out the last syllable, she leaned to me, tilted her head. The plane rocked with our kissing groove. We were being backed out of the gate so we could taxi to the runway.

She slid the box over to me, slow and deliberate. Her face softened. I didn't believe how much my hands had already sweated when I snapped the case open. Inside, there was a piece of paper. The note said, YOU OWE ME A RING.

She chuckled. "When you buy it, we'll go visit Mom-Mom and you can ask me to marry you in front of her and Daddy."

"Are you gonna surrender the rest of your life to me?"

"Probably not. I like things the way they are. But since Kinikki has been pregnant, my biological clock has been ticking pretty loud lately."

"Hit the snooze button. I'm in between careers."

She laughed, then pulled me to her for more kisses. The plane rolled out to the runway and the pilot announced we had been cleared for takeoff. Told the flight attendants to prepare for departure.

Kimberly winked. "You hear that?"

"What?"

She whispered, "Cleared for takeoff."

Kimberly leaned across me, looked up and down the dark rows of the shallowly occupied plane. Only a couple of reading lights were on, but those were nearer to the front of the DC-10. She leaned forward, peeked at the backs of the heads of a couple about six rows up, then peeped at an older couple four rows back.

I asked, "What're you looking for?"

She unbuckled my seat belt, unfolded the airplane blankets, grinned, and draped them across us. She took both pillows, shifted around, put one under her head, the other under her butt. Kimberly yawned, wiggled backward, moved up against me, and pulled my hand up under her dress. I rubbed around and squeezed, touched her front, expected to feel undies. Nothing but skin.

She whispered an erotic "Kiss me on my neck."

Kimberly reached back and felt around for my zipper, then dug inside and found me. I scooted close to her, kissed the spot on her neck that makes her weak.